Praise for *The Dead Ex*

"Corry's skill at building suspense and creating characters with secret pasts, as shown in her earlier novels, is on display again here." —*Booklist*

"Corry expertly weaves [the] stories together in unexpected and clever ways." —CrimeReads

"Corry delivers strong plot twists, a fast pace, and devious characters, making this a perfect blend of Liv Constantine's *The Last Mrs. Parrish* and Alafair Burke's *The Wife* that will keep readers guessing until the end."

—*Library Journal*

"Gripping . . . Corry delivers several satisfying plot twists as well as a meditation on the nature of family." —*Publishers Weekly*

Praise for *My Husband's Wife*

"Full of twists and turns, [*My Husband's Wife*] draws you into its complicated world within the first chapter, and it doesn't let you go until you've turned the final page. Corry's talented storytelling and brilliant writing make [this] a must-read." —*Bustle*

"[*My Husband's Wife*] nicely fits into the psychological suspense genre that's riding a slipstream of popularity, thanks to the success of *Gone Girl* and *The Girl on the Train* . . . Addictive." —*The Washington Post*

"If you loved *Gone Girl* and *The Talented Mr. Ripley*, you'll love *My Husband's Wife*. It's got every thriller's trifecta: love, marriage, and murder."

—*Parade*

"Brilliant, original, and complex, with a dark triangle at its center. A compelling thriller that kept me turning the pages until the end."

—B. A. Paris, *New York Times* bestselling author of *Bring Me Back*

"Lies fester and multiply, undermining intimate relationships in this psychological thriller . . . Suspenseful."   —*Booklist* (starred review)

"A devilishly devious debut . . . This swiftly moving psychological thriller offers surprises right up to the finish."   —*Publishers Weekly*

Praise for *Blood Sisters*

"*Blood Sisters* is one of the most addictive books of [the year] so far. . . . It'll keep you guessing until the very end."   —*Hello Giggles*

"Gripping, intense, and masterfully crafted."   —Bookreporter.com

"Engrossing."   —*Publishers Weekly*

PENGUIN BOOKS

THE DEAD EX

Jane Corry is an author and journalist, and has spent time as the writer-in-residence of a high-security prison for men—an experience that helped inspire *My Husband's Wife*, her bestselling debut thriller, as well as her second thriller, *Blood Sisters*. *The Dead Ex* is her third thriller.

ALSO BY JANE CORRY

My Husband's Wife
Blood Sisters

THE DEAD EX

A Novel

Jane Corry

PENGUIN BOOKS

PENGUIN BOOKS

An imprint of Penguin Random House LLC

penguinrandomhouse.com

First published in Great Britain by Penguin Books, Ltd., 2018
First published in the United States of America by Pamela Dorman/Viking,
an imprint of Penguin Random House LLC, 2019
Published in Penguin Books 2019

A Pamela Dorman/Penguin Book

ISBN 9780525561217 (paperback)

THE LIBRARY OF CONGRESS HAS CATALOGED THE
HARDCOVER EDITION AS FOLLOWS:
Names: Corry, Jane, author.
Title: The dead ex : a novel / Jane Corry.
Description: New York, New York : Pamela Dorman Books/Viking, [2018] |
"A Pamela Dorman Book/Viking."
Identifiers: LCCN 2018041545 (print) | LCCN 2018042290 (ebook) |
ISBN 9780525561200 (Ebook) | ISBN 9780525561194 (hardcover)
Subjects: LCSH: Missing persons. | Man-woman relationships--Fiction. |
BISAC: FICTION / Contemporary Women. | FICTION / Literary.
Classification: LCC PR6103.O776 (ebook) |
LCC PR6103.O776 D43 2018 (print) | DDC 823/.92--dc23
LC record available at https://lccn.loc.gov/2018041545

Printed in the United States of America
1   3   5   7   9   10   8   6   4   2

Designed by Amanda Dewey

For my husband, who makes me laugh every day, and to my wonderful, talented, loving children. Also to my "babies," who light up my life.

ACKNOWLEDGMENTS

Behind every writer, there is always a team of supporters. I am indebted to the following:

Kate Hordern, my amazing agent.

The incredible Pamela Dorman and her assistant, Jeramie Orton, at Pamela Dorman Books for their clever "eye" and encouragement. Thanks, too, to the rest of the USA team, including my publicists, Carolyn Coleburn and Sara Chuirazzi, as well as Mary Stone and Allison Carney in marketing and everyone else at Viking Penguin. Also, to Katy Loftus, my incredible UK editor; her assistant, Rosanna Forte; Hannah Ludbrook; Sarah Scarlet plus her team and everyone else involved in the birth of *The Dead Ex*.

My loyal following of bloggers, reviewers, Facebook friends and Instagram buddies plus everyone else on social media who've championed my writing, including Dead Good and Pageturners.

The authors who have kindly given me quotes.

Gail Lowe, clinical aromatherapist and tutor at Devon Academy of Complementary Therapies, *www.devonacademy.co.uk*. Her deft touch on the couch gave me inspiration.

Vicky Robinson, deputy director of HMP Bronzefield, who kindly allowed me to spend time "inside."

Also other prison sources, whom I interviewed for research, including Sue Weedon and her partner, Bob.

Deborah Pullen, communications director of Epilepsy Research UK, *www.epilepsyresearch.org.uk*. I became interested in epilepsy when it hit my family out of the blue.

Several men and women who were kind enough to share their experiences of epilepsy.

Colin Grant, author of *A Smell of Burning: A Memoir of Epilepsy*, published by Vintage.

Richard Gibson, a retired judge who was so generous with his time when advising me on court procedure. There may be instances when liberties have been taken with certain legal and police procedures for the purposes of the plot.

Thanks, too, to all the foster parents, adults who were fostered as children and social workers who kindly spoke to me. Also Tim McArdle at UK Fostering (*www.ukfostering.org.uk*), Amie McArdle and the author Kit de Waal.

The Royal Literary Fund, of which I am an Honorary Fellow. Thank you for your friendship over the years.

My family, for their support.

THE DEAD EX

Daily Telegraph, *5 November 2018*

A body has been found, washed up on the shore at the outlet of Deadman's Creek on the North Cornwall coast. A police spokesman said that no further details are available at this time.

PART ONE

PART ONE

*S*age, savin, rue, red thyme. People assume that aromatherapy oils are safe. But these little beauties can be highly toxic if used in the wrong way.

Or so some say.

Often, it's hard to know the truth.

Take this woman I once knew, who killed the man she loved.

She didn't mean to.

Well, that's what she told the rest of us . . .

He'd been cheating, but he'd promised to give this other woman up.

Then she caught him on the phone.

So she reached for the object closest to hand—a screwdriver, as it happened—which she plunged into his neck.

Of course she meant to kill him, I thought at the time.

But now I'm not so sure.

I.

VICKI

14 February 2018

I unscrew the lid, inhale the deep, heady smell—straight to the nostrils— and carefully measure out three drops into the glass measuring jug. Pure lavender. My favorite. More importantly, perhaps, this clever little remedy is renowned for its healthy level of esters, otherwise known, in my business, as "healing properties."

Healing? Who am I kidding? Nothing and no one can save me. I might look like a fairly average woman in her forties, but deep down, I'm a walking time bomb.

It could happen any second. You might wait for weeks, maybe months: all quiet. And then, hey, presto, along it comes when your guard is down. "Don't think about it," they advised me. Easier said than done. Sometimes I liken it to an actress coming off stage to be consoled on her performance even though she can't remember a single damn thing.

Standing on my tiptoes, I reach up to the shelf for a second bottle and add ylang-ylang, or "poor man's jasmine." Second-best can be just as good. Or so I tell myself.

Now for petitgrain. I take down the third vial carefully, remembering the lesson in which I learned that the contents are made from the leaves of the bitter orange tree. Blend with grapefruit? Possibly. It depends on the client.

When you've got what I have, you have to find ways to minimize damage. But at the end of the day, if something goes wrong, the ultimate price is death. The oils need to be treated with respect in order to reduce the dangers.

I love aromatherapy. Its magic is both distracting and calming.

But tonight isn't about me. It's about my new client. Though she's not a fellow sufferer, her face bears similarities to mine, with those soft creases around her eyes, suggesting laughter and tears, and the slightly saggy, soft-looking pouches underneath them, which she has tried to hide with a light-reflective concealer.

Silently, I admire her peach lipstick. I no longer bother with it myself. I used to always wear "Beautiful Beige" to make a point about being feminine. The woman before me has blond hair, tied back loosely with the odd wisp escaping. What I'd give for a color like that! The "freckly redhead" tag from school days still stings, but David had loved it. "My very own beautiful Titian," he used to say.

Both my client and I wear brave smiles that say, "I'm fine, really." But she's not, or she wouldn't be here. And nor would I.

"I just need something to help me relax," she says. "I've had a lot of stress."

It's not my job to be a therapist. Even so, there are times when I want to interrupt and tell my own story to show these women (I've never had a male client) that they aren't alone. Of course, that wouldn't be wise, because it might scare them off. And I need them. Not just for my business. But to prove myself.

Time to go over my client's medical history. "Are you pregnant?"

I have to ask this question even though her disclaimer form states that—like me—she is forty-six. It's still possible. She gives a short laugh. "I've already answered all that. Why do you ask, anyway?"

"There are some aromatherapy oils that aren't suitable for expectant mothers," I say. I move on swiftly. "Do you have high blood pressure?"

"No. Though I feel I should have. Can this stuff affect that, too?"

She glances with suspicion at the bottles lined up above us with all the colors of the rainbow trapped inside. Red, orange, yellow, green, blue, indigo, violet. For a minute, I'm aged nine, in the small northern mining town where I grew up, reciting them to the teacher. Some patterns you don't forget.

"No, but it's good for me to know. The oils are like medicine." I hear my tutor's words tripping out of my mouth. "Very good for you when used appropriately."

We run through more details. She's declared on the form that she has no medical issues. Yet, for some reason, I feel apprehensive.

"Would you like to change?" I suggest. "I'll leave the room for a few minutes to give you privacy."

She's clearly nervous. Then again, so are many of my clients who've never had this kind of treatment before. As I go, I see her glancing at my certificate on the wall for reassurance.

Vicki Goudman. MIFA. ITEC LEVEL 3.

Member of the International Federation of Aromatherapists. Sometimes I don't believe it myself. It's certainly not what I'd planned.

When I return to the room, my client is lying facedown on the treatment couch as instructed. Her bare shoulders, which reveal a dark mole on the right blade, are thin, scrawny. Her skin is cold even though I've got the heating on high at this time of year.

"I haven't felt like eating much recently," she says. "I've lost weight."

Trauma does that to you. Or it can make you pile on the pounds. I've done both. I turn on the CD player. The angel music is soft, healing.

"Mmmm," she says in a sleepy voice as I massage the oil in deft circular motions down her spine. "You've got a real touch. I love that smell. What is it again?"

I repeat the ingredients. Lavender. Ylang-ylang. Petitgrain. Grapefruit juice.

"How do you know what to use?" she asks, her voice muffled because of her position.

"It's a bit like a marriage," I say. "You match the oil to the client's needs. And you follow your instinct."

There's a snort. I think, for a minute, that it's laughter, but then I realize she's crying. "If I'd listened to my own instinct," she sobs, "I might have kept my husband."

There it is again. That temptation to give away too much about yourself. You think you're doing it to put them at their ease. But really, it's giving in to your own need. Afterward, you regret it. The client feels awkward on the next visit. And so do you. It's a business arrangement, not a friendship.

So I hold back the longing to tell this woman that David and I would have been coming up to our sixth wedding anniversary in a few months. I also resist the temptation to remind myself that it is Valentine's Day. That on our first—and only—one together he had given me a pair of crystal drop earrings, which I can no longer bring myself to wear. Instead, I breathe in the lavender and imagine it's wrapped around my body like a protective cloak.

"Sometimes," I say, kneading the stress knots, "you have to go through the dark to get to the light."

My client relaxes more, and I'd like to think that it's my words that have soothed her. But it's the magic of the aromatherapy. The lavender is getting into my own skin, too. That's the thing about oils: they're always the same. A constant.

Unlike love.

"Is there anything in particular stressing you out?" I ask gently.

She gives a *Where do I start?* laugh. "The kids are driving me crazy, especially the little one. He's impossible."

"How old is he?" I ask.

"Nearly four. Going on ten."

Now it's *my* skin that goes cold.

"He's in trouble at school for biting this new boy in his class, and the teachers think it's my fault. They've actually asked me if there is violence in our family."

Is there? The question lies unspoken.

She wriggles slightly on the couch. "Do you have kids?"

My hands dig deeper into her muscle knots. "I have a son. He's four, too."

"What's his name?"

"Patrick."

"Is he a good boy?"

I think of the picture in my pocket.

"He's perfect."

"You're lucky. Who looks after him when you're working?"

I pause briefly. "He's with my dad."

"Really? You hear a lot about grandparents helping out nowadays."

My thumbs are really pressing down now.

"Actually, that's hurting."

"Sorry." I release the pressure.

After that, we continue in silence with only the angel music in the background. Some like to talk throughout. Others don't say a word. Many begin to confide and then stop, like this one. She might tell me more at the next session. I sense she'll come back. But I hope she won't. She's too nosy.

"Thank you," she says when I leave her to get dressed. I return to my notes. I write down, in purple ink, the exact treatment and areas of the body that still need attention. Those knots were stubborn. They are often related to the knots in the mind. After David, my shoulders were stiff for months.

"Would you rather have cash or a check?" she asks.

"Check, please."

Paper payment—or an electronic transfer—allows me to be absolutely certain who has paid me and when. My business must be aboveboard. If nothing else, I've learned that.

She puts on her coat. It's cold outside. The wind is rattling the windows.

"I like your place," she says, looking around as if seeing it properly now that she is about to go.

"Thank you."

I like it, too. One joy of being on your own is that you can decorate exactly as you wish. David had liked modern. I chose a converted

ground-floor flat in a Victorian house. My consulting chair is draped with
a restful duck egg blue woolen throw. The lighting is soft. Unlit lavender-
scented candles line the low table that I painted myself in a creamy white.
The pale purple rug, which I take with me every time I move, disguises the
stain on the carpet beneath. No stairs. The front door leads straight onto
the street opposite the seafront.

"Wish *I* could work from home," says my client. "I had to give up my job
in the bank after my second child."

There are pros and cons, I could say. You don't get out enough if you are
busy. You don't have office colleagues to talk to. To joke with. To share
problems with. A sudden wave of loneliness engulfs me.

"May I make another appointment now?" she says suddenly.

"Sure," I say, vowing to keep quiet about my personal life the next time.
No more talk about Patrick.

And that's when the door sounds. I specifically chose a place with its
own front entrance. I also, with the landlady's permission, disconnected
the bell. Sharp noises disturb me. A knocker is less strident. But this thud
makes me jump.

Why is someone here now, at nine o'clock in the evening? Have I forgotten about another client? Usually I am very careful to write things down,
but there have been one or two mistakes recently.

"Would you mind waiting a minute in the studio?" I ask.

It takes a while to open up. I have a thick safety chain, and I've double-
locked it, as always. There's another knock as I search for the key. There it
is, on the side table. Once more, I must have forgotten to put it in its place
on the hook. Not a good sign.

"Coming," I call out as the knocker thuds again.

The open door brings in the biting wind with a trace of fog.

I do a double take. A woman is standing on the doorstep brandishing an
ID card as proof of identity. Her face carries all the hallmarks of stress.
Immediately, my mind springs into action as I mentally concoct a mixture
to soothe her. Lavender. Maybe lemongrass, too.

The man next to her is sporting a fawn raincoat. He looks suspicious. I learned to read body language the hard way. Not that it did any good in the end.

"May I help you?"

"Vicki Goudman?"

I nod, taking in this man and his strikingly assured air.

"Former wife of David Goudman?" he continues.

I nod again. Less certainly this time.

Now he, too, is flashing ID at me. "Detective Inspector Gareth Vine. This is my colleague Sergeant Sarah Brown. May we come in?"

"Sure." I step back to let them inside. My throat has swollen with apprehension. I run my hands through my hair, which I've started to grow again as part of the "new me." Sweat trickles down my back. My mouth is dry.

"What's this about?" I ask.

"When did you last see your ex-husband?"

The question is so unexpected that I cannot think. I feel a sick knot in the pit of my stomach.

"Years ago. Why?" The sour taste of bile is in my mouth as I speak.

The woman in uniform is staring at me. Her eyes are sharp, appraising. "The present Mrs. Goudman has reported him missing."

Sometimes I wonder how it's possible for another woman to carry my name, let alone Tanya, his former secretary, or "the bitch" as I sometimes call her in my head.

"How long . . . ? When . . . ? Is he all right?"

Even as I ask the last question, I'm aware it's a ridiculous one. If he was OK, they wouldn't be here.

It's the inspector who answers. "That's what we're trying to ascertain." He rubs his chin. "David Goudman has been missing now for fifteen days. His wife is insistent that it is out of character, so we are exploring various lines of inquiry."

My body begins to twitch. Stress is a significant trigger. So, too, is lack of sleep, and even certain music pitches. It was one of the first things they told me. And if it does go wrong, well, I can't be held responsible for either myself or anyone else.

"You said just now you hadn't seen him for years," continues the detective. "Can you be more precise than that?"

"Since 2013." I swallow. "It's when we got divorced."

"I see."

He says this as though he doesn't. Or perhaps he does—all too clearly.

"Where exactly were you on 31 January this year?"

That's easy. I rarely leave this place. "Here. At home. Or maybe on the seafront. I usually walk along it once a day for some air."

"Can anyone confirm that?"

I stare hard at him. "No. I live alone."

"Any friends who might have seen you out and about?"

"Not been here long enough."

"Don't you want to check your diary?"

"There's no need."

There's a brief silence during which I force myself not to speak anymore, conscious that I haven't sounded very convincing.

"Mind if we take a look round?" asks the woman.

I'd like to ask if they have a warrant but I don't want to arouse suspicion.

"You can, although I do have a client here," I say.

"Ah yes. I believe you are a masseuse?"

Her tone suggests that I offer a different kind of service. It wouldn't be the first time that my occupation has been misinterpreted.

"Aromatherapist, actually."

The man stares at me blankly. Those who aren't familiar with alternative treatments can easily get the wrong impression.

"I do massage people, but with essential oils."

As if on cue, there is a forced cough behind me. My lady has clearly gotten tired of waiting. "I can see you are busy." She glances nervously at my two visitors. "I'll ring later to make that appointment."

She slips out into the dark, and I suspect I won't see her again. Despite my earlier wish that she wouldn't return, I am not comforted. That one will talk.

I gesture my visitors toward my studio, wondering momentarily whether I've remembered to close the trapdoor fully. Thankfully, I have.

They look suspiciously at the vials of liquid on the shelf above my desk. "Do you make your own potions?" says the woman.

I resist a smile at her use of the word that brings to mind witchcraft or black magic. "We call them essences. Actually, I buy them from a mail-order site."

"What does this stuff do?" asks the detective.

"Relaxes you. Helps restore memory. Gives you strength."

The woman is picking up the lavender oil and smelling it. "I've always wanted to try it out."

"I can give you my card if you like."

"We know where you are."

Of course.

"So you work from home?" says the man.

"I'm registered." My tone is more defensive now.

It doesn't take long to do the "tour." It's a compact, two-bedroom, one-level apartment with one of the bedrooms now functioning as my studio. It's right on the seafront, "boasting easy access to the amenities of Penzance," as described by the estate agents.

"Nice view," says the woman, looking out at the sea from my bedroom.

It's why I came here. This morning, the water was a particularly striking azure blue. Yesterday, it was green. The day before, black. Too dangerous for me to swim, even if I had a wet suit like some of the keen locals.

"You don't miss city life, then?"

It's as though they are purposefully ignoring the elephant in the room.

"David," I say desperately. "Where was he when he went missing?"

The woman swivels round. "We were hoping you could tell us."

"Why should I know?"

"Come on, Vicki." It's the detective this time. His voice is silky smooth and reeking of suspicion. "Mrs. Goudman tells us that she saw you near their home in Kingston just before Christmas." He gets out a notepad. "'Standing at the gate and staring at my house.' Those were her exact words."

"I had an appointment with a consultant," I say hotly.

His eyes narrow. "In London? That's a long way to go."

I shrug. "The outskirts, actually. He wasn't far from my old house, so I walked past. I felt nostalgic. Anyone would be."

I note a swift flicker of sympathy in the policewoman's face.

"They'd dug up my roses and replaced them with a hideous rock garden," I add. I've never cared for rockeries. Too cemetery-like.

"You can prove that?"

"The roses?"

"Your visit to your 'consultant.'" His voice is tight, as if he thinks I'm having him on. I'm not. I'm still livid about those roses.

I reach for my address book and scribble down a name and number. "There. Ring that."

"We will."

"The lounge is through here," I say, anxious in case they make too close an inspection of another room.

We go into the small room with its duck egg blue throw on the sofa, just like my studio.

"No television?" the woman remarks, looking around.

"No."

She raises an eyebrow and then hands me a card. I want to turn it down, as she had done earlier to me.

"If you do hear from your ex-husband, please get in touch immediately."

"Do you know any more about his disappearance?"

The detective has his suspicious face on again. "Why do you ask?"

"He was my husband. I'd like to know he's safe."

His voice is clinical. "At this stage, we're still making preliminary inquiries."

They go. I double-lock the door. Put the safety chain up. Run to my bedroom.

Then I pick up the phone and dial the number that is firmly engraved in my mind.

"This is David. You know what to do."

My ex's voice is deep. It's comforting, despite everything, in its familiarity.

"Please answer," I choke. "It's me."

2.

SCARLET

8 March 2007

What a clever, grown-up girl! That's what Mum was always saying. They didn't need anyone else. Just the two of them. They were a team. Especially when it came to the game.

There were three types: the swing, the seesaw, and hide-and-seek. Out of the three, Scarlet preferred the last.

"Sometimes, love, we have to do the others, too," Mum would tell her in that singsong voice that came from a place called Whales.

"Why?"

"You're too young to understand."

"But I look older, don't I? 'Cos I'm tall like my dad was."

"Yes," Mum would murmur. Then she'd kneel down and hold Scarlet tight. Sometimes Mum would put her dark hair into neat little braids. That was Scarlet's favorite thing. She would breathe her mother in. She always smelled the same. Pat Chew Lee. That's what the bottle of her mum's perfume said. P-A-T-C-H-O-U-L-I.

Scarlet was good at English. Her average reading age was eleven instead of eight. "I'm really proud of you," Mum said. Her favorite book was *Alice in Wonderland*. It had been Mum's when she'd been little. They read it together every night except when Mum had been smoking one of her magic cigarettes and was being all funny.

Back to the swing game. So scary! You never knew who was going to come up behind and push. Mum was nearby. That's what she always told Scarlet. But they mustn't actually see each other, because that might give the game away. All Scarlet had to do was sit on the seat and pretend that the pusher was someone she knew.

Even though she didn't.

Then she had to say, "Please, can I have something to eat?" It was really important that she spoke loudly in case anyone else was listening.

The reply was always the same. "Again?"

That's when she'd turn round and see the person behind her.

It might be a woman. Or it might be a man. Sometimes they smelled of beer or pee or the wardrobe that she and Mum shared. But they always did the same thing.

They'd hand her some crisps—the kind you got in a tube with a plastic lid. Then Scarlet would stop the swing for a bit so she could take off the lid and eat the crisp on top before putting the lid back on again.

"Give us the old one, then," they'd say. So she'd hand them the empty crisp tube in her little pink shoulder bag, which Mum had bought her specially for the game because she was so good at it.

After that, they pushed the swing a few more times. When she turned round to see why they'd stopped, there was no one there.

That was when she had to walk to the park entrance, and Mum would be waiting. "Where have you been? I've been worried."

Scarlet knew exactly what to say. "I wanted a swing. This nice person pushed me."

"What have I told you? Don't talk to strangers."

But Scarlet wasn't upset, because this was all part of the make-believe, just like the tales in her storybooks. Mum wasn't really cross. She was only pretending to be!

When they got back to the flat, Mum would snatch the tube that didn't actually have any crisps. Instead, there were lots of tenners inside.

After that, they'd share a packet of fish and chips for tea as a treat. The vinegar made her mouth sting. Then Mum would light up a cigarette and open a bottle of wine.

"Have a sip," she'd say. "It will help you sleep."

Yuck! But she took it anyway, just to be a good girl.

Sometimes they used empty cans of fizzy pop instead of crisp tubes. It was good, Mum said, to have a change every now and then. But you didn't need either for the seesaw game, which was her second favorite. The nice part was that you got to see the other person, so it wasn't quite as frightening. The girl or boy on the other side would start to go up and down very fast. It made Scarlet's head all dizzy. She'd have to hang on very tight so that the little parcel tucked into her jeans pocket stayed exactly where it was meant to.

The next step was to fall off carefully so that she didn't hurt herself. "Make sure you cry loudly," Mum had told her. "When the other person helps you up, use the confusion to do a quick swap."

This was more complicated than the swing game. "It takes a real pro like you to do it," said Mum.

Scarlet wasn't sure what a pro was, but it sounded good. Especially as Mum often gave her a shiny pound coin in return for bringing back the tenners. Sometimes she was allowed to touch the notes after Mum had done her counting. They were as crisp as autumn leaves.

But the best game of all was hide-and-seek. They did this in the shopping center. Scarlet liked this most because it was warm in the winter and also because Mum came with her. It made her feel safer.

First, they'd do something called a decoy—this meant trying on new clothes without buying.

"Give us a twirl," Mum would say when the assistant came to the changing room to see if she could help. "Pretty girl."

Then Scarlet would look at herself in the mirror and flick back those braids with the little red beads and wonder once more why her skin was darker than Mum's. Mum said it was because her father had come from a place called Trinny Dad.

"Where's my dad now?" she'd sometimes ask.

But the answer was always the same. "I don't know and I don't care. We're happy enough on our own, aren't we?"

One day, an older woman had come up to them in a shop and told Mum she was a "model scout." "Your little girl would be perfect." But Mum had said they didn't want any of that and had rushed her out of the doors. "We mustn't attract attention," she explained. It almost spoiled the game.

After they tried on more clothes, Mum would leave and Scarlet would burst into tears. This was called "role playing," said Mum.

Then one of the assistants or maybe another customer would ask if she was all right.

At exactly that point, a woman would come rushing in. Scarlet had to pretend she knew her. "*There* you are, love. Your mum's fallen ill, so she asked me to come and get you."

The next bit was tricky. As they were walking out, the woman would hand her a tissue. After she'd blown her nose, Scarlet would put it in her pocket. Then the woman would tell her to hand it back so she could throw it away. But Scarlet would give her a different tissue back. The first tissue had a whole £50 note in it, which she would then give to Mum. And the second had a little plastic bag in it with white powder.

Once, the game almost went wrong when an assistant asked the strange woman for identification.

"What do you think I am?" she'd demanded. "A child snatcher? Go on, Scarlet, love. Tell her!"

"This is my auntie Julie," Scarlet said, remembering what Mum had told her.

And the assistant had gone all pink and said she was sorry but you couldn't be too careful nowadays.

That's why they had to make sure they didn't do the tissue swapping bit anywhere near a See See TV camera.

But then came that Wednesday. It started off by feeling all wrong because Mum hadn't wanted her hair stroked or to sing along to the radio like she usually did. She also got cross because they had run out of bread. "It's all right," said Scarlet, even though her stomach was rumbling. "I'll just wait for lunch."

"That won't help. You're not going to school."

"But it's library day and News Story Hour."

"Forget it. We've got to do the swing game today. Don't look like that. If we finish quickly, you might be able to go in late. Just tell them you were at the dentist."

"But I said that last time."

"Then we'll pretend it was the doctor. OK?"

"They'll ask me for a letter."

"I'll do you one later when we've got more time. Now stop arguing and do what I say."

Scarlet shivered. "Wear this," said Mum, handing her a big, fluffy, yellow, fleecy jacket.

"Wow! It's just like the one we saw in the market." The market was one of her favorite places—you could get anything there.

Mum looked pleased. "I bought it for you because you're a good girl." Then she handed Scarlet a crisps tube for her pink shoulder bag. The lid was slightly open.

"Why is there sugar inside?"

"Don't touch!" Mum said sharply and shut it quickly.

"I'm sorry."

Mum's face went kind again. "It's me that should be sorry, love. I've got a lot on my mind. Tell you what—how do you feel about moving somewhere new?"

They often imagined going to different places. It was part of the game. "Where this time?"

"Somewhere warm." Mum's eyes went all dreamy, like they did when she woke up. "We could have a home near a beach and build sandcastles."

"Could we eat ice cream? The kind with chocolate flakes that melt in your mouth?"

Mum lifted her up into the air and swung her around. She wasn't dreamy anymore. She was awake and excited. "As much as you want."

"Yes, please!"

"We can only do it if you follow the rules. Got it?"

Scarlet nodded solemnly. "Got it."

They made their way down the steep steps outside their flat and past the big red letters that someone had painted on the walls. C-U-N and then another letter that had been crossed out. "We don't need to know what that means," Mum always said.

"Watch out for the dog shit. Jump! That's right. Hold my hand when you cross the road. Are you warm enough? Don't forget your words."

But Scarlet kept thinking about the book with the pretty pictures that she could have been reading in class.

The rain trickled down the neck of her new jacket. "Just a drizzle," said Mum as she kissed Scarlet. The Pat Chew Lee was mixed with the smell of the fags.

"Off you go. See you at the gates."

Scarlet ran over to the swings. No one else was there. Not even the mothers with the little ones who were too small to go to school. She kicked the ground to start herself off. Forward. Back. Waiting. Waiting.

"Shall I push you, love?"

The voice had the same friendly sound that had belonged to the man who had visited last night. It meant he was from "the southwest."

Back. Forward. Back. Forward. Don't forget your words.

"I'm hungry," she said.

"Want some crisps?"

Scarlet stopped as the man handed over the tube. Then she reached in her bag for the sugar. Just as she gave it to him, there was a shout.

"You there. Stop!" Another man was running up to them. "I am arresting you on suspicion of illegal possession of a controlled substance . . ."

"No. NO!"

Mum suddenly appeared, but then a woman in a cop uniform rushed up and held her back. A second one tried to take Scarlet's hand.

"Come with me, lass. It's all right."

"LET HER GO!"

"MUM! COME BACK."

"Scarlet! SCARLET! Let me talk to my little girl, you bastards." Mum's cries pierced her ears as they pulled her away.

Was this part of the game?

"It's all right, love," said the cop. "You're safe now. Come with me."

"GET AWAY," yelled Scarlet.

The man pulled his hand away, but not before she'd bitten it.

"You little cat!"

They were putting her in one car and Mum in another. Hers went first.

"COME BACK," she wept, hammering on the window with her fists. But Mum grew farther and farther away until the other car was a little black spot.

And then she was gone.

*R*ose. Neroli. Sandalwood. Ylang-ylang. Patchouli.

All are said to have aphrodisiac qualities.

Some days I love him still. Other days I hate him. Right now I wish he was dead. It would be so much easier. Then no one else could have him either.

3.

VICKI

_T_ his is David," says the smooth, husky voice. "_You know what to do._"

But I don't. In fact, I lost my way on the day that it happened. I end the call.

Stop. Don't think about it, or the stress might trigger the "thing" that sits on your shoulder, day after day. Teasing you into thinking everything's all right and then striking out of the blue.

Deep breath—that's better. Work this out calmly. Why not just ring again? He might pick up this time. Even though my ex-husband has said he never wants to hear or see me again, I miss him. That's why every now and then I call, just to hear his voice on the cell voice mail. Besides, this is an emergency, so I'll give it another go.

"_This is David . . ._"

His deep, assured tone takes me back to the evening we met. It was a fund-raising dinner in aid of a campaign to rehabilitate prisoners, and I'd been told, in no uncertain terms by the authorities, that my presence was "necessary."

David Goudman (as his place card read) was late, which meant I had an embarrassing gap on my right, limiting me to conversation with a very quiet woman on my left. When he finally arrived, he was deeply apologetic as well as courteous and charming. Dismissing my questions about his work—property development—he seemed far more interested in me.

"Tell me about your life," he'd said, straight out. David had a way of listening as though you were the only person he wanted to hear in the whole wide world. I found myself wondering how old he was. Those crinkly lines with a hint of a tan suggested middle age, like me. How had he gotten that slightly hooked nose that somehow didn't detract from his good looks? Maybe a sporting injury. He looked like he might play rugby.

"That's amazing," he said when I gave him a brief outline. His brown eyes—with a hint of green in the middle—locked with mine. But it was his deep voice that really struck me. There was laughter there: something I'd been missing for so long! It seemed at odds with that strong, set jawline. I had a sudden urge to run my finger along that faint hint of stubble as he continued to talk. "I'd love to know more, Vicki. May I call you that?" He glanced at my place setting.

He was still there at the end of the evening when everyone else had filtered out. "I don't suppose you have time for a drink?" he asked. "My place is near here." He raised an eyebrow. "My ex-wife always said I was handy with both a corkscrew and the coffee machine. One of my few pluses, apparently!"

Ex-wife. I glanced at his left hand. No ring. To my embarrassment, he noticed.

"Single," he said, with a directness I admired. "You?"

"The same."

Sometimes we act completely out of character. Of all people, I should know that. Or perhaps my boldness was due to something one of the girls had said when she'd seen me earlier, all dressed up in heels and a lime green suit that seemed to complement my hair.

"Letting you out for the night, are they?"

She must have sensed how nervous I was. It can be daunting after being inside for so long.

I'd walked on, conscious of the titters behind me.

If only they could see me now.

"You're not what I expected," David said later.

We were lying face-to-face in his huge bed in a massive loft conversion overlooking the London Eye. I knew I could get into trouble for being back late, but for once I ignored the nagging voice, telling myself I was entitled to some fun for a change.

"In what way?" I asked.

I often wonder how people really see me. But very few have the courage to tell me. Instead, others usually look at me with curiosity, apprehension and fear.

"You're more . . ." He hesitates. "I was going to say 'feminine,' but that sounds disparaging."

"Yes," I agreed. "It does."

He stroked the side of my face as if memorizing the texture of my skin. "Let me start again. You're strong. You've done things that many women—and men—wouldn't or couldn't do."

This talk was making me nervous. "I suppose. The last few years haven't been easy."

He nodded. "I'm sure they haven't."

It had been a long time since I'd had such a frank conversation. Despite the unease, I felt a sense of relief at meeting someone who seemed to understand.

His right hand was tracing the outline of my back. "Do you have any regrets?"

David's touch made it hard for me to concentrate. It's as though he already knew each curve of my body, despite the fact we'd only just met.

"Yes," I whispered. "You?"

"Several—if I let myself dwell on them. But I don't." He turned away to lie on his back, staring up at the ceiling. My body felt cold without his skin on mine, despite the warmth of the apartment. "Instead I keep myself busy."

This was my cue to question him. Physical attraction was all very well, but it's what lies beneath that matters in a long-term relationship. Then I caught myself. Long-term? What was I thinking? I didn't know this man. And he didn't know me. I wanted to tell him that I'm not the kind of woman who goes to bed with someone on a first date, but that sounded too much like a cliché. The truth is that I had to do this—call it intuition or lust or loneliness or a desire to prove that I could get a man if I wanted. But here I was. And now I wanted to find out everything about David Goudman. I sensed there was much more to him than met the eye.

"How did you start your business?" I asked.

"Through sheer hard work and luck. My old man pushed me to go into the army, which I did, but it wasn't for me." A strange look flitted across his face, and I wondered what horrors he'd seen. "I got out as soon as I could and hooked up with a bloke I'd met through the forces. He'd gone back to the States, where he ran a business. My old mate had wanted a UK presence, and I began developing land. Then I was able to set up on my own." He spread out his hands. "The rest, as they say, is history!"

I was impressed.

"What do you do when you're not working?" I asked.

He laughed. "I usually *am* working. Doesn't leave much time for personal relationships, but I'm happiest being active."

"Me, too. I need fresh air."

He nodded approvingly. "I thought as much. Do you like walking?"

I thought of the long corridors and the outside exercise yard with its jogging track. "Can't get enough of it."

His eyes looked as though they were somewhere else. "I love to drive down to Devon when I'm not working. You can't beat places like Dartmoor."

"I love it, too!"

"Your favorite part?" He placed a finger on my lips. "No. Wait. Say it together. One, two, three . . ."

"Haytor," we both blurted out together. Then he moved toward me, and we rocked in laughter and amazement, his body against mine.

"When I climb right up and look down," he said, "it's like being on the top of the world."

"Exactly. But I have to come down on my bottom. It's too difficult otherwise."

He gave mine a gentle slap. "I'd like to see that."

"What else?"

"What else would I like to see?"

"No." I giggled. I hadn't felt this carefree for years. "What else do you do apart from walking or working?"

"Give away my money." He laughed when he saw my skeptical face. "Really. It gives me pleasure. I'm a great believer in giving back if you have good fortune yourself."

I had a flash of the homeless woman I'd passed earlier that night who was selling street magazines for a living. "Who do you help?"

"I like to go for smaller causes that don't get the big handouts. One of my favorites provides holidays for inner-city kids. And then there's a hospice in Oxfordshire. In fact, I'm driving down tomorrow to open its new wing." He reached across me for a brochure on the bedside table, brushing my breast as he did so. "My mother died of cancer when I was twelve. Dad and I nursed her together at the end. We could have done with a place like this."

A large lump sprouted in my throat. "I'm so sorry."

He made one of those *It's fine* gestures.

"My mother died of cancer, too," I ventured. "I was eight."

There was a sudden connection between us—one that hadn't been there before, despite the passionate sex.

"I'd like to see you again," he said. "Do you think that's possible?"

I thought of the many rules that governed my life. "I hope so," I said.

Over the next few weeks, he rang me every night and took me out to lunch on the days when I was able to meet. We usually went to bistros that were understatedly chic, tucked away in pockets of London that I hadn't been to before. David actually had a Porsche! But he was a careful driver, I noticed, constantly checking his mirrors. He didn't like to talk when he was driving, concentrating instead on the road. I liked that.

David was well-read. We shared a love of Somerset Maugham's short stories and went to a reading of one of his plays at the British Library. Like me, he couldn't paint for toffee, yet he admired art, as was apparent from the huge, colorful contemporary oils on his walls. This was a man who took his hobbies seriously. He listened when I allowed myself to cry at some of the things I had to endure, day after day. "You're the strongest woman I've ever known. A one-off. I've never met anyone like you before. And I don't think I ever will."

He didn't judge or ask why I had done certain things. Instead, he made me feel special in a way that no one had done before. He opened my body. My mind, too.

Men like David would have had several lovers. Common sense told me that. But right now, he wanted *me*.

Two months later we were married, with a prison officer as one of the witnesses. My only regret was that Dad wasn't here to see it.

I have to stop right here with my memories. Stress is bad. Hadn't they told me that over and over again?

Lavender. Quickly. Calming lavender. I reach for the oil next to the sofa. Inhale three deep breaths. Now massage into the pressure points. Two on the sinuses. Behind the ears. Above the eyebrows. That tender part on the top of the head. The two spots at the back of the neck. Press until they stop hurting. I learned that as part of the training.

I suddenly yearn for a lovely warm bath with orange blossom oil. Showers aren't the same. You can't lie back and relax. Sit still, I tell myself. I resist the temptation to pick up the phone and hear David's voice again. Then again, hadn't he gone walkabout enough times during our marriage?

My mind returns to the month after the wedding, when it all started to fall apart.

"I had a deal to sort out," he'd said casually when I hadn't heard from him for two days. "I told you. Don't you remember?"

I didn't.

"That's because you were tired."

Nonsense! Nothing wrong with my memory.

"I *did* tell you," David insisted. But I couldn't see his face because our conversation took place on the phone. And even if I could have, I might not have known if he'd been lying.

Eventually, it became easier to go along with it, rather than argue. Perhaps now, I tell myself, he's simply repeating his old patterns. Good luck to Tanya with her low necklines, little-girl voice and excessive black eyeliner. There's a certain justice that she's having to put up with the same thing.

Unless she knows something that I don't.

15 February 2018

When my eyes open the next morning, the sun is streaming in through the window. Gingerly, I do my usual checks. No obvious bruises. My muscles aren't aching. No feeling that something "isn't quite right." So far, so good.

I ease myself slowly out of bed and pad across the beige carpet to the window. The sea spreads out calmly before me. Yesterday, it had been furious, spitting pebbles up and onto the promenade. I'd had to walk round them, frightened of tripping.

How had I managed to live so long without being next to the sea? The colors alone are to die for: sometimes turquoise, or pale blue, or gray. Red from the rocks. I marvel at the soothing regularity with which the tide goes in and out, day after day.

Missing now for fifteen days.

The policeman's voice returns to me. Tossing me back to last night's visit, which means it's been sixteen days now. Despite my earlier resolution, I reach for the phone.

"This is David. You know what to do . . ."

Don't play that message again, I tell myself. Get out. Breathe in the air.

It might be cold, but it's good for you! You need to buy some nutty rye bread anyway. And pick up your prescription. Sort yourself out before the next client. When is she coming again? Check the diary. Not until to-morrow.

Since David, I've fallen into the habit of talking to myself. It makes life seem less lonely. The same goes for the radio. Most of the girls had gone for Radio 1, but the psychologist had introduced me to Classic FM. "Music makes such a difference to your state of mind," he would say.

I tune in now, but the reception isn't great. Radio Cornwall is clearer—more intimate, too. It makes me feel as though I belong here.

"More delays expected on the Great Western route to Paddington after a week of heavy storms . . ."

Might this explain David's disappearance? Could he have come down here—maybe to find me? No. Get real.

To have a break, then? No to that, too. "Can't think of anywhere worse," he used to say, "than a cold British beach." It turned out that he'd only been to Dartmoor once. In reality, he was a London man with holidays in the Caribbean, usually tied in with deals all over the world. That way, he could pass off "leisure" spending as business expenses. Was that legal, I'd asked in the early days. He'd laughed that deep, rich laugh of his. Of course it was.

All these memories, I warn myself as I put on my bright red waterproof jacket, are making my head hum. Or is it because I'm hungry? It's reason-ably early—only 7:30 a.m.—although the girls would have been up for some time by now. I pick up my bottle of tablets, think about it for a sec-ond, knock one back and then tie up my hair. They advised me to keep it short in case it proved a "hazard," but I needed to create a "new me" in order to keep going.

But suddenly, I think about everything that could trigger me, and the idea of going out scares me. I feel safer inside. So I stay in all day, blending my essences. But by the time it's dusk, I have cabin fever, so I put my jacket on once more and open the door, flinching as the wind hits my face.

I walk along the promenade, concentrating on the fine line between the

land and the sea to distract myself. Then a cracked paving stone makes me
falter, but I manage to right myself just in time. After that, I look straight
ahead. It helps that it's off season, with few tourists to bump into.

I freeze. There's a child walking toward me, carrying a yellow bucket
and spade, even though it's not the weather for it. He seems the right age,
and his fringe is cut straight across. His eyes lift up as if he knows me.

"Patrick," I whisper in my head. But the word escapes into the air for all
to hear.

The woman next to him grabs his hand and gives me a strange look, and
they skitter past.

Breathe deeply. Pretend it didn't happen. Think of something else, like
sea salt. Not just the smell but the taste on your tongue and the freshness
in your nose. Until I moved down to the southwest, I hadn't realized how
different the air could be.

A man on a cherry red disabled scooter is now approaching. I move to
one side to allow him by. Would it be easier if my own problems were
more obvious like his? Then others might not be so shocked when it happens. Past a woman in purple leggings playing a recorder, perched on the
seawall. The music is hauntingly beautiful, but experiences such as this
need to be shared. Yet who would want to share my dark life? Not David,
as it turned out.

The humming in my head is back. A warning aura—that's what they
told me. Not everyone gets it. Sometimes it passes. A small white dog goes
by, sniffing curiously. Animals often have a sixth sense.

I reach into my pocket for the lavender oil again. I quickly massage it
into my pulse points before clutching the chipped green promenade railing
for support. There's a yapping noise behind me. I look back. Next to the
dog and its owner is a pretty young woman, wrapped up against the cold.
For a moment, my eyes lock with hers. Don't I know her from somewhere?
But then she turns round and walks off.

Now I can smell burning. This isn't good. Experience has taught me
that I have a few seconds left, if that.

"Are you all right?"

A woman's concerned voice comes at me from a distance. I need to get under something. Fast. I need to move away from the railing, or I might fall through to the beach below. A car is going past. Avoid the road.

The bench. The one to my right. FOR MARJORIE—WHO LOVED THIS PLACE. I've seen the inscription before, along with all the others along the promenade. Each has a story behind it. But I'm in no fit state to read them now.

I'm vaguely aware of being on all fours.

"Are you all right?" repeats the voice.

I can feel something wet against my face. The dog?

And then nothing.

4.

SCARLET

"MUM! MUM!"

Scarlet kept screaming all the way from the park to the police station. Hammering the car window with her fists and then with her head. Her throat was sore and her hands hurt. A big blue bruise had already started to show on her knuckles. Rain was dribbling down, and the glass was misting up, so she couldn't see out. It made her scream even more, in case Mum was out there waving and she couldn't see her.

"Stop that awful noise right now," said the woman cop. "Bloody hell, she's bitten me again."

"Little beast." This was the other cop in the back of the car. She had a thinner face. Meaner. "Like mother, like daughter."

"I WANT MY MUM!"

"You'll see her if you behave yourself. Got it?"

Scarlet couldn't cry anymore. Her throat was so rough that it was hard to swallow, and she felt sick. But worst of all was that empty pit of fear inside her. "I'm scared I might never see my mum again," she whispered.

That was when she saw it. The look.

Scarlet was good at working out what looks meant. She'd had practice. There was the look Mum gave her before the game that meant, "Be a good girl." There's the look purple-haired Auntie Julie had given her in the shop that said, "Pretend you know me." And the look that the uncles gave her that meant, "Get lost—I want time on my own with your mother."

But this one, between the two cops, was different. It said, "Don't let on."

"You'll see her. I promise," said the nicer one.

"You're lying!" screamed Scarlet. And then she started banging her fist against the car window until they had to hold her arms, and even then she wouldn't stop trying—not even when they got to the big black building in the high street.

"What we got here, then?" said the man at the desk. He had a shiny head with patches of hair in between.

"WHERE IS MY MUM?" Scarlet kicked the desk so hard that her toes hurt through her sneakers. It's what Mum had done when the lady at the council had said their rent was going up. But it hadn't worked, because they'd told her to behave or else she'd lose all her Benny fits.

"You'll see her when we say so," said the man. "In the meantime, you'd better behave, miss."

Then he jerked his head toward a door. It had a black and gold sign on it. Scarlet mouthed the letters. C-H-I-L-D-C-A-R-E. "Through there."

The mean-faced cop took hold of her left arm. "If someone tries to get you," Mum always said, "buckle your knees. It's more difficult for them to carry you then."

But it didn't work, because the man from behind the desk had grabbed her right arm. Between them, her legs slid across the floor toward the sign and into a room with chairs and a table. There was a plate of biscuits on top. Chocolate. Her favorite.

"Scarlet?"

For a minute, she thought it was Aunt Julie. This woman had the same sort of messy purple hair, shaggy fringe and black makeup smudges under her eyes. But it couldn't really be her, because there wasn't a gold stud in her nose. This one was silver.

"Scarlet is your name, isn't it?"

"What's it to you?"

That's what Mum had always told her to say if someone asked her a question she wasn't sure she should answer.

"It was on your passport, love."

Passports had to be kept safe in secret places so the cops couldn't find them. Mum always moved theirs around—sometimes she hid them in the back of the oven, or under the loose dirty brown carpet tile in the kitchen, or even behind the cracked washbasin, which leaked, because the bloody council still hadn't fixed it.

"How did you find it?"

"Your mum had it on her, love."

"I WANT TO SEE HER!" Scarlet kicked the chair so hard that it fell over.

"Pick that up now and sit on it," roared the thin-faced cop.

But Shaggy-Fringe shook her head. "Let her stand if she wants."

Then she crouched down beside Scarlet so they were almost the same height. "My name's Camilla, and I'm a social worker. I know this is a shock, love. And I know you want your mum. But—and you've got to trust me on this—you can't see her right now. Not for a bit, until we've got a few things sorted."

"What kind of things?" whimpered Scarlet.

"Grown-up stuff."

She knew what that meant. Go to bed. Leave Mum and the uncles to it. Don't say anything when Mum slips a tin of supermarket beans into her bag without paying.

"Scarlet, love, listen to me." Her voice sang like a bird with a squeaky voice. "Do you have a dad or a nan or a gran or an auntie or someone who we can call?"

Scarlet hesitated, twisting one of the red beads in her hair. Should she mention the uncles? Maybe not. Mum always said she didn't trust any of them. "It's just Mum and me. We don't need anyone else."

"Just what the mother said," grunted the mean-faced cop.

"But I can stay on my own! I've done it before when Mum has to go out."

"Really?" Camilla with the shaggy fringe began to write on the big piece of paper in front of her. "Well, I'm afraid that's not allowed. You're too young."

Scarlet began to panic. "But I'm safe at home with my mum! She doesn't always go out at night. Anyway, it's not dark yet, and I'm late for school." Scarlet's eyes began to fill with tears again. "It's my favorite day. We get to choose our own books and do News Story Hour."

"What's that?" asked the cop.

"It's when children describe what they've been doing with their families," said Shaggy-Fringe slowly.

"Interesting . . ."

"Mum said I could go in to school later, after the game . . ."

"What game?" The cop's voice came quick and hard.

Scarlet bit her lip. "I can't tell you. It's a secret."

"Tell you what, Scarlet. We were talking about news stories just now, weren't we? I like them, too. So here's a pencil. Why don't you pull up your chair? That's right. Now write down a few sentences about the game. It sounds really fun."

Don't tell anyone anything, she'd always been told. But if it helped her mother, that was different, wasn't it?

"Promise I'll see Mum after that?"

"Promise."

It took a long time.

"Just put what you can remember."

By the time she had finished, her wrists were aching.

"Good girl." Even the mean cop looked pleased with her.

"Can Mum take me home now?"

Shaggy-Fringe was kneeling next to her again. "You'll need to stay somewhere else tonight. Let's see what happens after that, shall we?"

Scarlet felt a flash of panic. "But I gave you my story. So you have to let me see her, like you promised."

"We will, as soon as we find somewhere for you to stay."

"Why can't I just go home?"

"Because there's no one there, love. It's not allowed."

"Where's my mum? WHAT HAVE YOU DONE TO HER?"

The mean cop was holding her hand, yanking her into the corridor outside.

"I don't think that's necessary . . ." began Shaggy-Fringe behind them.

Then she saw her! Mum! Going through another door to the right.

Mum's voice stabbed her chest.

"Let me go!" she could hear Mum screaming. "I want to speak to my baby. It's my fucking right."

"Not now."

Then the door slammed, and Mum was gone.

"Why have you taken her away from me again?" Scarlet flung herself on the floor, sobbing. "Why? Why?"

"Poor little lamb," she heard above her.

"Some mothers don't deserve to have kids," said another.

"That's enough. Who's on the emergency placement list? Let's see . . . The Walters. They'll do."

"Listen, Scarlet. I'm going to drive you to see some nice people who will look after you. It will be much easier if you stop kicking and screaming. All right? We'll sort you out with fresh clothes when we get there and get someone to let your school know what's happened."

"Mum," gasped Scarlet. Her breath was running out, and it was hard to say the words. "I need to tell her where I'm going."

"It's OK, love. She already knows."

"When can I see her?"

There was another sigh. "We have to wait to see what happens in court. But don't worry. You're safe now."

*M*yrrh: uplifts your mood and soothes anger.

        Orange. Similar effect and can also reduce anxiety.

And don't forget chamomile.

"Anger aromatherapy," my tutor called it.

But sometimes you need something else as well.

I started keeping a diary when we had a writer in residence. She said it would help us to write things down—and she was right. It's an emotional release. I honestly think that letting it all out on paper has stopped me from seriously hurting someone physically.

But others might argue that I've done that already.

So if anyone does happen to pick this up and read it (which they shouldn't), I'd just like it on record that I didn't start off this way.

Believe it or not, I got into this mess to do some good.

5.

VICKI

I can tell from the jolting motion that I'm moving.

A man in white is bending over me. He's checking my pulse and wrapping a band of elastic round my arm and pumping it up. That's when it sinks in. I'm in an ambulance.

"Vicki? Can you hear me? My name is Adam, and I'm a paramedic. You've had an epileptic seizure."

Epileptic! Seizure! Two words that have changed me forever since they entered my life. I feel a flood of dread and unease.

Adam's voice is urgent but steady. He is looking at me the way people usually do when this happens. As though I'm a bit soft in the head.

If someone has a heart attack or breaks a leg or does something normal, then it's acceptable. But my condition—well, it's different. People can't always get their heads round epilepsy, not even paramedics. Besides, at this stage, there's not much they can do apart from the usual checks. Heart rate. Oxygen levels. The basics.

"What happened?" I ask.

"You were found under a bench."

Really? It's possible, I suppose. My natural instinct when I feel it coming on (and not everyone does) is to find somewhere safe. In the past, I've been discovered under a children's playground slide, a café table and a supermarket checkout desk. The last was by far the most embarrassing when

I came round to a queue of faces, an hysterical cashier and wet pants. In-continence doesn't always happen. The small saving grace about today is that I feel dry right now.

"Is there any family we should contact, Vicki?"

Dad. If only.

Mum. Long gone.

Patrick. *No!*

David. Does an ex-husband still count as family?

"No one," I manage to say.

A sympathetic look flashes across the paramedic's face. "What's the last thing you remember, Vicki?"

I always struggle with this bit. Think, I tell myself. "Putting on my jacket," I manage finally. "Going out to get some bread before the shop closed. Looking at the sea."

"Did you feel odd before that?"

"My ears began to hum, and then I smelled burning rubber. It's usually a sign; an overfiring of nerves, apparently."

He nods. "So you're one of the lucky ones that get an aura. At least that gives you some warning."

I'm impressed. Clearly, contrary to my suspicions, this man knows his stuff. But *lucky*? I almost laugh. Still, at least I'm alive and allowed to walk freely. Not so very long ago, I might have been locked up. That's what one consultant told me, as if he was trying to make me feel better. According to the statistics I read online after my diagnosis, 1 in every 103 people will be formally diagnosed with epilepsy. About 1 in 26 will experience a sei-zure. In approximately 60 percent of cases, the cause of epilepsy is not known. Staggeringly high when you think about it.

Premature death is by no means inevitable, but you increase the risk if you hit your head or have a seizure when you're in the bath, pouring out hot liquid, crossing the road or doing—well, quite a lot, actually. So I don't swim, drive or cook on a naked flame. You never know when you go to bed if you are going to wake up or not.

The good news—for some of us—is that it can heighten brain function. There are even toddlers who can recite their two times table.

"How long did it last for?" I ask.

"About a minute."

Average, then. Most of my observers in the past have reckoned that my fits—which are technically known as seizures—can be anywhere from twenty seconds to three minutes.

"How do you feel now?"

"My head is hurting."

I'm aware that there's a cold compress on my forehead. My muscles are aching, and the inside of my right cheek tastes of blood where I must have bitten it.

"Not surprising. There wasn't much space under the bench when you were thrashing about."

A memory surfaces. FOR MARJORIE—WHO LOVED THIS PLACE. I'm barely able to keep my eyes open; it's an effort to talk, but I have to keep going. My emotions are all over the place, though I know this is normal.

"How do you know what I was doing?" I'm always intrigued by this bit. It's weird blanking out and then not remembering anything about it, including the events leading up to the seizure. One girl, whom I read about on the Internet, sent a text to her boss to say she was going to be late when she started fitting but then couldn't recall anything about it afterward.

"Luckily, the woman who saw you was a nurse and realized what was happening."

That's not always the case. Often people think you're drunk, mad or having a heart attack (a Good Samaritan once tried to give me mouth-to-mouth, even though I was still breathing).

"She rang for an ambulance."

If she was a nurse, she probably didn't panic. It's probably why I feel relatively calm myself. When people freak out, it's catching—especially if they're still doing it when you come round. It makes it harder to compose yourself afterward.

I'm so sleepy that Adam is now drifting in and out.

"Did something upset you, Vicki?" His voice comes at me through a mist. "Something that might have brought this on?"

They usually ask this. It's all part of building up a profile. But my eyes are heavy, and I can't think properly.

"Not sure," I murmur. But something is nagging inside me. Something *did* upset me.

I just can't remember what.

When I awake, I'm in a hospital bed. I'm wearing a green gown. If I twist my neck, I can see a small wooden table with a jug of water. Blue and white striped curtains are surrounding me, although I can hear muffled sounds coming from the right: "Nurse. I need the toilet. *Nurse!*"

What time is it? It's not dark. But nor is it very light either. That's the thing about the seizures—you might think you've been out for hours when it's only been minutes. And vice versa.

Either way, I always feel as though I've had a long, deep sleep. It's a bit like when you've come out from an anesthetic.

I hate hospitals. They're so hot and airless. The heat always amazes me, given the cutbacks. Right now I'm sweating, even though I've just realized I'm not wearing anything underneath this hospital gown. What have they done with my clothes?

Places like this (and I've seen a few) always leave an unpleasant taste in my mouth of liver and bacon: a meal I always hated as a child and that still comes to me when I have to do something I don't want to. I simply want to get out. Be normal.

On the other side of the curtain I hear a trolley rattling past. "Break-fast!" says a cheerful voice.

That answers my earlier question, then.

"What do you want to do about that one?"

"She's waiting to see the nurse," said someone else. "We need to see if she's allowed to drink or eat."

Are they talking about me? There's a gnawing hunger in my stomach. I'm often ravenous after a seizure. I'm about to call out when there's a high, persistent beep that makes the hairs on my arm stand up. At least it's not coming from the machines I'm attached to. Although I can't see anything, I can hear tense voices and movement from across the room. "ICU. Now!"

My heart goes out to the patient. I've been there a few times myself.

Someone else—I think it's the occupant on my left—is on the phone. It's an oldish, wavering voice. "So the doctor said I had to take these tablets. Two, he said. Every day. I only did what he told me. And now the consultant says I should have been on something else."

I'd forgotten how noisy the hospital could be, even though it's only been two months since the last one. That was in Devon, before word got round my clients and I had to move again.

"Vicki?"

The curtains are being opened now. Why is it that hospital staff always speak as though they know you intimately? It was reassuring in the ambulance, but I'm not too keen on it now.

"How are you feeling?"

"Fine."

I ease myself up on my elbows, wincing at the pain. One of them, I notice, has a big blue bruise, presumably from my thrashing around under the bench. "Where are my clothes?"

"They got torn and muddied during the incident. Don't worry. We'll sort you out later."

I feel a sense of panic. "But I need something to wear so I can go home."

"I'm afraid we can't allow that unless you have someone who can be with you for at least twenty-four hours after discharge."

She glances at her notes again. "It says here that you don't have any next of kin. Is there a neighbor or a friend you could call?"

And that's when I remember. The thing—or rather, things—that had upset me. David. The police. And then that familiar girl on the promenade.

"I'll be all right on my own. I've done it before."

It's true. I've lied to other hospitals about having someone at home. Too late, I realize I should have lied this time, as well.

"It could be dangerous." She speaks as if I have never been through this before. Then again, she's young. Maybe I'm her first. "You've had . . . well, quite a traumatic experience."

I put on my firm voice. "I'm better off just getting on with it, taking the medicine and hoping I don't have another one."

Superstition makes me stop and touch the wooden table.

"You shouldn't be getting many at all if you're on medication, so we need to check that out. There's something else, too. I'm afraid you have some visitors."

Afraid?

Her eyes won't meet mine. "We wouldn't allow them in until we were sure you were up to it, but . . ."

Her voice trails away as she opens the curtains. Everyone on the ward is looking. And no wonder.

The couple in front of me is all too familiar.

The nurse backs away. "I'll leave you to it, then, shall I?"

"Mrs. Goudman. Vicki." Detective Inspector Gareth Vine's voice is as firm as the last time.

I feel dizzy. "How did you know I was here?"

He waves away the question as if this isn't important. "Your name came up on the system when you were admitted. Sorry to hear you're not well."

"I don't see it that way," I say defensively. "Epilepsy is part of me."

This was a phrase I'd picked up from one of various forums on the Internet.

"Is that why you didn't mention your condition when we spoke before?"

That lovely feeling of having woken from a deep sleep is beginning to evaporate. Instead, my skin is prickling with discomfort. The woman in the bed opposite is staring. She has a drip at her side and a bald head. Cancer, maybe?

"May we close the curtains, please?" I ask.

"Of course."

Just the three of us in an enclosed space. Two against one.

I put my hand over my eyes to shield them from the fluorescent strip above.

"Does light make it worse?" he asks curiously.

"Only strobe flashes," I retort. "And stress. Your previous visit didn't help. Or the news about David."

His eyes flicker. I can see he doesn't want to be held responsible for another attack. He's out of his comfort zone. Good. The sergeant says nothing, but she's writing everything down. I need to be careful.

"Then maybe," says the inspector, looking hard at me, "you should have been honest with us at the beginning."

"I was."

My mouth is dry. I know exactly what he's going to say next. I've been waiting for this ever since I told him why I was near my old home.

"Have you found my husband?"

"Your *ex*-husband? No." His voice is emotionless, but he is watching me carefully as he speaks. I feel a flash of fear, although I try to tell myself that it has to be OK. David is always all right. It's other people who aren't, thanks to the devastation he creates in his wake. Before me, there had been other deceits, such as his "charity interests." He'd told me this as if this was a credit to him. But by then, it had been too late. I'd been hooked.

The detective takes a seat close to my bed. "You told us two days ago that you were near Mr. Goudman's home because you were visiting your old doctor."

"Yes. I gave you his number."

"You did. And that was very helpful. But it might have been even more useful if you'd told us at the beginning that you had epilepsy."

What? "How did you know?" I splutter. "What about privacy laws?"

He looks pleased with himself. "It was a guess. One of the witnesses told us she thought you were having a fit. Thank you for confirming it."

I'd walked right into their trap!

"So why didn't you tell us?" he continues.

I shrug. "I didn't think it was relevant."

"Not relevant?"

Is it my imagination, or is he repeating my words on purpose to trip me up?

"You're on medication, aren't you?"

He's right, of course, but there are days when I choose not to take it because of the side effects. Besides, the stuff doesn't always help. I'm one of those unfortunate people for whom nothing really works.

I don't usually lie, but this feels necessary. "Yes. So what?"

"I gather that both the fits and the meds can affect your memory."

"Actually, we call them seizures."

"My apologies. But according to our research, 'seizures' can lead to mental blackouts."

There's the sound of a gasp from the other side of the curtain. The woman in the next bed must be having a field day.

"I don't know what you mean."

"I think you do, Vicki." Clearly, the detective had been to the same school as the medical staff. Repeat someone's name often enough, and they'll see you as a best mate.

"It's beginning to fall into place," he continues. "Now I see why you don't have a television in your home. Flickering lights can affect you. No bath either. Bright colors," he continues, "like your red anorak, are good because they make you stand out if you get into a dangerous situation. Looked that one up on Google, too."

He seems almost proud of it. He's right. Red isn't really right for my dark auburn curls, but I wear it for practical reasons.

"As far as I know, it's not illegal to have seizures."

"Vicki." He is standing up now. Bending over me so his square chin is close. Suddenly, I'm aware of how vulnerable I am with almost no clothes on.

You're intimidating me, I want to say. But I'm too scared of what's coming next.

"Vicki," he repeats, "let me put this another way. When we first paid you a visit, I asked where you were on the night your ex-husband was last seen. You said you were at home."

There are black curly hairs growing inside his nose. Why do we notice irrelevant things like that when more important stuff is happening? "Are you sure of that, Vicki?"

He pauses. His sidekick's pen is poised. There's no getting out of it now.

"Or is it possible," he says softly, "that, because of your condition, you genuinely don't remember?"

6.

SCARLET

Where are we going?"
Scarlet's sobs made the words come out all mushy.

Shaggy-Fringe Camilla glanced across from the driver's seat and patted her hand. "I've told you, love. To a nice family who'll look after you until the courts sort everything out."

"What if they won't let my mum come back?"

There was a second's hesitation. Camilla's eyes softened as though she was sorry for Scarlet. "Let's see, shall we? Now why don't you have a bit of a nap, love? It's a longish drive, and you must be very tired after everything that's happened today."

"But I need to go back home to get my stuff for school tomorrow."

Her voice was gentle. "We won't worry about that now."

Suppose this was a trick? What if she was being kidnapped? Scarlet began to panic. She should never have got in this car in the first place. "Mum said I wasn't to go off with strangers. I don't know you. Let me go home."

"STOP THAT!"

They swerved into the shoulder by the side of the road, brakes screeching. "You can't grab the wheel like that, Scarlet. It's dangerous!" Then she burst into tears, and Camilla's face softened. "I know how you feel, dear. I really do. But I'm a social worker, like I said before. Here's my identity pass. See? All we want to do is help you."

"If I can't go back home," Scarlet said quietly, "could I go back to your place?"

"Just now you said I was a stranger."

"You are." Scarlet tried to explain what she was feeling inside. "But I don't want to have to stay with *another* stranger."

"Sorry. But if I took in every kid I tried to help, there wouldn't be any room. Cheer up. You'll like the Walters. They've been fostering children like you for years, and they've got a son of their own, too. I think he's fifteen."

"What does 'fostering' mean?"

"It's when someone looks after children who aren't their own until they can go back to their mum and dad or . . ."

She stopped.

"Or what?"

"It doesn't matter. We must get going again. Just sit back and enjoy the scenery. We're leaving London now, and on our way to Kent. That's where the Walters live."

"Can I get to my school from there?"

"No. But there'll be a new one that's just as nice."

"How do you know?"

"I just do. Let's have some music on to help you doze. I'll turn up the heat, too. Is that better?"

Scarlet found her eyes closing.

When she woke up, the sky was dark, and there were buildings everywhere with lights on. Scarlet felt scared again. "Where are we?"

The social worker's voice sounded tired. "In Kent."

"Will Mum be here?"

"I've told you before. You can't see her for a bit. I know it's hard, but we're nearly at the Walters' house. With any luck, we'll be in time for tea. Are you hungry?"

Scarlet's stomach was rumbling as though she ought to be starving, but she felt sick at the same time. If she were at home, she'd be getting Mum her dinner.

"What do you like to eat, Scarlet?"

"Pizza. Burgers. Whatever we can . . ."

Scarlet stopped. She'd been going to say "nick." Ages ago, Mum had taught her to put one thing in her supermarket basket and then slip some other stuff under her sweatshirt or in her bag at the same time. But then she remembered that this had to be their secret.

Luckily, Shaggy-Fringe had slowed down now and was too busy looking at the houses to notice that she hadn't finished her sentence.

"I'm sure it's here. On the corner. Ah yes. They've built an extension since I was here last. That's why I didn't recognize it. Out we get."

Wow! The Walters' house actually had a garden in front. There was a bicycle lying on its side, and the wheels were still spinning like someone had just gotten off. Scarlet had always wanted a bike, but they were too expensive.

There was a doorbell, too, which made a pretty tinkly noise. A woman opened the door. She had deep-set eyes, and her lips were a straight pink line. "You're late."

"I'm so sorry, but the traffic was bad, and I got a bit lost toward the end." The social worker seemed nervous, rather like Mum before a game. "This is Scarlet. Scarlet, this is Mrs. Walter, who's going to be looking after you. It's very kind of her at such short notice."

"Bring the money, did you?"

"It will be paid into your bank account tomorrow morning."

"That's not what we agreed."

"I'm afraid this was all rather last-minute."

"Always is, isn't it? Well, you'd better come in, then."

Scarlet's eyes widened. There was proper carpet—with a red swirly pattern—instead of floorboards! It went all the way up the stairs. Was this really one house? She could hear a telly somewhere and children shouting.

"I want to watch my program."

"Piss off, it's my turn."

The woman gave a laugh, but it wasn't a nice one like Mum's. "Kids," she said shortly. "You know what they're like."

"Sure. I expect you're about to have tea, are you?"

"All finished now. Had it early tonight, we did."

"Ah. The thing is that Scarlet hasn't eaten much. She's had a bit of a traumatic day."

"Tall, isn't she?"

Scarlet felt the woman's eyes measure her up and down.

"Well, yes. I'm afraid Scarlet's only got the clothes she's standing in, and she doesn't have a toothbrush either."

"Now why aren't I surprised? Come along then. Let's see what we can find."

"Bye, love. You might see me again, or you could have one of my colleagues next time."

Suddenly, Scarlet didn't want the social worker to go. "Will you tell Mum where I am?"

Mum had always been really firm about that. She couldn't go off on her own. Not in their neighborhood.

"Of course I will."

"I'm worried about her." Scarlet's chest grew tighter. "Mum sometimes forgets to eat unless I remind her."

"I'm sure they'll give her food. Now you go and have your own. In the morning, you'll be off to your new school with the other children here. Won't she, Mrs. Walter?"

"Well, she's not staying in the house during the day."

The front door closed. Scarlet's stomach rumbled loudly as Mrs. Walter led the way into the kitchen. What a huge oven!

Maybe that's where she kept her stash, like Mum. Or perhaps it was in that massive fridge.

"Don't touch! That one over there is for you lot."

"You've got *two* fridges? You must be very rich!"

Mrs. Walter stared at her. "You teasing me? Let me tell you, Scarlet. I get pin money for looking after kids like you, considering the amount of trouble you lot give me. Now choose something—just one, mind—and go and eat it in front of the telly."

There was only an egg and something green at the back with black spots on it. The smell made her sick.

"Little bastards must have cleaned it out earlier. There's no way I'm cooking at this time of the evening. Here, take this."

"Wow, thanks!"

"You taking the piss again? It's instant noodles—not bleeding caviar."

"They're my favorite."

There was another stare. "Funny little thing, aren't you? Give it here, then, and I'll put some boiling water in the carton. Don't want you hurting yourself on your first night and getting me into trouble. Here's a spoon. Go into the room on your right and you'll find the others."

Scarlet felt her stomach falling in. "But I don't know them."

There was a hoarse laugh. "You soon will."

There were four boys lying on the sofa. On the floorboards—no carpet in this room—was a crowd of girls. One had thick black makeup round her eyes like Mum sometimes put on when she was going out. The telly in here was so loud that it hurt her ears.

Uncertainly, Scarlet crouched down next to the girl with black stuff, who gave her a dirty look. "Not another kid. If Mrs. W thinks she's putting down an extra bed, I'm going to bloody well report the cow."

"Right. And how are you going to do that?"

This question came from a boy with ginger hair. "You know you can't win."

"And you know you can't keep coming into our room. I'll tell on you. I've said it before."

"But you don't mean it, do you, Angie? 'Cos you love it really."

"Fuck off."

"Maybe I will now someone else has just arrived."

"Her?" Angie was glaring at Scarlet. "Call that competition?"

"You wasn't much when we first . . ."

"Shut up. Or I'll smack your bleeding gob."

"All right, you lot." Mrs. Walter was at the door. "Enough arguing. Off to bed."

"It's only seven o'clock."

"You know the rules. We need time to ourselves."

"Excuse me." Scarlet put up her hand like she did at school when she wanted to ask a question. "But I still haven't got my pajamas or toothbrush."

"Then you'll have to sleep as you are, won't you?"

What about the stuff Mrs. Walter had promised to find?

"And there's a mug of shared toothbrushes in the bathroom; just help yourself."

That wasn't clean! Mum had always been very particular about the uncles keeping their mitts off Mum's and Scarlet's pink ones.

"You'll be sleeping next to Dawn," Mrs. W continued. "You're lucky. I've found a mattress to put on the floor. Your toilet's at the end of the corridor. Don't use the one at the top of the stairs. It's ours."

"That's right," muttered Angie. "One for three of them. And one for nine of us. Ten now with you."

"It's OK," said Scarlet. "I'm not going to be here for long. Just until they let my mum come home."

"That's what they told me," said a girl with a turned-up nose who seemed a lot nicer. Her name, she told Scarlet, was Dawn. "That was at Christmas."

They were queuing up now to use the toilet. She could smell it from here. Ugh!

"What's school like?" Scarlet asked her new friend Dawn, whom she was going to be sleeping near.

She shrugged. "I don't go that often."

"Why not?"

"Don't like it."

"Really?"

"Who does?"

"I do." Scarlet felt herself going red. "I love reading and writing stories and drawing pictures."

"Fucking hell. We've got a swot." It was Angie. "I don't know what your last school was like, but you won't like this one. I give you that for nothing. Tell Mrs. W you've got a stomachache. Then you won't have to get on the bus, and she'll pretend she's keeping you at home so she doesn't get reported to Social Services. But as soon as the bus has gone, she'll push you out of the house and tell you not to come back until four. Then you can do what you want."

"Won't the teachers check?"

"Depends. They can't always keep up. If they do, you might have to go to class for a bit, but then you can drop out again."

"I don't want to do that."

"I don't think you get it, Scarlet." Angie came closer. "It's not what you want. It's what *we* want you to do."

"That's right." It was Darren, the ginger boy with a rash of red spots all over his chin. "If you want us to be nice, you've got to do exactly what we say. Just wait for the word. It might be tomorrow or next week or the week after that. We've got to make sure it's safe first." He stepped toward her, looking angry.

"Shit." Angie was pointing. "The new kid's just pissed herself."

Scarlet went red. Sometimes when she got frightened, she couldn't help it.

She wanted to hide. Everyone was looking.

"Baby, baby," chanted the boys.

Footsteps pounded up the stairs. "What the hell's going on?" demanded Mrs. W. Her beady eyes took in the damp patch on the swirly red landing carpet.

"I don't believe it! They've only gone and sent me another bed wetter! That's it. You're out, my girl. First thing in the morning."

Sometimes I'll get a phone call from a husband who wants to buy a voucher for his loved one, to celebrate a special occasion. One man said his wife was "too shy for her own good." So I treated her with eucalyptus for confidence, and—because I hadn't cared for the husband's arrogant tone—I blended it with basil for mental enthusiasm and concentration. With any luck, that might sharpen her mind and she'd get rid of him.

I should have taken a dose of my own medicine when David cut our honeymoon short for "an important meeting." Was Tanya there, too? Bet she was. That woman deserves to be punished. And so does my ex.

7.

VICKI

16 February 2018

They insist they'll have to keep me in the hospital for another twenty-four hours because I don't have anyone at home to look after me.

Still, at least the detective and that policewoman with her narrowing eyes have gone. I try to brush away my fears. Tell myself that they can't accuse me of having something to do with a walkabout ex-husband just because I have memory lapses. But I get the distinct feeling they will be back.

A chirpy orderly with a HOSPITAL FRIEND badge comes round with a trolley. Its wheels click as she rams it by mistake into the bottom of my bed. Drinks. Sweets. Newspapers. Would I like anything?

I'm about to say no. I've ignored the news for years now as part of my "determined to stay positive" attitude. But then I spot a tabloid with the headline: WEALTHY BUSINESSMAN STILL MISSING.

He is staring right at me. My skin goes cold with goose bumps.

Fears are growing for missing property dealer David Goudman. Police are appealing for anyone with information to get in touch.

My fingers trace the distinctive outline of his nose. I can almost smell the expensive musky cologne he used to wear. Imagine his arms around me. The touch of his lips on mine.

Until now, none of this has seemed real, despite the visits from the police. Men like David are invincible. Bad things don't happen to them. But the news story means I can't pretend anymore: my ex-husband has disappeared. And I might—or might not—have something to do with it.

When I get home the next day, the first thing I do is take the little book that was behind the pillow and slip it under the mattress instead. Just in case.

Then I put on the radio for company and microwave some parsnip and carrot soup. There's a hint of ginger and curry powder, which I've added for kick. I'm feeling hungry. Seizures often do that to me, but it's not the same for everyone. When I was finally diagnosed, I was told there are over forty different types of epilepsy, and each person will be affected differently.

There were other "helpful tips," too.

You might find that your character changes. This could be due to the medication rather than the condition. Yes. I used to be so much more confident.

Some relatives and friends find it difficult to accept. Too true.

Someone with epilepsy is not advised to live alone. If only I had a choice. "You do have an alarm, don't you?" said the nurse when she discharged me.

"Sure," I'd said. But the truth is that I quite often don't wear it. Especially when I have clients.

"What's that round your neck?" they might ask.

"Just a little red button that I press if I think I'm about to have a seizure—assuming there's enough time."

How well would that go down? An aromatherapist is meant to help others—not be in need of healing herself.

I brush the thought from my mind and instead attempt to concentrate on the client whom I'd rescheduled for tomorrow. It will do me good, I tell myself. I need to get back to normal. That was another piece of advice from the consultant. *Try not to let it ruin your life. Keep taking the meds. Don't alarm yourself over the statistics. Plenty of people still have jobs and families.*

But what kind of employer wants someone with an official record like mine? The only option was to go self-employed. It would be, I told myself, a new start.

Now, to clear my head, I go for a walk along the promenade. Below me, the beach drops away.

When I get back, I spray lavender onto my pillow for a calm sleep. It doesn't work. In my dreams, David runs after me along a beach. "I'm sorry," he's shouting. "I'm sorry . . ."

I wake with a start, the night still black outside and the clock showing 4:12 a.m. next to me. For a moment, I think that it's true. That he really is sorry for not sticking with me. And then I feel a huge gray wave of regret and sadness, because if he'd supported me, things would have been different.

All I can do now is hope against hope that David turns up. Soon.

Mrs. M—one of my regulars—is five minutes early, but I'm ready for her. The room is warm, and my usual soothing "angel" music—like the sound of a light breeze or gentle waves—is playing. I like this woman with her soft, kind manners. Indeed, there have been times when I've been tempted to explain my condition to her.

I've a feeling she might understand. But I daren't risk it.

"How are you?" she asks when I answer the door.

When rescheduling, I'd deliberately not mentioned my hospital stay. Now I'm nervous. My hands begin to sweat. She lives in town, so maybe someone has told her. I can almost imagine it: *That aromatherapist with the red hair who lives in one of those converted flats? Found her having a fit under the bench on the seafront, they did.*

"Fine," I reply tersely.

"I'm still having my migraines," she says. And then I realize that her "How are you?" was simply a matter of courtesy.

Immediately, I snap into professional mode. "Let's see what we can do, shall we?"

Lavender, of course. Citrus scent. Clary sage. Jasmine. Now blend. She lies back on my couch, her head in my hands. I massage the oils into her temples in a slow, circular motion. "Lovely," she breathes. "You've got such a deft touch. Have you always been able to do this?"

I stiffen. Even though this woman has been here before, she's never asked questions about my past. She's just taken it for granted that the black-and-white framed certificates on the wall are a measure of my competence.

"Not always," I say hesitantly.

"So what made you become an aromatherapist?"

I swallow the tension in my throat. "I went to one when . . . when I needed to tackle some of my own issues. I found it calming. And then I decided to train as one myself."

"Fascinating," she murmurs, eyes still closed. "What were you doing before?"

I can't tell her the truth. "Just running a home, actually."

"Don't undersell yourself." Her voice is gently admonishing. "I was a full-time mum until my youngest went to uni."

I have a sudden vision of rosy cheeks and a soft brown floppy fringe. A strong nose. Freckles. That wonderful baby smell.

"How old are yours?" she asks.

My hands slip.

"Ouch!"

"I'm so sorry."

"My left eye." She sits up. "Your finger went right in it. The oil is stinging."

I've never done that before.

She leaves without making her next appointment. That's two clients I've lost in the space of a few days. One thanks to the police, the other due to my own stupidity.

I try telling myself that it's not the end of the world. I still have other clients on my books. Even though I haven't been here long, I've had some good responses to my ads and through referrals. But this is a small seaside town, and people talk. What if the last client spreads the word about her eye? How many onlookers had spotted the ambulance at the bench?

It's not going to be long until my secret is out once more, and I'll have to move. Again.

Because the truth is this: no one really likes the thought of someone who can—at a minute's notice—go "crazy." That's what he said to me when it first happened.

David. The man whom I have every right to hate. The man I could easily destroy if I wanted. And maybe now's the time.

I walk across to the desk where I keep my important papers. I open the file marked BILLS. The document is still there, hidden between the neatly filed copies of receipts, in case I ever need it. Should I have told the police? Probably. But although I'm angry with David, it's Tanya I really blame. She's the bitch who lured him from me. I suspect she was there all the time, even before epilepsy stole my life.

And this piece of paper implicates her, too.

Is David's disappearance connected? There's only one way to find out.

I feel myself babbling on in my head. It's sometimes hard to speak or understand things after a seizure. My memory is vague, and I feel generally confused. It can take hours or days to get back to normal, and often I sleep during this period.

Yet right now the effect on me is different. I just want to *do* something. And right now, that means having it out with the woman who stole my husband.

I lock the windows, which are rattling in the wind. Turn off the music. I pack my meds in my small case with a change of clothes in case I get an incontinent seizure. Put on my red jacket.

I'm at the door now. I open it. And jump back in surprise.

"What are you doing here?" I demand.

Detective Inspector Vine looks down at my bag in a movement clearly designed to be casual but which is more of a risk assessment. "Going somewhere?"

"To see a friend," I retort with more confidence than I feel.

"I need to show you something first."

He is waving a file in his hand. Sergeant Brown is at his side.

"May we come in?"

It might sound like a question, but it isn't. I could refuse him entry—he hasn't mentioned a search warrant—but if I do, it makes me look guilty.

I find myself being marched to my own kitchen table. He opens the brown envelope. There's a photograph inside.

I stare at it, and after a minute, I manage to speak. "Where did you get this from?"

"Someone who works for your ex-husband. She didn't realize the significance until recently."

"Significance?" I repeat, partly from shock and partly to buy myself time.

"The thing is, Vicki," chimes in Sergeant Brown, "that this picture was taken just before your ex-husband disappeared. You told us that you hadn't seen him since 2013. Five years ago. Yet here you both are. Is there something you'd like to tell us?"

8.

SCARLET

12 March 2007

The phone call came on Scarlet's fourth day at the Walters' house. They were having breakfast, and Darren was fighting for the last piece of toast.

"Listen," hissed Dawn, the girl with the turned-up nose. "She's talking about you."

Mrs. W was just outside the kitchen door in the hall. She kept repeating the same words loudly. "All right, I'll make an exception and keep her."

Then she came back in and said that Scarlet could stay, as long as she was a good girl.

Being a good girl at home meant putting out the bins for Mum and doing her homework. But Scarlet hadn't done any homework since she'd come to number 9 Green Avenue, because her new friend Dawn hadn't let her go to school. "It's for your own good. Trust me," she'd said.

Instead, Dawn, Darren and some of the others pretended to wait for the bus but then hung around the park and smoked and drank the last few drops that people had left in beer bottles. Scarlet didn't want to join in but felt she ought to so she didn't stand out. The others had been right about the teachers. No one had complained to the Walters.

"We'll forge a sick note when we go back," announced Dawn. "Not that they even give a shit about us foster kids. Now, about today. We're going to do something different. You did say you was eight, didn't you?"

Scarlet nodded.

"You look older."

"I know."

"That's cool."

"Why?"

"No reason. We need to get going."

Scarlet felt an unexpected beat of excitement along with the fear. "Are we going to play the game?"

Her friend's eyes widened. "How do you know about that?"

"Mum told me."

"She was hustling?"

"I don't know what that is. We called it playing the game. We'd do it in the park or shopping center."

Her eyes widened. "You went with her? You poor kid."

They were walking now. "I didn't mind. I got pocket money sometimes."

"I've got you wrong, haven't I? You're actually pretty cool."

Scarlet flushed with pleasure. It was nice to have a friend. "Have you got the cans?" she asked Dawn. "Mum either took drink or crisps." A big lump came up in her throat. "Then they took her away. I really miss her."

They were standing outside some shops, just like the center where she and Mum used to go.

"They said I would see her soon." The tears were pouring out. "But I don't know when."

"If you want to help her, you've got to do what I say. See the boys?"

They were outside a music shop with stickers on the window.

G-R-E-A-T V-A-L-U-E.

"There's a big stack of DVDs just inside. Darren's going to push Kieran into it, pretending to have a row. They'll come falling down. While the assistants are distracted, you've got to go to that other display—see? The one on the right. Grab a load and scarper. OK?"

"But what if I get caught?"

"You won't if you're quick. And if you do, you say nothing. Got it? Not even 'No comment,' 'cos then it looks like you've done this sort of thing before. Just act scared and cry."

Scarlet began to walk unsteadily toward the shop door.

There was a loud clattering noise as the DVD display fell over. "Those kids are at it again," shouted one of the shop assistants.

Quickly! Scarlet's fingers were shaking so much that she could hardly pick up the DVDs. One, two, three, four.

"STOP THAT GIRL," she heard someone yelling after her. "The black kid with the braids and red beads."

No! She'd dropped one. Too late to bend down. Running out of the door, she dashed down a corridor. Where should she go now? Dawn hadn't said.

Then she saw it. A sign. L-A-D-I-E-S.

"If you ever get into trouble, go to the toilet," Mum had always said. "Lock yourself in and then scream for help."

Scarlet shut the first cubicle door behind her. There was shit all over the floor and no toilet paper. Sitting on the seat, she panted with terror. Someone was coming!

"That one's occupied," said a voice. "Take the next one."

Scarlet waited until the loo had flushed and the footsteps had gone.

Creeping out of the toilets, she started to walk as fast as she could across the center to the main doors. Round the corner maybe? And down this road here toward McDonald's?

"There you are!"

It was Dawn.

"Got the stuff? Good girl. Time to pass them on."

Scarlet didn't want to ask what that meant in case Dawn stopped being her friend.

They walked through the rain until they reached a market on the other side of town.

"I'll give yer a fiver," one of them said to Dawn.

"You've got to be kidding me. These are the latest."

"Seven then. Not a penny more. Or I'll hand the two of you in."

"You wouldn't dare. Or they'll get you, too."

"Go home, the pair of you."

"Mind your own bloody business."

"All right. Eight quid. And that's yer lot."

They had to hang around the park until four p.m. so it would look as though they'd been to school. Scarlet was beginning to learn not to question her new friend. You never knew when she was going to be nice or not.

That night, Scarlet stayed very quiet when Darren came into the room. He and Dawn made lots of strange noises, a bit like Mum and the uncles used to.

When the boy left, her friend went straight to sleep; her snores sang in the dark. Outside, car brakes squealed in the rain. Scarlet tossed and turned in the too-big brown pajamas Mrs. W had finally found her. When Scarlet was little, Mum had taught her to speak to the universe. "You can ask for whatever you want," she'd told her. "Sometimes it works and sometimes it doesn't. So you might as well try."

"Please, universe," prayed Scarlet now, "can you fix it so I see Mum? As soon as you can?"

9.

VICKI

I am still staring at the photograph.

There's no denying it. There I am, wearing the same pale blue high-necked sweater that I have on now. Wagging a finger at the man standing in front of me.

David.

A red London bus is going past behind us, and the Embankment is clearly visible in the background.

"You two look as though you're having a bit of an argument," says Inspector Vine. His voice is steady, balanced. It strikes me that his name is perfect for him. Vine. Clings tenaciously to whatever support—or clue—it can find. My ex-husband and I used to have a rather lovely Virginia creeper that clambered all over the balcony at the back of the house in Kingston. We spent ages one weekend fixing little green supports onto the wall. David was up the ladder, and I was at the bottom, keeping it firm. I remember thinking how good it was to work as a team. I wonder if the creeper is still secure.

"Do you see that *Evening Standard* placard in the corner?" he continues. "When you enlarge it, the front page shows the date, 30 November 2017. Yet you told me you hadn't seen your ex-husband since 2013."

"Perhaps," I say unsteadily, "I just forgot. My medication . . . it affects my memory."

"Ah yes." His eyes are cold. "We talked about that before, didn't we, in the hospital? How very convenient."

"That isn't fair." Panic is making my throat tight. "I need to speak to my solicitor."

The detective sighs. His breath smells of mints. "No solicitor in the world is going to be able to deny this photograph." Then his voice softens. "I've got to tell you, Vicki. I feel for you. I really do. I'm not sure I could deal with it. Not being able to trust my mind. Never knowing when I'm going to have another seizure . . ."

"I sometimes get a smell of burning," I say suddenly. "Just before it happens."

His eyes light up with interest. "Really?"

"And I've got one right now."

It's not true, but I can see I've scared him.

"Stress can bring it on." I sit down heavily on the sofa. There's a nervous glance between my two visitors.

"Go ahead," she says quickly. "Make that call to your solicitor."

The only one I know is the woman who handled my divorce. Her name was Lily Macdonald. I'd liked her. Professional and also understanding. She'd sent me a routine e-mail some years ago, to say she'd relocated from London to the southwest. I still have her number on my phone. I call, but it goes straight to voice mail. It is a Sunday, after all. I stammer a message, stressing the urgency and apologizing for bothering her on the weekend.

"Now what?" I say to my inquisitors. "Are you going to charge me?"

Instantly, I realize I've said the wrong thing.

The inspector's eyes narrow. "What exactly do you think we should charge you with?"

"I don't know," I say.

"Are you sure about that?"

He's trying to confuse me. I need to get the upper hand somehow. There's no proof, I tell myself. The photograph just shows that I had seen David nearly two months before he'd disappeared. But it doesn't mean I have anything to do with his disappearance.

"May I look at the photograph again?" I say.

I turn it over. There's a silver and black sticker with a name on it. HELEN EVANS.

"Who's she?" I ask.

"The photographer. She was with Mr. Goudman at the time."

"Handy," I say acidly. I notice that the sergeant is no longer in the room.

"Where are you going?" asks Vine as I try to move past him.

"To find my diary."

"I have it here," says Sergeant Brown, coming in from the lounge. She is tapping a thick black book. I think back to the psychologist who'd suggested keeping one. "It's good for mental health," he'd said, "because it releases emotion safely without hurting anyone physically."

Luckily, this is my office diary for appointments. Not the personal one.

"How dare you? That's private property."

"Come on, Vicki," says Detective Vine. "If you've got nothing to hide, then surely you won't mind me looking."

"Fine." I nod, after a moment's hesitation. He's right. Much better to show goodwill.

He turns a page. "Your diary says you had a client at eight a.m. on the same date that the photograph was taken."

"There you are, then," I say triumphantly. "I couldn't have gone to London. There wouldn't have been enough traveling time."

"Then how do you explain the woman in the picture who looks just like you?"

"I can't."

"Can't or won't?"

I want to scream. "Can't."

He taps his fingers on the page as if sending Morse code. "Even if you'd seen this client, you would still have had enough hours to have left Cornwall and got to this part of London."

"But apart from medical appointments, I hardly go up to town anymore," I say, choosing not to share the fact that I had just been about to pay Tanya a visit when the detectives had turned up.

"Town?" queries the woman officer. "That suggests you used to be familiar with it."

"I was," I snap. How much do they know? Why haven't they brought up the big thing that's missing here?

"None of this proves anything," I say.

DI Vine glances around the room. "We'll decide that when we've finished looking around. How's the burning smell, by the way?"

I'd almost forgotten.

"Gone," I say lamely.

"That's good."

He turns and walks into my studio. I follow meekly, feeling wretched, conscious that he doesn't believe me. Too late, I tell myself that I shouldn't have lied.

They start with my desk: one of the few items here that belongs to me and not my landlady. After David, I walked away from material possessions. Besides, when you are constantly moving, it's easier not to have too much. I bought the desk the other week from a local antique shop in the mistaken belief that I might stay here for a while.

I can hear the policewoman in my bedroom. More drawers are being pulled out. Cupboard doors open and shut.

I ring Lily Macdonald again. I leave another message.

Outside, the sky is turning pink. It's nearly evening. I yearn to get out. Walk along the seafront. Hear the waves gently lapping on the shingle. Smell the salt air. Pretend that none of this is happening.

The inspector has my Bills file out and is flipping through it. My heart catches in my throat. Any minute now, I tell myself, he will see it. Any minute.

He puts the file down. Either he hasn't noticed the document hidden amidst the other financial papers or else he doesn't realize its importance.

"May I look in your kitchen?" he says.

"It hasn't changed in the last ten minutes."

He ignores my sarcasm, spreading his hands as if apologizing. But I know he isn't.

I shrug. "Be my guest. I'll come, too. I need to get my medication anyway."

"Really?"

"Yes." I follow him and reach for the bottle, which—because it's a controlled drug—I keep on a high shelf as advised by the consultant.

The detective is watching me closely. "Do you ever forget to take it?" he asks.

"No." I neglect to mention there are times when I choose not to. Sometimes I think I'm damned if I swallow the stuff and damned if I don't.

I point to the DON'T FORGET board on the wall with its jaunty border of flowers around it. There's a mark for each date. I add to it now.

"Go on," I say. "Take a look for the day that David went missing."

It's there. We can both see it. So is the mark for the day before and the day after.

"It can't be easy for you," he says in a softer tone.

"It's not." This time his kindness seems genuine, causing my eyes to blur. I turn to one side. "I'd make you a cup of tea," I say, "but I don't have a kettle, as you can see."

He raises an eyebrow.

"Hot liquids," I add. "I might scald myself. Some people use microwaves to make hot drinks, but there's still a chance you could get burned."

I'm definitely striking a chord there. I learned that in my old life. Find something that makes others sympathetic. It's the first chink in the armor. Then you start to get in there.

But has this man found *my* chink yet?

There's nothing for it but to wait and see.

10

SCARLET

13 March 2007

The next morning, Scarlet woke to Dawn prodding her in the ribs. "Get up. Quick. Mrs. W is going mental. She wants us out early."

Yesterday began to float back to her. The DVDs in the shop. The man they'd sold them to. Darren in Dawn's bed. Still, thought Scarlet with a fresh spring of hope, maybe they'd let her see Mum today.

"We're going to have to go to school," said Dawn. "Or they might get suspicious. But we'll do a sick note first and pretend it's from Mrs. W."

"Won't they check it with her writing?"

"They're too busy to bother. You do it. My spelling's crap."

"After school, will you help me get to see Mum?"

Dawn was pulling up her tights now. They had holes in the knee. "She's locked up. Didn't get bail, according to what I heard Mrs. W say."

"What's bail?"

Her new friend's voice softened. "It's when they let you out before the trial. But they won't give it to you if they think you'll run away or try to hurt someone."

"My mother wouldn't hurt anyone."

Dawn was pulling up her skirt now. It didn't cover the holes in her tights. "Then count yourself bleeding lucky. Mine tried to strangle me once when she was pissed."

"That's really bad."

"No, there's worse than that." Dawn had a weird look on her face. "My brother stopped her. It was the next bit that was shit."

Scarlet said nothing. This was something she'd learned from Mum. Sometimes you had to wait to get someone to give you an explanation.

But Dawn was silent for a bit, looking as though there was a bad taste in her mouth. "Anyway," she said at last. "It don't matter now. Someone told on him, and then the authorities got me."

What had her brother done? wondered Scarlet. But she didn't want to ask.

"You done that note yet?"

"Shall I tell them we all had a stomach bug?"

"Can you spell stomach?" Dawn frowned. "I'm not sure I can. We need to get it right or they'll know we wrote it ourselves."

"S-T-O-M-A-K."

"You're clever, Scarlet. I'll say that."

Then Scarlet got dressed in the same clothes she'd worn the day before because there weren't any others.

"Bloody hell, you've wet the mattress again. You'll get it from Mrs. W like last time. Get some toilet paper to soak it up. Quick."

But the bathroom door was locked.

"IF YOU LOT AREN'T DOWN HERE NOW, YOU WON'T GET NOTHING TO EAT!" roared Mrs. W from downstairs.

"C'mon." Dawn was pulling her by the hand. "Not that it's worth rushing for."

"The cereal's all gone," moaned Darren.

"That's because someone here's had more than their fair share," said Mrs. W.

"Yeah. Your own brat," murmured Dawn. "He nicks ours even when he's got his own."

"What's that you're saying?"

Dawn put her chin up defiantly. "Nothing."

Instead, there was one cold slice of toast each. Scarlet ate her piece slowly, chewing each mouthful the way she and Mum always did when there wasn't much to eat. Then she put her hands on her lap to show she had finished.

"Posh manners," sniggered Darren.

"Fuck off," said Dawn.

"Your new best friend, is she?"

"I'm training her. And I don't want her upset."

"Training me for what?" asked Scarlet.

Dawn made a *shut up* face just as Mrs. W came back in the room.

"What are you lot talking about?"

Nervously, she put up her hand. "Please, Mrs. Walter. Can you tell me when I'm going to see Mum?"

"When the Social says you can. Now get out of here. All of you."

"But it's too early for the bus."

"Tough. I'm going out."

It was freezing, waiting at the bus stop.

"Someone stinks," said Darren. "Ugh! The new girl's pissed herself again."

"Stinky Scarlet. Stinky Scarlet!"

Soon everyone was saying it over and over again.

As soon as they reached school, she ran behind some bushes and peeled off her knickers from under her skirt. That was better. Then she followed the trail of children through the gates. It was big—like her old school—and the classes were ginormous. "'Cos of the cuts, we're divided into abilities and not age," explained Dawn. "Looks like I'm in the same class as you for math." She tugged at her arm. "I'm bloody hopeless, so we'll sit at the back. Come on."

At last! Something fun to do. "Fuck, you're quick," said Dawn when Scarlet had finished her worksheet. "Can you do mine for me, too?"

Luckily, there was so much noise that the teacher couldn't hear her.

"Who can tell me the answer to number one?"

"Eleven."

The teacher looked surprised. "Well done, Dawn. And number two?"

"Five and . . . and a small one over two."

"Brilliant. It just goes to show what hard work can do. Now what about you?" The teacher glanced at the class list in front of her. "Scarlet, isn't it?"

"Get it wrong," hissed Dawn.

"What?"

"Then she won't suspect you gave *me* the answer."

But six times six was thirty-six. Everyone knew that, didn't they? Mum was good at sums. She'd been going to learn math at university before she'd had Scarlet.

"Thirty-four," said Scarlet dutifully.

"Thirty-six, actually. Never mind."

"That's not fair," hissed Scarlet when they moved on to the next sheet.

"'Course it is. I'm looking after you, aren't I? So you've got to do stuff for me in return."

At last it was lunch: chips and baked beans!

"I'll let you off lightly," said Dawn. "You only need to give me half."

"Why can't I eat it all?"

"Because I'm your protector, stupid. It's how you pay me to keep you safe."

"Safe from who?"

Dawn pointed toward three girls by the window. "See them? They're real cows. Scratch your eyes out in the playground unless I'm around."

As she spoke, one of them looked across and gave her a hard stare. Scarlet felt a cold shiver pass through. "They live in public housing. We call it the Badlands."

Silently, Scarlet pushed her plate across the table to Dawn.

A few minutes later, there was a sharp whistle sound. "Outside, everyone."

"This is it." Dawn's voice was low. "Stick to me."

The biting air hit Scarlet as soon as she stepped outside. The old anorak that Mrs. W had given her was too small and had a broken zipper.

"Someone cold, are they?" asked one of the Badlands girls. She was wearing a black top so low you could see her bra.

"No," said Scarlet, but her voice quivered.

"Maybe it's 'cos you're not wearing no knickers."

How did she know?

"One of my mates saw when she dropped her pencil on the floor. Trying to flash your fanny around, are you? Or maybe you're used to being somewhere hotter. Which country do you come from?"

"Here."

"Yeah. Right. I heard there was a new girl in the center yesterday nicking stuff." The eyes narrowed. "Same color as you. With red beads in her hair."

"I could belt you for that," cut in Dawn.

"Just try. Ow! She's broken my nose."

"What's going on?" A teacher had appeared.

"It was *her* fault." Dawn was pointing to the girl on the ground, who was yelling, her face covered in blood. "Go on, Scarlet. Tell her."

If anyone asks you what happened in the game, Mum used to say, always blame someone else.

"This girl," said Scarlet, pointing, "upset me because she said I was black. Dawn was just sticking up for me."

"You made a racist remark?"

"So? My dad says they should all be chucked out and sent back to where they come from."

"Get up. You're coming inside with me." The teacher nodded at Dawn. "You take care of the new girl while I sort this out."

That afternoon, when they got back to the house, Mrs. Walter was waiting.

"Upstairs," she said grimly to Scarlet. "What the hell do you call this?"

She was pointing at the damp patch on the sheet with bits of toilet paper still stuck to it.

"I don't like bed wetters. I told you that before."

Scarlet went bright red. "I'm sorry."

"I do the sheets once a month. I'm not spending money on extra laundry just because your waste-of-space mother never bothered potty training you. You can sleep on them until the next wash day. Now come downstairs for tea. You lot are going to bed early tonight."

For supper, they had one and a half fish fingers each, a handful of peas and a few cold chips. Dawn was sitting next to her. Scarlet already knew what to do. When Mrs. W's back was turned, she quickly handed over the whole one to thank Dawn for being her friend. The peas were only half cooked, so Dawn didn't want those. Scarlet devoured them ravenously.

"What's for dessert?" asked Darren.

"There ain't none."

"You're meant to give it to us."

"And you lot aren't meant to nick stuff from our fridge."

They all froze. The voice came from a short, fat man standing at the doorway. Scarlet hadn't seen him before but guessed who he was from what Dawn had already told her. Mr. W was a truck driver, and he was away a lot. Sometimes he took his son, Wayne, with him. That must be the teenage boy next to him that the social worker had mentioned. They both had huge ears, like cauliflowers, that looked too big for their heads.

Mr. W's beady black eyes searched the table.

"Come on. Own up. I'll find out sooner or later."

Silence thudded in Scarlet's ears.

"I'll be watching you lot. Every one."

To her horror, his eye fell on her. "So this is the new girl. The bed wetter."

The other kids sniggered, including Dawn.

"Well, Miss Pee-In-Your-Bed, I've got some news for you." He waggled a finger, and she noticed that, like his ears, his hands seemed too large for the rest of him. "The social worker's taking you to visit your jailbird mother on Friday."

"Thank you, thank you!"

She wanted to jump up and down.

"But if you wet your bed again, miss, you won't be going. Got it?"

Scarlet's heart sang all the way upstairs. It didn't stop singing even when Darren and Dawn went at it nearby. Instead, she closed her eyes tightly and prayed to the universe that Mum would somehow escape from prison and get her out of here. Then everything would be all right again.

II.

VICKI

It's not like in the films. It doesn't happen immediately. The noose feels quite loose at first when the police start to question you. But then it begins to tighten.

At least, that's how one of the girls on my wing described it. At the time, I'd put it down to fanciful prose on her part. She was prone to making things up. My own experience of going inside was quite different. But now I'm beginning to see what she meant.

The policewoman has a plastic bag out; the type used for evidence. I've seen a few of those in my time.

"We're taking your office diary," says Inspector Vine, cutting into my thoughts.

"Fine," I say, forcing myself to sound calm. "You might not be able to read my handwriting though."

It's true. Since it happened, my hands have been shakier.

"Is that all?" I ask. Too late, I realize this makes me sound suspicious, as though I had expected them to take me with them.

"For now." The detective eyeballs me again. "We'll be in touch. And I strongly suggest that you have your solicitor ready."

I turn the key in the lock behind them and shut the windows, too. I know this is daft. One of the rules I was taught after my diagnosis was to make sure that access wasn't barred in case I needed rescuing quickly. But I have to ensure my privacy.

As soon as they have gone, I grab the Bills file. The document's still there. Maybe I should put it in a safer place.

Crawling into bed, I make a cocoon out of the duvet, which smells of lavender. I feel safer that way. It's not nighttime, but the meds are having their usual effect. My eyelids are heavy. I can't keep them open anymore. It's a relief to give in.

I must have fallen into a deep sleep, because the phone initially sounds like an echo in my dreams. Often, when I wake, I get an uneasy feeling that I have somehow emerged, miraculously unscathed, after battling some un-remembered terror. But on this occasion, I recall my dream all too well.

I was dreaming about the photograph that the police had shown me with the name on the back. I am chasing Helen Evans along the beach even though—as in real life—I have no idea who she is. Her hair flows out be-hind her, and I'm willing her to turn round. Then, just as she starts to do so, the phone rings. I bolt upright and grab my mobile. It slips out of my sweaty hand, but I manage to press the Accept button just in time.

"Vicki?"

At last. It's the solicitor. So late on a Sunday night? That's surprising.

"I'm sorry I couldn't speak earlier. I had clients with me, and this is the first chance I've had to ring back." Her voice tightens. "You say you're un-der investigation. Would you like to tell me more?"

"Do you do criminal law?"

"We do." There's a brisk tone to her voice.

Sweat runs down my armpits, and I find myself stammering. "I'm . . . well I'm being investigated by the police for . . ."

I stop. *What* exactly? The word "murder" hasn't been mentioned.

"Because my ex-husband has gone missing, and they think I have some-thing to do with it."

"*Do* you?"

"I don't think so, but . . . well, it's complicated."

We're back to brisk now. "Sounds like we need to make an appointment as soon as possible."

We fix a date and time. I'm not sure, to be honest. If the police don't return, I will cancel it. If they do . . . I don't even want to think about it.

I glance at the clock. It's ten p.m. I should go back to sleep, but I'm no longer tired. Suddenly, I have a yearning for fresh air.

So I wrap up against the cold and take myself for a walk along the front toward the distant cliffs. In the daylight they're red, but I can't actually see them now in the dark. The promenade, on the other hand, is lit up with streetlights. I love it when it's empty, like now, apart from a few fishermen who are standing silently, leaning over the railings. One is wearing a headlamp and has a bucket of bait by his feet and a line that reaches out into the sea. We nod at each other in companionable silence.

The tide is up tonight, and the waves smack the shingle with purpose. The spray hits my face, and I laugh spontaneously. It makes me feel like a child again. When life was normal. When I could remember things. When I didn't get a burning smell or wake up wondering if something bad had happened.

I walk past the bench, but I don't look at it. Place or name associations are all potential triggers.

When I get back home, my answerphone is flashing. One of my clients has canceled. She doesn't give a reason, but I'm pretty sure it's because she's heard about the bench incident or my uniformed visitors. I think about running away to another town, but if I do, I'll only look more suspicious in the eyes of the police.

Damn you, David.

Not just for what you did but for making me miss you still.

Perhaps it's time to put an end to it.

12.

SCARLET

Scarlet couldn't sleep that night—and not just because of the noises coming from Dawn's bed.

"Mum," Scarlet kept whispering. "I'm coming to see you."

Saying it out loud made it feel more real. The scary bit was that she couldn't picture Mum's face clearly. She could remember the name of her perfume—patchouli—but it was hard to recall exactly what it had smelled like. But if Scarlet closed her eyes tight, she could almost feel the touch of her mother's face against hers.

Friday, Mr. W had said—that's when the social worker was going to take her to see Mum. She had special permission to be absent from school.

"Please let her be all right," Scarlet whispered into the darkness. "Help her to remember to take those tablets that make her feel happy. And clean her teeth, because sometimes she forgets. Oh—and eat properly, too."

That's when she heard it. The crackle of a packet. Muffled laughter. Someone munching.

"Want some?" asked Dawn.

In the half-light, Scarlet could see her holding out some crackers. Darren, who was meant to be in the room next door, reached out to grab a handful for himself.

"Where did you get them from?"

"Nicked them from the family cupboard, didn't we?"

"We'll get into trouble if they find out," said Scarlet between mouthfuls. The crackers stuck in her throat, but she still couldn't get enough.

"Then they ought to feed us right. 'Sides, we're careful. We only take bits every now and then. Store the rest under the bed. Look, we've got chocolate, too."

Scarlet's hand shot out. Fruit and nut. One of the uncles used to bring this sometimes. Her favorite.

"Don't get the sheet dirty," warned the boy, "or Mrs. W will think you've been shitting yourself as well as peeing."

Scarlet felt her cheeks grow hot with shame.

"Don't be so mean." Dawn was shoving the boy out of bed.

"Fuck off. You'll wake the others."

Footsteps were coming along the landing. "What's that noise?"

To Scarlet's horror, the door opened. Mr. W glared at her.

"Nothing," whispered Scarlet, glancing across at Dawn, who was now pretending to be asleep. "I just rolled off the mattress."

"Careful. Or you'll get a bruise."

His voice was gentler than his wife's. He padded toward her. His feet were bare, and he only had pajama bottoms on, and his stomach flopped down over the waistband. "Let me sort you out."

Scarlet held her breath. Surely, he'd see the shape hiding under Dawn's duvet?

But no. He seemed to spend a long time, kneeling down beside her and rearranging the duvet. "That's better," he grunted, getting up. "Should keep you nice and safe now." He stood over her for a bit, looking down. Scarlet's skin began to crawl. Then he seemed to shake himself and began walking toward the door.

"No more noise, do you hear me?" he said in a loud voice. "Or there'll be trouble."

"Fucking hell," breathed Dawn, emerging from the covers. "That was close. Ta, Scarlet. You was great."

"Reckon he's got the hots for you," whispered Darren. "Just like Kayleigh . . ."

"Fuck off," hissed Dawn. "If that man ever comes near one of us again, I'll cut his balls off. See if I don't. And yours, too, if you don't behave."

"Who's Kayleigh?" whispered Scarlet after Darren had gone.

"It doesn't matter."

But Dawn said it in the kind of voice that Mum used when something *did* matter.

"What did he mean when he said Mr. W had the hots for me?"

"Come off it. Means he wants to get into your knickers."

"I don't get it."

"You're not kidding me, are you?" Dawn tiptoed out of her bed and perched on the end of Scarlet's mattress. It was so narrow that there was only just room. "Listen, love. I don't know what your life was like before you came here. But I'll tell you something for free. There are blokes out there who would do anything to you. Sometimes that's great, 'cos you can use them. Sometimes it's bad, 'cos they use you." She made a strange sound in her throat. "That Mr. W. He's not a good man."

"Did he hurt Kayleigh?"

"I'm not saying."

The streetlight, streaming through the gap in the curtains, lit up the pain on her friend's face. Maybe, thought Scarlet, she'd guessed right.

"Mr. W seemed so kind. He didn't want me to get any bruises."

"Hah!" Dawn rolled her eyes. "That's 'cos he doesn't want any awkward questions asked by the Social. If they spot any marks, they might blame the foster parents. Then Mr. and Mrs. W will lose their money."

"What money?"

"For Chrissake, Scarlet. You don't think they take us in here 'cos they're nice, do you? They do it 'cos they get paid."

"Really?"

Dawn groaned. "I can see I've got my work cut out with you. Just as well I'm your friend. Mind you, it's a bloody nuisance about you seeing your mum on Friday. We was planning to do the next job then. So we'll do it the day after tomorrow instead."

"Do you mean I've got to take *more* DVDs?"

"You've got it." Dawn patted her on the shoulders. "Now move over. I'm fucking freezing."

She slid in beside her, arms around Scarlet's back. She and Mum used to sleep like that. It was comforting. And suddenly, it was morning again.

"*Right,*" said Darren on Thursday when the bus dropped them outside school. "Remember the plan. We do the roll call so they think we're here, and then we slip out as soon as we can. Good thing we're in different classes today. With any luck, they won't notice till it's too late."

But Scarlet couldn't concentrate for excitement. Tomorrow, first thing, the social worker was coming to pick her up. They were going to drive to a place called Aitch Em Pee Something to see Mum.

"Soon as you can, get out," carried on Darren, "and go straight to the shopping center. You—Scarlet—do what you did before. Wait by the door until we've pushed a stand of stuff over. Then run in and grab what you can. Got it?"

It all happened so fast. Darren knocked over the stand, then Dawn gave Scarlet a shove, which sent her flying. She stumbled over her shoe and then righted herself, remembering her instructions. Go for the section marked NEW RELEASES. One. Two. Three. Maybe a fourth. Scarlet hugged the DVDs to her chest and ran back toward the door. But a big man in black trousers was standing there, his huge arms folded and feet wide apart. He was glaring at her like his eyes were on fire.

Crouching down, Scarlet flung herself between the man's legs and out the other side. She knocked into an old lady with a walker.

"My leg!" she screamed.

"I'm sorry." Scarlet ran back toward her. "Are you all right? I didn't mean to—"

That was when she felt those big arms on hers. She was being marched now toward the main doors of the shopping center. *You're hurting me!* she tried to say. But fear kept the words inside.

Everyone was looking. There was no sign of Dawn or Darren or any of the others.

She was pushed into a police car where there was an unsmiling uniformed woman in the back. "What's your name?"

Don't tell them nothing if they catch you. That's what they'd told her. Scarlet pressed her lips together.

"What do you think you were doing? Stealing's bad enough. But knocking an old lady to the ground is wicked."

Her eyes filled with tears. This time she couldn't stop the words. "I didn't mean it. Is she going to be all right?"

"Would *you* be all right if you were old and some kid attacked you? Now, empty your pockets."

Reluctantly she handed over her eraser, pencil and new spelling book. *Scarlet Darling.*

The policewoman shook her head as she read the name on the cover. "Right, Scarlet. So what's your mum called?"

Her voice was squeaky with nerves. "Zelda."

"Got a mobile phone number for her?"

"She has to use a pay phone 'cos she's in a place called Aitch Em Pee, where they don't let you have mobiles."

Something changed in the policewoman's face. "Right."

"I'm seeing her tomorrow! The social worker's going to take me."

"We might have to see about that."

Scarlet got a sick feeling in the pit of her stomach. *Might have to see.* That was something Mum said when she really meant *I don't think so.*

"But I've *got* to see my mum. I have to. I haven't cuddled her since they took her away from me, because of the game."

"What game?"

Maybe she shouldn't have mentioned that.

"I can't remember."

"How convenient. Well, when we get to the station, maybe you can remember what those other kids asked you to do. Don't think you've got to cover for them. And don't go getting excited about seeing your mother tomorrow. You'll be up before the judge instead."

I sell oils to my clients sometimes.

   One of the most popular is frankincense, which is part of my special "Escape" gift pack. After all, we all want to get away, don't we? Including me.

   Looking back, I wonder how on earth I got into this mess. My only excuse is that I was bruised. Vulnerable. Then I met David, who made me feel special.

   If only I'd known then what I know now.

13.

VICKI

1 March 2018

I wait for the police to call me, but the phone stays silent. So I cancel my appointment with Lily Macdonald. Perhaps they've forgotten about me. Perhaps they're building a case. But I'm still uneasy. Eventually, my uncertainty triumphs, and I ring them.

"There's something you should know," I say.

They ask me to come down to the police station. When I get there, Vine buzzes me through to the interview room. It's more modern than the ones I'm used to. Streamlined desks. Big-paned windows. Comfortable chairs.

"Just been done up," says the detective, following my gaze.

I suddenly have a flashback of handcuffs on my wrists. Do they know about that side of my life? If not, it can only be a matter of time.

There is no one with Vine, but I suspect that at least one person—if not two—is listening in.

"So, you said you had something to tell us."

I twist my hands under the desk, wondering if I am doing the right thing.

"The fact of the matter is," I say, "that my husband . . . I mean ex-husband . . . has done this before."

He's waiting. Silence is an effective weapon. I've been taught well. I also know that the right words are crucial when it comes to defense.

"He used to go walkabout when we were married," I say.

His right eyebrow rises. "What exactly do you mean by that?"

"My ex would disappear, sometimes for days on end. Then he'd claim he'd told me where he was going. But he hadn't."

"I see."

It's obvious he doesn't believe me. I lean forward in my desperation. "It began soon after we were married. He didn't come home one night. I thought he'd had an accident, and I even phoned the police. Why don't you check? It must be in your files somewhere."

"Can you remember the exact date?"

I know when Mum died. Patrick's date is engraved in my heart. So, too, is the evening I met David. But I can't be certain of this one. "Only the year and the month."

He makes a half smile, as though humoring me. "So where was he?"

"On a business trip to Hong Kong, he said."

"And you're sure he didn't tell you? Or is it possible you'd forgotten?"

"It was before I got . . ." I start to say.

He nods. I'm glad. I try to say the word "epilepsy" as little as possible.

"How often did this happen?"

"Several times. At the end, I'm not sure if it was work or . . ." I swallow hard. ". . . or pleasure."

I spit the last bit out with bitterness. He doesn't miss it.

"Why haven't you mentioned this before?"

"I was embarrassed."

"Your ex-husband married his secretary very soon after you broke up, I believe."

I nod curtly, not trusting myself to say anything.

"And you think that's what he's doing now? Taking a business trip, or even seeing someone else?"

"Well, it's possible, isn't it?"

He shrugs. "Mrs. Goudman says she has no idea where he is."

I laugh. "Nor did I!"

I almost tell him my suspicions that Tanya might know where David is. Then again, he might think I'm trying to deflect attention away from me.

"Do you have any proof of what you've just told me?" he asks.

I think of my surety hidden in the Bills file. Isn't that why I'm here? To hand it over? But the detective's cool attitude makes me wonder if he will believe me. He might even think I've forged it to get David into trouble. It seems I can't win.

"Not exactly."

"What do you mean by that?"

"I'm not a detective like you. Just a woman who is trying to make the best of things after her whole bloody life has been turned upside down."

I'm not the swearing type. I don't mean to be angry or hit my fists on the desk like this. Yet I'll do anything to make this man understand that I honestly don't know why my ex-husband has disappeared. But most importantly, I need to convince *me*.

The detective pushes a box of tissues in my direction. They're man-size. I am reminded of the one occasion when I found David crying—he was watching a TV drama about a boy whose father beat him up for some minor misdemeanor. It was the only time I ever saw him shed tears. When I asked if he was all right, my husband quickly changed the channel, saying he didn't want to talk about it.

My anger is subsiding now. I want to go home to snuggle up on the sofa with a soft blanket. To dab lavender on my temples. Besides, I've got another client coming over soon. Unless she's canceled, too.

Detective Inspector Vine is tapping his index finger on his left wrist, thinking to himself. Then he frowns. I find myself wondering if he's ever cried as an adult. I suspect not.

"And you honestly still can't explain the photograph that showed you arguing with your husband two months before he disappeared?"

"No. I can't. Maybe it was doctored. They can do that sort of thing."

"They?"

"Experts. Someone who has it in for me."

"And who might that be?"

So he *doesn't* know about my background. Unless he is playing double bluff and waiting for me to tell him.

"You're the detective," I say.

He shrugs. "You're obviously upset. Would you like someone to drive you home?"

His voice is gentle. I don't trust it. I knew where I was with the blunter approach.

"Can it be an unmarked car? No uniform? I don't want the neighbors to see."

"I'll do what I can."

I'm escorted through the door and into the main waiting area. And then I see her, sitting on a chair: smudged black eyeliner. Short black skirt. Opaque black tights. Knee-length black suede boots with a high heel. That heavy floral scent that sickens me from here.

What is *she* doing here in Cornwall? Is it possible she's come to lodge a complaint against me?

"Tanya," I croak. But the woman ignores me. Then I realize it's not her after all. It's another tarty-looking bitch.

"Are you all right?" asks the policeman.

I nod, feeling stupid. What must he think of me, saying the woman's name out loud like that?

Crazy. That's what. And maybe he's right.

14.

SCARLET

"P-O-L-I-C-E," spelled out Scarlet, eyeing the letters on the outside of the tall gray building.

The policewoman's face softened. "Like reading, do you?"

Scarlet nodded. "My mum taught me before I even went to school."

"Is that so?" The lips tightened. "How old are you exactly? Eleven? Twelve?"

"If I tell you, will you let me see Mum?"

"I'll do my best."

"Eight."

There was a frown. "But you're so tall."

"I know." Scarlet nodded again so that the beads in her braids flew into the air. "So was my dad." This was one of the few facts she knew about him, so she always hung on to it tightly.

The policewoman groaned. "Now what the hell am I going to do with you?"

Scarlet felt a stab of panic. Had she done something wrong again?

They were inside now, standing before a glass screen. Behind it sat a man in a black uniform with a scar on his cheek. It reminded Scarlet of the time she'd cut herself on a kitchen knife, peeling potatoes for dinner as a surprise for Mum before she came home. She ought to have had stitches, Mum had said when she'd found her covered in blood. But instead, she put a plaster on it 'cos Social Services might ask questions.

"Got a problem here, Joe," called out the policewoman. "This one might be younger than she looks. That's if she's telling the truth. Won't tell us where she lives, and her only ID is the name on her schoolbook. *Scarlet Darling*. Fancy, eh?"

Groaning, the man picked up the phone. "Get Social over here, can you? We could have an under the age of criminal intent here."

"What's that?" asked Scarlet.

The policewoman was looking pissed off. "It means you won't be going to court after all. Tell me, Scarlet. Did the other kids put you up to this?"

Don't tell.

"What other kids?"

"She might be a baby, but she's good," sniffed the man with the scar.

"I'm not a baby!" Scarlet was indignant. "I'm as good as any adult. That's what Mum says. I help her with the shopping and cleaning when she's not feeling good. At least I did until they took her to the Aitch Em Pee."

"If you don't start behaving, you'll end up in the same place yourself. Do you get what I'm saying?"

Not really, but it seemed safer to nod. And after that, they sat and waited as the clock ticked by.

"Scarlet!"

It was Camilla, the social worker who had taken her to Mrs. Walter's house. "How are you doing, love? Fancy seeing you! I've just been sent down here for a bit and was wondering if I might bump into you." Then she frowned. "Are you in some kind of trouble?"

Scarlet didn't know what to say but the policewoman got in first. "Know this kid, do you? Caught her nicking stuff. An old lady got her ankle sprained."

There was a sigh. Then Camilla whispered something to the policewoman, but Scarlet managed to hear. "Her mother's on remand, and she's under an interim care order. Poor kid's in emergency foster placement with the Walters."

"So there's nothing we can do about it apart from giving her a bollocking and sending her back to this family."

"It might change if the mother goes down."

Scarlet looked up. The man three flats away had "gone down." Mum had told her that meant he'd be in prison for a long time.

"I want to see her! Can you take me?"

"Promise you'll be good in future?" asked Camilla.

"Yes. Honest."

Anything so she could have Mum's arms around her again. Bury her face in her neck and feel Mum stroke her hair and tell Scarlet that she was her "best girl."

"Because if you break the law when you're older, the judge can send you to a juvenile offenders' unit."

Kieran at the Walters' had been in one of those!

"I'll be good. Honestly. I won't play the game anymore."

"This is no game, Scarlet. It's real life. So if someone tries to get you to do something bad, you've got to say no. Do you understand?"

She nodded. "Can I see Mum still? I miss her so much."

The policewoman sighed. "They don't learn, do they?"

Camilla patted her arm. She had long red nails.

"I'll try and sort it out, Scarlet. But please. Remember what you've been told. We're just trying to do our best for you. Really."

Camilla was as good as her word. The next day, she took Scarlet to see her mum as arranged. The Aitch Em Pee had a high wall with curly metal loops above. Camilla's hand tightened over hers as if she was scared, too.

"Where are the windows?" asked Scarlet as they went past a sign that said V-I-S-I-T-S.

"On the other side. There aren't any here. It's all part of security."

They were going through a big door now, where a man on the other side of a glass screen told her to sign her name. A woman in black uniform and with a green dragon tattoo on her wrist made her lift up her arms. Then she ran her hands up and down the rest of her body. It tickled.

"This way."

The door bleeped, and it opened into another room, after which was a second door followed by a third. It was like going down a really long school corridor.

"You said there were windows here," whispered Scarlet.

"There are," said Camilla, squeezing her hand. "Just not in this bit."

They finally arrived in a huge room that stank like someone who didn't wash. In it were loads of tables and chairs but no Mum. Scarlet's chest did a little dip as though it was going to fall out of her body with disappointment.

"She'll be here soon," said Camilla, patting the seat next to her. "Let's just sit for a bit. Look, there are some children's books for you to read."

They waited for what seemed like ages as families came and sat at the other tables. Then women wearing bright blue sashes came out to talk to them. The outfits showed they were prisoners, Camilla explained. The long clock hand on the wall went halfway round, but still Mum didn't come. "It is a bit odd. Let me have a word."

Scarlet watched her go up to one of the uniforms, aware of a woman with round gold earrings at the next table who kept staring at her. At last, Camilla came back.

"Your mum—well, she had a bit of an accident this morning, and it's made her late. But she'll be here quite soon and . . ."

"SCARLET!"

The voice sounded like Mum. But the face wasn't right. Her lovely long blond hair was shorter, and there was a big bruise around her eye. Scarlet hurled herself at her. Mum didn't smell the same, yet her warm hug was exactly as Scarlet remembered. She had a blue sash like the others.

"I've missed you so much." Tears were streaming down Mum's face as she knelt down in front of her. "I told them it wasn't my fault, but they won't believe me. You have to know that your mummy isn't a bad person. I can't sleep at night without you. I can't eat. I made you a special picture in craft class, but one of the other women tore it up. They're all nasty to me here. Look." She pointed to the bruise. "They did this."

"Shhhh." Scarlet patted her mother's back in reassurance, just like she did at home when the water went cold because they hadn't paid the bill or when there wasn't anything to eat. "It will be all right."

"How can it be?" Mum's eyes were bright and angry. "I can't breathe without you, baby. I don't know how I'm going to manage in this shit-hole of a place. My cellmate pisses herself because she can't hold it in. It's inhuman."

"You're upsetting your daughter," interrupted Camilla, who had been standing near them. "Please calm down."

"How fucking dare you tell me how to behave with my own child? Who are you, anyway?"

"Her social worker." Camilla was folding her arms, but she seemed a bit nervous. "We're responsible for Scarlet's well-being. Are you aware that she's committed a shoplifting offense? If she'd been older, she could have been in serious trouble."

"Bollocks. My daughter wouldn't do anything wrong. She's a good girl. Like me."

"TIME," said one of the men in uniform in a loud voice.

"NO!" Mum howled. "I've only just got here."

"That's your fault for being late."

"I was in the fucking nurse's room, wasn't I? Getting this sorted out."

Scarlet leaned forward and stroked the bruise. "All better now."

"You let her treat you as though you are the child," Camilla murmured.

"I need to look after Mum," said Scarlet proudly. "It's my job."

The other women were queuing up at the door. "TIME!"

Mum was gripping her arm so tightly that it hurt. But one of the officers was pulling her.

"SCARLET! SCARLET!"

"Please don't take my mum away," she cried.

Mum was being dragged out of the door. "Don't you dare try to bite me," shouted one of the uniforms, "or you'll go straight to Solitary."

"GIVE ME BACK MY LITTLE GIRL."

The door slammed shut. Mum was gone. Again.

*R*ecipe to cure loneliness: two drops of bergamot and three drops of clary sage.
But it isn't working for me right now. My bed is still empty and cold. I try to lie diagonally to take up the space, but it's not the same.

I used to love watching David sleep. He looked like a little boy. So vulnerable. Sometimes he used to talk, but it was hard to make out the words.

Once, I was shocked to find myself thinking how easy it would be to put a pillow over his head. I knew a woman who did that once. She got Life.

The weird thing is that my husband hadn't done anything wrong then—well, nothing I knew about.

I loved him. Everything was good.

But I still couldn't stop thinking about the pillow. It was as if I knew what was to come.

15.

VICKI

2 March 2018

Just as I am potting some rosemary—a symbol of good luck—on my kitchen windowsill, the door knocker thuds. It's DI Vine again, with a different sergeant this time. He doesn't introduce her. I've been waiting for this. The police often follow up quickly after an interview to unnerve suspects.

"There are just a few more things we need to check. Mind if we take another look?"

"It's becoming a habit," I say.

They don't smile.

I gesture inside. "You know the way."

Be calm, I tell myself.

"Would you like something to drink?" I ask the woman, who is waiting with me. She's younger than the last with a slightly foxy face and two silver stud earrings in one lobe. I decide to get on her side. Might be easier.

"Cup of tea would be nice. Milk with two sugars."

"I don't have a kettle in case I burn myself. I told your inspector that before."

"Ah yes," she says heavily. "You have epilepsy, don't you?"

She says the word with a certain amount of skepticism. I'm used to that. Unless someone has seen you have a seizure, they often don't get it. I've actually heard of people like me being accused of being "benefit cheats." Sometimes I wish others could go through it—just the once—and then they might be more understanding. Mind you, it's the babies that really upset me. The parents' stories on the websites reduce me to tears.

"Can't be easy to do your aromatherapy stuff," she says, interrupting my thoughts. "What if you have one of your turns when you've got a client?"

My mind shoots back to one of my worst early experiences. When I came to, I found my client—still in her underwear—dialing 999. "Ambulance," she was babbling in the way you do when you're scared stiff. "Quick."

"Are you ill?" I'd asked sleepily.

She'd given me an *Are you mad?* look. "No. But you were. Your eyes started rolling, and you began thrashing all over the place. You hit me. Look!"

There was indeed a bruise starting to show on her arm.

"You must remember!"

But I didn't. That was when I'd explained my condition. At least, I'd tried to. I was feeling very tired and woozy, which is what always happens.

"Then you shouldn't be treating people," she said. "You could have seriously hurt me. Isn't there a law against it?"

No. Someone with my condition can still carry on working. Yet, as it was explained to me at the time of diagnosis, you have to be sensible and not take risks. As if that were possible.

On the other side of the wall, I can hear cupboards being opened.

"What would you do," I ask the sergeant, "if *you* suddenly started fitting?"

The woman looks as if I've asked something quite ridiculous. "No idea. I've never been in that position."

"Nor had I," I said quietly, "until it happened. And I've never been in this one either. I don't have anything to do with my ex's disappearance, you know."

Her eyes sharpen. "Then who might?"

I have a flash of the trip after Hong Kong.

"Why didn't you tell me you'd gone to Paris?" I'd asked David when he finally came home.

"I did."

"No, you didn't."

"You've been busy. Probably didn't hear me."

At the time, I'd accepted it. After all, I'd had a lot on my plate and might well have not taken this in. Now I know better. David could worm his way out of anything. Is that what he's doing now?

I turn to face her. "Like I told your boss, I think he's just taken himself off somewhere."

"Is there anyone you can think of who might want him harmed?" Her voice is softer, as though *she* is the one who is trying to get me to be her friend.

I laugh, even though it isn't funny. Her face turns suspicious. Instantly, I know I've made a mistake. I try to get out of it. "When you're a wheeler-dealer like David, you are bound to make enemies."

"What about his family? His wife, for instance. What do you know about her?"

I hadn't trusted Tanya from the moment David had introduced me to her at the staff party. We'd been married for barely a month. "My right-hand woman," he'd said. Tanya's eyes had glittered.

"Not much," I say tightly.

"David has a daughter from a previous relationship," perseveres the policewoman. "Right? In her early twenties?"

They've clearly done their homework in that department, even if they haven't questioned me about this. Surely, they must be aware of my past by now? Then again, it wouldn't be the first time I'd discovered a lack of communication in the police or a failure to follow things up. So perhaps they *didn't* know. Our justice system has more inadequacies than people realize.

I swallow the hard lump that has suddenly sprung up in my throat. "That's right."

Nicole never cared for me, even though I had nothing to do with her parents splitting up. They'd been so young that they'd barely been together. Nicole's grandmother had brought her up so her own daughter could finish her education. David had only become interested in his child's welfare when she was older. Yet he'd been excited enough about the baby.

Patrick . . .

A mental image of a pram flashes into my head. "Will you excuse me?" I blurt out.

Without waiting for a reply, I go into my bedroom and close the door of the en suite behind me. Then I reach for the bottles at the back of the cabinet. Lavender. And two other essential ingredients, too. That's better.

I return to the sitting room. DI Vine is back with a white box. The silver ribbon that was around it has been untied.

"Your wedding album, I presume," he says.

Oh no.

Without waiting for a reply, he opens the first page. There's a picture of David kissing me on the steps of the register office. I've blacked out his face with a thick felt tip. In fact, I've done the same in all the other pictures, too.

"So?" I say defensively when he looks up at me, eyebrows raised. "I bet lots of women deface their wedding albums after they get divorced."

"Why not chuck it?"

Because then it would be gone forever. And I'm not ready for that. I'm not ready to admit this either, so I just shrug. That's when the policewoman comes in. She is holding a small black book. My heart sinks as she holds certain pages out for her boss's inspection. His face darkens.

So they've looked behind the radiator I'd turned off. And I thought I'd been so clever.

"Victoria Goudman, you are now under arrest . . . do not have to . . . on in court. Anything you do say . . ."

I don't hear the rest of it. I smell something burning. Feel dizzy. I need to get under a table. Quickly.

Voices come in and out.

"What's wrong with her?"

"She's faking it."

"I don't think so, sir."

"Catch her, Sergeant."

16.

SCARLET

Sure you didn't snitch on us?" Dawn had demanded after the police brought her back.

Scarlet made a sign on her chest. "Cross my heart and hope to die."

Mum used to do that when she was at something called a "convent school." It was one of the few things she'd told Scarlet about her own childhood. It upset Mum too much to say more, especially when Scarlet asked why she didn't have grandparents like some of the others in class—so she'd learned to keep quiet.

Once, though, she'd found a photograph in Mum's bag. It showed a little girl in a red spotted dress and blond hair in a bouncy ponytail. A smiley man stood on one side and a woman with curly yellow hair on the other. A black-and-white dog next to them. There was nothing written on the back to show who was who.

"Is that you?" she'd asked.

"Yes." Mum's voice had been quick and hard.

"I like the dog."

Mum's voice melted. "He was called Charlie. We used to go everywhere together."

"Who are the other people?"

"No one."

This was the quick, hard voice again.

"But how can someone be no one?"

"They're nothing to do with you or me. OK? It's not important. Just leave it."

If it wasn't important, why did the photograph go everywhere with Mum in her red velvet bag? But Scarlet kept that question in her head, because she was a good girl.

Scarlet had kept quiet after the prison visit, too. She didn't feel like talking in the car on the way back to the house, so Camilla did it instead.

"Don't be too upset by your mum. It's not easy for her, being away from you. Just as I know it's not easy for you either, love. But the Walters are good people. They'll look after you."

That isn't true, Scarlet wanted to say. She almost told her then about the two fridges and the shouting and the having to leave the house early so Mrs. Walter could get rid of them. But if she did that, she might get into even more trouble.

"Just make sure you stay on the right side of the law from now on," added Camilla. "There are still things they can do even if you're under ten. They might put a child curfew order on you. Do you know what that means?"

Scarlet shook her head.

"You can't be in a public place between nine p.m. and six a.m. unless you're with an adult. Or you might get placed under the supervision of a youth offending team."

The traffic lights were red. Scarlet could feel the social worker's eyes on her. She looked away, out at the street. A girl about her age was walking along, holding a woman's hand. Her heart lurched.

"When will they let Mum get out of prison?" she whispered.

"We won't know until the trial, love. We just have to be patient."

Nearly a week went by, and to her relief, the others didn't make her play any more games. They needed to "lie low," according to the whispers from Dawn's bed at night.

"Your social worker rang, Scarlet," sniffed Mrs. W as she put their tea on the table. "She's picking you up on Saturday afternoon to see your mum."

Scarlet jumped off her chair with excitement.

"Get back to the table. There's another thing, too. Your mum's got her pin numbers approved now by the prison, so she's going to ring you in a bit on the landline." Mrs. W sniffed. "Seven on the dot. Very inconvenient."

This was when Mrs. W watched her favorite program on telly in her private lounge. They all had to be upstairs by then, getting ready for lights-out. But that night, Scarlet was allowed to stay downstairs, waiting by the phone in the hall. It was warmer than usual, because, according to Dawn, the Walters raised the downstairs heating when she and the other foster kids had gone to bed.

"Scarlet's jailbird mum is late," snapped Mrs. W to her husband. "Reggie. You'll have to wait with her."

He frowned. "Why?"

"'Cos you've got to make sure the kid doesn't say something she shouldn't." Then there was a whisper.

When the phone rang, Scarlet jumped, even though she'd been waiting for it. "Mum?"

"Scarlet!"

Mum's voice sounded different. Sharper. "Is there anyone with you?"

Mr. W was playing on his own mobile phone with those fat fingers of his. Was that an excuse to pretend he wasn't listening to her call?

"Yes."

"Then don't speak. Just pay attention. When you come out of school tomorrow, there's going to be a man at the gate. You might recognize him."

"Is he one of the uncles?"

"I said not to talk, didn't I? He's going to give you something. Keep it safe. When you come and see me, hide it in your sleeve, wrapped up in a tissue. They don't always search kids. Then, when we give each other a hug at visits, I'm going to sneeze. You'll pass me your tissue. Got it?"

"But what's in—"

"SHUT UP. It's a new game. OK?"

Scarlet glanced across at Mr. W. He was still busy with his phone. "I can't wait to see you, Mum."

"Me, too. Be a good girl and do exactly what I've said. Now blow me a kiss so I can catch it."

This had been another of their games for as long as she could remember. But it wasn't the same doing it over the phone instead of face-to-face.

"I love you, Scarlet." Mum's voice was thick with tears. "Always remember that."

It was Mum's friend with black cornrows, a bit like hers, who was outside school. Scarlet liked him because he was always smiling and didn't shout at her.

"For your mother," he said quickly, and then pressed a tiny envelope into her hand. "Doing all right, are you?"

He ruffled the top of her head and then walked away before she had a chance to answer.

"Who's that?" asked Dawn.

"No one."

"What did he give you?"

"Mind your own business."

Quickly, she stuffed the envelope into the gray backpack that Camilla had got her.

"You can keep a secret. I'll give you that." Dawn said it in a way that suggested this was good.

But inside, Scarlet's heart was all fluttery.

"Excited?" asked Camilla on Saturday as they walked toward the visitor center.

Scarlet nodded. The envelope felt heavy inside her sleeve. She'd wanted to open it, but it had lots of brown tape round it.

"Put anything you're carrying in the lockers," barked the dragon lady.

Camilla placed her large black briefcase inside. "You haven't got anything, dear, have you?"

Scarlet shook her head as her heartbeat quickened.

Another uniformed woman was running her hands over Camilla. Then she nodded at Scarlet. "Off you go."

Phew!

This time, Mum was already waiting for them. "Thought you weren't coming," she said accusingly to Camilla. "Felt like a right prat, I did. The other girls thought I'd been stood up."

"The traffic was bad, and we had a long queue to get in here," said Camilla. "Didn't we, Scarlet?"

She nodded. Mum hadn't even hugged her—she was all snappy instead. Maybe she didn't love Scarlet anymore. Dawn said that might happen.

"Give us a kiss, then."

Overcome with relief, Scarlet flung herself into her arms.

"No touching," said one of the guards.

Mum sneezed.

"Bless you," said Scarlet.

Mum sneezed again. At home, this had always been a sign that she had to do something that no one else must know about.

She'd almost forgotten!

Carefully, just like Mum had said, she passed over the folded tissue.

Mum wiped her nose and then put it in her own sleeve.

Nervously, Scarlet glanced at Camilla. But she was looking at the woman at the next table, who was arguing with her visitor. "You promised," one of them was saying. "You can't let me down."

Then Mum stood up. "Officer, I've got to go to the toilet."

Two uniforms were marching toward her. "Haven't you heard of TV surveillance? We saw you. Training your daughter to be a mule now, are you?"

"She was just bloody giving me a tissue . . ."

"This it?" One of the uniforms was shaking it out. The package fell to the floor. Camilla gasped.

"Scarlet?" Then she turned to Mum. "Your daughter is already in enough trouble as it is."

"Get off. There's been a mistake."

"You can say that again. This way."

"I said, get your fucking hands off me."

"MUM! I'm sorry. I tried to . . ."

"SHUT UP, YOU SILLY LITTLE COW."

Scarlet burst into tears. Mum never talked to her like that.

Camilla had her arms around her. "It's OK, Scarlet. It's OK."

But it wasn't.

The police came to the Walters' house the next day. Camilla was with them. They had a video recording of a shop where Dawn had nicked some jeans. Scarlet hadn't known about that. Her friend was taken away. "You've made a mistake," she said, pointing to Darren. "It was his idea."

"Then he'd better come as well," they said.

That night, Scarlet couldn't sleep. The bedroom felt so empty without her friend. "Mum," whispered Scarlet into the darkness. "Where are you?"

Then, as if by magic, the door opened.

The universe had answered her prayers! Then she smelled sweat.

"Be a good girl," he whispered. "Or I'll tell my wife about those crisps and chocolate that you lot have been hiding under the beds. Think I didn't know about that? If I blab, you'll go to prison like your mum. And you'll never get out."

"What's up with you?" demanded Mrs. Walter as she put cold toast on the table for breakfast. "Cat got your tongue?"

Mr. W wasn't normally around in the morning. But right now, he was staring at her. Scarlet couldn't help it—she started to heave.

"Someone get her a trash can, quick!" squealed Mrs. W. "Get out, all of you. Go to school. Someone can clean you up there."

When Scarlet got back, Camilla was waiting in Mrs. W's kitchen. "In a few days, we're going to be moving you to another family, love. You'll have more restrictions. You won't be able to go to a shopping center with the other children. The new place is in the middle of the country. There aren't many shops there, just lovely green fields. You'll go to another school, too."

What about Mum? Scarlet wanted to ask. But the words wouldn't come out. They'd stayed stuck inside her mouth ever since the bedroom door had opened last night. At school that day, she'd been given a black mark for refusing to talk.

"I'm afraid there's something else. Your mum did something wrong, you see. It's to do with drugs. Never take them when you're older, Scarlet. They wreck people's lives. I've seen it over and over again."

Camilla stopped. When she began again, her voice sounded different. "You'll have another social worker at your new home. Your mum's not allowed to see you for a bit because she made you bring in those drugs. If she asks you to do that again, you must say no. Do you understand?"

Scarlet nodded.

"She's sent you this. Said you'd always liked it."

It was the photograph of her mother when she was little in the place called Whales with the two grown-ups and the little dog. The one that she always carried with her.

"The prison lets people keep certain things when they go inside. Your mum got special permission to give it to you because she thought it might give you comfort."

Scarlet held it against her cheek, pretending that Mum was right next to her and that everything was back to normal again.

17.

VICKI

I'm sleepy when I come round. Although I've never taken drugs, I imagine this is what it feels like to be high.

"Vicki? Are you all right?"

It's someone in black. Slowly, it dawns that this is the policewoman from earlier. She is kneeling over me.

"Water," I say. Then, because I'm dimly aware this sounds rude, I add the word "please."

My wrists ache. That's when I realize I have handcuffs on.

"Take them off." The metal is cold against my skin. It chafes against my bones as I shake them furiously. I hear my voice rising in hysteria. "I SAID, GET THEM OFF!"

The woman's face registers a sympathy that hadn't been there before. "I'm afraid we can't. Not until we've been to the station. Do you feel well enough to come with us now?"

Might as well get it over with. I stumble to my feet. She takes my arm to help.

"We can get you checked there," she adds, almost apologetically. "Unless you want us to call an ambulance."

"There's nothing they can do."

"Why?" cuts in the inspector. "Because you've just pretended to fit?"

"How dare you? Is that why you haven't called for help already?"

The flicker in his eyes shows that I've hit the mark.

"I could report you for that," I add.

He looks distinctly uncomfortable now. I've a mind to carry out my threat. But he's not the only one to react like this. David hadn't understood either. You can rarely cure epilepsy, one of the doctors once told me, but you can learn to live with it. The same can't always be said for your nearest and dearest. Or your enemies.

I turn to the policewoman. "Can you fetch my tablets, too? They're in the high cupboard in the kitchen."

She looks at the detective as if seeking approval. He nods abruptly. And then we're on our way.

I was hoping not to come back to this police station. There's a couple sitting on metal-backed chairs by the wall. The woman is silently weeping, holding a scrunched-up tissue in her hands.

I smile in what I hope is a comforting gesture. In return, the woman turns away. No doubt this is related to the fact that there are two police uniforms on either side of me. At least they've taken off my handcuffs. Presumably, they no longer think I'm going to make a dash for it.

I am led into a side room. A young nurse is waiting. She asks me the usual questions. Did I feel unwell before the seizure started? Yes. I was under stress because I'd just been arrested. Was I hurt in any way? Only a bruise on my right arm where I had fallen. Nothing serious, she declares. Had I had anything to drink? A glass of water but I need more. Please.

I gulp it down.

The nurse has my tablets. I see her checking the strength. She asks what normally happens after a seizure. I explain that sometimes doctors increase the dose. But there's a limit on how far you can go. I've almost reached that now.

"Is she fit for an interview?" asks the policewoman. I sense from her pink cheeks that she's been slightly rattled by our conversation. Maybe she knows now that epilepsy isn't to be taken lightly.

The nurse turns back to me. "How do you feel?"

Terrible. But what's the point in complaining? It would only delay the inevitable.

I am led into another, smaller room. The window is dusty, and the sun-rays shining through are dancing with little white specks. There is a worn oak desk. Two chairs with stiff backs. The man in uniform indicates that I should take the one on the left. Maybe the other is for my solicitor, whom I've asked to be contacted. Don't say anything about David until she arrives, I tell myself. But it's tempting. I have to make them see this is all one big mistake.

"Doesn't look good, does it, Vicki?"

DI Vine speaks as though we are old friends. I fix my gaze on that chin, which merges into the throat without the usual folds or curves. It helps me to remember that no one is perfect.

"We've already got that photograph of you with your ex plus your wedding album. And now there's this."

He places in front of me the small black book that the policewoman had shown to him earlier. My personal diary.

"I didn't mean any of it," I say quickly, forgetting my earlier pledge to keep quiet. "They're just . . . you know . . . thoughts."

He gives me a disbelieving look.

"I was encouraged to write them down."

"Therapeutic, is it?" His voice is mocking.

I feel the old anger rising up inside along with the bitter taste of bile. I was physically sick for days on end after Mum died. And after Patrick, too.

"Actually, yes."

He opens one of the pages, which has a yellow Post-it sticker on it. Not mine. "So when you say, 'I wish he was dead,' you don't mean it?"

"No. Of course I don't. It's just one of those silly ideas that might pass through your head. It relieves the pressure inside."

For a minute, I think I've convinced him. "So the 'him' and the 'he' in this diary of yours do actually refer to your ex-husband, David Goudman, then?"

Instantly, I realize I've walked into a trap. I could have pretended this wasn't mine. That someone had forged my distinctive neat handwriting, or that I'd been talking about someone else.

"Yes . . . No . . ."

The door swings open to admit a tall woman with blond hair and a swanlike neck. She is well-dressed in a tailored navy blue skirt and an elegant cream jacket. Her handshake is warm but firm. "I'm Penny Brookes. I'm filling in for Lily Macdonald. She's got a lot on, so she's asked me to step in."

I don't want someone who is just a reserve. I need a sharp solicitor who can get me out of this hole. How old is this woman? What kind of experience has she had? I suddenly feel cold. My future is in the hands of a complete stranger. How often have I heard that?

"Is it all right if I call you Vicki?"

I nod. "One c, one k, two i's."

When you're different, like me, you feel defensive about your identity.

"I noted that from your records, although I should add that your divorce files are separate. Because I wasn't involved with that, I don't have access to them unless you give me permission."

"It's not necessary," I say quickly. "This isn't connected."

She bends her head as if accepting my point. "I should also say that you don't have to answer any questions from the police if I don't feel they are appropriate."

Maybe she knows her stuff after all.

She takes a pen from her brown leather bag and addresses the inspector.

"Can you show me the evidence that, in your view, links my client to the disappearance of David Goudman?"

I watch, mouth dry, as she flicks through the diary. Then, to my horror, she reads a passage out loud.

"I wish he was dead. It would be so much easier. Then no one else could have him either."

"I've already told them that they were just feelings," I burst out. "I would never actually do anything."

The detective makes a dismissive snort.

My solicitor mutters something like, "Have you never said or written anything you didn't mean?"

He immediately picks up on it. "Our own personal feelings are not the point, as you know very well. As I've told you in the past, it is unprofessional and unusual for a solicitor to get involved in arguments with the police on certain points."

So my solicitor is a bit of a maverick who isn't afraid of doing things differently! I'm now relieved that she's fighting in my corner. But I'm still nervous.

Penny looks unrepentant. "This diary merely expresses the views of my client at a time when she was under stress. It would not, in my belief, stand up in law as definitive proof of complicity in Mr. Goudman's disappearance."

Inspector Vine bristles. "That's a matter of opinion. What about the photograph of your client with the victim, taken shortly before he disappeared? She told me that she hadn't seen him since 2013 and couldn't remember being there."

The victim?

He hands over a brown envelope. My solicitor seems to take an age studying it. Then she looks at me. "Is that right, Vicki?"

I feel myself going red. "OK." I swallow hard. "I did go to London . . ."

The detective slaps his knees. "I knew it!"

"I'd . . . I'd missed David. I know he behaved badly, but . . . well, he left this hole in my heart. It's like he still had this hold over me . . ."

There's another scoffing noise from the detective, which I try to ignore.

"So I went to some of the places we used to go to together, like this restaurant near the Tate. And then I saw him through the window."

"So you went in to see him?" he asks.

"No." I am hot with embarrassment. I can feel the heat rising to my face. "He came out to tell me to stop following him."

"You had an argument?"

"Yes. Of course we had a bloody argument."

Penny puts her hand on my arm as my voice rises in distress.

The detective is looking triumphant. "Then why didn't you tell me before, instead of lying?"

I try to keep my voice level. "I felt embarrassed, and I . . . well, I thought it would make me look guilty."

"I'd say so."

"But it's still not proof that she had anything to do with David Goudman's disappearance." My solicitor's voice is calm but firm. "Besides, I gather that Vicki has already voiced her opinion that Mr. Goudman may simply be away on a business trip."

"Then why wouldn't his wife know?"

I can't not interrupt. "I told you before. He often went off when we were married."

My solicitor lays a hand on my arm again. Just briefly, as if to indicate that I shouldn't be too aggressive. "My client's ex-husband appears to have had some questionable business practices," she says.

"That doesn't mean we can dismiss his disappearance."

"Of course not. But there may be a valid explanation for it."

"What about the stalking?"

"I gather from the notes that my client has already explained she was merely in the vicinity of her ex-husband's house at the end of last year in order to see her doctor."

"And the phone calls she kept making to her ex-husband after they broke up. Would you say that's not stalking either?"

"Actually, I'd call it the sign of a woman who'd been bruised after a divorce." My solicitor's voice is brisk, yet I get the feeling that she has been hurt, too. There's no wedding ring on her left hand, although that doesn't mean anything nowadays. "I would suggest that unless you can come up with a stronger case against my client, you should release Mrs. Goudman immediately."

He is shaking his head. "You're making a mistake here, Pen."

The shortened version of her name suggests they know each other.

"I don't think so."

Then I hear him mutter something under his breath. It sounds like *It wouldn't be the first time.*

Great. So my solicitor's made a mistake in the past. But right now they're both missing something. "Where *is* David?" My voice is full of anguish. "What if he hasn't gone on a trip? Supposing he has been hurt? Why can't you find out exactly what's happened?"

I'm aware that I sound like a worried wife rather than an ex. But the truth is that I do still care.

I can still feel him touching me. Kissing me. Telling me, before it all went wrong, that I was the most amazing, unique woman he had ever been with. Despite everything, it's hard to get that out of my head. A court can dissolve a marriage. But it can't do the same to the heart. After all, there were plenty of good times.

"I'm sure the police are doing what they can," says my solicitor as she gets up, indicating that I should do the same.

Inspector Vine stands between me and the door. "I fully expect to see you again, Mrs. Goudman."

My solicitor cuts in. "That sounds like intimidation, Inspector."

"Just making our position clear."

Outside the police station, I gulp in the air, despite the fumes of the passing traffic. Penny Brookes appears to do the same. Then she shakes my hand. "Go home," she says. "Look after yourself. Let me know if there are any more developments."

"What do I owe you?"

"Nothing. It's pro bono. We take on a certain number every year."

Would she feel like this if she knew about my past? "So you believe me?"

"Yes. I do."

I'm changing my mind about this woman. "Will you represent me?"

"As long as you don't do anything daft."

"Such as?"

"Well," she says slowly, "if it was me, I would want to find out what happened to my ex. Please resist that temptation. It could do more harm than good."

"I know what it looks like," I protest. "He cheated and lied to me, and now he's dead, but . . ."

"What makes you think he's dead?" says my solicitor sharply.

"I don't know." I want to curl up in a hole. "I've just got a bad feeling about this. And I'm scared."

"Are you sure there's nothing else you want to tell me?" she asks.

I curse myself for my stupid outburst, which has—let's face it—made me look guilty.

"No," I say firmly. "I've told you everything."

"You're sure?"

I go red again, the way I always do when accused of something. It's a childhood habit. "Quite sure."

If my instincts are right, there's only one person who might throw some light on all this.

Tanya. I'd been going to see her before the police had arrived.

Now it's even more important. I just have to sum up the courage.

18.

SCARLET

1 April 2007

What was that funny smell? Scarlet began to sneeze. The new social worker, noticing, wound up the car window on the side nearest to her.

"Oil seed rape," she said brightly. "Makes your nose tickle. They get a lot of it out here. Not far now. You're going to love it. Dee and Robert are *super*. They've got horses and cows and sheep. You'll be able to describe all this to your mum when you write to her."

But writing wasn't the same as seeing. All she wanted, thought Scarlet miserably, was to feel Mum's arms around her and her soft face against hers.

The car swung round a bend, lurching Scarlet into the door. "Sorry about that. These lanes can be a bit narrow. What do you think, then?"

Scarlet gazed at the house in front of her. It was white with a strange brown roof that looked all bristly like a hairbrush. Yellow flowers were growing up the walls, and there was a dog running around the car, making horrible growling noises.

"Let's get out then, shall we?"

"I can't," whispered Scarlet's thoughts. "It might bite me."

"No need to shrink back like that. He's really friendly."

A man was walking across toward them, wearing green boots with a camera round his neck.

"Hello," he said, opening the car door. "You must be Scarlet. Get down, Aztec."

Scarlet's scream rang in her ears.

"Don't be afraid," said the man again. "He's just saying hello in his own way. Look, he's licking your hand."

"Scarlet!" The social worker's voice was cross. "Don't hit the poor thing like that."

"Robert!" A woman was running out of the big door by the roses. "I told you not to let him out. The child looks terrified." Then she put her fingers to her mouth and whistled.

To her amazement, Scarlet watched the dog turn around and slink back into the house. The woman walked over and knelt down beside her. She wore her hair in a ponytail, and she smelled of roses.

"I was scared of dogs when I was little, too. But you'll get used to him soon. Just as you'll get used to us." She waved her hand around. "All this must be rather different for you."

Scarlet nodded, but the "yes" stayed stuck in her mouth.

"Tell you what, why don't we go inside and I'll show you your bedroom? I'm Dee, by the way, although I expect they've told you that already."

Silently, she followed. To her relief, the man didn't join them. The ground made her feet slide from one side to another.

"Cobblestones," said Dee. "They're really old. Just like the house. We've been here for years. The farm used to belong to my husband's parents. It's too big for us, so when we couldn't . . . when we decided the time was right, we opened up our home to children who needed somewhere to live."

They went inside. Scarlet put her hand on the smooth staircase banister. There were funny pictures carved into the wood. A lion's face. An apple.

"We don't have any other children staying with us at the moment, so you can have the big bedroom. It's rather pretty, with a fantastic view over the river. Look!"

This room was all hers? But it was bigger than the flat where she and Mum had lived.

"You don't need to come to the window if you don't want to. Maybe you'd like a bit of a lie-down on the bed."

It was a proper one! Not just a mattress. Big enough for her *and* Dawn, if she'd been here. But she didn't deserve something nice like that, Scarlet told herself. Not after what she'd let Mr. Walter do. Why hadn't she tried to stop him? She was a bad, bad girl.

"Or perhaps you're hungry?"

Dee was looking at her with such a kind face that Scarlet knew it had to be a trick. "You poor dear," she whispered. "You've been through so much. No wonder you don't want to talk. And there I am, prattling away like there's no tomorrow."

There was a cushion on the bed. A bright red one with a flower on it. Slowly, Scarlet lifted it down and put it on the floor. Then she laid her head on it.

"Are you sure you're comfortable there?"

Scarlet put her hands over her ears to block her out. Dee was nice enough, but it was too much: it was everyone. *Everything.* Mum. Dawn. The police. But especially Mr. W's soft white hands that had stroked her body and taken her voice away.

"You know, I find it helps to jot things down when I don't want to say them. I write poetry myself. Robert is a photographer. He specializes in nature. In fact, he's had quite a few pictures printed in magazines. Maybe later, when you've settled in, you'd like to go on a walk with him."

Scarlet began to shake. What if he hurt her, too?

"You could leave the dog behind, if that's what's scaring you."

Still no.

"I'm going to leave you on your own for a bit now, Scarlet. I've a feeling that's what you want. But I'll be downstairs if you want company. Your social worker is there, too. I baked a cake this morning—a Victoria sponge. It's got plum jam inside that I made myself. Next year, you can help me make some more."

Next year? But that was ages away.

Dee seemed to understand the thoughts in her head. "The plan is,

Scarlet, that you're going to stay here for some time. We'll help you, Robert and I. Everything's going to be all right now. I promise you. Now remember. When you're ready, just come downstairs."

But Scarlet stayed as still as she could, pretending to be asleep.

Only when she heard the footsteps going downstairs did she get up. Slowly, she went to the window. Robert was down by the water.

Uh-oh. He was turning and looking, as if he knew she was staring out of the window! Getting down on the floor, Scarlet crawled across the carpet so he couldn't see her anymore.

"Scarlet?"

There was the sound of knocking.

"Are you all right in there?" It was the social worker's voice.

Her eyes darted round the room to see if she could push something against the door to stop them getting in. The chest of drawers was too heavy, but this chair might do.

"It's OK if you want to move things around." This was Dee's voice. "But don't hurt yourself, will you?"

Back at the window, Scarlet could see the man walking up to the house again. He disappeared out of sight. Then she heard heavy footsteps coming up the stairs.

If anyone tries to get you, just run. Wasn't that what Mum had always said? The window catch was stiff.

She could hear the chair behind her, moving across the carpet as the door began to open.

"For God's sake, child. What are you doing up there?"

The drop below made her feel dizzy.

"DON'T JUMP!"

She hesitated. For a moment, Scarlet thought she was going backward into the room. And then she fell.

*E*very client is a blank sheet. They come to me for so many reasons. More happiness. Less stress. More libido. Better sleep.

I love working out what oils to use.

But it's the return visits that are important. I need to check that my blends have worked. That I am creating a new person.

In some ways, it's like writing in a diary. You can start a fresh page whenever you want. You choose your ingredients.

And you can begin all over again. Now that the police have taken my diary away, I have simply started another. Old habits die hard. I need to let out my emotions somehow.

If only I could start life over again.

There's so much I'd change.

But it's too late now.

19.

VICKI

31 March 2018

It's nearly a month since I decided to visit Tanya. I've been mulling this over for too long. Putting it off. Waiting for the police to arrest me again. But they haven't.

Finally, I make a decision. Tomorrow, I tell myself. I have a new client scheduled for nine a.m.—it's actually Easter Sunday but she said it was the only day she could do because of work. I text her, explaining I have to cancel for "personal reasons." Then I realize the date—April Fools' Day—and almost change my mind. Traveling from Cornwall up to London on the train is a big deal when you could have a seizure at any time. So, too, is the prospect of visiting your ex-husband's wife. But it must be done if I'm going to get anywhere.

"It's work," my husband used to tell me when I questioned why he had to have so many late meetings. And I accepted this. I was even concerned that he was working too hard. How stupid was that?

All these thoughts are whizzing round my head as I try to leave the house the next day. It makes me even more stressed. I've massaged lavender into my wrists, but it isn't working. So I take some deep breaths and tell myself firmly that I have to lock up the house, walk down the high street to the station, get on a train and sit there for the best part of six hours without having a seizure. Then I have to make my way across London to *my* house, where they now live.

It can't be that hard. I've done it before. The police reminded me of that.

But that was before they discovered my personal diary and wedding album. What else might they find if they dig deeper?

Meanwhile, my solicitor's warning rings round my head. *If it was me, I would want to find out what happened to my ex. Please resist that temptation. It could do more harm than good.*

That's all very well, but I can't shake the suspicion that Tanya knows something. That woman stole my husband. What else is she capable of?

The train is packed. Just as well I reserved a seat. It's on the aisle, because it's easier to get to the loo that way. Of course, that will only help if I sense a seizure coming on. I don't always get the burning aura, and the humming is becoming increasingly rare for some reason.

I glance at the man sitting next to me on the window side. Is he the type who will freak out if I roll to the ground and thrash around? Will he pull the emergency cord? I've never actually had a convulsion on a train before, but there's always a first time.

When it initially happened in front of David, he was hysterical. I know this because, when I came round, he was screaming—that made me scream, too. We were in the kitchen right by the phone, but he hadn't even had the presence of mind to ring 999. I did it instead. I didn't even know what had happened, so I described my own symptoms as falteringly recounted by David. Falling on ground. Eyes rolling. Body shaking.

"A possible one-off." That's how the young duty doctor had described it at the hospital. "Go home and rest. Let us know if it happens again."

These thoughts—and more—go through my mind as the train rattles its way toward Paddington. I reach into my bag and feel for the bottle of tablets. Did I take one or two this morning? The more I think about it, the less sure I am.

I wake with a start. Someone is nudging me. It's an elderly woman. Her face is creased with concern. Instantly, I know I've done it again. The other seats around me are empty. People tend to clear the room when an epileptic is in full fling. "I'm sorry," I stutter.

"No need to apologize," she says. "I'm always doing it."

"Really?"

"So easy to doze off on trains. At least that's what I find. I'm relieved I could wake you. Deep in the land of Nod there, you were."

I am swamped with relief. "So I was just asleep?"

"What else could you have been, love? Anyway, we're here."

"Thanks," I say. But she's already on her way, gathering great pace with her cane. Hastily getting down my stuff from the overhead rack, I make my way onto the platform and head for the Underground. I can't get a taxi, or there will be a record of someone dropping me off.

That shouldn't matter. It's not as though I'm going to do anything to Tanya. Merely ask her a few questions. But even so, the fewer witnesses the better. Mind you, when she sees what I have in my bag, I bet she won't want anyone else to know either.

Then I stiffen. There's a broad-shouldered woman in police uniform talking to one of the orange-clad transport officials at the barrier. She glances at me. My mouth goes dry. There's no law that says I can't be here, but I feel as if I've skipped bail. Then she goes back to talking again. I insert my travel card (included in the rail ticket, which I'd paid for with cash) and go through. I wait for someone to tap me on the back, but it doesn't happen.

I hover now at the top of the escalator. Heights always do this to me. I'm all right if I can't see the bottom. But there is no one in front. So I have to wait until someone else arrives.

When they do, I am so relieved that I step in quickly after them. But they walk down on the left. The space in front falls away from me. I grip the rail tightly.

I'm going to fall.

And that's when I see him.

On the escalator going up on the other side.

A tall man. Slightly hooked nose. Rugby build. Well-cut gray overcoat.

"DAVID!"

People are turning round, staring as I scream his name.

He looks straight ahead. He hasn't heard me. Or else he doesn't want to.

My fear of falling is now replaced by the fear of losing him all over again.

I run down the escalator, fear forgotten, my bag bumping against my hip. Down to the bottom. Up the adjoining escalator. I emerge at the top, panting. The policewoman is still talking to the worker at the gate.

He's nowhere in sight.

I want to fall to the ground and sob with relief that my husband (for he'll always be that) is alive. And I want to weep with anguish that I can't put my arms around him and tell him that I don't really wish he was dead. I'd only said that in anger. I'll tell him how much I miss him and that I understand he made a mistake with Tanya. Of course I will take him back. All he has to do is to come to terms with my epilepsy as I have done. It would be so much easier if there were two of us to fight it.

"Excuse me."

My heart stops as I hear his deep voice.

"I'm having problems with my fare card, I've added twenty pounds, but it's not showing."

It's the tall man with the slightly hooked nose. The rugby build. The gray overcoat. He's come up to the transport worker.

I can see him more clearly now.

It isn't David.

20.

SCARLET

She was lucky. If the window had been higher and there hadn't been long, soft grass below, it could have been much worse. Lucky, too, that it was her left arm that was broken. It meant she could still use a pen when she started school the next day.

Dee said that she would like school. "The whole class is excited about seeing you. It's only just down the lane. We'll walk with you on your first day, and after that you'll probably want to come back with one of your new friends. Then you can write a letter about it to your mum."

Scarlet liked Dee. But Robert scared her because his deep voice reminded her of Mr. Walter. The very thought of him made her feel sick, even though Robert's hands were lean and brown instead of white and flabby.

"Why do you think she still won't talk?" she'd heard them say when they returned from the hospital. It had been dark by then. Scarlet was meant to be in bed, but she'd moved to the ground again. She still couldn't sleep. Everything creaked. The floorboards below the carpet when she turned over to get comfortable. The ceiling, too, as though someone was walking around above. Scared, she crept out of the room and sat on the staircase near the lion and the apple, listening to the voices floating out of the kitchen.

"Traumatized, poor kid. Imagine if you'd been through all that with your mother. It took me years to get it out of my system—if indeed I have. You're lucky, Robert. You and your golden childhood."

Dee sounded cross.

"I know, love. I'm sorry. But I want to make it right for her."

"She's frightened of you."

"Really?"

"I can tell from her eyes. Yet she's all right with me and the social worker. If you ask me, a man has upset her. Maybe she's even been . . ."

"Don't you think you're jumping to conclusions, love?"

"NO." There was the sound of something heavy. A fist on the table? "You don't understand."

Dee was crying now. Scarlet almost felt like running down and putting her arms around her like she used to with Mum when she cried. But then she'd be discovered.

"It's all right. I'll never let anyone hurt you again."

That was Robert's voice. Something stirred inside Scarlet. Not just fear in case he couldn't be trusted, like Mr. Walter, but jealousy, too. Dee had someone to look after her. She and Mum—they didn't have anyone.

Quietly, Scarlet tiptoed back and put the pillow with its little blue and yellow dots over her ears to block out the creaks around her. Just as she finally drifted off, Dee was knocking on the door and gently telling her that it was time to get up.

This was a school?

Scarlet looked with amazement at the pretty red house at the end of the lane. There was grass instead of concrete as well as swings like a proper park.

"It's a very small church primary," said Dee, placing a hand on her shoulder. "So they'll make you feel at home. I know it will seem strange to begin with, but you'll be all right. I promise."

She spoke in the same voice that Mum used when she was trying to make Scarlet feel better.

"Scarlet still isn't talking," she heard Dee tell the teacher. "We don't want to force her. She'll do it in her own time."

It was so much easier to stay silent. That way she wouldn't have to tell anyone what happened when Mr. Walter had opened the bedroom door.

Everyone looked at her when the teacher showed her where to sit. Instead of a shared table, she had a desk all of her own with a lift-up lid. The girl next to her had a picture of a pony on the inside of hers. Carefully, Scarlet took her own precious photograph out of her pocket and stuck it to the lid with bits of sticky tape that were already there.

"Who are they?" asked the girl with the pony.

My mum and some other people, Scarlet wanted to say, but the words stuck in her throat again.

"Cat got your tongue, has it?"

"We heard you're living in the home for weirdos."

This was a boy whose desk was on her left.

"The ones that take in kids without parents."

Not true! She still had a mother, even if she was in prison. Then a terrible thought struck her. What if Mum had died, and no one had told her?

The teacher was pointing to a map now, but Scarlet felt too sick to listen. As soon as the lesson finished and they were sent into the playground for break time, Scarlet knew what she had to do.

"Was it school?" asked Dee a few hours later when they collected her from the railway station. "Was anyone horrid to you?"

Scarlet looked out of the car window. Fields, fields and more fields. Yellow and green and yellow again. She still felt sick but hungry, too. It had been a long time since breakfast.

"Then why did you run away? If the station master hadn't called us, you might be on a train to goodness knows where by now, and anything could have happened to you."

Because I wanted to visit Mum, of course, said Scarlet in her head. *Make sure she's all right.*

"You've got to say something, love, or we can't help you."

This was Robert.

DON'T CALL ME "LOVE"! Scarlet wanted to shout. Mr. W had done that. And other names, too. She should have stopped him. But then she might have got into trouble again.

"Can you write it down instead?"

No. That would make it even more real.

"Did the other kids tease you about the color of your skin?"

Scarlet was about to nod when Robert spoke again.

"Don't be daft, Dee. The teacher would have put a stop to that."

"I know you want to see your mum." Dee's voice was softer. "I wasn't able to live with my parents either when I was your age. It's not that she doesn't want to see you. She's not allowed to at the moment for lots of different reasons. But she's safe and well. I promise you."

How did she know Dee wasn't lying?

"In fact, she's sent you a present. It's a CD that we can play when we get home. It's got her voice on it."

Robert, who was driving, made a noise in his throat. "I'm still not sure this is a good idea. It might upset her even more."

"Let me handle this, OK? You go back to taking your precious pictures."

After that, no one said anything until they got home. When they asked if she was hungry, Scarlet shook her head, even though Dee put a bowl of pasta in front of her with a cheesy homemade tomato sauce.

"Shall we hear your mum now?"

They went up to her bedroom. Dee plugged in a CD player.

"Once upon a time, there was a little girl called Scarlet."

Dee had been right. It *was* Mum's voice!

"She recorded this specially for you! Isn't that nice? The people in the prison helped her."

"Scarlet lived in a pretty house far away from her mum. But her mum still loved her very much."

"See?" Dee was cuddling up to her. "I told you she was all right."

"*She hoped,*" continued Mum's voice, "*that her little girl would always re-member that she loved her whatever happens.*"

Sometimes she did wonder if Mum really cared, but this was proof that she did!

They listened to the story right to the end. When it finished, Scarlet wanted Dee to play it again, but the words wouldn't come out. Then Dee said good night. "Won't you use your bed now? I think your mother would want you to."

So she did, but she hid under the duvet all night, listening carefully in case the door opened and Robert came in.

They made her go to school the next day. "It will be good for you," Dee had said when she'd walked with her down the lane. "Watch out for that pud-dle. It would help you settle in if you could talk," said Dee as they got closer. "Your social worker thinks you should see the educational psychologist."

When she got to the classroom, everyone stared again.

"Heard you tried to run away," said the girl with the pony next to her.

Scarlet ignored her. Instead, she lifted her desk lid to say hello to Mum.

I'm sorry I left you here, she said silently. *But I just wanted to find you.*

Mum smiled back at her. But now she had something black above her mouth. A mustache.

"It wasn't me that drew on it," said the girl. "It was him." She pointed a finger at the boy on the left.

"It was only a joke. GET OFF ME. YOU'RE HURTING."

Scratch. That's what Mum had told her to do if she really wanted to hurt someone. And put your fingers in their eyes. It gave you time to run away, because they wouldn't be able to see.

"WHAT ARE YOU DOING?"

This was the teacher, trying to pull Scarlet away.

"DON'T KICK ME LIKE THAT!"

Then another teacher rushed in and held her good arm behind her back. The first one was standing in front of her. "Why did you do that, Scarlet?"

"He messed up Mum."

The words came out of her mouth without her realizing.

"So you can talk, after all. What do you mean?"

Tears were pouring down Scarlet's cheeks now. The words stopped again.

"Kevin drew a mustache on her photograph." The girl was pointing to it. "That's when she got upset."

"It was only a bit of fun. And that picture can't be her mum, 'cos she's blond and not a darkie."

"Kevin! You know it's wrong to make racist remarks or mess with someone else's belongings. It's also wrong, Scarlet, to be violent toward anyone. I am going to have to call your foster parents."

"BUT I WANT MY MUM." Scarlet lunged at her photograph. "GIVE HER BACK."

"When you've apologized," said the teacher. "Say sorry to Kevin."

To the boy who had hurt Mum? No way.

"Then you can't have your picture. No good crying like that. We operate a zero-tolerance policy toward aggression here. Into my office. Now."

Robert seemed almost as sympathetic as Dee.

Of course, Scarlet told herself, that was a trick to make her like him.

"I can Photoshop that," he said when the head teacher gave her back the photograph after he'd had a "little word" with her.

"What does that mean?"

"I'll use some special photographic techniques to wipe out the mustache. Nice to hear you talking. Maybe it was because you got upset, and the words fought their way out." He patted her shoulder as he spoke. Scarlet jumped backward.

Dee noticed. She took Scarlet's hand. Her skin felt soft, but it was a nice soft. Not like Mr. W's. "There's no need to be scared of Robert—or me," she said gently. "We're here to help you. That boy is going to get told off, too. But you need to write a letter of apology to him. It's all right. I'll help you."

"Would you like me to show you how I can take away the mustache?" asked Robert. "We can go into my darkroom in the studio outside."

Scarlet began to shake. What if he touched her?

"I'll come, too," said Dee. "It's all right, love. In fact, it's like magic."

Later, Scarlet watched with amazement as Robert put Mum into a special machine that made her come out as good as new. "Are these all your cameras?" she asked, without meaning to.

"They certainly are," said Dee, rolling her eyes. But she said it in a nice voice, as though she was pretending to be fed up.

"Tell you what." Robert took one down from a high shelf. "Would you like one? I can teach you how to take pictures."

Dee was nodding. "A hobby's always a good thing."

"Will you be there, too?" Scarlet took her hand again.

"This is Robert's thing, dear. But he'll look after you."

"I'd rather take pictures on my own."

"But you'll need to learn first. Trust me, Robert's a good teacher. Now how about an early night? You've had quite a day. And you can listen to your mum's story again."

"*Once upon a time, there was a little girl called Scarlet. She lived in a pretty house far away from her mum. But her mum still loved her very much.*"

Scarlet closed her eyes. And the funny thing was that as soon as she heard Mum's voice, she didn't feel scared anymore.

She felt strong. And that's what she needed to be if she was going to help Mum escape from prison.

I love him and I hate him.

  How is that possible?

I want them to find his body.

But I'm terrified, too.

  Note to self: vetiver. Can be added to Roman chamomile and clary sage to instill relaxation and calm. Warning: the aroma of vetiver on its own can be very strong. Should be well diluted or blended with other oils.

21

VICKI

I want to sink to the ground with the discarded train tickets around me and curl up in a ball of shame. Of course, the man with the deep voice isn't David, any more than the woman in the police station had been Tanya. I'm going mad. How could my ex-husband be on the up side of the escalator as I am going down? Yet coincidences happen. Just not to me. At least, not today.

The worst of it is that it means David is still missing. So where the hell is he? And why is it that everyone I've ever cared for eventually leaves me?

The other passengers are no longer staring. That crazy woman who was calling out a man's name? They've already forgotten her, moved on.

But I can't. I need to know what has happened to the man I once trusted. So it's back to Plan A.

I take the tube to the station nearest to Kingston. Tanya knows something. I'm sure of it.

My old road—which still has a public phone box on the corner—screams nouveau riche. It's not the kind of house I would have gone for, but David had persuaded me, and I'd wanted to keep him happy. It was too modern for me. Diamond-paned windows that would have been all right if it wasn't for the brown windowsills the planners had insisted on. Triple garage. Wide driveway. Tanya has a little yellow Audi convertible.

I used to have an open-top, too. David and I made love in it once in the early days. I'd never done that before. It made me feel naughty, but in a good way. No one would believe it now to look at me. I'm not even allowed to drive.

Twice I walk past the house. Three times. Partly through nerves and partly because I'm testing myself. Am I going to have a seizure? The last thing I want is to knock on the door and then collapse in a heap of rolling eyes and stiff limbs.

On the fourth circuit, I tell myself I am looking suspicious. This is a small cul-de-sac. There are only eight houses: all the same on the surface. Only different if you look very carefully.

I take a deep breath and walk up the drive. The front door has one of those twirly black iron boot scrapers in an open porch. It's shiny clean. My successor doesn't strike me as the walking type. There's also a notice informing cold callers that they will be reported. My old brass lion knocker has gone. Instead, there's a bell that makes a tuneful sound when I press it.

Was that her choice or David's? What kind of woman *is* my replacement? I hadn't had many dealings with her apart from the odd conversation. In fact, it was only after everything had fallen apart that I'd pummeled David mercilessly for details. When precisely did the affair start? The date. The time. Where? Our house? Or the apartment in London?

In return, he'd fed me a million different cliché lines that answered none of these questions. I'd changed. He was scared of the person I'd become thanks to the seizures. It wasn't my fault; it was his. He was sorry, but he'd fallen in love with someone else. It happens. And so on.

If you love someone, you stay with them through thick and thin. He just wanted an excuse to run away with his new younger model. Well, actions have consequences. And this thing that I'm about to do is one of them.

No one is answering, so I go round the back. It's a beautiful day—quite warm for April. The first thing I see is the fishpond. On the patio is a pair of smart green-striped canopy swing chairs and a rectangular wooden table with a candle in the middle. An outside heater. Sliding glass doors leading into the conservatory. The doors are ajar.

Tanya is just inside, lying on a sunbed.

She opens her eyes. "What the fuck . . ."

I'm inside before Tanya can close the patio doors on me.

"Where is he?" I say, grabbing her arms.

She pulls away. "If I did know where he was, I'd have thrown him out by now for playing around. Now get out of my house."

"When did you last see David? What kind of mood was he in?"

My husband was always in moods, although he'd kept that hidden at first.

Tanya was staring at me, hate shooting out from her black eyes. "Who do you think you are?" she snarls. She has tiny white teeth. A bit like a rat. "The police?"

That squeaky little-girl voice is irritating. There's no way she'd been born with that. I can just imagine her cultivating it as she grew up to snare the right kind of man.

"I just want to clear my name," I say, trying to be reasonable. "The police are after me. I need to prove that I had nothing to do with his disappearance."

What the hell is she doing now? Tanya has grabbed something from the top of a pretty cane chest of drawers. I recognize it immediately. It's a wooden love spoon that Dad had bought Mum during their honeymoon in Wales. I'd brought it back with me after Dad's death, revering it as one of Mum's few remaining possessions. In the divorce, it must have ended up in David's pile. I'd been looking for it for ages. How dare he? It wasn't as though it was valuable. He must have known I'd miss it. Maybe that was the point. Now Tanya is waving it in front of me as if she is considering poking my eyes with it. There are red blotches on her face and arms.

I need to distract her, so I hold out the papers I've been keeping safe. It was my surety, I told myself. A get-out-of-jail-free card. One day I might need it. And now that day has come.

"Did you know that our husband has been money laundering?" I say softly.

"'Our' husband?" Tanya laughs, putting down the spoon. "You're deluding yourself, Vicki. I'm his wife now."

Once a wife, always a wife. Did David's first ex, Nicole's mother, feel the same about me?

"Look. He's been buying houses for cash."

I flourish a page from the deeds I'd come across when going through David's study just after he'd announced he wanted to split. For a clever man, my husband could be rather stupid. Why hadn't he hidden them better?

"The paperwork has got you down as a co-owner every time."

Tanya's face goes rigid. "That proves nothing. It's just business."

"With all these houses? I've got evidence to show there are eleven of them, each worth several million. What would the company want those for?"

Her eyes glare. "An investment."

"Then why not put the money in the business account? He told me that he was short of cash toward the end of our marriage."

"That was five years ago. Things have changed."

It's possible, but I don't believe her. Lying is an art. And I should know—I've learned from the masters.

"I know a bit about money laundering, Tanya."

"Hah! How?"

I think of a woman I'd come across who'd been done for fraud. She used to boast that she still had a "hidden stash" for when she came out.

"You'd be surprised. But I do know that people often buy houses with cash to get rid of large quantities of dirty money. Where did it come from? What's David been doing?"

For a minute, I think Tanya's going to say something, but then her mouth tightens. Her face is getting redder, and she seems slightly unstable. Clearly, I've hit a nerve.

"Perhaps," I say, "the sensible thing is to hand this to the police."

"Why haven't you done so already?" Then she notes my expression. "You can't bring yourself to snitch on him, can you?"

I ignore the question, because the true answer would make me look like one of those pathetic divorcées who can't get over their exes. Which I suppose I am.

"Maybe he's hiding to avoid being caught. Come on, Tanya. I know there's something going on here."

Tanya steps toward me, her face registering pure hate.

"Don't do anything stupid," I say softly, "or you'll be in even more trouble."

"Prove it," she hisses, right in my face. A shudder of fear runs right through me. It's so strong that for a minute I think I'm going to have another seizure. Then she grabs the papers out of my hand and rips them up. Pieces flutter to the ground.

"I've got more copies," I gasp.

She gives me a shove. I fall against the piano but right myself.

Her hands seize my wrists just as I'd grabbed her arms earlier. She twists her grip like some spiteful schoolgirl. Two can play at that game. My nails cut into her skin.

"Ouch," she screams. "You cow!"

She lunges at me. I step sideways, pushing her away. She falls, hitting her head against a table with a sickening crunch.

For a minute, I panic. Then my old enemy gets onto all fours and staggers to her feet. "Get out," she screams, her face puce with fury. "Do you hear me? You haven't heard the last of this, Vicki. Just you wait."

22.

SCARLET

January 2013

What do you think?" asked Scarlet nervously.

Robert held the print up to the light. "Good shade contrast. Nice angle, too. You have to look at it twice to realize what it is."

Phew. Robert's approval was worth a lot. He was the expert.

"What's it meant to be?" asked Dee, peering over their shoulders.

"A leaf," they both said in unison.

"Really? Wow, Scarlet. That's great."

A warm feeling flooded through her. Over the years, Robert had taught her so much. How to find the right subject. What speed to use. Arranging a composition. Shooting in black and white. Entering competitions. Last year's award certificate for runner-up in Teenage Photographer of the Year was displayed in the hall, right by the front door.

Dee had insisted. "It's an amazing honor," she'd said, flushing as if she had won it herself. "I'm so proud of you."

Scarlet had hugged her back warmly, but she'd felt sad, just as she always did. It was Mum whom she should be hugging. Mum who should be hanging her certificates on the wall. Mum who ought to be helping her braid her hair with the little red beads. Mum she should be living with. Mum who should be here to help celebrate Christmases and birthdays. She'd be fifteen in June.

"Do you think it's good enough to enter?" asked Scarlet.

"For this year's award?" Robert patted her on the shoulder. Scarlet flinched.

"That man," Mum would sometimes demand when she visited. "He doesn't try anything with you, does he?"

"Of course he doesn't," Scarlet would say, glancing nervously at the social worker who always had to be with them. Her initial fears when she'd first come here, that Robert might come into her room like Mr. Walter, had proved unfounded. Even so, it had taken her a long time to trust him, and she still couldn't help shuddering if there was any physical contact, however slight.

Dee was different, though. Scarlet liked hugging her. And if she closed her eyes, she could imagine it was really her mother . . .

At times, Scarlet felt her heart was literally going to break—especially when Mum rang. "Is that my little girl?" she'd ask, and Scarlet could hear the tears in her voice. Kind as Dee and Robert were, it wasn't the same. No one else at school was in a foster home, though thankfully it was all so different from the horrible time she'd had at the Walter house. But at least since she'd started to gain recognition through her photographs, her classmates had been much nicer and actually admiring. She didn't have a best friend, but Scarlet didn't need one. All she wanted was Mum.

The first year had been the worst—Mum had been forced into rehab. Scarlet hadn't been allowed to see her much, because she had been put on restricted visiting, but when she did, Mum didn't ask Scarlet anything about school or what it was like with Dee and Robert. All she wanted to know was whether Scarlet had brought her some weed. "*Why* not, you silly girl?"

Then Mum would start screaming and shouting so that the officers took her away, leaving Scarlet in tears.

It was Dee who had comforted her when the social worker brought her home. Dee who sat her on her knee even though she'd been a big girl of nine then. Dee who told her that her own parents had done drugs, too, and how they could really mess up your brain. "Your mum loves you," she'd sighed. "She just needs time to get cleaned up."

Her foster mother had been right. In the last couple of years, Mum had got her privileges back, and Scarlet was allowed to visit more often. Mum stopped pestering her for drugs, but she was still thin, and her lovely blond hair was lank and greasy. Mum had laughed when she'd asked her why she didn't wear patchouli anymore. "It's not on the canteen list, love."

When Scarlet had asked what that meant, Mum had explained that you could only buy things like shampoo or toothpaste that were on this special list. But you had to have money to get what you wanted. Mum's cellmate had loads of money that her family sent in. But Mum only got a few quid from doing jobs in the prison like cleaning or ironing.

"I wish I had money to buy you presents," she often said. "But I wrote you this poem in our creative writing class. Look.

> "A daughter is special.
> A daughter is forever.
> A daughter is a friend.
> A daughter is a treasure."

"That's lovely, Mum," said Scarlet, her eyes brimming with tears.

"I mean it, love. Every word. I just wish I could get out of this place."

"And I wish I could make it easier for you, Mum."

That's when Scarlet started entering photos for competitions through Robert's photographic magazines that came in the post every month. She'd won £50 for the first one.

"Are you sure you want to give it to your mum?" asked Dee. "I don't know if it's allowed, love."

So she'd asked the social worker, who made inquiries and found out that they could pay it into a special account that the prison would then give to Mum to spend on canteen items. When Scarlet visited next, Mum immediately asked if she'd won any more competitions. "Not yet, but Robert says I show promise . . ."

Mum's eyes had narrowed. "I can't buy my fags on promise. You'd better get snapping, my girl. Don't you want to help me?"

It was almost, Scarlet told herself, as if prison was making her mother into a different person. Someone who was harder and even selfish at times. Then Mum would go the other way, especially at Christmas and birthdays, when she'd cry down the phone and say—once more—that she wished she could afford to send her nice things instead of the crappy purple felt handbag she'd made in the prison craft class.

"I don't want any presents," Scarlet would say. "I just want you."

That made them both cry even more.

At school, Scarlet put on a brave front, just like Mum told her. When the other kids had boasted about what they'd done in the Christmas holidays and how they'd been to visit grandparents, she just kept quiet. When she got home, she'd go straight up to her room and talk to Mum's picture, the same one that Robert had mended, which she now kept next to her bed because it was safer. "It won't be forever," she would say. And the little girl in the red spotted dress seemed to understand.

But gradually, Mum had started to become more cheerful. "Not long now, if my parole goes well." Then she'd rub her eyes with her hands. "I could have been out of this sodding place if I hadn't started using again."

"Using what?"

"It doesn't matter. I'm so sorry, love. I really am. I don't deserve a daughter like you. I'm so lucky."

Then Scarlet began to get her old nightmares all over again. "Shhh," soothed Dee, who would come into her room when this happened and hold her against her shoulder, patting her back. It was so comforting. "I've always wanted a daughter like you," she murmured. If Scarlet closed her eyes, she could almost imagine she was a child again and that it was Mum who was soothing her instead. Yet in the morning, Scarlet would always feel guilty and she'd go quiet and not want to talk to Dee.

"Would you like me to go with you to the prison next time?" offered Dee during one of their better days. "It might help her to know you're safe with us. I could tell her how well you're doing."

It had seemed like a good idea at the time. But as soon as they got to the room called "Domestic Visits," her mother's jaw set as she took in Dee. It probably didn't help that Dee had had her hand on Scarlet's shoulder, the way she sometimes did to give her courage. Scarlet moved away, but it was too late. Mum had seen.

"Hello. How very nice to meet you. I thought it would be reassuring for you if I came along so you can see who your daughter is living with. She's very happy with us. Aren't you, love?"

Scarlet cringed. This was awful. Dee might be trying to be nice, but she was making it worse. *It's all right, Mum*, she wanted to say. *I'd rather live with you. You do know that, don't you?*

But that would seem rude in front of Dee!

"I know it can't be easy for you being in prison," she continued.

Mum was looking really upset. Dee was sounding all schoolteach-ery now.

"I can promise you that as your daughter's foster mother, I . . ."

"Shut up!" Mum's face had gone blotchy red, and her eyes were glitter-ing with fury. "Don't you dare use the word 'mother.' *I'm* her mother. Do you hear me? No one else, especially not some bleeding-heart do-gooder like you." Then she lashed out at Dee and had to be taken away.

"I do understand that your emotions are divided," Dee told her later. There were still marks down her cheek from where Mum had scratched her. Scarlet tried not to look. "I really do. Remember I was in foster care myself when I was a kid?"

But could this be a lie to make Scarlet love Dee again?

After that, Scarlet wasn't permitted to visit for a bit because of Mum's behavior. Didn't they all realize it was a punishment for her as well? When she was finally allowed back, the social worker went with her. Mum seemed much quieter. "I'm sorry about before," Scarlet had whispered. "You know that you're the only person I love."

"I hope so," whispered Mum. "Cross your heart?"

"And hope to die," added Scarlet, just for good measure.

"I miss you, baby. I don't know if I can go on for much longer with-out you."

But now it was all going to change.

"I've got my parole!"

Mum's voice screamed the news down the phone.

At first, Scarlet thought she was crying. But then she realized it was laughter.

"I don't get it. What does that mean?"

"They're going to let me out. Isn't that great? We can live together again."

Scarlet's heart began to pound with apprehension. Why? She should be happy. "Where will we live?"

"I don't know where, but it doesn't matter, does it? Just as long as you and I are with each other." Mum really did start to cry now. "It's made me ill not to be with you. All I think about is my little girl and how they've taken your childhood away from me. I'll never get over it. None of this was my fault, love. You've got to believe that."

Of course she did. Scarlet knew that. Mum had told her enough times. But she also couldn't help worrying. "Will we have to go back to the old flat?" she asked.

"No bloody way. They'll have to rehouse us somewhere else."

"Maybe you could come and live here with Dee and Robert."

"Why the fuck would I want to do that? Don't you love me anymore, baby?"

Then Mum burst into tears all over again, but before Scarlet could comfort her, the line went dead.

Dee was in the kitchen when Scarlet had come in after the phone call. "Everything all right?"

She put the kettle on.

"Sort of."

Then she told Dee about what Mum had said about coming out and how she was *so* excited but also scared about where they would live.

"I'll miss you," she said suddenly.

Dee's eyes were wet. "I'll miss you, too, love. But we'll always keep in touch."

"Promise?"

"Promise."

A few days later, a visitor arrived.

"What's going on?" Scarlet demanded, her body shivery with frightened goose bumps.

She was sitting at the kitchen table with Dee and Robert and a different social worker. This was, they'd explained, an "emergency conference." Usually, they had a weekly "family meeting" (as Dee called it) to talk about homework or tidying her room or any other issues. The best bit was that there was always a homemade chocolate or Victoria sponge cake with warm jam oozing out.

But today there were plain biscuits and a scary feeling in the air that caught in her throat.

The social worker answered.

"I'm afraid that your mother has done something very wrong."

Scarlet felt a sharp blast of cold running through her, even though it was really hot in the kitchen. "What?"

"I'm not allowed to say."

"But *you* know."

"Yes . . ."

Scarlet wriggled uncomfortably in her special kitchen chair with her name on the back. Dee had stenciled it on in blue letters soon after she'd come here, and even though it seemed a bit childish now, she loved it. "So why can't you tell me?"

"The point is, Scarlet," continued the social worker, "that your mother isn't going to be released now for at least five years—and that's only if she behaves herself."

"But she promised me," whispered Scarlet. "They're going to find us somewhere to live, and we're going to be together."

"She did something bad in prison again, Scarlet. I'm sorry. But that's the way it is."

This was her fault! It was because she'd been nervous about Mum coming out. She'd jinxed everything. "If you're wondering what will happen to you, love, it's all right." Dee was taking her hand. "You can carry on living with us."

There was a crash. Scarlet hadn't meant to throw her chair to the ground. But there it was. One of the legs had broken. It felt as though someone else had done it.

"I don't want to live with you anymore. I only want Mum."

The social worker's voice was clipped. "That's impossible while she's in prison, as you know. Right now, we need to think about your best interests."

"Exactly." Scarlet felt her scream rise into the air. "That's why I need to see her. When can I visit?"

The adults glanced at one another in a funny way. "I'm afraid it might be some time," said Robert.

A bolt of fear shot through her. "Why?"

Dee took over. "She's been sent to a different prison, love. It's a long way off."

"WHY?"

Both Dee and Robert looked at the social worker. "It has a special secure section," she said slowly, as though choosing her words very carefully. "Like I said before, your mother has done something very wrong."

"I don't believe you. She's a good person. You're all lying to me. I know you are."

"Why would we do that?"

CRASH! The biscuit plate went flying. Scarlet looked at the fragments of blue and white china on the terra-cotta tiles. Had she really just done that?

"How dare you!"

"Robert!" This was Dee. "Stop shouting. Look. She's shaking."

"We've got to do something! This is becoming intolerable. Locking herself in her room, throwing things around. What's next?"

Dee tried to put her arms around her. "She's been through so much."

But Scarlet pushed her away.

"Ouch!"

"Don't you dare push my wife."

"I think that's more than enough." This was the social worker. "Can everyone calm down right now, or I will have to take Scarlet to another placement."

Dee had looked scared then. "I'm sorry, love. Robert didn't mean to get cross."

The social worker left soon after that, but her words planted an idea in Scarlet's head. Mum was still jealous of Dee—she kept asking how "that foster woman" was during visits. And although Scarlet always reassured Mum that no one could ever take her place, the truth was that she *had* learned to care for them. After all, Dee had been so kind and Robert had shown her how to take photographs. But now the news that Mum was going to stay inside for five more years changed everything.

"It's all right, love," said Dee, gathering up the broken china. "We understand. Don't we, Robert? Be careful not to cut yourself. Let me help you."

But the nicer Dee was, the angrier Scarlet became. Every minute she spent here made her feel even more disloyal toward Mum. "I'd rather live with someone else," she told the social worker during the next visit.

The woman looked worried. "Why? Don't they treat you well?"

"Yes, but . . ."

"Then you'll have to stay. We usually only organize moves if the foster families or the children do something wrong."

Scarlet felt a leap of hope. Dee and Robert wouldn't do something wrong. But *she* could.

The fire started at night. When Scarlet looked out of the window, there was a ball of flames flickering up into the sky. It was just like bonfire night, except it wasn't the right time of the year.

"FIRE," she yelled out, running onto the landing. "HELP!"

Robert stumbled out of their bedroom, his eyes wild with terror. "Where?"

"Your studio," cried Scarlet.

"I've got to get my stuff out," he yelled.

"No!"

They raced after him and only just managed to hold him back as the shed roof came crashing down. The heat was fiercer than anything she'd ever known. Lumps of wood—lit up like giant matchsticks—came hurtling toward her.

"Careful," Dee implored. "Robert—stand back. We've got to get Scarlet into the house. Be sensible."

The three of them watched from the kitchen window in stunned silence as the final plank was consumed by the flames just as the fire engine came screaming down the lane.

It was only when the police came round to talk to them that they found the small can of petrol under Scarlet's bed along with a box of matches.

"How could you," wept Dee, "after everything we did for you? I loved you like my own daughter."

Robert refused to speak to her. In a way, that was worse.

"What will happen to me?" asked Scarlet in a small voice as she was led out in handcuffs.

"Youth court," snapped the policewoman. "Then, if there's any justice, to a juvenile center. With any luck, you won't be out for some time."

23.

VICKI

The train from Paddington to Penzance is as busy as it was when I came up this morning. Someone bumps against my bruised wrist as I search for a seat, and I wince. Maybe I should get it checked out, but if I do, it will go on my medical file.

I'm not sure I can risk that.

As we leave London, I run over the last few hours in my head. None of it seems quite real.

For a minute, back in Tanya's house, I'd really thought she was going to hurt me when she'd flown at me. If it hadn't been for the self-defense course all those years ago, she might have succeeded. Instead, she was the one who had ended up on the ground.

I'm still shaking—I'm glad to be on my way home.

On the other side of the aisle is a family, chattering about catching the ferry to the Scilly Isles. I'd tried to persuade David to go there during our marriage, but then I'd gotten pregnant, and he said I needed to rest.

Patrick.

The seat next to me has a slip of paper marked EXETER to indicate it's reserved. I'm reminded of the time I lived there before moving to a village near Totnes where I thought I could start again. After that it was Cornwall.

Now it looks as though I am going to have to find somewhere else again. Shame. I would have liked to have put down roots.

Even when David eventually turns up—please let it be *when*—I can't stay in a place where the neighbors will have seen the police going in and out or gawped at me thrashing about under a bench.

The very thought of the seizure makes me nervous. I begin to massage my wrist and gasp with pain again. The man on the other side of me looks up curiously.

I glance away, watching the countryside whiz past. An oxbow lake catches my eye. An outlying farm comes into view and then goes in a flash. A perfect place to hide a body. Then I shiver. The thought of David lying dead somewhere is simply too awful to contemplate.

"How long now?" squeals one of the children in the carriage, snub nose pressed against the window.

I feel a stab in my chest as I think about what might have been. As soon as I get home, I will call Inspector Vine. This time I'll show him the evidence. And when he asks why I didn't hand it over before, I'll try to explain that when you love someone—even if they've crushed you—it isn't always easy to betray them.

Will the detective believe me? Who knows. At times, I don't believe myself. Epilepsy does that. It makes you wonder who the real "you" is. The person who others see, thrashing around? Or the one who looks back at you in the mirror?

We're in Devon now, and my mind turns to Dartmoor. One hill—or "tor," as they are called—after another. Once, in my old life, I'd climbed up Haytor.

I must have dozed off for some time, because when I wake, the train is slowing down. The man across the aisle from me is staring in a concerned way, just like the elderly woman on the way up to London had done. A bolt of fear shoots through me. Was it possible I really *did* have a seizure this time?

"I was just wondering whether to wake you," he says. "Penzance is the next stop. The last one on the line. We're nearly there."

Slightly rattled, I thank him and reach for my coat. I can see the water now, glittering in the darkness. I feel my body relaxing, even though I am dreading the prospect of handing over the "evidence" that could damn my ex for life. Maybe, before I do that, I will take a nighttime walk along the beach. The tide will be out at this time. I'll take off my shoes, even though it's still nippy, and feel my feet sinking into the sand. I'll gather some shells and remember what my dad used to say: *Hold it to your ear and you'll hear the waves.* Those were the days of happy, rainy trips to the coast with hard-boiled eggs that crunched with sand when you bit into them, and that early childhood certainty that everything was safe.

"I can see the sea!" cries one of the children in the carriage. I wince. *Patrick.*

The agony in my heart is so intense now that I can barely walk to the train door. There's an emergency alarm box on the wall. I have a crazy impulse to smash it. Do other people sometimes feel the same? I wonder.

Calm down, I tell myself. After I get back from my beach walk, I will blend something to help the stress. Lavender, rose and bergamot. I will massage it in when I take my shower.

I must get home.

But there's a queue of people waiting to get off. The man who'd spoken to me earlier gesticulates that I should go first.

There's some kind of holdup at the outside door of the carriage. They're not easy to open. Such a heavy mechanism. I've struggled before. We're moving forward now, but slowly.

Then I see it: a flash of fluorescent yellow jacket. Three men and one woman, waiting. Watching. They're scanning the faces of everyone getting off. Sweat begins to trickle down my back. Something has happened. I know it. Have they found David? Is he . . .

I make to turn round, although I'm not sure why. The man who'd been on the other side of the aisle from me puts a hand on my shoulder.

"There's no point," he says softly. "Just come quietly."

A shock wave goes through me. He's an undercover cop!

The family is staring as he grips my arm. The mother draws the small boy with the snub nose close to her, as if I might hurt him. My legs feel as though they are going to melt.

I almost fall as we go down the step.

"Victoria Goudman," says one of the yellow jackets. "I am placing you under arrest for the murder of Tanya Goudman . . ."

PART TWO

24.

HELEN

10 November 2017

I've never been to a big "do" like this before, and I've got to get it right. Everything depends on tonight.

Shall I wear my hair up or down? I experiment both ways. An updo looks more sophisticated. Not like me at all, but then that's the whole point. From what I've found out about my quarry, he likes a touch of class.

Now what about clothes? I stand in front of my cracked mirror, trying to see myself from a different perspective. The lace creamy top looks good with the black leather trousers—both had been lucky charity shop buys, along with the purple velvet jacket that I've also put on for tonight. But is it enough to catch a man like David Goudman?

"The best way to get a job nowadays is through work experience," our tutor had said at the beginning of term. "Be prepared to do it for nothing. The most important thing is to build up a portfolio." He'd looked directly at me. "I suggest you approach some property companies, Miss Evans."

So I e-mailed the Goudman Corporation, enclosing some of my photographs. But I didn't get a reply.

"I'm afraid that's pretty common in today's market," my tutor reassured me. "Just keep sending out your CV. Make sure you network, too. Google individual companies, and find out what they're up to."

I heard back from two others. Each one offered me work, but I turned them down. There was only one employer I really wanted, so I kept tabs on him.

Then I had a breakthrough. On Twitter, I discovered that David Goudman had won an award for building some big glass office block in Bow. There was going to be a grand opening on-site. Swiftly, I contacted the press office and asked if I could come along because it would be "useful" for my portfolio. To my amazement, they sent me an invitation.

It was so simple I could hardly believe it. And now here I am. Getting ready to meet the man at last. I take another look at his profile picture on Facebook, where he is standing next to his wife at some swanky party. She's in flats. So I slip on a pair of black high heels at the last minute.

I'm not the boastful type—at least, I don't think so—but heads turn when I walk in. Then they go back to the people they were talking to. No one comes up to chat with me. I stand there, feeling like a dope and clutching the stem of my glass until I almost drop it because my hands are sweating with nerves. Look around, I tell myself fiercely. Find him.

The place is so packed that it's hard to see my target in the crowd. But then someone shouts out for silence and introduces him: "David Goudman, one of the leading property developers of our time."

His face mesmerizes me. It isn't that he has traditional good looks—far from it. But there's something about that strong jawline, the slightly crooked nose and the tall build that makes him stand out.

Intuitively, I sense that this is a man who knows what he wants. I just have to make sure he wants me.

As he delivers his speech—all about responsibility and caring for the public's needs—I wonder if everyone else knows what kind of man he is. Mind you, blokes like this can get away with murder.

After he finishes, everyone clusters round him like bees, each vying for his attention. I try to get near, but it's difficult. A waiter takes pity on me and offers to top up my champagne. I choose sparkling water instead, along with some kind of fish pastry thing, and try to make my way a bit nearer.

Eventually, I get to a spot where I am almost within touching distance. A man with a press badge is interviewing him, but there's a short gap in the conversation. If I don't say something now, I might never get another opportunity.

"Sorry to bother you, Mr. Goudman, but I'm a photography student, and I e-mailed you recently about work experience. You didn't reply."

"Really?" says the journalist sharply. "But, David, you've just been telling me how important it is to help young people get onto the career track."

David Goudman swivels round to look at me. A shiver goes down my spine. Now that I am up close, I can see that he looks different from the man on the podium. In fact, he appears almost like a caricature with those cartoonlike chiseled cheekbones and black eyebrows. Then he smiles at me, and he is transformed into the most attractive man I have ever met. His gaze suggests I am the only person in the room. That deep voice, with the hint of a South London accent, speaks just to me. This man oozes charm. I need to be careful.

Then he stops smiling as though someone has flicked a switch. "It *is* important," he says briskly, taking in my velvet jacket. "But I prefer to give a hand to those from challenging backgrounds."

"I know all about that," I retort. "My mum and dad believe in working your own way up. I live in a council flat and am doing a government-funded photographic course. Is that challenging enough for you?"

My sharp repartee is a bit of a gamble. But during my research, I read an article about David in which he was quoted as saying he likes "people who stand up for themselves." The journalist is scribbling furiously.

"E-mail me again." David thrusts his right hand into his pocket. His gray-striped suit looks expensive. He brings out a card, which he presses into my hand for a touch longer than necessary. "This is my personal address. I'll be in touch. Promise."

The journalist looks up from his pad. "You know what? This could make a good feature. A week in the life of a work-experience student at the Goudman Corporation." He turns to me. "Would you be up for that?"

"Sure," I say excitedly. That means he's got to give me a break now. And I can tell from David's expression that he's thinking the same.

"Let me think about it," he says.

He makes me sweat for ten long days. Then, just as I've almost given up hope, the e-mail falls into my inbox. He's granted me a week's work experience, starting on Monday.

I am finally in.

25.

VICKI

Tanya's dead? It seems impossible. Yet here I am. In a prison cell, waiting for my solicitor to arrive, under arrest for murder.

Goodness knows how long I've been here. There's no clock. The room is cramped—barely space for the blue plastic-covered mattress down one side. In the corner is a loo minus a seat. The previous occupants have left brown stains in the bowl. It's airless, and I start to feel sick. Disorientated. Dizzy. None of these are good signs.

"My tablets," I blurt out when the door finally opens and Penny comes in. "They're in my bag. I keep telling them, and they say they'll bring them down, but they haven't."

Her face tightens. "Leave it to me."

She bangs loudly on the door. I sink to the floor, head in hands, but I can hear the odd word. Human rights . . . nurse . . .

Finally, I find a plastic bottle of water in my hands. "How many?" she asks gently.

"Three," I say.

"You're sure?"

"I'm not trying to overdose myself," I snap.

She seems convinced, although she shouldn't be. Three will make me extra drowsy, and that's what I need right now. I want to crawl into a hole and not be here.

"I'm going to get straight to the point. They're telling me your DNA was found on Tanya's body." She sits down next to me. "And you were seen by a neighbor, coming out of the house."

"I didn't kill her," I whisper.

There's a sigh. "I wish I could be certain you're telling the truth. You've been holding things back from me, haven't you, Vicki? Like your career before you became an aromatherapist. Why didn't you tell me you were once a prison officer?"

Finally, my secret is beginning to leak out.

It started with the Prasads. I was in my first year at uni when I spotted a notice asking for volunteer students to help teach English to local immigrants. Dad had always taught me to look out for others, and I was matched with Mrs. Prasad, who had recently come to the UK from India with her family to make a new life.

"My wife has found job in lampshade factory," her husband told me when I first visited their small terraced house. They had a baby plus a toddler who was wandering in and out with a pacifier, and a quiet adolescent boy who was their nephew. "But she does not understand the difference between round and square, or pink and blue. I am working away on building sites. I do not have time to help her."

After that, I would cycle down to the other end of town every Wednesday to help Mrs. Prasad master the complex and sometimes inexplicable mechanics of the English language. "The boss he promote me," my pupil told me a few months later. "It is thanks to you."

She'd grasped my hand and insisted that I join them for dinner. I left with a warm feeling in my heart that I hadn't had for a very long time.

Then, toward the end of my third year, shortly before finals, I arrived to give the usual Wednesday lesson only to find the nephew being dragged out of the front door in handcuffs by a pair of policemen.

Mrs. Prasad was in floods of tears. "He is good boy. They have made mistake."

It transpired that the nephew had been accused of stealing money from work. He was refused bail because he "might abscond" and was put behind bars until his case was tried. I knew very little about the prison system in those days, but it seemed most unfair to me that someone could be sent to jail until he or she was proven guilty.

"Please," Mrs. Prasad pleaded a few days later. "Come with me to visit him. My husband is away. I am too scared to get train on my own."

I had no idea what a prison would look like. The red and gray Victorian building that rose forbiddingly before us gave me a feeling of unease but also, unexpectedly, excitement.

Mrs. Prasad was trembling with fear as we followed the signs to the visitor center. Naively, I'd presumed I could go in with her but was curtly told by an officer on the other side of the glass screen that I wasn't on the list.

I promised to wait on a nearby chair while Mrs. Prasad's ID was checked and she was taken through a door, throwing a terrified look over her shoulder.

I wanted to go with her, but at the same time, I was riveted by the goings-on around me.

The other prison visitors, queuing up to get their IDs checked, weren't what I'd expected. One had a posh southern English accent like the mother of one of my uni friends. The staff weren't what I'd imagined either. The woman in prison uniform with the stylish layered haircut had been talking articulately about "inmate psychology" to her colleague. Somehow, I'd expected jail staff to be less educated.

Standing up to stretch my legs, I wandered over to the noticeboard.

LOOKING FOR AN EXCITING CAREER? WANT TO HELP OTHERS? NO TWO DAYS ARE THE SAME IN PRISON. YOU WILL NEVER BE BORED.

A career in prison? How crazy was that? I was a history graduate—or soon to be one. But at the same time, I had no idea what I was going to do with it. "How about teaching?" Dad had suggested. But it just didn't appeal.

I found myself walking over to the glass screen. "I've already told you," said the woman. "You can't visit. You don't have permission."

"Actually," I said, almost without meaning to, "I'd like a job application form."

Is there anything else you want to tell me, Vicki?" says my solicitor, standing up.

I gulp back a sob.

"It can't be easy," she says. "I'd be upset, too, in your situation."

I know what she's doing. Personalize. Identify. Make vulnerable. Then swoop in.

"How would you feel if the man you were married to suddenly disappeared?" I demand. "What if you suspected that someone knew where he was?"

There's a flicker of interest in my solicitor's eyes.

"And what if you then began to wonder if your ex-husband—whom you still care for even though he hurt you—might actually be dead and that you were responsible?"

She looks stunned, as though I've just slapped her.

"Are you?"

"I hope not. But my meds and the seizures. Sometimes I don't remember stuff."

Her eyes harden. "That sounds like an excuse for lying, just like you did about the photograph showing you and David arguing."

"*No*. Like I said before, I was scared and embarrassed. But there is one other thing I should have mentioned."

She stays silent. I sense she's losing confidence in me.

"I told the police about David being a bit of a wheeler-dealer."

"So I gather."

"But I didn't tell them I have proof that he might have been money laundering."

Penny looks at me sharply. "What kind of proof?"

"Several deeds, showing he bought houses for cash. Some were worth millions. As you know, it's a recognized way of getting rid of money gained from illegal activity."

"Are you an expert on this?"

"I know a bit."

"And would you like to tell me why you haven't revealed this before?"

It's a question I have been asking myself, desperately trying to find another answer, even though there is only one.

"Because I still love him," I blurt out. "Crazy, isn't it? He's hurt me more than anyone has ever done, but I still care for him."

To my surprise, there's a flash of sympathy in her eyes.

"Where are these deeds?"

"Hidden. I went round to the house to show one of them to Tanya, because it implicated her, too. I just had this feeling that she knew more about David's disappearance than she was letting on. I thought that if she admitted she knew where he was, it would get me off the hook with the police. But she claimed ignorance, and then she attacked me. It's how I hurt my wrist. I defended myself, and she fell onto the floor."

Then another thought comes to me: she'd crashed against the table on the way down. She was conscious when I left. But what if she'd passed out afterward? Suppose she'd had a bleed to the brain. Oh God.

"But you didn't strangle her?"

"What?"

"Forensics suggest that a heavy dog-tooth metal chain was used. Rather like the key chains that prison staff wear, attached to their belts."

Sweat breaks out down my back. "But you can't mean . . ."

Her eyes are cool. "I have to ask, Vicki. Did you ever take one home and keep it?"

"No. Of course not." I am loud in my indignation. "They won't find my fingerprints on this chain. I can assure you of that."

"That's the thing. They can't find it."

"So they think I've got rid of it?" I bluster.

Penny nods. Then her mouth tightens. "There's something you haven't asked me, Vicki. I have to say I'm quite surprised."

So she's found out. It was only a matter of time. I brace myself.

"Don't you want to know who found Tanya?"

It's not the question I am expecting.

"Yes," I splutter. "Of course."

"Your ex-husband's daughter."

"Nicole?"

"She'd come over for lunch at her stepmother's, apparently."

Poor kid. Even though I don't care for her, it's a terrible thing to have happened to her.

"Vicki, can you describe the relationship between you and Nicole?"

"There's no love lost, if that's what you mean. She always disliked me, but I put that down to jealousy. David had her when he was very young. He didn't take his obligations seriously, but later, he'd decided to remember he was a father again."

"You sound jealous yourself."

"I suppose I was. He began spending more time with her than me after we got married. I know he was trying to make up for the past, but she didn't want me around. So I was left on my own a lot."

"And then he went off with someone else." Penny is looking at me carefully. "You must feel upset about that, too."

"Not enough to kill Tanya, if that's what you mean."

"Or your ex-husband?"

"No! Whose side are you on?"

She puts her head to one side, quizzically. It's as though my solicitor is asking herself the same. "I'm just asking the kind of questions the prosecution will ask you in court."

In court? I might have been arrested, but I haven't been charged yet. This doesn't sound good at all. "The thing is," I say wearily, "that as I've told you before, I can't remember everything."

"Even if I do believe you—and I want to—a jury might not buy that."

Then she stares at me hard. "There's one more piece to this puzzle, isn't there, Vicki?"

A huge lump comes up in my throat.

"You told me earlier that you used to work in a prison. But that's not the full story, is it?"

I go cold.

"Come on, Vicki. Did you honestly think the police wouldn't find out? Mind you, I'm surprised they've taken this long. I have to say," continues my solicitor, "that it didn't look good when they told me earlier today, and I had to explain that my own client hadn't revealed this rather crucial piece of information. It's going to make everything very difficult."

She shook her head. "I can only help if you are totally honest with me. Tell me. I want to hear it from your own mouth. You weren't just a prison officer, were you?"

"All right." I want to curl up with embarrassment.

"I used to be," I say slowly, "a prison governor."

26.

HELEN

27 November 2017

It's my first day in the office. The place is massive: big and white and modern. There are even security guards at the front door. I'm both terrified and excited. According to my research, Tanya started off in a junior role just like this.

Mind you, I have an intuitive feeling that Perdita, David's glossy-lipped assistant, might be after Tanya's wifely position. She flushes every time someone mentions his name. Like now.

"You mustn't, under any circumstances, bother Mr. Goudman. Your job is to follow me around and take photographs—providing the subject matter is not confidential. Is that quite clear, Helen?"

She emphasizes my name as though I'm not paying attention. But I am. It has taken me a long time to make it here, and I intend to get as much as possible out of it. Including the boss himself.

We are walking down a wide corridor with bare walls on either side. No chance of that in my Deptford council block. Any space—no matter how small—is immediately taken up with brightly colored graffiti.

"Frankly," murmurs Perdita, tossing her flame red hair, "I don't know why you're here at all. Still, David does pride himself on his community work."

Clearly, my new boss hasn't told her about being shamed into giving me a break thanks to the journalist. Still, if there's one thing I've learned in life it's to keep my enemies close. Perdita clearly doesn't like me, and the feeling is mutual. But if I can buddy up to his haughty PA, she might tell me something useful about the man we're both interested in.

"When am I having my meeting with Mr. Goudman?" I ask as we turn another corner.

I receive a cool look. "Ah, that. I'm afraid he won't be able to see you personally after all. He's busy all week."

"But he promised to give me some one-on-one time for career advice! And besides, a newspaper is doing a piece on us. The journalist is coming in on Friday to interview me." I give her what I hope is a winning smile. "It will be very good for the company. I'm going to tell the reporter how everyone—especially you—has made me feel really welcome."

She shoots me a look that suggests she's not sure whether to believe me or not. "Mr. Goudman makes his own decisions on matters like this. He will e-mail the paper a quote." She opens a door. "This is the design department. You can take some pictures here, if you like."

I am still reeling from this bad news. Somehow, I have to engineer a face-to-face with the man I've been pursuing for so long. He's got to appear sometime. But meanwhile, I must pretend I'm only here for the job.

A woman is sketching on the desk. It looks like the design for a house.

"This is Helen," says Perdita with another hair toss. "She's a work-experience photographic student."

She speaks in a heavily sarcastic tone, as though I have made it up.

"Mind if I photograph you?" I ask nervously.

"Sure. Go ahead."

I concentrate on her right hand and the way it cradles the pencil.

"What will you do with your pictures?" asks the woman.

"They're going in my portfolio. But they could hang on the walls in the corridors here."

There's a brief laugh from Perdita. "That's news to me."

It will be news for David, too. I was going to suggest it to him, hoping it will show initiative. But if he's too busy to see me, how is that going to happen?

"Could I photograph you, too, Perdita?"

"Why?"

"You've got such amazing hair—I know you'd look great in my portfolio."

"If you insist." She sits half on the desk and half off as if she's been practicing this pose before.

Arrogant bitch.

By my third day, I'm getting panicky. There's still no sign of David. I don't even know where his office is. I am running out of time. And to make it worse, Perdita is watching me like a hawk. Either she doesn't trust me or she has something to hide. I've tried my best to be friendly—even admiring the brand of her bright coral lipstick and asking where she got it from—but she's as cold as ice toward me. Today I expressed an interest in photographing the company's healthy snack bar that David has recently installed, and we are on our way there when Perdita's phone sings out. She speaks sharply into it and then signs off, clearly annoyed. "I've got to sort something out. Wait a sec, can you?"

She indicates a room at the side with a watercooler in the corner. I sit for a while and examine the shots I've taken, deleting the ones that don't work and editing the ones that do. Then I get itchy feet. I stand up and look out of the window to take some pictures of the street outside and a couple walking arm in arm. I wander down the corridor.

I can always pretend I was looking for the Ladies.

That's when I see it: a door with a plaque saying DAVID GOUDMAN. My skin breaks out into excited goose bumps.

There are voices inside.

"You're wrong. I've told you."

It's that same deep voice I'd heard at the launch.

"Don't play games with me, David. You promised we'd have tonight together." That was definitely Perdita!

There's a sigh. "I was looking forward to it, too. But Tanya wants us to go out to dinner with some of her friends now."

"Why can't you just make an excuse?"

"Because my wife knows all the tricks, and it won't help us in the long run. Look, darling, if I was free, I'd be with you in a shot. You know that. We've got to be patient."

"What do you think I've been doing? It's nearly a year now."

"Sweetheart, some things are worth waiting for. Don't you think?"

"I don't know what to think anymore, David. And that's the truth."

"Then come here and I'll show you."

There's silence for a minute. Then a sigh. "Gorgeous as you are, I've got to get back to work. Did you get me out of seeing the work-experience girl?"

"I told her you were busy."

"Good."

"So when am I going to see you next?"

"As soon as I can, sweetheart. Just leave it with me. Don't look like that. I'll do my best. Promise."

"But . . ."

One of the secretaries walks round the corner at that moment with a tall blond woman with long hair and clearly fake bronze skin. "I really don't need you to accompany me," the woman is saying crossly. "I'm perfectly capable of finding my husband's own office. I used to work here, you know."

Tanya! Quickly, I pretend that I am checking something on my phone and then head back to the watercooler room.

It takes a while for Perdita to come back, and when she does, she doesn't seem so haughty anymore. Her eyes are red, and her pale, freckled skin is blotchy.

"You know what?" she sniffs. "I'm going to make sure you get your slot with Mr. Goudman. How about tomorrow at 5:30 p.m.?"

27.

VICKI

My solicitor is sitting back, arms folded. "If we're going to work together, Vicki, I need total honesty. No holding things back. Do you understand?

"Sorry." The tablets are beginning to kick in. I'm feeling sleepy. It's been a long day.

"You need to be careful. Not many former prison governors are accused of murder. They're going to charge you. The likelihood is that you'll go to a remand prison until the trial for your own safety."

I shiver, remembering the slamming doors, the click of electronic locks.

In those days, I was in charge.

Now I'll be on the other side of the bars.

"The women will tear me to bits," I whisper. "You've got to help me."

"I'll do my best."

Then she goes, leaving me alone with my memories.

"You mean to tell me that you've got a degree only for you to end up behind bars, looking after the likes of Billy Jones?" my dad had said all those years ago when I told him what I wanted to do after uni.

Billy had been three years older than me at school and had got life for knifing an innocent father of four when he was high on heroin.

"It's a good career, Dad. They run this special graduate training program. I'm not going to be a prison officer all my life. It's where you start. Then you work your way up."

"To what? The bleeding prison governor?"

He laughed hoarsely at his own joke and then took another swig from his third bottle of stout that evening. "I was so proud of you, lass. A first-class degree in history. I've told the whole bleeding street. Now what am I going to say?"

This wasn't fair. "You're the one who's always telling me to stand up for myself. To not be scared of standing out in a crowd."

Dad slammed the bottle down on the table so the foam ran over his thick, rough hands. "You're not old enough to remember the strikes, lass. The police were bastards. And so were the screws to the poor sods who got put away. Memories run deep, including mine. I can't stand by and see you becoming one of them. You'll get lynched by folk round here, and so will I."

After Dad's outburst, I'd nearly decided not to do it. But a week later, I'd found myself in the interview. I'd assumed the assessment would take place in a prison. But it was held in a large government building in Central London. *Be prepared to engage in role play and to complete written papers in English and math*, the letter had warned.

"Heard they bring in special actors," said one of the other interviewees as we sat in the corridor waiting our turn. "I know a woman who applied last year, and she freaked out when an actor pretended to assault her."

"At my old school," I couldn't resist saying, "you had to learn to fight back." They all stared at me.

"It's the written bit I'm dreading," said someone else. "I haven't done math since I was sixteen."

"You don't even get to work as a prison officer to begin with. There's six months' training first. You have to . . ."

"Vicki Smith."

I leaped up as my name was called out by a woman with a clipboard and followed her into a room. There were three men on one side of the table. The woman joined them.

Which one was the actor? Or did that come later in the day? And what about the written test?

One of the men leaned forward. "Tell us about yourself, Vicki."

"What would you like to know?" I asked hesitantly.

"What kind of person are you? How would you describe your personality?"

If in doubt, be honest. That's what Dad always said.

"Well, I'm not stupid."

"Why do you say that?"

"I got a first-class honors degree in history."

"Do you think that's a measure of intelligence?"

"In some ways."

"Go on."

"I want to help others."

Was it her imagination, or was there a brief roll of the eyes there?

"I've been helping an immigrant woman to learn English, and . . . and I went with her to a prison when her nephew was arrested."

The woman on the panel looked interested. "Why?"

"She needed someone."

"Did you help her?"

I thought of poor Mrs. Prasad, who was inconsolable after the trial. "I don't think so."

"Then you didn't do much good, did you?"

"Maybe not. But it was better than not trying at all."

"What's your biggest achievement, Vicki?" This was the first man again. "Apart, of course, from your first-class degree?"

The last three words were uttered with sarcastic emphasis.

"Getting Billy Jones arrested."

Why the heck had I said that?

"Who is Billy Jones?" asked the woman.

"He was a boy at school who got into drugs and killed a man. The police issued a sketch. No one back home would shop him. So I did, providing they didn't reveal me as the source."

"That must have taken some courage," said one of the men.

"I didn't tell anyone." I was feeling sick now. "Where I come from, people stick together. My father, like everyone else, knew Billy was bad news. But they also thought it would bring shame on the town if they identified him."

"So why did you?"

"Because it was the right thing to do."

"Weren't you scared of being found out?"

"Of course! If the rest of the gang knew, they'd have killed me. But it was better than staying quiet and feeling bad about it for the rest of my life. That man who died had a wife and four kids."

The first man was sitting back in his chair, scrutinizing her.

"You're an attractive woman. How do you think that would go down in a male jail?"

I felt a wave of irritation. "My dad's a union man. My mum died when I was young, and I've learned to stand up for myself. And by the way, I don't think you should ask questions like that in this day and age. It's sexist."

"Thank you." The woman was writing furiously on the pad in front of her. "I think we've got all we need now."

Six weeks later, after working a stint at McDonald's to pay the studio rent, I came back to an official envelope.

I'd been accepted into the prison service.

It's the day of my directions hearing.

I'd had my share of these as a young prison officer when I'd accompanied defendants to court. Each time I'd been struck by how quick they were. The lawyers outline the case, and the judge makes a decision to grant or deny bail, almost as though the choice were between a cheese and pickle or ham and mustard sandwich.

This judge is a woman. Is she going to incarcerate me in a jail or allow me to go home under certain conditions? She observes me with interest as I give my "not guilty" plea.

Desperately, I try to concentrate on the barrister whom Penny has chosen to represent me in court—so confident with her navy suit and well-cut hair. "The defendant used to be a prison governor," she says.

The judge eyes me with a new interest.

"Is that so?"

I feel myself flushing with shame. I've already sensed an undercurrent of glee among the officers who escorted me here. There's a great deal of hidden jealousy in my old profession, especially when it comes to promotion.

"If Mrs. Goudman goes to prison," continues my barrister, "it is possible that her life might be endangered because of her previous position. It's feasible that she might encounter inmates whom she once supervised."

The judge does not seem moved by this. "But if she is convicted, this will happen anyway."

It is all too true. I can see it now. This is a small world. Prisoners are frequently locked up, released, and then locked up again. Staff move around. People you knew ten years ago turn up once more. There really is no escape—for either employees or the convicted. And that's why it doesn't do to hold grudges. Someone, somewhere will track you down.

"My client is also epileptic, which can be triggered by stress. She would be safer at home."

I feel myself redden as the judge's eyes take on a keen look.

"Is that the case? Surely, she is on medication."

"She is, but it doesn't always control her condition."

"In what way?"

"She can have seizures at any time. Her memory has also been affected, and she sometimes has no recollection of certain events."

The judge frowns. "Then I rule that bail is denied. The defendant would be better off in prison, where her medical state can be constantly monitored."

My worst fears have been realized. Many defendants are terrified because they don't know what lies ahead. But I know it all too well.

I will be eaten alive in prison. Inmates love it when another has a vulner-ability such as mine. Jail can bring out the basest of natures, partly because the bullies are scared, too, so they hide their fear by tormenting others. A former prison guv is a top prize. They will make mincemeat of me.

I also know the score from a practical point of view. In a minute I'll be escorted down to the cell below the courtroom, where I'll be allowed a few more words with my solicitor, and then into the van. Women's prisons are divided into open, restricted and closed. I will be sent to one of the last two, where security is tight. Then I will wait there until I am tried in court. The judge didn't set a specific date, but I know from experience that it will be at least three months, although sometimes someone decides there's a backlog and bumps things along. The barrister, meanwhile, will be preparing my case. I will be allowed legal visits once the paperwork is sorted.

Yet when I get to the court cell, my solicitor tells me that someone wants to see me.

I'm not expecting this, though it's true that a defendant who is not granted bail or who has just been convicted is often allowed to see a close relative before being taken away.

But I don't have anyone. Not anymore.

"Who?" I ask.

"Nicole Goudman."

David's daughter?

"OK."

Penny hesitates. "You're sure?"

I nod.

I hear the voice before she comes into sight. Shrill. Well educated. Spoiled. Those had been my first impressions when David had introduced us. Now her voice is hysterical. I brace myself.

"What have you done to my father, you coldhearted bitch?"

Once more I am struck by the similarity between her and David. The same dark hair and brown eyes. Those high cheekbones.

"You've killed him. Just like you killed my stepmother."

"No," I say. "I haven't. I didn't."

"I don't believe you." Tears are streaming down her face. "You were obsessed with him. Dad told me you were always ringing him. Following him. Said you were a nutter. I told the police you were dangerous all along. WHERE HAVE YOU PUT HIM?"

She is lunging in my direction now, lashing out. For a minute, I let her. After all, look what happened when I defended myself against Tanya's outburst. But then my survival instinct kicks in. I go for her right arm and twist it back so she can't get me.

"Help!" screamed Nicole.

Officers are flying at me in all directions. My own arms are now behind my back. I am handcuffed. Then I am led away, with Nicole still screaming, to a courthouse cell. A stark concrete floor. Stained mattress. No window.

"The prison van will be here shortly," says one of the officers sharply. "So don't get too comfy."

Somehow, I've got to survive.

I remember those early days of my training—when they taught us exactly how to do that.

Attacks on staff were not unknown, apparently. It was why the self-defense course had been included in our instruction.

"Nice work, Smith," one of the officers had said when I'd twisted a colleague's arm behind his back. I was surprised to find how good that felt—even though my "victim" was yelling in agony. At least it meant I could defend myself.

Then there was the survival week on Dartmoor, to show your mettle, as one officer had put it. We'd been sent out there with basic equipment (torch, tent and thermals) to see how we got on. I was selected as the leader of the group, encouraging everyone, even when we walked for two whole days without finding the next spot on our map. Rations were running low, and the rain was teeming down. I found us shelter near Haytor. When we finally reached our destination, one of the other trainees threw in the towel and said he'd had enough. I didn't admit that part of me felt the same.

We were also taught how to put on handcuffs and deal with a hostage situation. Another crucial part of the training was to put yourself in the minds of your prisoners. So I spent a night in a cell on a hard, narrow bed with a pot underneath.

By the end, only twelve of us were left out of a group of fifty. I was exhilarated. But if I expected congratulations from Dad, I was mistaken.

"Can't believe you're still going ahead with this," he said gruffly on the phone. "Thought you'd have seen sense by now. And how are you going to find a decent man to marry in one of those places?"

I decided not to repeat the warning we'd already been given. "The divorce rate among staff is high due to stress and the unsociable hours," one of the instructors had said.

So what? Marriage seemed far too big a commitment to think about. The right man would come along at some point. What I wanted now was an adventure.

"Where are you going to live, anyway?" Dad had continued. "Not in the prison itself, I hope."

"There's a modern staff accommodation block in the grounds," I'd reassured him. "I'll be fine. I promise."

"Reckon you'll rue the day you stepped foot in that place," he snorted. "Mark my words."

The only saving grace is that Dad isn't here to see he was right.

28.

HELEN

30 November 2017

L ift your chin to the right," I instruct. "No. Not so much. That's better. And your eyes need to be looking up."

Is this really David Goudman I'm talking to? Speaking to him as if he's my equal instead of my boss? When Perdita said she'd get me a slot, I didn't really believe her. But she was as good as her word. I gave her a tube of "luxury" lavender hand cream to say thank you, hoping she didn't realize it came free with a women's magazine that had been in the reception area. And now here we are in his office. Just David and me.

I can smell his aftershave. It seems like a mixture of pine and lemon. I hope he can smell me, too. I took a peep inside Perdita's handbag the other day to check the brand of her perfume. Then I went into a department store on my way to work today and gave myself a free squirt of the same. "Think of something nice," I urge. "What do you like to do when you're not working?"

He shoots me one of his looks. I've already learned that there are several. This one is mixed. It tells me that he is interested, which is encouraging. Not that I'm flattering myself. I've already heard the odd office remark that David Goudman "can't keep his hands off anything with breasts." But the same look also tells me to keep the hell out of his space. This is a man of contradictions. He would eat me up if he knew why I was really here.

"Very curious, aren't you?"

I shrug. "It's part of a photographer's job to know the subject."

My eyes deliberately turn to a picture on his desk. It shows a pretty young woman with long dark hair, leaning against a doorway and oozing with confidence.

"Is that your wife?" I ask, even though I know it's not.

"That's a bit of a presumption." His face returns to me. Sharp and keen. "Actually, that's my daughter."

I hold my breath. "By your previous wife?"

Instantly, I know I've gone too far. His mouth tightens. "Thought you were a photographer, not a journalist."

"I am," I say quickly. "But our tutor says that we need to know about our subjects in order to capture their souls."

He puts his head to one side as if considering this. "What an intriguing concept."

I click. This is exactly the expression I've been looking for.

"Let me see that," he demands.

"My tutor says it's not always a good idea—"

"To hell with your tutor."

He holds out his hand for my camera. I have a distinct feeling that if I don't give it to him, he will snatch it from me.

"You need to press this button," I explain. "Then you can go through the frames."

We are standing so close that I can smell that lemon and pine mixture. It's intriguing, rather like the tweed jacket and the jeans he's wearing along with the formal shiny brogues.

His hands brush mine. It feels deliberate on his part.

"You're good for someone so young," he says slowly. "We might actually consider using these for our next brochure."

"You'd be welcome to buy them from me. They'd look good on your blank office walls."

He shoots me another look. I am about to apologize and say that of course I will allow him to use them free of charge. But he gets in first.

"Ambitious, aren't you?"

"What's wrong with that?"

Something happens then. It's small, almost imperceptible, but there is a definite reaction there. I only noticed because I've had to learn to read others.

"Actually," he says, rubbing his chin. It's as if he has an itch and is massaging it into submission. "I'd like to know more about you, Helen. May I take you out for dinner tonight?"

"No, thanks."

But inside I am jumping up and down with excitement. Isn't this just what I wanted?

"No?" He tilts his head to one side, as if flirting. "Aren't you even going to give me an excuse, like a previous engagement or washing your hair?"

"No." I pick up my camera.

"You don't care for my company?"

"That's not true." I glance at the picture of the daughter. "I . . . It just doesn't feel very professional."

"Then take it as part of your induction, if you like. I'll meet you here in the foyer at, say, seven. OK?"

I am twenty minutes late on purpose. *Treat them mean. Keep them keen.* It's a piece of advice I was given years ago.

And it's worth it. David looks relieved to see me even though there is a touch of annoyance there, too.

"Sorry," I say smoothly. "I decided I'd go home to change."

David takes in my short black skirt and boxy denim jacket. I sense his approval.

"Where do you live?"

"Deptford."

He does one of those nods as if recognizing it's what politicians might call "an area of diversification" but doesn't say anything.

"The car's outside," he says, gently touching my elbow.

I'd expected a chauffeur, but instead, he leads me to a two-seater red sports car parked round the corner. "I've never been in one of these before," I say. "Wow, the seats are low."

He seems to find this funny. "Just what I thought when I bought my first."

This man must be loaded. But it's not his money I'm after. He drives carefully, constantly checking his rearview mirror, almost as if he's expecting someone to be following him. I think of the security guards back at the office. Is this man scared of something?

I try to make conversation, but he cuts me short. "I like to concentrate on the road."

We pass Pimlico tube station and then Tate Britain. The river runs alongside us. It looks prettier in the dark, lit up like this. I usually walk in London or take buses, but David drives through each street with a sureness that can only come through experience. This man knows what he is doing. We pull up on a corner. A valet in uniform is waiting for us. David opens the passenger door for me and then tosses him the car keys.

He touches my arm briefly, indicating a redbrick house that, as we get closer, turns out to be a restaurant even though it doesn't have any signs outside. "Do you like steak?"

I shake my head. "I don't eat meat, although I'm happy with fish."

"That's OK. This place has a comprehensive gourmet menu. I used to take my . . ."

Then he stops. I have the distinct feeling he was going to say "wife." But the sentence lies unfinished in the air between us, and my intuition tells me to leave it there.

Slowly, slowly, I warn myself as we go inside and someone takes my coat. I've waited a long time for this. I can't afford any false moves.

29.

VICKI

4 April 2018

The officer in the van doesn't tell me which prison we are going to until we've been on the road for over an hour. I suspect from the frantic flurry of calls that I have caused a certain number of admin issues. As a former prison governor, I can't be taken to a jail where I've worked before or where I might know one of the inmates. They might have a grudge or even try to kill me.

Eventually, I'm informed that we are going to a brand-new prison that has recently opened in the West Country. How ironic that I am being taken back to the very area I have just left.

I'm stiff when they finally let us out. I want to stretch my legs, so I am quite relieved when I am marched through a wide courtyard and into a modern-looking room with "SAFETY FIRST" posters on the walls. After being frisked, I am allowed to get back into my own clothes. Only if I am convicted will I have to wear a prison uniform.

This particular prison is made up of what they call "houses"—rather like a posh school. I've seen a few like this. There's a huge hub at the center of each house with different corridors leading off like spokes from a cartwheel. In the middle of the hub is a glass office, or "watchtower" as it's known, where the officers monitor activity.

Prisons are usually noisy with constant shouting. But right now, it's silent and everyone is looking at me. Even though I've never worked here, word has clearly got round about my arrival. A prison governor—past or present—equals the enemy.

Suddenly, the noise starts up again. A very pale-faced woman in prison green—indicating garden duty—yells at another who is pushing a massive kitchen trolley. "Get out of the fucking way." A young woman with scraped-back hair and a weary expression begins to sweep the floor around my feet as if I am not there. I am escorted toward a double gate that forms the entrance to one of the houses. On the other side is a table where women are eating lunch. One is chewing with her mouth open; another catches my eye for a second and then looks away dismissively.

I'm led up a flight of stairs but have to stop halfway.

"Move it," snaps one of the two guards escorting me.

"I can't." I grip the handrail. "I feel dizzy."

"How convenient," says the other.

Don't they know what happened at my last jail?

My cell is by the stairs, on the right. It has bars on the window and overlooks the mother-and-baby unit. Another deliberate act? Hard to know. I force my face to stay neutral, as if this means nothing to me. But inside I am quivering.

There's a shower in the corner and a loo. A narrow bed takes up one side, and there is a long shelf that acts as a desk/dressing table. By some prison standards, this would be a palace.

"You're just in time for tea," says one of the officers. His voice has a sarcastic edge, as though I have dropped in to pay a courtesy visit.

I sit on the bed. It's hard. "Not hungry," I say.

He shrugs. "Suit yourself." His eyes become even colder. "Is it true you used to be a prison guv?"

I ignore the question. Instead, I remind him that I'll need my meds soon.

"You'll get them when they do rounds."

Don't cause any trouble, my solicitor had warned. *It won't help at the trial.* So I nod and take out the picture they've allowed me to keep and place it gently on the table. Then I try to breathe calmly. I wasn't allowed—unsurprisingly—to bring in my lavender essence or any of the other oils that might calm me down. I've had to leave those behind in the flat.

A loudspeaker announces that an "emergency lockdown" is about to take place. Immediately, there's a click, indicating that the door has been electronically secured. No further details are given—maybe a prisoner has attacked someone or tried to escape. As I know all too well, this can be common in prison. Tea could be a long time coming.

That's when I finally let myself cry. I cry for David because, despite everything, I don't want him dead. I cry for Tanya, even though part of me still hates her. But there's one person I can't cry for. It hurts too much.

30.

HELEN

Talk about a posh restaurant! Some of the women are in long, backless dresses, making my short skirt look like a serviette. But I chose it purposefully to show off my legs, and it's worked, because when David met me tonight, he couldn't take his eyes off them. The men, like David, are in striped shirts and chinos. Waiters are bobbing and bowing all around us. But the best bit is the view, looking out toward all the buildings along the Embankment.

I'm itching to take a picture, but instead I feel bound, out of politeness, to read the menu. "I usually eat baked beans for dinner," I say.

"I remember those days."

"Really?"

"Why do you look surprised?"

"Because you seem like a man who's been used to luxury all his life."

He gives a half laugh. "I come from a tough background. My dad was a laborer till he joined the army. I had a spell in the forces myself for a few years, but shooting people wasn't for me. So I went back to civilian life. Tell me, how old are you?"

I am pretty sure he's pretending not to know. "Didn't you read my CV?"

"No. Not the first or the second. You rather put me on the spot, if you remember, by telling me in front of that journalist that I'd ignored your e-mail."

"At least you're honest."

"Only sometimes." His eyes go hard again. "I suspect that you're the same, Helen."

I don't know what to say. Luckily, the waiter comes to take our order.

David senses my hesitation. "Don't take this the wrong way, but would you like me to choose for you? I don't know why they have to use such fancy descriptions. No one knows what they mean—they just pretend to."

Usually, I'd have taken offense at this. But he says it in such a gentlemanly way, blaming the menu rather than my own inadequacy, that I agree.

While we wait, we make small talk. It's very different from that terse conversation in the office about the picture on his desk. "So, what got you interested in photography in the first place?" he asks, topping up my glass.

That was easy. "An art teacher at school." I smile at the memory. "I was hopeless at anything academic, so I hid away in the art department. I wasn't that good at drawing or painting, but then Miss Hughes joined. She'd actually had stuff published in a magazine. I was so overawed."

He is smiling as if he understands.

"Then I found that taking photos made me feel good about myself."

David nods. "And maybe disguise your shyness?"

I rest the side of my cheek against my hand, quizzically. "You said I asked too many questions before."

"That's a sign of shyness, too. You create a veneer to disguise what you see as failings. It's all right, Helen. I get it. A lot of people are the same. I find it rather endearing, actually." He takes a sip from his glass. "Now I'm going to ask the same question you put to me earlier. What do you like doing in your spare time?"

"Walking. I love London. There's so much to see and photograph."

"You grew up here?"

"No. I was brought up in the country, but . . ."

A cheese soufflé arrives with a fancy sauce that melts in my mouth even though nerves have dulled my appetite. He has chosen the same dish. I wonder if he did that to put me at my ease. Is this a game on his part, or is David Goudman genuinely nicer than I'd given him credit for?

Then his phone goes. He excuses himself and turns to one side. His voice is hard. "Just sort it, will you?"

Then he turns back to me. "So sorry."

I was wrong just now—I mustn't underestimate this man. He is a pro. And what's more, I'm pretty sure he knows I'm out for something. Hopefully, he just thinks it's his money.

"You were telling me about growing up in the country. Was it boring?"

"Not at all." I close my eyes. I imagine the green fields and . . .

"Fuck," he says suddenly.

"Are you OK?"

He's staring through the window. Outside is a woman of medium height and build. But it's her hair that stands out: a mass of red corkscrew curls. She is staring back at us.

Clearly, they know each other.

He leaps up. "Back in a minute."

I watch them through the glass. Suddenly, he grabs one of her arms, but she shakes him off, waving her finger at him angrily. Swiftly, hands shaking, I reach into my handbag for my phone.

When David returns to the table, he is clearly edgy, rearranging the as yet unused cutlery and making no apology for his absence. Nor does he explain who the woman was. Our next course arrives, and we each pick at our separate plates. "You've lost your appetite, too," he comments drily.

I nod, not mentioning it had never been there.

"I'm sorry."

"Don't be." I gaze around the restaurant with its crisp white tablecloths and fancy napkins, trying to stay calm. "I've never been anywhere like this before. And I probably won't again."

"I very much doubt that." He is looking at me again, appraising me as though seeing me for the first time. "How about coffee? I make a great cappuccino."

What a sleazeball. I've met men like David before. They are never happy with what they have. Instead, they are constantly trying to prove themselves by going one better or, in my case, one younger. I swallow my mouthful. "Don't you need to get home to your wife?"

"She's in our Kingston house tonight. I have another place round the corner from the office for when I work late. We can chat properly there."

It's an offer that's too good to refuse.

31.

VICKI

5 April 2018

The key turns, disturbing my thoughts. My heart jumps.

Then I take in the woman standing at the door and am swamped with relief.

It's my solicitor. A visit so soon might mean that something important has happened. When I was a governor, a woman was released before she'd even spent a night inside. New evidence had emerged that showed she was innocent.

"Take a seat," says Penny. Her face is serious. "I'm afraid a second witness has come forward after hearing about the case on the news."

She sits down facing me. Her eyes are on mine. "She was walking her dog in the cul-de-sac where David and Tanya's house is. You ran past her, apparently, carrying something in your hand. She thought it might have been a chain."

Shit! I don't remember seeing anyone. "It wasn't."

"Then what was it?"

My mouth is dry. I suddenly feel very foolish.

"If you want to know, it was a Welsh love spoon that my father had given my mother. David must have taken it in the split. It didn't belong to him, so I took it."

Her face expresses disbelief. "Weren't you rather preoccupied to think of that?"

"Actually, I saw it immediately. Why should they have it?"

"So where is it now?"

"The police took it from me when I was arrested. It should be with my possessions."

Penny sighs. "The thing is, even if we can prove that, there's been another development. Apparently, when you left the prison service, there had been a series of thefts. Equipment had been stolen. Whistles, regulation jackets, ligature knives . . . that sort of thing."

"Yes. It was one of the reasons I'd been unpopular with some of the staff. I came down heavy on them about the thefts."

"Your key chain also went missing."

"So it did. I reported it myself."

"And you didn't think to tell me this earlier?"

"It had slipped my mind."

She gives me a pointed look.

"You'd signed in for it that very day, I believe."

"But I put it in my locker when I went for a shower, and when I came back, it had gone. The keys weren't on it. I'd handed those in. It was just my prison key belt and chain."

"OK . . . ," says my solicitor slowly. "But the trouble is that the police searched your apartment again. They went through it with a fine-tooth comb. And now they've found a prison belt. With a long dog-tooth metal chain."

"What?" I go cold.

"It was wrapped up in your old prison uniform in a packing crate in the cellar with other bits and pieces from your previous job, including a mobile phone that should have been handed in. The same cellar that you neglected to mention when they first took a look around."

To be honest, I'm surprised they hadn't found it before. The trapdoor lies beneath a loose piece of carpet in my studio, and sometimes I forget to close it.

"I didn't know there was a chain there. Or a phone. Honestly."

My solicitor gives me a doubtful look.

"Unless," I say uncertainly, "it got caught up with my uniform by mistake when I left. I was in quite a state mentally at the time. And I haven't been through that box since." I shiver. "I haven't had the strength to do so after what happened there."

My solicitor sighs. "Even if the jury does accept this, they're not going to take too kindly to your admission that you attacked Tanya."

"I told you. She attacked me first. I was just defending myself."

"So you say."

How can I, a former pillar of the justice system, be in such a hole? I hang my head in shame as Penny leaves the room. I can see Tanya's face all too clearly in my head. Of course I'd fought her back. That was one of the first things I'd been trained to do . . .

I was still a raw recruit. "You're on the landing today." The prison officer spoke as if inviting a challenge. "Know what that means?"

Sure. The landing was where the men slept. Sometimes there was a second community lounge up there, too. Visitors weren't allowed in this area. But it was my first day on the job, and I wasn't meant to be doing high-risk work yet. Surely this wasn't right.

"You've got to make sure they stay in their pads. Don't take any shit about how they need to see the nurse."

"Who's my partner?"

"Off sick. Just you today."

He was grinning. Testing me. Just like Dad had said they would.

There was nothing for it but to go up the stairs. They were broad and modern with open struts just wide enough to see through to the floor beneath. Along the walls on the landing itself were rows of doors like a cheap hotel. Men were banging them deafeningly. "I need my meds, for fuck's sake," one was shouting.

"Thank God I'm out of here," said an officer, walking past me on the stairs. "I've been on all night, and they haven't let up. Still, that's what you get with perverts."

I felt my stomach dipping down with fear. "What do you mean?"

"Didn't they tell you, love? This is the sex offenders' wing."

I stared at the officer. Surely, there'd been a mistake. No one had said. Then I recalled the nudges and the winks when I'd started that morning. Someone had set me up. Or else I was being tested to show my mettle.

"Never been in one before, Smith? Good luck."

By 11:30 a.m., my head was ringing with the shouts, pleas and threats.

"Officer, I need a crap, and there's no fucking toilet paper in here."

"Get me out of here, I'm going to be sick."

"What about my rights? I'm going to get my solicitor to sort out you bastards."

This wasn't right. It couldn't be.

"Miss, do something. PLEASE."

This was after I'd made the mistake of talking back to one of them through a closed door. Instantly, they'd seized on the fact that I was a woman.

Even worse, I needed a pee myself, but there was no one to keep watch while I went. Surely, this was against employment regulations.

At last—a loud bell sounded, accompanied by a metallic click. Each door opened at the same time. How was I going to manage all these men?

"Stay in line," I shouted as they pushed past me, jostling down the stairs. So much for an "orderly fashion."

"Fuck that, miss," retorted a man with a closely shaved head. "I'm bleeding starving. You need more bloody staff. Going to talk to the IMB, I am."

The Independent Monitoring Board is a panel of volunteers from the public who visit prisoners to make sure that the proper standards of care and decency are being observed. An inmate, for example, might complain about the temperature of the cells or that the food portions are too small. The IMB then forwards this to higher authorities. It's a good system in my view. Frankly, I had some sympathy for the man with the shaved head. As I was beginning to learn, staff shortages caused huge problems for all of us.

There were just two men left now. One walked with hunched shoulders, revealing a large red dragon tattooed on his neck. Another was loitering at his door as if he didn't want to leave, despite the fuss he'd been making earlier.

"I need to show you summat, miss," he said in a soft voice. "Look."

He was beckoning inside.

Never go into a pad unless someone knows your whereabouts. That's what our training manual had said.

Hesitantly, I put my head round the door.

"Look at my bloody toilet. It's fucking bunged up."

I walked over to inspect. That was when I felt his hand on my head, tugging at my roots and pushing me toward the feces that were rising up over the bowl.

Dad's words rang round my head. "They'll eat you alive."

No bloody way.

I kicked backward. The sound of my boot against his shin bone rang out. "You bloody bitch!"

He lurched toward me. Somehow I managed to grab his head with both hands and push him away. The force sent him flying against the radiator. Oh my God. I've killed him!

Then he got up and lunged toward me again.

Swiftly, I twisted his arm behind his back in the holding position while shouting for help. *Make as much noise as possible*, the self-defense instructor had told us. *Then others will be aware of your location.*

"What's going on?" yelled two officers bursting in.

"She bloody assaulted me!"

"It's all right," I panted, wiping the sweat from my face. "Everything's under control."

If only I could say the same all these years later. But one thing is clear. If a jury hears about my self-defense training, each one of those twelve might well assume I am capable of inflicting serious harm on someone else. And they'd be right.

32.

HELEN

I've seen fancy loft conversions like this in magazines. You could put five other flats plus mine in this open space and still have room for more. There's even an L-shaped white leather sofa by the huge paned windows overlooking the city, seven floors below. The security system downstairs was something else. David had to enter a code on the alarm pad before we could even get into the lift. Talk about Fort Knox.

At the other end of the room is an enormous bed with a black-and-white frieze behind it, showing famous London silhouettes like Big Ben and Buckingham Palace. There are no dividing walls apart from a door that leads into the bathroom, as I discover when I need the loo. It has automatic lighting and taps.

When I come out, David is opening a bottle of wine. The cork seems to be a bit of a struggle. But eventually, it pops open. "My first wife always said I was handy with both a corkscrew and the coffee machine. One of my few pluses, apparently!"

He sounds rather bitter. "So, what do you think of my place?" he says, handing me a glass. I decide not to point out that this is not the cappuccino he promised.

"There's so much space," I reply, not wanting to flatter him. I suspect he gets enough of that.

He nods. "I have a phobia about being cooped up in small places."

"Why?"

He turns away. "Reminds me of the army."

"It must have been scary," I say gently, in case he wants to tell me more.

He looks back at me with a hard face that suggests it's none of my business. "It doesn't matter."

"What *does* matter to you?" I find myself asking.

"Sure you're a photographer and not a journalist?"

I laugh lightly, crossing my legs as I sit on the sofa, just to remind him of my good points. "Quite sure."

"Well . . . you should make a trip to Dartmoor. You could take some amazing shots there. Have you ever been?"

"Where is it?"

His face now softens. "In the southwest. There's this tor—that's like a really steep hill—with these mountainous rocks at the summit. I love to climb right to the top and look down. It's like looking down on the universe."

"Sounds wonderful." This is a lie. Although I sometimes pretend to like the countryside, I'd much rather be in the city.

I glance at the pictures on the walls in chrome frames. Most look like the girl in his office—his daughter. But there's one of an older man with a top lip so narrow that it almost isn't there. He has piercing eyes and a bald head.

"Who's that?"

"You *are* a journalist, aren't you?"

I try to make light of it. "Like I said before, a photographer needs to be curious."

David bends his head slightly as if conceding my point. "He's my father." His face tightens. "Taught me a thing or two, I can tell you."

"Such as?"

"You really don't give up! He . . . well, I suppose he showed me how to stand on my own two feet."

"Like me," I say. "My parents started off without any help, but now they're doing really well. They say we have to learn to do the same."

"We?"

"I have a brother and a sister."

"Are you close?"

I consider. "Reasonably."

He looks wistful for a moment. "I was an only child. Shame, really."

I can't help placing a sympathetic hand on his arm. He looks up startled. Then his mood seems to change.

He moves closer to me on the sofa. "My mother died of cancer when I was twelve. That's why I support this hospice in Oxfordshire. In fact, I'm driving down in a few weeks to open a new wing."

That's actually rather touching. But it's time to stop talking now and get down to business. "What a lovely man you are," I murmur. Then, my heart pounding in case I'm being too daring, I lean in toward him and nibble his right lobe. He makes a low guttural sound in his throat; I had a feeling he was an ear man. Then I press my lips to his, sucking him in and trying to ignore that soufflé breath. He seems to be waiting, not wanting to take the lead. Is this a good or bad sign?

So I trail my fingers along the inside of his thigh, and I can see him getting hard. I straddle him, inviting him to slide his hand up under my bra and squeeze my nipple. It hurts, but I don't want him to stop. His breathing quickens, and he takes me by surprise and rips my top off altogether before flipping me on my back so that now *he* is on top.

I gasp as he bites my neck. His eyes are closed as if he's in another world. I feel his hands move down my body toward my knickers.

I can't believe it's this easy.

33

VICKI

9 May 2018

I've just been to the showers. There was a used tampon blocking the drain. When I complained, the guard just said she'd "look into it." No attempt was made to clear the offending item.

Now it's eight p.m. Lockdown. Bedtime is early in prison. Despite being here a month, I'm still not used to it. When I was a governor, this used to be my quiet hour to catch up on admin. Some prisoners have televisions in their rooms. I have chosen not to because of the flashing light that can sometimes set me off.

Instead, I sit and read, although it's difficult to concentrate now that they've moved me from a single cell in Solitary (for my own safety) to a double in the main prison because of overcrowding. I have a cellmate who spends her time either pacing or crying.

"Do you have kids?" she asks me fiercely.

I shake my head.

"Then you'll never bloody understand."

Patrick . . .

"My three are with my mother-in-law," she continues.

Three? She barely looks old enough for one.

"That cow has always hated me. God knows what she's telling them about me now. My solicitor says I'll get ten years. By the time I come out, they won't even know me," she sobs.

I try to comfort her. "They'll be able to visit," I suggest.

She snarls. "Think I want them coming to this place? 'Sides, I'm ashamed. I should never have done what I did."

I suspect her crime has something to do with drugs. There are needle marks all the way up her bare, sinewy arms. She reminds me of someone I met in the mother-and-baby unit a long time ago . . .

It was September 2008. I'd come a long way since that incident in the sex offenders' wing fifteen years ago. Rather than being reprimanded, I'd made my mark. My "ballsy" actions had helped me to win respect: "Vicki Smith," I overheard one officer say in the dining hall. "Tougher than she looks. You don't want to mess with that one. Rising up through the ranks. One to watch."

He was right. Several promotions followed, and I was now a senior governor at a woman's prison. When I rang to tell Dad, he was only interested in telling me about the girl next door who'd just had her third baby and had been four years below me at school.

"Don't leave it too late, lass. I'd like to be a grandad one day."

To be honest, I had never felt much of a maternal stirring. But then, at the new prison, I discovered the MBU. The mother-and-baby unit.

Of course, we'd covered this in my training. Women prisoners were allowed to keep their babies until they were eighteen months old. After that, they were either brought up by a member of the family or fostered or adopted.

But now the reality was in front of me with bright blue and pink pastel murals of Snow White and the Seven Dwarfs lining the corridor. At the far end was the "play area," where twenty or so women sat about in ordinary jeans and baggy tops while the children played with an assortment of toys. Several had arms around each other. Are they just good friends or is it something more? Hard to tell. Women prisoners, I'd already noted, were more physically demonstrative toward one another than their counterparts on the Outside. Some became attracted to the same sex even if they'd been straight when they'd been free. "It's all to do with needing someone," I was once told. But those two over there, scrapping over a push-along toy train, looked like they could kill each other.

"That's my Alice's," snapped one with a shaved head.

"She's just pinched it from our Jimmie," hissed another. Her thin arms bore a large tattoo of a bluebird on one and a heart on the other.

"No, she bloody didn't."

"What's going on here?" This was the prison officer who'd been assigned to show me round.

The shaved-headed woman pointed to the other. "She's always hogging all the best stuff from the cupboard. Just 'cos she's going to lose him before I have to give my Alice, she wants him to have the best."

"BITCH!"

The tattooed arms flailed. Then the pair were sprawling on the ground. "She's scratching me. Get her off."

We took one each. I found myself with the tattooed woman.

"In the cooler, both of you."

"Actually," I butted in, "I'd like to talk to this one privately."

The prison officer gave me a stony look. Tough. I was the superior here. I addressed the young girl with the tattoo. "What's your name?"

"Sam."

"Well, Sam. Shall we chat in your pad along with your Jimmie?"

The room was only just big enough for a single bed down one side and a cot on the other. Baby stuff littered the floor. Packets of nappies. Rusks, some of them half eaten. A pair of small denim dungarees. And toys—lots of them.

"Do all these belong to you?"

The young girl nodded, protectively hugging the small boy in her arms. He sneezed, producing a large lump of snot that Sam tenderly wiped away with her sleeve.

"I thought you were only allowed to have a certain number of personal items in your room."

"I've borrowed some of them."

"So you were lying just then."

There was a shrug.

The little boy wriggled out of his mother's grasp and began walking uncertainly toward me.

"There's no one in my family what can have him." The girl's voice was tearful. "Only me sister, but she's done time, and they say she's not responsible enough. So he's going to be fostered or maybe adopted. He'll grow up without me."

The boy was playing with the buttons on my jacket. I could smell him; a mixture of biscuits and milk. "How long have you got?"

"Ten years."

Something serious, then. It wasn't "done" to ask what someone's offense was, but the question lay there, hovering.

"I killed the bastard."

"Who?"

She looks down at the ground. "My uncle. Said my mother had dishonored the family name by going out with this bloke he didn't approve of. So he slashed her throat."

She says this with such matter-of-factness that I almost wonder if I've heard correctly.

"How terrible."

She shrugged. "That's why I killed him. Life was too good for him."

Maybe. But even so, you couldn't just go round taking the law into your own hands, or the world would be even more anarchic than it was already.

"You might be out early with good behavior."

There was a sniff. "I've got into trouble already."

Jimmie was now playing with my keys instead.

"I was pregnant when I came inside. If it hadn't been for him, I don't know how I'd have got through. And now they're taking him away."

Tears were streaming down her face. As if sensing his mother's distress, Jimmie began to cry, too. "When?" I asked quietly.

"Next month."

The girl reached out and clutched my hands. "You're important here, aren't you? Do something, please. He likes you."

The child was staring up at me, through his tears. Such long, dark lashes!

"I'll look into it," I said, handing the little boy back to his mother. "But I can't change the rules. Do you have a counselor to talk to?"

"Just the other girls. And they're in the same situation. We're the forgotten island. That's what some of us call the MBU."

I spoke stiffly to hide my feelings. "I'll do my best."

It wasn't until I'd reached the staff loo and locked the door behind me that I allowed the tears to flow. *Mum.* As a little girl, I'd pretended to cope with the separation when she'd been in the hospital and then later with her death. I'd wanted to be strong for my dad. So I knew all too well what these toddlers—and their mothers—were going through. If I could help only one girl, it would be something.

Yet, when I asked my superiors, there was nothing that could be done in this particular case. Long-term fostering was the best they could offer, but adoption might well be in the cards. It depended on committees, et cetera, et cetera. Any decision had to be in "the child's best interests."

I decided I'd break the news to Sam myself. It was the least I could do. But when I went to see her, she was out, walking Jimmie round the grounds.

Meanwhile, I had a lot to learn in my new role. A prisoner had to be moved quietly overnight to another prison for having a mobile phone. Another was on a hunger strike because, she told me, she wasn't allowed to go to her mother's funeral. I declared at a staff meeting that I considered this "grossly unfair." Then Jackie, one of the senior prison officers who had been helpful when I'd arrived, told me that the woman's mother had died five years ago and that the deceased was actually her cousin three times removed.

"Prisoners love funerals because it means they can get out for the day," she explained. "But I respect the fact that you're not afraid to make a stand. Know what the others say about you? You've got breasts *and* balls."

"Hope that's a compliment," I said, half joking.

Jackie'd touched my arm briefly in a chummy fashion. "It is. By the way, we've started an all-girls squash ladder in the new gym. Fancy joining us?"

It was just what I needed. There's nothing like physical exercise to block out the stuff we have to deal with. Afterward, we sometimes had a coffee together. My new friend was conscientious like me but also fun. And she could stand up for herself. "Clear off," she'd say to some of the male married officers who made passes at her. "Or I'll tell your wives at the next social."

Privately, I sometimes wondered why she hadn't found someone. Jackie was one of those women who looked good even when she wore her hair pulled back off her forehead for work. As a friend, she was a breath of fresh air. Bright. Intelligent. And with a wicked sense of humor. One day, Jackie confided that she'd broken off her engagement to an officer in a previous prison. He insisted she keep the ring, so she sold it to go on a solo breakup holiday to Thailand. "It was worth every minute," she told me with a twinkle in her eye. I'd never had a "free-spirited" friend like her before. It was refreshing.

Then, about three months later, the phone rang in the middle of the night. There was a "situation." No details were given, but my presence was needed.

My house—which came with the promotion—was in the staff estate block, a short walk away.

The Main Gate—where staff and visitors sign in and out—had a grave, subdued air about it; not good, considering how many people were there. Three officers. A medic. The chairman of the IMB. My heart sank. The latter would have only been called at this time of night if something terrible had happened that required an independent witness. An ambulance had silently appeared outside, too.

"What's happened?"

"Samantha Taylor," said one of the officers, stepping forward.

It took a second for the name to register. Then I got it. Samantha with the bluebird tattoo and mother to little Jimmie.

Numbly, I followed him. Why weren't they going to the mother-and-baby unit? Of course. The boy would have gone for fostering or adoption now. Sam would have been moved to an ordinary cell.

The knocks behind the doors on the landing were persistent. Furious. Demanding. "What's going on?" shouted one woman.

"Tell us," screamed another.

One cell door was open. A visibly distraught prison officer was standing outside. "I found her. She'd been upset ever since she got here. But then tonight she went quiet. Thought I'd check everything was all right, but when I went in, I found her . . ."

The officer stopped. No need for him to say any more. There was the chair. And there was the body on the ground, still with the blue cord round her neck.

"I cut her down. But she was gone."

The man's eyes were red. "Same age as my daughter. Couldn't cope without her kid, she couldn't. Do you know how she did it?"

I shook my head numbly.

"She'd hidden the kid's harness. Just learned to walk, he had, before they were parted." He rubbed his eyes. "Makes you wonder why we do this, doesn't it?"

34·

HELEN

1 December 2017

When I wake in the morning, David has gone. His side of the bed is almost uncreased, as though he was never in it. The kitchen area is immaculate. Gone is his wineglass. In fact, there is no evidence of last night at all. If I wasn't physically in the apartment, I might think I'd dreamed the whole thing.

My mouth is parched, so I help myself to orange juice from a fridge that takes up half the wall. It has an ice cube dispenser on the outside. I spend a few moments trying it out just for the hell of it.

Then I see the note on the massive island in the middle of the kitchen. It's entirely in capitals, almost childlike.

YOU'RE A REMARKABLE GIRL WITH A BIG CAREER IN FRONT OF YOU. I'M SURE YOU UNDERSTAND THE NEED FOR DISCRETION. JUST SHUT THE DOOR BEHIND YOU. THE SECURITY SYSTEM WILL KICK IN.

Naturally, he wants to be careful. But he can't forget last night. I won't let him. My mind goes back to the angry woman with red hair on the other side of the restaurant window. I wonder if she had a similar letter once.

———————

Half an hour later, I head toward his office. Inside, there are raised voices. "Just bloody find them." David's deep voice is unmistakable. "They want to see them. It will look suspicious if we can't produce the paperwork."

"I've tried." I'd recognize Perdita's indignant tone anywhere.

"They have got to be somewhere in the archives."

"Could you have kept them at home?"

"Maybe. I'll check. Meanwhile, get rid of that hack in reception."

"Are you sure? He's waiting right now to do an interview with you and that irritating work-experience student . . ."

"She's just ambitious. Nothing wrong with that."

Suddenly, David's door opens. I manage, just in time, to look as though I was walking past. "Ah, there you are, Helen." His deep voice is detached and professional. His face friendly but not overfamiliar. There is no sign to show he'd been up half the night making love to me. "Ready for the interview, are you?"

Then his eye takes in the cardigan I am wearing. I'd found it in a wardrobe next to his immaculate line of suits, immediately spotting it as his daughter's from the picture on his desk. It's my size. Turquoise with pretty pearl buttons. Soft to the touch and smelling of something expensive.

I give him one of my innocent looks, which I've been cultivating. "Sure. Let's go for it."

"So what have you learned from your week's experience, Miss Evans?"

I look up through my eyelashes at my boss and then back to the journalist, a seemingly earnest young man with tortoiseshell glasses. "You need to be resourceful if you're going to work in this kind of business."

David looks distinctly nervous.

The journalist is scribbling. "Would you like to define that?"

"Well, you need to take all the opportunities you are given." I am rather enjoying this. "I've got some great shots as a result, and they're going to really boost my portfolio."

My boss smiles, looking more relaxed.

"Perdita, Mr. Goudman's PA, has been really kind to me, too. She's been super efficient."

Next to me, David shuffles in his chair as if he feels awkward.

"Of course, there's one problem."

They both look at me. David's eyes are wary. The journalist's are keen.

"What's that?" They speak as one.

"A week's work experience is all very well. But it hasn't led to a paid internship. We're meant to find one this term. It's part of our course, and if I don't, well, I might not get my diploma."

"She has a point, Mr. Goudman."

A flash of distinct irritation passes over my boss's face. "It's not as simple as that."

"Really?" I finger the buttons on my cardigan. "I could be useful to you, Mr. Goudman. Maybe you'd like some photographs showing one of your many homes. I heard you had a loft conversion with a fancy shower that plays music."

David is rubbing his chin. Not in that relaxed fashion as he had over dinner. But fast, angry. Have I gone too far?

"I will definitely consider it."

"Is that a 'yes'?" persists the journalist.

I undo one of the pearl buttons and then fasten it as though I am the twitchy one.

"Like I said, I'll consider it."

The journalist is still writing. "This is going to make a nice piece on how companies like yours are helping young people get onto the career ladder. Thank you, sir."

David finds me at the end of the day. I've stayed late, hoping for this.

"What the hell did you think you were playing at?" There are little dots of sweat on his forehead. They make me feel pleasurably powerful.

"I thought you'd be pleased to have me around," I retort.

"I don't like being pushed into a corner."

As he speaks, he begins to do exactly that to me. The wall is cold and hard against my back. His face is close to mine. "It so happens that I was thinking of offering you a job anyway, Helen."

"I'm sorry," I whisper. "I was just desperate to work for you full time. I shouldn't have put you on the spot in front of that journalist."

Of course, I'm not sorry. I know that this man likes me to stand up to him. It's what makes me different from the others. "No. You shouldn't." He pulls up my skirt.

"Here?" I whisper. "Your note said we had to be discreet."

"The door's locked," he growls.

He presses his mouth against mine. I can feel his body hardening. Power and excitement surge through me. I suspect he feels the same. Might as well let him enjoy that for a while longer. I'm under no illusions that this is going to last.

"OK," he says, doing up his trousers afterward.

"Better than OK, surely?" I retort, pretending to look offended.

He laughs with a smile that actually reaches his eyes. "Actually, it was amazing." He gives me a quick kiss. "The 'OK' referred to your earlier request regarding a job. I'll employ you for six months. After that, we'll see what happens."

It was almost too easy.

"Thank you!" I jump up and put my arms around him. He seems frozen for a second, and then hugs me back.

"Go and tell my PA. She'll sort out the paperwork."

Perdita is going to get the shock of her life.

35.

VICKI

17 May 2018

I've got another pad mate. The last woman kicked up a fuss when she learned she was sharing with a "murderer," even though I haven't even been tried yet. So much for "innocent until proven guilty."

The new one is keen to tell me that she's here for fraud, even though she didn't do it. "They" say she embezzled several thousand from the company books, which seems a hard one to get out of. She spends hours in the prison library, leafing through legal textbooks. "I can't afford a barrister," she says. "I'm going to argue my own case."

I can't help being impressed. In a way, I'm amazed my solicitor is still with me. She's already said that she only wants to represent me if I am telling the truth. Perhaps I should have been honest from the beginning, but if I had, I'm pretty sure no one would have believed me.

Right now I'm having lunch with the other girls on the wing. We eat outside our cells at a large table in a communal area. It's quite casual, with drinks machines at the side. The setup might surprise some people who are used to seeing noisy prison dining halls. They're not all like that, but if I am found guilty, I will be sent to a high-security prison with fewer privileges.

My cheese roll is actually quite tasty. It's weird how you can appreciate things like that even in situations like this one. I've almost finished when one of the officers comes in. "Legal visit for Goudman."

Penny isn't due to be here for another half an hour. My heart starts pounding.

"You took all the chutney," says one of the girls as I get up.

I shrug. "Sorry."

"That's not fuckin' good enough."

"Shut up." This is from the woman I used to share a pad with. "You don't want to mess with that one. She's evil."

It's not true, I want to argue back as I follow the officer to the legal visits room. Then again, who am I to say?

Penny Brookes is there, waiting for me, sitting on the other side of the desk. I can almost imagine that this is a normal working office environment—except there are signs on the walls warning that VIOLENCE WILL NOT BE TOLERATED.

After asking how I'm doing, she comes straight to the point. "I'm concerned about the jury's reaction when the new witness tells them that she saw you coming out of Tanya's house holding something."

"It wasn't a chain," I remind her.

"But we can't prove it. Even if they found the Welsh spoon, it's not enough. What we need is a character witness who can vouch for your good behavior in the past. How about this Patrick M—"

"No." I stand up abruptly. My solicitor jumps. For the first time since we've met, I see fear on her face.

"I'm sorry," I say quickly, sitting down again. "But he's the one person I can't ask."

It was December 2008 when I met Patrick Miles.

"You're going to another women's prison," one of the deputy governors had told me. He paused as if about to say something else and then stopped. "There aren't many in this country, as you know. This one needs someone like you to shake it up. There've been, let's say, some issues with management that the press have got wind of. If you do a good job, Vicki, you'll be well on your way to the top."

My heart thudded with excitement. Maybe I might even make deputy governor one day or—the real cherry on top—governor itself? That would show Dad and the neighbors.

"What kind of problems?" I asked.

"The usual. Overcrowding. Rebellions. Hunger strikes. Racist attacks. Arson. You name it." His eyes searched mine. "Are you up to it? I know you like a challenge."

"Is there a mother-and-baby unit?"

"No."

"OK." I felt slightly more reassured.

"But there should be. And that's partly why we've picked you, Vicki. We want you to start one."

My skin went cold. I could see all too clearly Sam Taylor's body lying on that cell floor.

We're the forgotten island.

"Here's the thing." My boss took in my expression. "The government's been embarrassed by some of the inmate revolts. It's prepared to spend some money—providing we can get the right person to turn it round."

"Is there a psychologist in the prison?"

"Well, there's the usual medical staff. Doctor on call. Resident nurses."

"I want one." I heard my voice coming out cool and clear. "Someone who specializes in family relationships."

"I'll see what I can do."

"No." I could hardly believe I was speaking like this. "I will only go if I have a definite 'yes.'"

He looked annoyed.

"And if there isn't one?"

"Then I will have to consider my future in the prison service."

It was a gamble. But it paid off.

The mother-and-baby unit was opened to fanfare in the press.

One journalist wrote a profile of me in a national tabloid, describing me as the "driving force." He declared that I wasn't afraid to do a fair job and mentioned how I'd suspended a prison officer in possession of a mobile phone, made sure that smokers weren't housed with nonsmokers and initiated regular drug tests that had become infrequent because of staff shortages. It meant more employees had to work overtime (including me), but it reduced the number of offenses.

When an anonymous cartoon caricature of me arrived in the internal mail, I pinned it up on the staff noticeboard to pretend I didn't care—even though the sender had portrayed me as being at least three sizes larger than I was, with hairs sprouting out of my chin.

"I wouldn't do that if I were you," said Jackie. I'd asked her to come with me from the old prison, along with Frances, another high-ranking prison officer whom I trusted. The three of us got on well, although we were quite different. My two friends always had an eye on new male staff and constantly badgered me to come on out to the socials. But I was focused on my career, and besides, I thought the right man would just come along at some point.

"No point in hiding anything," I said in reply to her comment. "I'd rather embarrass them than pretend it hadn't happened."

She gave me a quick, friendly hug. "Whoever drew that picture was downright unkind. You're a very attractive woman. Frances and I think you're a great boss."

"Thanks," I said, flushing. I told myself that I wasn't there to be popular. I was there to do a good job. All too often I'd seen prison staff flaunt their power and sometimes abuse it. It was a crowd mentality thing: only a few had to do it before others followed suit. It was why I'd initiated an investigation into two officers who had punched an inmate in "self-defense," even though his cellmate swore it was because they'd demanded his cigarettes and he'd refused to hand them over.

But the most important achievement in these prison changes was my appointment of Patrick Miles as the psychologist.

He'd stood out among the applicants not just because of his credentials but because of his empathy. "The bond between mother and baby is stronger than any other," he'd told me during his interview. "It's inhuman to break it and then expect both to carry on as though they had never been joined together."

"Is it possible for the mother to cope?" I asked.

"Yes, but only with the right counseling and care." Then, to my embarrassment, he'd glanced at my left hand.

"I don't have children myself," I said quickly, checking his CV. *Marital status: single.*

I took a deep breath. "I knew a woman who hanged herself because she couldn't face being separated from her toddler."

He nodded. "I read about that. In your last prison, wasn't it? A Samantha Taylor?"

So he'd done his homework.

"She had no one to talk to?" he asked.

"Just the other women."

He shook his head. It was a kind face, I thought, with those lovely dark brown eyes. Then he ran a hand through his short black curly hair. "They can often do more harm than good. Where I worked before, there was great jealousy among mothers who were about to lose their children and those who still had some months to go. We will have to be very careful."

"You speak as though you have already got the job."

"I apologize." He spread out his hands. His nails were neatly clipped, I noticed. "I am, as usual, being carried away by my enthusiasm."

I could say the same. And it proved to be my downfall.

36.

HELEN

5 January 2018

I didn't see much of David last month because he was away on business in the States, and then, apparently, he took his wife to the Maldives for Christmas. My own Christmas was busy with family. One of the geeks from the IT department at work asked me to a New Year's party, but I told him I was already going out with a friend. The truth was that I needed to think.

David's absence made me nervous. There was still so much I needed to do. It was like letting a slippery fish off the hook, hoping that it would come back so I could finish the job.

When he did return a few days ago, he was cool with me, declaring that I would have to do some general admin in order to pull my weight.

I hoped it was part of an act, especially as he'd said it again yesterday in front of Posh Perdita. But what if he's genuinely lost interest? Supposing Tanya has lured him back?

This morning, though, in the Ladies, I heard some of the girls talking. "Boss is in a bad mood. Sounds like he's had another bust-up with the wife, judging from his manner on the phone to her. I had to go into his office with something and caught the tail end of it."

I need to know more. "Thought you might like this," I said, bringing in a prawn salad roll to Perdita's office at lunchtime. "I could see how hard you were working and thought you might not have a chance to get out."

She appears taken aback, but in a good way. "Thank you."

"David working you hard, is he?"

"I don't think that's any of your business."

"You're right. Sorry. It's just that you look tired, and I was worried about you."

"Well you don't need to be."

Yet her eyes fill with tears. If I was a betting woman, I'd say that Perdita's hopes of being the next Mrs. Goudman are pretty slim. Good news for me.

Shortly afterward, David came into my office, where I was captioning some of my photographs. "Thought I'd see how you're getting on," he said loudly, before shutting the door behind him. I carried on working. I'm pretty certain that David doesn't like being rebuffed, and I'm proven right. Within seconds I could feel his fingers massaging my shoulder blades from behind.

I stood up and opened the door. "Mind if we keep this open? It's quite hot in here."

The disappointment on his face was suitably gratifying.

"I'm only being careful," I whispered, "like you said before."

I watched him eyeing my legs under my short black skirt and a skinny-rib jumper that showed off my shape. I rather missed that nice cardigan that belonged to his daughter. But I got enough money for it to pay for two months' worth of groceries.

"Come to my place tonight," he whispered back. "Eight p.m. Don't be late."

It's nine by the time I reach his smart block of flats near the London Eye.

"You're late again," he says through the intercom when I press the button on the security pad in the foyer.

"I got lost."

It might have been true. After all, I've only been here once before.

When I enter his apartment, he hands me a glass of champagne. "You're lucky," he says curtly, still clearly irritated by my timing. "The monkfish could have been ruined."

"You've made me a meal?" Perhaps this man has hidden depths after all.

"Not exactly. I had it brought in. But I did do this myself." He gesticulates toward the beautifully laid table with its pink glasses and flashy gold-plated cutlery.

I am almost touched. "That's really sweet. No one's gone to this much trouble for me before."

His anger seems to melt away. "Why not?"

We are on dangerous territory now. "They just haven't. I thought you might like this."

I hold out a CD of "mood music" that I bought cheap at the market.

"I've got enough music here."

I pretend to look hurt. "But it's one of my favorites. Put it on." I make a little face. "For me."

He reluctantly obeys. The music is haunting. Silky. Seductive.

"Not bad," he says. "There's this fantastic singer from Iceland—have you heard of him?"

He names some musician whose name I can barely pronounce and starts going on about how great he is.

I need to stop him talking. So I unzip my dress at the back. It slides onto the floor. He stops mid-sentence and moves behind me, cupping my breasts before running his hands farther down. Then he steers me toward the bedroom. "What about the monkfish?" I murmur.

"Bugger the fish."

"And what about your wife?"

"You didn't bother asking me that last time."

My last thought, before I let him throw me onto the bed, is that you never know where you are with David Goudman. Then again, although he's not aware of it, he doesn't know where he is with me either.

Just like my previous visit, I wake to an empty space beside me. Obviously, this is the kind of man who doesn't go in for morning cuddles.

HAD TO GO INTO THE OFFICE. HAVE A GOOD DAY. THE CLEANER WILL BE
IN AT 9 A.M. I'D APPRECIATE IT IF YOU LEFT BEFORE THEN.

I'm not surprised that he's gone into the office, even though it's a Saturday. David is a workaholic. Perfect. It's now 8:30 a.m. I have precisely thirty minutes.

After opening various cupboards, I finally find the dishwasher—cleverly disguised so that it looks like part of the kitchen island—and put my plate in before washing my hands with the expensive shea butter soap by the sink.

Then I get down to business. If I don't do it now, I might not get another chance. He's clearly getting bored already.

I check the wardrobe again—just clothes. Then the modern-looking pale wooden desk in the corner by the sofa. I expect it to be locked, but it opens easily. There are a few bills, marked "paid," but nothing else. I sit down briefly on a beige recliner chair and fiddle with the remote control. Instantly, it begins to massage my back. Nice. If I wasn't in a rush, I might stay put for a bit. Then I leaf through some heavy books on the glass shelves, just in case something is hidden inside. They're not the kind I would read. In fact, they look like they're for show. One bears the title *Fifty Best Hotels in the World.* It's still in its plastic wrapping. At the other end of the room is a designer side table with about twelve different-colored pullout drawers. Each one is empty.

Perhaps he's cleverer than I'd thought.

37.

VICKI

11 June 2018

Time goes slowly in prison—for inmates, that is. When I was in charge, there were never enough minutes in the day to get everything done. Now I try not to look at the clock, because otherwise I might hit the walls with frustration as the seconds crawl by. All I have to do is sit and remember. And those thoughts scare me. I'm also terrified that someone is going to have a go at me because I used to be on the "other side."

Every day when they unlock us, we have to walk down the stairs to the dining room. I grab the rails each time, my heart pounding at the drop below, palms sweating. Once I made the mistake of looking down and tripped on a step. One of the women reached for me, and for a second, I thought she was going to send me flying to the bottom.

"Get off me," I'd screamed.

One of the officers had come running. "I was only trying to help," protested the woman.

"You don't want to do that," hissed another. "She's scum. Used to be a bleeding governor herself."

"Fuck. You're kidding."

Meanwhile, one of the officers was helping me up. "You all right?" she said in a kindlier manner than I'd expected. "You're as white as a sheet."

No wonder. I'm even more scared going up the stairs when we have to return to our pads.

How I miss my aromatherapy: the only thing that helps to calm me. What I'd give for some lavender essence right now. I yearn for the day-to-day contact with clients, the warm feeling that comes from helping others and the distraction of work in the real world.

I'm on kitchen duty this week, in charge of potato peeling. My hands are red raw from the water, and I've got small nicks all over them from the peeler. Health regulations demand that you're meant to go to the nurse if that happens, but she's been on leave with stress for the last week, and they're still trying to find a stand-in.

Actually, I quite like peeling potatoes. The banal rhythmical action is soothing. It also helps to distract me from thinking about the trial. It's due to start in a month's time, and I haven't heard from my solicitor for some time. I know she's annoyed with me for not allowing her to contact Patrick.

But I can't go through that shame. I can't see his face full of pity. It would kill me. I wonder if he actually knows that I'm in prison. I'd imagine that he does—the gossip lines are hot inside. But if he does, he hasn't been to visit me—even more reason why I'm not going to ask him to be a character witness.

Ouch! I glance down at my potato, bringing myself sharply back to the present. I've cut my skin. The pain feels like a release.

"You've created something here," said my Number One Governor back in late 2009 after my prison was given an award for its outstanding mother-and-baby unit. When I started in the justice system, I learned that there are several governors in one prison but that some were more senior than others. Number One usually meant the top. "Well done."

"It's not just me," I replied quickly. "It's Patrick, too." We'd been working together for almost a year by then.

He nodded. "That's why we want you both to do the same at HMP Longwaite. As a team."

Another move? But I liked it here. Mind you, this new prison was close to London. I could spend my days off in museums and art galleries.

"It will help you with your career," added my boss.

It was tempting. Yet . . .

"I'll do it," I replied slowly. "But I don't know if Patrick will be happy to uproot."

"He will." He looked at me meaningfully. "If you do."

"We are professional colleagues," I retorted briskly.

"You work well together."

"I'd also like to take Jackie and Frances with me," I added. It would be good to surround myself with people I knew and trusted.

All three agreed. But it was Patrick's acceptance that really excited me. If I was honest with myself, there *was* something there. I had never met a man like him before. He was intelligent, kind and attractive. And he was different—not just because of his poor upbringing back in Uganda, but because he was a good, honest man who was not afraid to stand up for what he believed in. I loved all these qualities. But there was something else, too, that was hard to put a finger on. All I can say is that I was drawn to him like a magnet. I wanted to be as close to him as possible.

But, amazing as Patrick was, he seemed oblivious to me as a woman. On the rare occasions when our shifts meant we had a night off together, he never suggested a meal out or even a drink.

Instead, we would both go back to our separate prison bedsits. "I'm thirty-seven," I reminded myself. How had the years gone by so fast?

"You need to get out more, lass," said Dad when I went back during one of my longer leaves. "Aren't there social nights in your line of work?"

"Yes. Bar quizzes. Darts. The odd staff party."

I might have added that I had to be careful in my senior position. I could hardly snog someone and then work with him the next day. Maybe that's why Patrick hadn't made a move . . .

That night, I got a call. One of the mothers in the unit had gone missing. She'd taken her child with her. "There's going to be hell in the papers when they find out," said my superior, as if this was the only thing to worry about.

By the time I got back to the prison from Dad's, the pair had been found.

"It's my fault."

Never had I seen Patrick in tears before. Not all men have the strength to show their feelings. It made me want him even more.

"We had a counseling session booked, but I had to cancel it for a bloody financial meeting."

I'd never heard him swear either.

"You can't blame yourself."

"I should have been more forceful when they refused to reschedule."

We were sitting in his room. It was more colorful than my own safe beige scheme, with a bright red and blue throw on the bed, matching cushions and a yellow rug on the floor. In the corner was a deep, comfortable armchair where I was sitting now.

"But it all turned out all right."

He rubbed his eyes. "Yes, they're safe, thank God. But it's not going to change the situation, is it? No parent can survive being divided from their child. I should know."

Had I heard right? "You said you didn't have family."

"I lied." He turned away. "I'm sorry. I had a wife in Uganda, and a son. He was two months old when they were killed."

"How . . ."

"I don't want to talk any more about it. Yes, I know I'm a bloody psychologist, but that doesn't mean I have to practice what I preach. My wife and child died when I wasn't there to protect them. Now I've made a new life, and I pretend they never existed to deflect questions. That's all you need to know. All you need to forget."

I tried to find the right words, but they wouldn't come. How I wanted to put my arms around him and comfort him. But I didn't have the courage. Supposing he rejected me? It would be the end of our friendship.

He stood up. "It's been a long day."

After going back to my room, I sat up all night, shocked by what he'd told me.

How did anyone even start to get over a tragedy like that? Yet at the same time, I couldn't help feeling flattered. He'd confided in me.

"I'm so sorry," I said to him the next day, when we found ourselves leaving our accommodation block at the same time and walking to the prison. "I can't bear to think of you going through such pain."

He shook his head. "I'm not the one who went through pain, Vicki. It was my wife and child."

What could I do to help him? "Jackie and Frances tell me there's a dance on Saturday in the mess," I hear myself saying. "Do you feel like going?"

There was a short, awful silence. Did he think I was coming on to him? "Just as friends, of course," I added quickly. "You'd be doing me a favor; I don't get out much."

His face cleared. "Why not? It might be good to do something different." He made a half-mocking, half-rueful face. "It's what I advise my patients to do. So perhaps I *should* take a leaf out of my own book."

We had a great time. Patrick was a natural dancer with a rhythm that made my feet come to life, especially when he tried to teach me to jive. He'd learned, apparently, as a boy where music was "big" in his family.

The two of us were in stitches! "Not the right arm—the leg!" he instructed. Then he spun me round. "That's right!" he said breathlessly, face close to mine. "You've got it!"

Jackie and Frances were both dancing with two new male recruits, but they stepped back to admire us. "Go, girl. Go!" yelled Frances while Jackie let out a wolf whistle!

Later, he walked me back to my door. To my surprise, he gave me a big bear hug. That night, I couldn't sleep. "Just as friends," I'd said earlier. So why did I have this buzz of excitement going through me?

Over the next few months, we spent more and more time together. Each time it was the same. We had fun. One night, on a whim, he suggested going bowling. I hadn't done this for years. He helped me choose the right ball size for my strength, gently placing my fingers into the holes in the correct way. It sent shivers down my spine. Our bowling nights, followed by a pizza in the café attached, became a regular fixture whenever our time off coincided.

On another occasion, when we found ourselves with a full weekend off, we got on a train and got off whenever we felt like it. "I don't usually do things spontaneously," he admitted over a pub lunch.

"Nor me."

He reached out and touched my hand. "But it's great, isn't it?"

"Yes." I flushed. "It is."

We hugged at the end of each "date." But that was it. Meanwhile, I was falling more and more in love with him. At last, I knew what it was like. That tingle when he was near. The acute disappointment if our shifts didn't coincide. That sense of panic in case he didn't feel the same. The replaying in my mind of our conversations in an attempt to convince myself that he did. Why else would he spend so much of his free time with me?

"Are you around tonight?" I asked him after we'd both been at an internal meeting one day. "There's something I need to discuss with you."

"Me, too. Shall we go to that Italian restaurant again?"

This is it, I told myself. Tonight I would summon up all my courage and tell him how I felt. I was pretty sure, from the small gestures he had made—touching my hand and the hugs—that he felt the same. He just needed a little encouragement, that's all. In fact, his shyness was endearing.

"So," he said, his warm eyes meeting mine over the table that night. "What was it that you wanted to discuss?"

My mouth went dry. "You first," I said.

"OK." He sighed heavily. "I've put in for a transfer."

It was as though he'd put a knife in my body. Had I really heard him right?

"You're leaving Longwaite?" I gasp.

"That's right." His eyes hold mine steadily.

"Why?" My voice is shaking so much that I can barely speak.

"The truth is that I find it too upsetting to work with mothers and babies. I thought I could do it. But I can't."

"Where are you going?" I blurt out.

He named a men's prison in the north of England. "It will be a challenge. Just what I need." Then his hand reached out and briefly covered mine. "What was it you wanted to tell me?"

Quick, I told myself. Think of something to avoid embarrassment. "There's a woman who's just been admitted to D wing. She seems very withdrawn, and I'm concerned for her."

"Eileen? I'm seeing her first thing in the morning." He stood up. "You don't need to worry."

That night I couldn't even go to bed. I just sat on the floor, my head leaning against a chair, and wept. I knew, beyond doubt, that I had just lost the love of my life. When I did eventually fall asleep, I dreamed that he got on a train, leaving me to stand on the platform waving good-bye.

I was surprised to hear that Patrick is moving on," said a colleague at his leaving do. "I thought you and he might have . . . you know."

"Not at all," I said briskly. "We're just friends. That's all."

Only then did I realize Patrick was standing right behind me.

Later that night, he shook my hand formally. No hug. "It's been an honor to work with you, Vicki," he said. "Good luck."

38

HELEN

8 January 2018

When I get into work on Monday morning, I'm almost beside myself. How frustrating that my search of David's place had proved fruitless. Maybe I'd missed something. There has got to be a clue somewhere. Some little detail. I can't get this far and leave the company empty-handed.

There's only one thing for it. I'll have to go into the lion's den. David's personal office.

But when? It's locked over the weekend. David is the only one who goes in then. It's true that he's often out during the week for external meetings or business trips. But I can't rely on his absences, because Posh Perdita is always flitting in and out.

So I have to find a time when no one is around. It's not unknown for David's staff to work until eight or nine p.m. Even after that, there's often some nocturnal straggler keen to gain points for dedication, especially with appraisals coming up.

My best bet, I decide, is to try to be the last one there so I can get on his computer. We all have to change our passwords every last Friday of the month, and I know for a fact that Posh Perdita writes down David's on a pad on her desk for when she needs to send an e-mail on his behalf. I've seen her.

So today I have come prepared, including packing a small parcel in my bag as I leave my flat. My plan might have gone all right if the geek in the IT department—who'd asked me to the New Year's party—wasn't still working in the next room, having stayed late, too. Finally, he puts his head round my door. "I've just finished. Fancy something to eat?"

I pretend to look disappointed. "Really sorry, Nigel. I'd have loved to, but I've got to go through this lot." I indicate the camera on my desk.

"Looks fascinating. I'd like to know more about your work."

I shrug. "I'm just taking pictures that might, if they're good enough, go into a new brochure for David, that's all."

Well, that's what he'd promised, I recall silently. Whether he'll deliver or not is another story.

"David?" He raises his eyebrows.

"Mr. Goudman," I say quickly, correcting myself. Even Posh Perdita addresses him by his surname in front of others.

"OK." He still appears hesitant. "Don't work too late. You know what they say about all work and no play."

Great! He's gone. I quickly check the other offices. No one there. I'll need to be fast, or Security will be here to close up for the night. Perdita's office is empty, too. The notepad is on her desk. There are a series of symbols on it. At least, that's what they might look like to anyone else. Teeline shorthand—it was one of the other subjects I did at sixth form college, thinking I might go into journalism. I wasn't great at it, but I could just about make out some of the letters.

My heart falls. It's a shopping list.

"*Buy cheese. Milk. M* something. That was it! *Mascara.*"

That won't get me anywhere. Then I flick back to the previous page. There it is!

I've half expected David's office to be locked, but it's not. Everything is neat, just like his apartment. Swiftly, I key in the password. *Nicole01.* Very touching. I scan the inbox. Everything relates to various property deals.

Shit. I freeze at the sound of footsteps. Terrified, I duck down—as if that will stop me from being noticed—but they go past. I didn't think anyone was still here. I can't risk this anymore.

Then my eye falls on something else. Trash files. And there it is. Fingers shaking, I scribble down the words.

Footsteps sound again. Quick. Switch off the computer. Shutting down . . .

The footsteps come closer. They're at the door.

"Helen? What are you doing here?"

It's David. His eyes are hard and narrow.

I make an attempt at a half laugh. "You've caught me. I admit it."

His voice is steel. "What?"

I shake my head. "I'm sorry. It was meant to be a surprise."

"What was?"

"This."

I indicate one of his desk drawers, which is still open from my foraging. Then I hold up the little package that I'd just taken out of my bag. Thank goodness I'd thought of that.

"I wanted to plant a little birthday present for you. It's nothing very special, I'm afraid. Just . . ."

"How the hell did you know it was my birthday?"

I can hardly tell him I had to go into considerable research on the Internet to find out. It would look too stalkerish.

"I heard one of the girls say something."

"But no one knows when my birthday is."

He's drawing closer. Suspicion is written all over his face. Suddenly, I am scared, thinking of the stories he'd told me about his spell in the forces. He could break my neck and make it look like an accident. No one is here. Anything could happen to me, and no one would know.

"Someone must have told them," I suggest, trying not to shake. "Perdita, perhaps? She's good at research, isn't she? Maybe she found out somehow."

I can see his face struggling to work out if I'm telling the truth.

"Would you like it?" I ask, holding the package out toward him.

"No, thanks. My wife is waiting in the car outside. I only came in to get some papers."

He is examining me now just like he did when we were in bed. Except this time, although I am fully clothed, I feel more naked than I have ever been.

His voice is still firm but less angry. "I suggest you leave now."

Then, as I pass, he reaches out and grabs my arm. "I'd like to see you. Tomorrow. At my place."

"But that's your birthday. Won't you be spending it with your wife?"

"No."

I take a gamble and step closer to him to stroke the lobe of his left ear. "Why not?"

His mouth makes that strange shape it does when he's aroused. I lean in closer, willing him to kiss me. But then he steps back.

"Because dates like that don't matter. It's what you do with your days that count."

I think of all those expensive properties in his files. "You mean make money?"

"Got it in one." He chucks my chin. "Know what I like about you, Helen? You're ambitious, like me. You take chances."

I hold my breath.

"Just look at how you put me on the spot in front of that journalist in order to get this job."

I relax.

Then his eyes harden. "Just don't ever try to get one over on me, Helen. I don't like to be messed around. See you at eight o'clock tomorrow night. And this time, don't be late."

39.

VICKI

20 June 2018

I need to ask some personal questions about your marriage," Penny says.
We're in a special room for legal visits. It's cold and bare with metal
chairs. The atmosphere doesn't encourage confidences.

"How exactly did you meet your ex-husband?"

I suddenly feel dizzy. "Why is this relevant?" I stutter.

"I don't know yet. It might not be. But you know as well as I do that you
have to tell me as much as you can so I can brief the barrister who will be
pleading your case in court. The smallest detail might be relevant."

I look down at my bare left hand. There hasn't been a white band of skin
there for some years now. There's nothing to show that David and I were
man and wife apart from a decree absolute and my broken heart.

"It was at a dinner," I say . . .

My fortieth had come and gone without celebration. If life had turned out
differently, I kept thinking Patrick might have been here with me to celebrate it. How I missed his kind, singsong voice; his sense of fun; his warm
hugs. One of the members of the IMB had asked me to go to a Rotary dinner with him, but I'd pretended I was busy. No one could compare with
Patrick. And yet I was aware that I wasn't getting any younger, especially
if I wanted a family.

Then, out of the blue, I was invited down to London for a prison fund-raising dinner. There were going to be various philanthropists there, and my superiors thought it might help if I was there to generally raise awareness.

Ironically, it fell on Dad's birthday. Except that he wasn't alive to see it. Three years earlier, when dealing with a woman who'd been hiding weed in her prison library book, I'd received a phone call from one of my uncles to say that Dad had died suddenly of a stroke. In the months after, I was numb with grief, guilt and regret. Sure, my shifts had made it difficult for us to see each other frequently, but I could have put myself out by going back more often than just Christmas or birthdays. I should have spoken to him more on the phone, too. In fact, I could barely remember our last conversation.

"Still enjoying life as a screw, are you?" asked one of Dad's union friends as they'd filed past me at the funeral, offering their condolences.

"Actually, I'm in senior management now."

The face tightened. "'Course, it was your job that helped kill him."

My blood ran cold. "He had a stroke."

"Yes, but stress added to it. Had to cope with a lot of flak, he did. People round here don't like screws, or the police."

Later, when going through Dad's things, I had come across a faded newspaper cutting about Billy Jones's arrest. There was a yellow Post-it sticker on top with Dad's distinctive loopy handwriting.

I knew about Billy Jones. Least, I always had my suspicions. You did the right thing, lass.

Why had I never talked to him about it? So many things left unsaid.

Drained, I left by the first train. Burying my head in a newspaper to hide my grief, my eye fell on a marriage announcement. It was an old university boyfriend who was now an eminent academic.

That could have been me, I thought, looking at the name of his wife, also a professor. "Why can't I have a normal life, too?" Ever since joining the prison service, I'd only ever had the occasional date, and nothing that had got past the third meeting.

After that, more challenges followed, not least of which was exposing a gang of prison officers who had been smuggling in drugs for the prisoners. More heartache watching mothers parted from their children. More successes, too, including an award for a prison beauty salon where women could train for qualifications so they could do jobs outside the prison. All of which led to my next promotion to deputy governor.

Some of the other staff weren't so happy—especially those whom I suspected of abusing their power and bullying the inmates. I made it clear I would be on their case. Most of my "friends" had deserted me as I climbed the ranks, not just because I'd shopped them but also from jealousy at my success. Even most of the genuine ones fell by the wayside because I had no time for socializing. I was beginning to feel there was no escape.

The last thing I needed after all this was to go to some smart dinner and put on a bright face. But it had more or less been an order, and besides, it would give me the chance to plug the cause for our own mother-and-baby unit, which desperately needed money to expand. So I'd made a particular effort with my appearance and had my hair styled more softly. Instead of trousers, I'd treated myself to an expensive lime green suit that flattered my curves *and* my hair, according to the assistant. To top it all, I was wearing high heels for the first time in years. Jackie had lent them to me—we were the same size. "You look great," she told me. "Now go and let your hair down for a change."

But after changing in my office, my confidence took a hit when some of the prisoners on C wing caught wind of it. "Got a date, has she?" I overheard one say.

"Nah," said another. "She's not interested in men."

It wasn't true, but I wasn't going to demean myself by correcting them or dishing out a punishment for insubordinate behavior.

When a tall man with a charming smile and a striking, chiseled face slid into the empty seat next to me—extremely late—I was relieved to have someone else to talk to. "Tell me about your life," he'd said, even though it emerged during the evening that he'd clearly done his homework. (We'd been given a delegate list in advance.) David knew all about my career and my campaign for more MBUs. He asked the right questions. His admiring glances made it clear he thought I was attractive. For the first time since Patrick had left and Dad had died, there was a lightness in my heart. David was totally different from Patrick; he was streetwise and a businessman. Yet for reasons I simply couldn't explain, I felt an almost animal-like attraction to him. What would it be like to make love to a man who clearly knew how to flirt?

So when David gently touched my hand again—he'd been doing a lot of that during dinner—and suggested a nightcap back at his place, I found myself in bed with him. Why not? If I couldn't take a chance at this time of my life with a handsome near-stranger, when was I going to? Besides, the comment from the prisoners before I'd left still rankled.

"I don't want this to be a one-off," David had murmured. "When can I see you again?"

"Next week?" I suggested, blocking out the imaginary picture of Patrick in bed with me right now. He'd made his feelings clear on this score. It was time to move on.

David showed me how to have a good time. After the austerity of the prison, everything about him was refreshing. During my days off, he took me to nice restaurants and bought me beautiful clothes from the sort of shops in Knightsbridge that I had only walked past before. Once, we actually went to Ronnie Scott's Jazz Club—something I'd always wanted but had never had the opportunity to do before. I'd never thought of myself as the kind of woman who would be interested in this sort of thing. Yet it *was* nice to be spoiled! But it was David himself who really made an impact on me. Such charm and wit! For someone like me from such a restricted environment, he seemed to be so wise. And, of course, there were all the charities he supported—proof to the world that he was a good man.

Nearly every woman we passed on the street would look at David admiringly. Then their gaze would rest on me, and I could feel them wondering what on earth he was doing with me. It was the same if we went out to dinner or to parties. He'd engage the women in conversation and make them feel as though they were the only ones he wanted to talk to. Then, just as I began to be jealous, he would stroke my leg under the table or squeeze my hand.

"What do you see in me?" I'd ask, more often than any self-respecting girlfriend would.

He'd trace the outline of my breast and nibble my ear, making me squirm with pleasure, before answering. "You're different, Vicki. You're the strongest person I know. You've done things that no one else I've met has ever done. You don't pretend to be someone you aren't or attempt to flatter me like the others. You're just . . . you."

Then he stopped for a second. "What do you see in me?"

A picture of Patrick's face shot into my head. I pushed it away. "You've taught me about another side of life. And you know what you're doing." It was true. Whether it was making love—with a skill that could surely only have come from experience—or overtaking another car in pouring rain with confidence, David was a pro. I also felt flattered that out of all the women who fell over themselves to attract his attention, it was me whom he wanted.

Then came a weekend trip to Oxford and a spontaneous visit to an antique shop where David slipped an emerald ring on my finger. I hadn't needed to think twice before saying yes.

"Are congratulations in order?" asked the head of the prison trustees when he spotted it a few days later.

I nodded, both embarrassed and flattered.

"I hope this won't mean you're going to turn down our offer," continued the trustee head.

My mouth went dry. Did he mean—?

"You've achieved a lot here with your mentoring schemes for the newly released offenders and the awards for the mother-and-baby unit. The way you handled the drug scam was most impressive. So we thought you might like to try your hand at running your own show. You're aware that the governor is stepping down for health reasons. We'd like to put you forward as acting governor. With a view to making it permanent."

David cracked open a bottle of champagne when I broke the news during my next visit down. "It's an amazing promotion. My future wife. Number One Guv!"

Female governors are few and far between, so my promotion thrust me into the public eye. The features editor of the *Daily Telegraph* rang to ask if she could interview me. The result was a full page on the "attractive woman" in charge of a high-security HMP who had just gotten engaged to a handsome property developer. The journalist enthused about my "radical ideas for prison reform" and described how the "happy couple" had also just bought a house in Kingston, close to the river.

I couldn't help wondering if Patrick had read the piece.

"You've given our David some respectability," said a man at one of his many business dinners that I now attended.

"What do you think he meant by that?" I asked later in bed.

"He's jealous." My fiancé drew me to him. "That's all."

The old me might have probed further. But a new one had taken my place.

40.

HELEN

9 January 2018

Eight o'clock," David had said. "Don't be late." This time I'm five minutes early. I press the button on the security pad and wait.

Nothing.

Is he in? I hope that decoy present did the job. It was only a cheap copy
of a designer pen, but it looked pretty good.

I am carrying something bigger now. A framed photograph of his office
taken from a rather unusual angle that involved some gymnastics on my
part, leaning out through my own office window. I am rather proud of it.

But if he doesn't bloody open the door, I can't give it to him.

I try again. Still nothing. I am nervous now. Freezing, too. I should have
worn something warmer than a short skirt on a cold winter night like this.
But I know he likes my legs. And I need to keep him happy.

It's dead-on eight p.m. now. Where the hell is he? I ring the bell once
more. "Hello?" says the voice on the intercom. Finally.

"It's me. Helen."

"Come on up."

He's waiting for me as the lift door opens. He kisses me long and hard.

"I've been ringing the bell for ages," I say, finally breaking away.

"Really?" He checks his watch. "But I thought we said eight."

"I was early."

He gives me a sideways look. "That can be as bad as being late. My dad would lock us in the cellar if we weren't exactly on time."

So that explains his fear of being cooped up in small spaces. I'm sure that David has kept me waiting deliberately, but it won't serve my purpose if I accuse him and get on his wrong side. So instead I follow him in. The lighting is low.

"Sit down. Please. Champagne?"

I take a small sip. It tastes sharper than last time.

"I could get used to this," I joke, trying to introduce some levity into the air.

"I expect you could."

There is no sign of food. My stomach feels empty.

He gives me another hard look. "What are you doing next weekend, Helen?"

"Seeing friends," I say casually. "What about you?"

"Working."

I wait for him to suggest a date, but there's silence.

"That's pretty cool," I say, eyeing the huge TV on the wall. It's one of those designs with a static screen picture, presumably to make it a feature in its own right before it's switched on. I've seen them advertised in glossy magazines. This one shows a beach with a long line of palm trees and parasols.

He seems amused. "You like it?"

"'Course I do."

"I love hot places," he says, as though talking to himself. "Especially when they're remote and no one can get to you."

I'm still eyeing the telly. "Shall we watch a film?"

"Like a couple, you mean?"

"That would be nice."

"But we're not an item, are we? Come on, Helen. I know you're only here for one thing."

My throat goes dry in terror. Somehow, he's sussed me out.

Then he drapes an arm along the back of the sofa behind me and kisses me so hard that it hurts.

"Hey," I say, trying to push him away. But he doesn't apologize. Instead, he moves away and is now studying me closely.

"You weren't really in my office to hide a birthday present for me, were you?"

"I was!" Fear makes me sound indignantly righteous. "OK. I know that pen was crap. But it was all I could afford. That's why I've made you something else. It's not great but . . ." I hold out the package. "Sorry—I didn't have any wrapping paper."

He pulls the photograph from the supermarket carrier bag and examines it. "You have a certain knack for showing the ordinary things in life in a different light."

"I brought a candle, too," I say. "It's got this special scent that . . ."

The next bit happens so fast that, at first, I barely realize what's going on. One minute we're looking at my picture, and the next I find myself being yanked up and pushed against a wall, face-first. My hands automatically go up against the cold surface, palms flat, like in one of those films where the heroine is about to be shot and knows it. Except that there is a hot body behind me. David is pulling down my knickers and pressing me into the wall even harder.

"You're hurting me," I gasp, but he puts a hand over my mouth. Presumably, it's to stop me making any noise in case someone hears us, but for a few minutes I am genuinely scared. His urgent movements and deep grunts are so very different from the gentle side of David that I've seen in the last few weeks. This David is out of control. Dangerous. To my shame, I find myself coming harder than I've ever done before.

Then it's over. Just as abruptly as it had begun.

I sink to the floor, trying to gather myself. When I look up, he is gone.

41.

VICKI

26 June 2018

I'm on the cleaning work party today. This can mean anything from scrubbing floors to wiping excrement off bathroom walls like I'm doing now. I wish I could wipe away my memories, too. It's been five months since the night David went missing. I remember the last words he spoke to me all too well.

I rub harder now on a dried brown lump to try to block out the thought. The action makes a hole in the rubber gloves. They're the cheap, thin variety. I could lodge a complaint, but I'm not sure it will do any good. They all hate me here.

Indeed, the staff take pleasure in belittling me at every opportunity. "Don't fancy the food, then?" asked one last week when she saw me picking through "vegetarian pasta" that tasted of cardboard with tomato ketchup on top. "Not like the governor's posh dining room, then."

"Actually," I retorted, "I used to eat in the staff café, like everyone else."

"How very democratic of you."

The other women on my wing regard me with a mixture of disdain and interest. "Heard you killed your ex-husband," says my new pad mate.

"Actually—" I start to say.

But she continues before I can make a denial. "Reckon they'll make an example of you because you used to be a prison guv?"

I've wondered that myself. And now my biggest fear has come to pass.

I've been told to report to the MBU with my cleaning trolley. The thought of facing all those poor mothers on countdown to losing their babies is too upsetting to bear. "Couldn't I go somewhere else?" I ask.

The prison officer fixes me with a glare. "What do you think this is? A menu at the bleeding Ritz? You'll go where I say."

My heart thuds as I press the security button next to the MBU sign. One of the officers lets me in and then checks my trolley. A previous cleaner had smuggled in drugs that way. "You can start in the nursery," I am told.

I walk past the huge hand-painted murals on the walls depicting farm-yard animals and a smiley sun. There's a sign to say that this is the work of inmates.

A little voice now comes floating out of the room on the right. "Mummy!" it sings. My stomach feels as if it is plummeting out through my body and into the ground.

Then there's a furious screech. "Mine! Mine!"

I push my trolley in. Before me are two women arguing over a push-along toy, each fiercely clutching a child as if brandishing a shield. "My son had that first," snarls one.

"Then it's about time he bloody learned to share," hisses the other.

I want to intervene and suggest that they take turns, as I might have done when I was on the other side of the fence. Instead, I stand stock-still. I am transported back to the day that Zelda Darling came back into my life . . .

"Congratulations on your engagement, by the way," Patrick said as we walked toward the mother-and-baby unit together that day in 2012.

I'd felt slightly apprehensive about asking him back to work for me in the new prison, but told myself that my old romantic feelings toward him were long dead. Besides, he was the best person for the post, and that's what counted. I'd expected Patrick to turn down my offer since he'd found it hard working in the mother and baby unit before. But he'd accepted, saying it was a challenge he now welcomed. I took that as a sign that he'd moved on.

Nevertheless, I experienced an uncomfortable twinge when he mentioned the engagement. "I presume you've learned this from the staff."

His voice softened. "Jackie and Frances told me. They're really pleased for you, and so am I. You deserve some happiness."

An unexpected pang of regret shot through me. Hadn't I told myself that I'd put all thoughts of Patrick behind me? Concentrate on the job, I told myself fiercely. So I began talking about the changes I had in mind for the MBU. As long as we stuck to business, it was as if nothing had changed between us.

Much as I loved David, he didn't fully appreciate my work—mind you, I didn't understand his either. But Patrick's world centered around prison life, and just as importantly, he loved it. He got the intensity and the excitement and the terror and the responsibilities—and the danger—that came with the job. The other month, a woman had threatened to throw boiling water over another during kitchen duties. I'd been on the wing at the time and had managed to talk her out of it.

My fiancé's initial admiration of my job frequently turned to irritation when my shift work interfered with our social life. "Can't you just cancel it?" demanded David when I explained I couldn't meet his daughter, Nicole, on a particular Tuesday because of an appointment with the board. He wasn't pleased when I replied that I couldn't.

When I was finally introduced to Nicole, I was faced with a sulky little thing who was rudely ungrateful for the Mini that her father had given her for her eighteenth birthday. "I wanted silver," she'd pouted. "Not black."

"That's not what you told me," he'd said, almost as if he was amused.

"I changed my mind."

At no point during the dinner did Nicole look at me.

"Only jealous," David said simply as if this was perfectly normal. "It's a father/daughter thing. She's never liked any of my girlfriends."

Nor, it seemed, did David's PA, Tanya, who was distinctly frosty every time I rang. Maybe they wondered, as did the rest of the world, what he saw in me: a redheaded prison governor without the style favored by David's previous girlfriends. I still thought about the chic cream linen dress I'd found at the back of his wardrobe when I'd moved into the London apartment. Apparently, it had been left behind.

One day, Patrick and I were on the way to see a tricky new inmate. I remembered her from 2008 in a previous posting. She was the woman who had been fighting with Sam Taylor that day—someone I still can't get out of my head. Like poor Sam, she'd been separated from her child a few months later and had blamed me for it. I'd tried to help her with extra counseling, but the woman had taken out her grief by lashing out at whoever was nearest, accusing me of "picking on her."

Now she was back—and as angry as ever. To make it worse, she'd recently managed to get into the mother-and-baby unit by escaping from her work party and pretending to be one of the cleaners. "I only want to cuddle the babies," she'd told the officers who found her there. But when they'd tried to make her leave, she'd bitten one of them.

She was punished by having visiting privileges removed and a spell in Solitary.

"Imagine never seeing your child again," I found myself saying to him on our way to see her. Then I stopped, appalled by my blunder.

"It's all right." He bit his lip. "I'm coming to terms with it; more than when we last worked together. Time is a great healer. You never forget, but you learn to live with it."

We were approaching the security gate now to A wing. All personal chitchat had to stop. We signed in. The officer looked serious. "You'll need someone with you. Been sounding off all day, she has."

"I'm sure we can manage," I said briskly. What sort of message would it send if a prison governor needed hand-holding?

We knocked on the cell door, more out of courtesy than anything else. Then I unlocked it from the outside. Zelda was sitting on the narrow bed, her long hair greased and matted. She had scratches all down her arms, which I suspected were from her own fingernails.

"You!" she roared, leaping up. "You took away my daughter."

"That's enough," Patrick started, but I put my hand up.

"I didn't do it personally," I said firmly. "You know that. We went through it before at the time. Children over the age of eighteen months can't be with their mothers in prison. They have to be fostered or adopted or brought up by a member of the family. I understand your distress. I really do."

"Do you have kids?" Her eyes were glaring.

"No, but . . ."

"Then you don't know what it's like to lose one. To not feel that soft cheek against yours or a little pair of arms around you. I know I did wrong, but why do the kids have to be punished, too? What kind of law separates a mother from a child? You say it's not your fault, but you're the one with power. *Do* something about it."

"I'm sorry. I can't. It's the law."

"Then make someone change it."

Her eyes were red. Raw. Angry. I couldn't even look at Patrick, who had remained silent. Then I remembered what he'd once told me. Sometimes you just have to listen. I felt a wave of grief as I thought of poor Samantha Taylor. "Can't you even say anything to me? Stuck-up bitch." Then suddenly, Zelda lunged toward me.

Thanks to my training, I was faster. I caught her hand before it had a chance to hit me, placing it in the restraining position.

"Officers," yelled Patrick.

It was all over in seconds.

"Are you all right?" Patrick asked me, briefly touching my shoulder in concern as we walked away.

I nodded, quaking inside. But if I'd known what the repercussions were going to be, I'd have run. As far as possible.

42.

HELEN

31 January 2018

I go into the office early before anyone else, knowing that David often did the same. This isn't a conversation I want anyone else to overhear.

"Hi," he says, looking up from his desk. "Didn't you get my text, asking if you wanted to come over last night?"

"Sorry. I was calling my parents."

My fingers are clammy. There's a strange taste in my mouth. "The thing is, I was asking their advice. But really I should have just asked you."

"Fire away." He looks flattered.

"I'm pregnant."

Immediately, he leaps to his feet, face tight with anger. "You silly little girl. If you think you're going to trap me like that, you're mistaken. Anyway, we always used something."

"Not on the last occasion," I point out quietly. "Believe me, I don't want to be pregnant either."

"Don't give me that."

His fists are clenched. I try to move back, but my feet won't budge for fear. Then he seems to realize what he's doing and turns away. "I haven't got any money to pay you off."

"Of course you have! You own a massive company. Look, David. I meant it when I said I didn't mean to get pregnant. But you can't just expect me to manage on my own."

"What about your parents?"

"They'll be there for me. But why should they bail me out when you got me into this mess in the first place? That's what Dad said, anyway. Perhaps you'd like to talk to him about it." I hold out my mobile.

He brushes it away.

"Why can't you just get rid of it?"

I can't pretend I haven't considered this. "You won't change my mind, David. If you don't promise to do your bit, I'll tell everyone—including your wife. And Perdita, too."

He scowls. "How do I know it's mine?"

"When it's born, we can do a DNA test. Then you'll see it's yours." I spit the words out, furious. "I can assure you that I haven't slept with anyone else."

His mouth twists in a way I've never seen it do before. "You expect me to believe that? Just get out. Do you hear me?"

I can't help it.

"How dare you!" He's staggering back, rubbing his cheek where I've slapped him. I'd never done that to anyone before. But if anyone has earned it, David has. In fact, he deserves a whole lot worse.

Not long afterward, I hear him leaving the office, declaring he's going to a meeting.

The next day, Perdita comes into my office. She looks terrible without makeup. I hadn't realized how much she relies on under-eye concealer. "Have you seen Mr. Goudman?"

"Not since yesterday."

"Are you sure?"

Something's up. Perdita isn't just looking terrible. She's scared, twisting her hands and interlacing her fingers like she's playing an invisible cat's cradle.

"He didn't turn up at an important meeting last night. That's really out of character."

She's staring at me as if she has X-ray vision.

"Sorry," I say. "I've no idea where he is. By the way, I love your outfit."
Actually, it's a hideous red shift dress that doesn't suit her at all.

She stares at me. "How can you think of clothes at a time like this?"

So I'm right. Perdita doesn't know anything. As far as she's concerned, I'm in the clear.

43.

VICKI

27 June 2018

Penny still wants to know more about my relationship with my ex. She thinks it might help in the trial. So I fill her in on our brief relationship, which had initially blown me away but ended by blowing me apart.

"David sounds a bit like a Jekyll and Hyde character," she says thoughtfully when I finish.

I give a rueful shrug. "He was. But I didn't realize how bad it was at the beginning."

My solicitor looks reflective. "How do we really know what someone is like underneath?"

Her words make me nervous. Is she talking about me? I think back to the woman I was when I married David. "I used to have a friend during my thirties who worried about not finding the right man. I thought she was silly at the time. But when I met David, I'd got to forty and was beginning to feel the same. I was also . . . well, I was recovering from a disappointment."

"Ah." Penny nods as if she gets this all too well. But I'm not prepared for the next question.

"Did David ever hit you?"

"No." I feel nervous. "But there were times when he could be quite forceful. He wanted his own way, even over silly things like where we'd go out for the evening. Sometimes he'd pick something for me from the menu and then get huffy if I didn't agree. Or he'd want to stay in when I suggested going out. Since we didn't see each other as often as other married couples because of our work, I usually gave in for a quiet life."

"So he bullied you?"

I'm feeling even more uncomfortable. "I didn't see it that way at the time. Maybe a bit controlling. Occasionally, I dug my heels in, and he didn't like that."

Penny is writing all this down. "So it wasn't the marriage you expected, then?"

"No," I say slowly. "It wasn't."

Our late July wedding in 2012 was going to be much bigger than I'd wanted. David needed to invite several important business contacts whom he said were far more like family than any blood relative. Apparently, the latter were almost as thin on the ground as my own. He'd lost contact. His father was long dead.

Despite not attending a service every Sunday, I'd always assumed I'd get married in church. But my fiancé persuaded me otherwise. "Sorry, darling, but I'm not into that. Anyway, it doesn't matter where we get married, does it, as long as we're together?"

I could hardly contain my nerves and excitement when the day arrived. "You look absolutely gorgeous," David said when he met me outside the register office in King's Road.

I smoothed down the size 14 cream knee-length satin dress that I'd only just managed to squeeze into. What did he see in me? Clearly, some of the other guests thought the same, judging from the whispers and the looks. But David loved me, and that's all that mattered.

"Let's start a family right now," he said during our honeymoon night in the Dorchester. I realized I didn't need any persuading. I wanted a baby. I wanted to build something that wasn't just my career.

I was worried that I was too old, but only two months later, I was pregnant. "Some women," said my doctor, "get a last-minute burst of fertility at your age." I kept the news to myself, not wanting to tell David over the phone but waiting instead until our work schedules finally allowed us to spend a night together in his London apartment. He was already coming home far less than before.

It was worth it, though, to see his face. "You're sure?" He'd picked me up and whirled me around gently. "That's amazing!"

The following week, he turned up unexpectedly at my house on the prison estate, bearing two packages. One contained an oyster-colored silk maternity negligee. The other was a little red knitted doll with a perky yellow hat. "I couldn't resist buying it from a designer craft shop in Chelsea." He looked as excited as a child.

"Congratulations," said Patrick when I told him the news, explaining that I didn't want it to be common knowledge yet. "Your husband must be over the moon."

I'd noticed before that he hardly ever used David's name.

"Yes. He is."

Any feelings for Patrick were now gone, I told myself. David was the man I was having a baby with. It put a different perspective on everything. "Hope you're going to make me a godmother," said Frances.

"And me," chipped in Jackie. "We'll teach it a trick or two! Don't look like that. I'm only joking. We'll be the models of respectability. Promise." She went quiet for a minute. "Having a godchild might be the closest I get to having a baby myself."

"There's plenty of time to settle down," I reassured her, feeling guilty about my own happiness.

David managed to get time off for the three-month scan. "You don't think I'd miss that, do you, darling? I'd move heaven and earth to get there."

We drove together to the car park. Just as he was reversing into a space, his phone rang. "Don't touch that," he snapped.

"I was only trying to help."

"Well, don't."

Shocked, I put the phone back on its dashboard holder.

We walked in silence toward the hospital. What should have been a really special time had been ruined. But then we both stared in wonder at the screen. "There's the head," said the radiologist. "See?"

"Our baby," breathed David. "It's like magic." Then he kissed me, properly, right in front of the woman. "I love you so much."

Our previous argument was forgotten. As if it had never existed.

We had two scan pictures done. "I need one as well," he said, tucking it into his pocket and patting it. Then he put an arm around me as we headed back to the car. "We're going to be the perfect family. Our child will want for nothing. I'm so proud of you, love. You do know that, don't you?"

By then, I was beginning to show. Not much—just a little bump. But that was enough.

Staff started to nudge one another. The inmates appraised me keenly.

Meanwhile, morale wasn't good in the prison. Nights were getting darker, and Christmas was coming up. The heating kept cutting out. A prisoner found a large lump of feces in her "clean" sheets. No one would admit responsibility, so I put them all on loss of privileges, which meant not being allowed phone calls or the twice-weekly gym sessions.

"Bitch," spat Zelda when she passed me in the corridor. So I ordered that her outside visits should be cut. I knew this would make her resentment worse, but I had to lay down the law. Zelda Darling was a troublemaker. If anything, no matter how small, went wrong, she was always first among the prisoners to summon in the IMB. In a way, I couldn't help thinking Dad would have admired her. In another life she'd have made a great union official. But Zelda seemed to have it in for me personally.

If only I'd known how deep her resentment went.

44.

HELEN

Are you sure you haven't seen David?" asks Perdita again, just before lunchtime.

"Of course not. If I had, you're the first person I'd have told."

But inside I feel nervous. Is it possible that Perdita knows something is going on between us? Perhaps someone had heard us in the office.

"He missed another really important meeting today. Very unlike him."

Hah! Clearly, she doesn't know him that well. Despite our brief acquaintance, even I can tell this is a man who doesn't play by the rules.

"I just don't understand it." She runs her hands through her hair, messing up the style completely. I almost feel sorry for her.

"Have you rung his wife?" I suggest.

Perdita makes a face. "She says she thought he was staying in the London flat. But when she went round, it was empty. He's not even answering his private mobile."

I hadn't realized he had one. But when I think about it, this stands to reason. In fact, he probably has two or three.

One of the men from HR then walks past. "Have *you* seen David?" Perdita demands.

"No." His brow creases. "And I need him to sign something."

By late afternoon, the rumors are flying thick and fast. David Goudman has been in an accident. He's left his wife. The business is going bust.

This last comes from a girl in Accounts—things haven't been good for some time, apparently.

"Bastard," says a young man who works in the design section. "How am I going to pay my mortgage if it all goes tits up?"

"What's going to happen?" I ask Perdita.

"I wish everyone would stop asking me that just because I'm his bloody PA."

"Have the police been called?"

"Tanya did. Apparently they told her 'to wait a bit' to see if he turns up."

"How long?"

"They didn't say. Maybe until Monday. Who knows?" She slumps down into her chair. I've never seen Perdita look so shaken. "The thing is—I know this might sound silly, but I can't help wondering if something might have happened to him."

"Like what?" I ask carefully.

"That's just it. The possibilities are endless. David had—I mean has—several enemies." Then she shakes herself. "Goodness knows why I'm telling you this. Just get on with some work, can you?"

"Would you like a cup of tea or coffee?" Maybe, I tell myself, she might be persuaded to tell me more about these enemies.

"No. Just get out of here and give me some peace. Haven't you got some work to do?"

But I can't concentrate. No one can. As one of the secretaries says, there doesn't seem any point when everything is so uncertain. Good thing I've already got what I came for.

45.

VICKI

My mouth is dry after so much talking. I take a slurp from the plastic cup on the desk and glance up at the clock. Why hasn't one of the officers knocked on the door to say it's lunchtime? I'll get a strike if I'm late. But my solicitor hasn't finished yet.

"I hadn't realized you were pregnant." My solicitor has a thoughtful expression on her face. "What happened . . . ?"

Her question hangs in the air.

"I can't talk about it at the moment," I whisper.

There's a sigh. "You're not making it easy for me. As I said before, I need to know as much as possible. But all right. We'll go back when you feel a bit stronger. Meanwhile, let's go on to your theory that David was money laundering. When did you first have suspicions?"

I'd come back to the Kingston house during a rare weekend off. I was nearly three months pregnant. I'd had that dragging ache at the bottom of my stomach that is apparently normal at this stage. It had been a tough week. A woman on B wing had thrown paint at another during the art class. The teacher had brought in her own materials (which wasn't allowed, although they had somehow got through security), and the oil paint had stung the victim's eyes. No long-term damage had been done, but her family had reported it. I'd had to suspend the teacher, which was a shame, as she had, until now, been a great asset.

Naturally, I was tense. So, too, was my husband. Instead of asking me how the drive had been or how I was feeling, he announced that he had some "urgent papers" that he needed me to sign.

"What are they?" I asked.

"Just to do with our investments."

David and I had decided at the beginning of our marriage that we would each maintain our separate bank accounts. So the sudden mention of shared investments was news.

"I didn't know we had any," I said, sitting down at the dining room table to read through the papers he'd put in front of me.

"I want to put something aside for the baby." As he spoke, he massaged my shoulders from behind. Mmmmm. "Couldn't we do this in the morning?" I suggested, leaning my head sideways against his arm.

"I need to get this sorted."

His hands stopped. His voice was abrupt. "It has to be sent off by tonight. Don't you want to make sure that our baby is provided for?"

"Of course." Keen to make the peace, I added, "It's really thoughtful of you."

"Just sign here."

"I haven't read it yet."

"There's no need."

"Come on, David. You wouldn't sign something unless you read it first."

"I would if you asked me to. Don't you trust me?"

"Of course." My eye had already scanned the first few paragraphs while we'd been talking. "You're buying a house in the States for 3.4 million dollars?" I was stunned. "I didn't realize we had that kind of money."

"I've done a big deal at work. And it's not just me who's buying it. So are you. It's got nothing to do with the company."

So that's why he needed my signature.

"But I haven't seen the house."

"You've hardly got time to come home, let alone go to the States. Anyway, it's an investment, like I said."

I was still reading. "You're paying for it in cash?"

He shrugged. "It's not uncommon."

An uneasy sensation began to crawl through me. One of the women at my previous prison had been jailed for money laundering after buying houses with the proceeds of drug deals.

"This deal that you did at work," I said slowly. "It was . . . aboveboard, wasn't it?"

Instantly, his face darkened. "Of course it was. What do you think I am?"

"Then why didn't you pay the money into the bank and do a transfer?"

"Because the seller is in London tomorrow and wants cash."

"There's no need to snap at me."

"And there's no need to ask so many questions." His finger jabbed at the space for the buyer's signature. "Just write your name, will you?"

"Why can't you buy it in your name alone?"

David began to massage my shoulders again, but this time, it didn't feel so good. "So that if anything happened to me, you and our baby would have an asset to sell."

That niggle of worry was getting bigger. "I'm sorry, darling, but it doesn't feel right, especially in my job. I have to be within the law, and . . ."

"I've told you. This is perfectly legal. Just sign it."

"Only when I've got my own solicitor to look it over."

Instantly, he snatched it away. "If you feel like that, don't bother. How are we going to be good parents if we can't trust each other?"

"Where are you going?" I asked, suddenly scared. Patrick, I couldn't help thinking, would never have bullied me like this.

"Out. Don't bother waiting up. I'll be sleeping in the spare room."

I stop for a minute. The pain caused by the memory has winded me. "What happened after that?" asks my solicitor quietly.

"When I woke up in the morning, he was standing by my bedside with a mug of tea." I shake my head, half laughing and half crying. "'Thought you might like this,' he said. He didn't mention the document, and nor did I."

"You wanted to keep the peace," she says gently.

"Exactly."

"And you think he was buying houses with cash that he got from something illegal?"

"Well, it makes sense, doesn't it? He asked me once more, but I refused. Clearly, Tanya wasn't worried about getting into trouble, though."

There's a knock on the door. It's one of the prison officers. "Lunchtime," she says.

I am saved. For now.

46.

HELEN

14 February 2018

There's still no sign of David. The office is now in a state of pure panic. The phone constantly rings with journalists wanting to know if there is any news. I try to keep my head down, but really, I'm putting off what needs to be done. Why don't I just get on with it? I've waited long enough. But the weird thing is that, now that I've got the information I've been looking for, I'm beginning to have doubts. What if it all goes wrong?

It's today's date that makes me finally do it. Valentine's Day. My blood boils just to think of it. Whatever happened to compassion, let alone love? Someone has to take revenge for what happened. The following day, I call in sick. No one seems bothered. From Perdita's panicky voice at the other end and the background chatter, it's clear that they are only interested in David.

"Still no news?" I ask.

"No," she snaps.

Then I head for Paddington and catch the first off-peak train, desperately hoping, as my credit card slides into the machine, that I haven't exceeded my limit.

Part of me wonders why David had her address in the first place. Is it possible he still has feelings for her?

Once more I think of that woman with red hair who'd given David a mouthful on the other side of the restaurant window soon after I'd started at the Goudman Corporation. She'd seemed like a force to be reckoned with.

The journey takes hours. Outside, the trees are bowed with the storm. The train rocks from side to side, making me feel a bit sick. The trolley rattles by, but everything is expensive. I make do with the bottle of tap water I'd had the foresight to bring and try to ignore my rumbling stomach.

By midafternoon, we finally arrive. WELCOME TO PENZANCE, says the sign at the station. My heart starts to pound in my chest. It feels unreal to be so close after all this time.

I walk along the seafront past a massive open-air swimming pool. I go down a side street and pause briefly outside an art gallery. PHOTOGRAPHIC EXHIBITION. FREE ENTRY. At any other time, I'd have gone in, but I've got a job to do. According to the map on my phone, I'm nearly there.

It's taken so long to achieve my goal that somehow I've neglected to work out a plan. So I go back into town and find a cozy coffee shop on the corner of the high street and order a peppermint tea. Then I try to think.

Yet by the time dusk is falling, I am still no clearer. The waitress is hovering. I need to get on with it. So I retrace my steps, but this time I force myself to take that final left and right. I stop outside a big house with a gable roof. Looking around—no one seems to be watching—I walk up the path. There's a series of names outside the front door, suggesting the house is several flats with different entrances round the side. My throat tightens as I take in the first.

VICKI GOUDMAN. AROMATHERAPIST.

47.

VICKI

4 July 2018

For the rest of the week, I think of nothing else but Patrick. I'm on the gardening work party now. We're picking carrots, which were planted earlier in the year. Many prisons grow their own produce for inmates to eat. When I was governor, I used to encourage this. It always amazes me that great things can come from small seeds. All you need are the right conditions and a certain amount of care.

By the time my solicitor visits again the following week, I am ready.

"All right," I say. "I'll tell you about my baby."

It was a wet, windy start to the new year in 2013. I was four months pregnant. So exciting and yet also daunting, given David's unpredictable behavior. Maybe he was scared, deep down, of being a father again.

Meanwhile, Christmas had left the women in prison with a deep sense of injustice. Whatever they'd done, surely they deserved to be with their families? I felt for them. But at the same time, as I reminded myself, each one of them had hurt someone else on the Outside, and all the victims had families, too.

Ironically, visits made it worse. "My kids kept telling me what a great time they'd had and all the presents they'd got from my bloody ex," said one mother. "It's like they didn't miss me at all."

Patrick was holding extra therapy sessions called "Moving On." But the rumblings and moanings in the wings had become louder. "It's like being a bloody battery hen," yelled one woman from inside her cell. It sounded like Zelda's voice.

"What does she expect?" pointed out Jackie, not unreasonably. "It's a prison."

Mind you, I could see the women's point of view. I couldn't think of anything worse than being unable to breathe the outside air. No wonder they all lived for their hour's exercise every day. But we were down on staff thanks to a flu virus that was doing the rounds, so it was suggested that the afternoon exercise walk round the courtyard outside be rescheduled for five p.m., when the evening officers arrived.

"It's dark then," pointed out Patrick at the morning briefing when this was announced. "The women need their vitamin D intake."

"Then give them some bloody tablets," muttered one of the officers.

Patrick's lips had tightened. "It's not the same, and besides, I thought we had a budget."

He'd turned to me for help, but what could I do? "It's a question of safety," I replied. Dissatisfaction with the situation caused me to be sharper than usual—so, too, did my pregnancy hormone levels, which made me want to cry one minute and laugh the next. On top of that was the added anxiety about David. He hadn't returned my calls for six days now. According to Tanya, he was still away on a US business trip, which was meant to have been a quick visit.

I could feel the odd "baby flutter" now and then. I should be sharing this with my husband instead of being here.

"How many extra staff would we need if we moved the exercise slot to three p.m. instead?" I asked.

"Two."

"Fine. Then I'll help out."

My deputy threw me a don't-be-crazy look. "You're the governor."

"I'll lend a hand, too," offered Patrick.

The deputy looked uncertain. "I would do the same, but Sharon . . ."

He stopped. We all knew that his wife was starting her chemo treatment the next day, and he'd been granted temporary leave.

"It's fine," I said quickly. "We'll sort it."

It might be a good idea to show willingness with the outside exercise issue, even though, as my deputy had pointed out, high-ranking staff weren't usually meant to get involved on a one-to-one level with prisoners. It would cause more of a problem if one of us was taken hostage. "Are you sure you're up for this?" asked Patrick. He eyed my swollen belly.

"Yes," I said. "Quite sure." My reply came out curtly, more because he seemed to care. Too late for that now. I'd made my bed with David, and I had to lie in it.

When I got back to my office, there was a message on the answerphone from David. "Sorry. The trip is taking longer than I thought. Expect you're in another meeting or sorting out some emergency. Love you."

Immediately, I rang back, but his mobile went through to voice message. I was going to be tied up for the rest of the day and the evening, too. Still, with any luck, we might be able to catch up tomorrow.

Meanwhile, word had got round that the exercise slot was being moved to later in the day. It would be done in strict rotation for half an hour instead of a full hour. So even though I'd slotted it during daylight hours, the inmates were still angry.

Zelda was furious at being left in the last group. "It's not bloody fair," she yelled while being shepherded out of her wing toward the series of double-locked doors toward the courtyard.

"Stop moaning," snapped Jackie, who'd also volunteered for extra duty. "If it wasn't for the guv, you wouldn't be going out at all."

"That's 'cos she had no choice. It's against my human rights to stay in all day."

"You all right, Guv?" asked Frances, who was there, too.

I held my hand against my stomach. Another flutter. "Fine, thanks."

"When are you due, Guv?" called out one of the women.

"Early summer," I said. No point in keeping it quiet. Nearly everyone knew now.

"At least you get to keep your kid," snarled Zelda.

Not again. I'd tried to be understanding, but now I'd had enough. Something inside me snapped.

"Look," I said, going right up to her and staring her in the face. "I'm sorry that you can't be with your daughter. But actions have consequences. You did something wrong, and you have to pay for it. Maybe you should have thought a bit more about your kid before you broke the law."

"You'll be sorry you said that," hissed Zelda. Her hard eyes locked with mine. "I've warned you before, but now I mean it."

"How dare you threaten me." I was livid. "You can go inside right now."

Zelda laughed. "Make me. You haven't got enough backup, have you?"

An icy chill ran down my spine. I looked around for Patrick, but he was farther down the line. It was cold, and the afternoon light was fading fast.

For a moment, Zelda just stared at me. I forgot to breathe.

Then she turned and started running back toward the building.

"Walking only," roared one of the officers.

The last few stragglers passed me.

"Back in now!" shouted Jackie from up ahead.

"You've cut us short," I heard Zelda shout. "Just 'cos we're the last group."

"I don't mind coming in," shivered another woman in front of me. "It's cold."

It was, too. I pulled my heavy-duty jacket closer around me and followed her. As we entered the building, the lights flickered. "Circuit playing up again," mumbled one of the officers. This often happened in bad weather. The electricians were meant to have sorted it by now. I made a mental note to chase them.

Right now, I needed to concentrate on getting this lot back through the doors to the rest area and then up the stairs. Jackie was running past to check the others. "I want to see Zelda Darling in my office as soon as we've got them all locked up," I called out.

"Sure. Anything wrong?"

"Tell you later."

"Keep moving," called out Frances. Patrick was somewhere here, although it was difficult to see where, with the lights flickering.

"Stay together," yelled another officer. There was a note of urgency in his tone. Then, suddenly, we were plunged into blackness. Fuck.

I waited for the lights to come on. Nothing.

"Into your cells, everyone."

The officers' torches were scattered like glow worms. I fumbled for my own, but the battery was fading. Why hadn't I checked earlier?

"This is fun," called out someone.

Another was giving a wolf whistle.

The smell of fear and excitement was tangible. The women were acting like schoolkids who had been let loose unexpectedly. Then, suddenly, the mood changed to one of mass fear.

"I can't find the handrail," whimpered a voice.

"It's not fucking fair. If I couldn't keep my kid, why should she?"

Footsteps. Running.

Face your attacker. That's what the self-defense refresher course had taught us.

But it was dark.

There was a sudden blinding pain in my head.

I reached out for the handrail, clutching instead at empty space. And then I fell.

"Vicki, Vicki. Are you all right?"

David's voice seemed to be coming from a great distance.

The ache between my legs—like a terrible period pain—made it hard to think straight.

"You're here," I murmured, struggling to open my eyes. I was in the hospital, judging from the drip in my arm and the white uniforms around me.

"Are you all right?"

My head hurt. I could barely talk. "What happened?"

"You were attacked. One of the women hit you."

It was coming back now. Outside exercise. The stairs. The agonizing, searing pain.

"The baby." David was sobbing. "You've lost our baby."

"No!" I screamed.

A nurse took my hand. David was now standing up, moving away from the bed as if he wanted to distance himself from me. There was a policeman, too, I suddenly noticed. Awkwardly, he came forward.

"Unfortunately, Mrs. Goudman, the power failure took out the CCTV as well as the lights. But we found a snooker ball in a sock in one of the prisoner's cells. It matches the injury to your head."

I tried to absorb this. The snooker table in the leisure area had been my idea. Lots of prisons have them, I'd argued when one of the officers had suggested that the balls could be "misused."

I struggled to sit up. "Which prisoner?" I hissed.

"Does it matter?" wept David. "We've lost our son."

"It was a boy?" We'd chosen not to know at the scan. I pummeled the bed with my fists, tears streaming down my face.

"We had to put you under, dear, while we got him out," said the nurse. "You were hemorrhaging badly, and—"

"I want to see my son!"

The nurse glanced at David. "Your husband thought it was best if he was taken away . . ."

"How could you?"

"How could *you*?" he roared. His eyes were red. Furious. "If you'd transferred to a less dangerous prison when I said, none of this would have happened."

"That's not true. You never suggested that."

"Yes, I did."

This wasn't the first time David had sworn he'd said something when he hadn't.

"Whose cell did you find the snooker ball in?" I demanded.

There was a silence.

"Tell me!" I screamed.

"Zelda Darling," said the policeman quietly.

Penny is holding my hand as if she's a friend rather than my solicitor. "Why didn't you tell me earlier about this?"

I pull my hand away. "Because it's too painful to talk about."

"I understand."

It strikes me that I know very little about the personal life of this woman.

"Do you know where Zelda is now?" my solicitor asks.

"Still in prison, serving time for her attack on me. They extended her sentence."

Penny writes something down.

"You think this is relevant?"

"I don't know." She continues writing. "I need to look into it."

48.

HELEN

I'm about to knock when I hear footsteps coming toward the door from the inside. It wasn't meant to be this way round. I'm the one who's meant to be calling the shots by summoning her, rather than Vicki Goudman discovering me on her doorstep. Of course, it doesn't matter—not really—but it throws me. So I run back down the path and over the road. There's a stone wall. I sit on it, pretending to fiddle with the laces on my ankle boots. When I look up, I see her making her way toward the promenade. I follow at a discreet distance. There are others between us, so it doesn't look obvious.

Vicki seems a bit unstable. Twice she stops to grip the railings as if she's trying to get ahold on herself. On each occasion, I have to stop, too, and hang back.

My fists tighten into a ball.

Then she stops again to hang on to the railings. Once more I do the same, but someone behind bumps into me. It's a woman with a small white dog. "I'm so sorry," she says, even though it's my fault for halting so abruptly.

"It's fine," I say in a low voice. But the dog begins to yap as if in protest at having its walk interrupted. Vicki Goudman hears the commotion and looks back. Her eyes lock with mine.

She can't know who I am. Yet I sense her wondering if she's seen me before. I watch her take in my face. There's a flicker of recognition.

I try to speak, but my words freeze in my mouth.

Then she falls to the ground. Her arms and legs begin to writhe as though she is trying to swim on dry land. Froth is coming out of her mouth. What is going on?

"Dear Lord," says the woman whose dog is tugging her toward the body. "The poor thing is having a seizure. Quick—ring for an ambulance."

But if I do that, the police could trace me. I haven't done anything wrong. Yet. But even so, I'd rather not be around when the cops come.

"Sorry," I lie. "I'm out of battery."

"Sit."

For a minute, I think she's speaking to me, but it's to the dog. She gets out her own phone. "Ambulance. On the seafront. By the lido."

I take a quick glance at Vicki Goudman writhing on the ground underneath a bench. Part of me feels this is no more than she deserves. The other part feels sorry for her. And then I run.

49.

VICKI

11 July 2018

L egal for Vicki Goudman," comes the announcement.

"Again? Has your solicitor got the hots for you?" snorts my cellmate.

"She's preparing my case," I reply. "My trial starts tomorrow."

Penny is already waiting in the legal visits room. She has a man with her. "This is Giles Romer," she says with an excited expression on her face. "He's going to be your barrister, and I'm delighted to say, he's one of the best in the business."

"Penny has already told me about your attack, Vicki." He speaks as though he already knows me. "I'm very sorry for your loss."

I look away. This isn't something I can discuss with a stranger. It was hard enough telling Penny.

"We need to know more, Vicki," she says gently.

"I've had enough."

"You're not helping your case. Your baby might be the thing that throws your case into a whole new light."

After losing my son, I was almost mad with grief. One minute I'd been pregnant, a child fluttering inside me, and now there was nothing. How was I meant to go on? I'd hoped for comfort from my husband, but David would barely speak to me. I knew he blamed me. So I found myself confiding in my old friend Patrick instead.

"Sometimes," he told me in the privacy of my office, "it can help to give your baby a name. Think of him as a person."

Your name, I thought instinctively. A good, solid, loyal name. And strangely, it did help. But naturally, I kept my baby's name to myself. Anyone else might have misunderstood my feelings. I wasn't even sure what they were myself.

I'd been so busy grieving for my son that I'd scarcely given a second thought to my own injuries, which included a broken arm on top of the bruising to my head. I'd also been deeply distressed by the D and C, which was apparently necessary after a miscarriage, especially one so late. "We need to scrape your womb to make sure it's clean," a nurse had told me. "Then you can be ready to start again."

But the very thought of having another baby seemed disloyal to little Patrick. Besides, with David's hostility toward me, it didn't look as though there was any possibility of that. He still maintained he had told me to transfer to a less dangerous prison, and he was so adamant that I almost believed him. Perhaps the blow to my head had unsteadied me more than I'd realized. I even forgot Valentine's Day, although David, in an attempt perhaps to make up for his behavior, gave me a beautiful pair of crystal drop earrings. But his kindness was short-lived, and he soon went back to being snappy with me.

Perhaps it wasn't surprising; I wasn't myself: constantly anxious and jumping at every noise. Post-traumatic stress, said the doctor, prescribing tranquilizers. I was even rude to poor Jackie and Frances, who came to visit with chocolates and flowers. "I'm sure that one day you'll get over it," said Frances awkwardly.

"How do you know?" I'd retorted. "Neither of you are mothers. You don't know what it's like to be pregnant and then lose it." The hurt on their faces was all too clear.

"I'm sorry," I said, turning my head away as hot, silent tears dripped onto my pillow. Jackie had squeezed my hand in comfort. It was more than I deserved.

Then came the first seizure three weeks later. The last thing I could remember was an argument with David in the Kingston house and then waking up on the sitting room carpet, feeling as though I'd had a deep sleep. Yet, at the same time, I was weirdly disoriented. When I pulled myself up, using a chair, I fell over again. At first, David panicked, but a change came over him, and he quickly became cross with me.

"What's wrong with you?" he had snapped. "Get a grip on yourself, Vicki."

"What are you talking about?"

"There's no need to go nuts just because I said I was going away again."

"Where? When?" I rubbed my arms and legs as I spoke. The muscles felt achy. Only much later did I find out this can be a side effect of epilepsy. "I think I need to see the doctor."

"A psychiatrist, more like."

How could he be so cruel? Once more, I found myself thinking that Patrick would never, in a month of Sundays, say anything like that.

The doctor sent me off for an MRI scan, which revealed I'd had a seizure. "This can happen after a head injury. With any luck, it's a one-off, but we'll keep an eye on it. Let's see you again in a month's time."

But before the appointment came up, I had another, this time in the prison staff room. Patrick had driven me straight to the hospital. "You need to test her for epilepsy," he'd told the duty doctor.

"What?" I demanded.

"I've seen it before," he said quietly.

Only later did I discover that my experience was quite common. After an accident, it can take weeks or sometimes months before an epileptic attack actually happens. Diagnosis can take even longer. Mine was finally confirmed after a series of complicated tests that measure the brain's electrical activity. I was also warned to avoid alcohol, which can be a fairly common trigger. By the time the results came through, I'd had two more seizures. To my deep embarrassment, one had taken place during a staff risk assessment concerning a new prisoner who'd been self-harming.

But if it wasn't for the witnesses, I could swear that nothing had happened.

"I don't remember anything about them," I told the doctor. "But I have noticed a sort of burning rubber smell just beforehand. I also got very thirsty on the last occasion."

He looked as though I'd said something exciting. "They can be forewarnings as a result of unusual brain activity. Not every epileptic gets them, so this is good news because it will give you a chance to be prepared. Always make sure you are somewhere safe. It's also best not to sleep alone."

I thought of David's frequent absences from home and my own demanding schedule, which meant I spent six nights out of seven in prison staff quarters.

"Some fatalities," added the doctor, "occur either because of accidents such as falling and hitting the head, or from drowning or from SUDEP—sudden unexplained death in epilepsy."

"Fatalities?" I repeated, shocked. "I didn't realize it was that serious."

"Try not to worry. Hopefully we can control it with the right medication and the correct dosage."

It took another three seizures before they finally found a drug that seemed to work best. The downside, they said, was that this particular medication might affect my memory recall. The other side effects, when I looked them up, were equally alarming, with several online "personal accounts" of degeneration of the brain. "The Internet can be dangerous," said Patrick crisply. "I'd follow the doctors' advice."

But the worst of it was that doubts were now being cast on my ability to do my job. "I'll be fine," I insisted when the chair of the board suggested I take more time off.

But a week later I had yet another seizure—despite the meds—on the mother-and-baby unit, which apparently made the children scream with terror, even though I could remember none of it.

They upped my dosage. The women began to give me a wide berth when they passed me on the corridor or on the wings. Staff looked at me differently. Another seizure happened a month later when I was showing a visitor from the Home Office around. That was the clincher.

"We have to be sensible," said the chair when they called me in for a full board meeting. "You'll get a good pension. I'm sorry, but we need to consider our duty of care to the inmates. What if you hurt someone when lashing out?"

"This only happened because one of them hurt *me*!"

Zelda had been found guilty and was given another sentence on top of her existing one. But her punishment couldn't bring back my child. I felt in my pocket for the three-month ultrasound pregnancy scan that I still carried everywhere, and bit back tears of frustration and grief.

"That bit about me naming my baby Patrick probably sounds mad to you," I now say to my solicitor. "But over the years it really helped me."

Her eyes are soft with sympathy. "I might well have done the same."

Giles Romer is still writing. "If you can tell the jury what you've just told us, Vicki," he says, looking up, "there won't be a dry eye in the house. How did you and David end?"

I've gone over this again and again in my head. "My husband came home late one night to the house in Kingston. He was drunk. Then he . . ."

I stop, fighting back the tears.

They wait patiently for me to continue. There's no getting out of this.

"He said that he'd fallen in love with Tanya." I raise my face angrily. "Not that he fancied her, but that he was in love with her."

I can still feel the shock when he told me.

"I never really loved *you*," he'd roared. "Anyway, I've no use for you now."

"You can't mean that . . ."

His face was close to mine, anger contorting his features. "But I do," he spat. "Do you know why I proposed? Because I liked the idea of being with a woman in authority. Someone who had status. A baby would have sealed it. Made us a proper family whom the world would take notice of. But that's all gone now."

"No," I howled. Despite everything, I was suddenly terrified of being on my own. "Can't we try again?"

He shook his head. "There's no point."

Then he'd packed a case and walked out of the house, slamming the door behind him. Despite everything, I still kept hoping that it was the alcohol coupled with grief over the baby that had made him say such cruel words. Surely, this also explained why he'd allowed himself to be lured into Tanya's arms. Illogically, I blamed her rather than him. But he never came back.

"He claimed he didn't have any money when we were thrashing out the divorce settlement. Tanya bought me out instead." I wince at the humiliation. "It's how they stayed in the Kingston house. She liked it, apparently.

"I had my payoff from the prison, too. To start with, I rented a flat in London while I decided what to do next. But I was restless. How could I stay at home all day, waiting for a seizure that might or might not come? I'd been used to a busy life."

My solicitor nods as though she understands this.

"That's when I got my idea. It would be difficult to work for someone else, because an employer might be nervous about my condition. But I could work for myself."

They both listen keenly.

"I'd helped to launch a beauty salon at one of my previous prisons. Women could train there for skills that gave them a chance of getting a job after release. I'd been particularly impressed by the aromatherapy treatment, which helped to soothe me. I thought this would reduce my tension— and also assist others. So I did my training and then moved to Dorset."

"But you didn't stay there," says the barrister, checking his file.

"No. I had to keep moving around, because every time I had a seizure, word somehow got out and clients were scared to see me."

I omit the fact that I often thought about calling Patrick, but each time I had talked myself out of picking up the phone because I felt embarrassed. I had shown such poor judgment in choosing David as a husband. And I knew if I started telling him about my problems with David, I wouldn't be able to stop myself from admitting my true feelings for Patrick. I couldn't cope with a second rejection.

"All this should go down well with the jury," says Giles. "I'm pretty sure they'll be sympathetic."

"Did you have any contact with David during this time?" asks Penny.

I could lie. But I've had enough of that. I always seem to get found out anyway. I take a deep breath.

"I would leave messages on David's answerphone to tell him where I was living—just in case he wanted to get hold of me. I kept hoping . . . despite everything."

"Not good," the barrister murmurs. "It could be seen as stalking."

Then his face grows even more serious. "We've also got something to tell you."

He glances at Penny. She looks nervous. I have a bad feeling about this.

"The thing is, we've done some digging." Giles gives a half laugh. "Lawyers have to be a bit like detectives at times, you know."

"What are you trying to say?"

"You told Penny on the last visit that Zelda Darling was still in prison. In fact, when we checked this, we discovered she was released soon after Christmas."

I go cold as I work out the dates. "So that means . . ."

"That's right," says my solicitor. "Just before your ex-husband was missing, she was let out early—for good behavior."

PART THREE

50.

HELEN

It's been a long time, but Vicki Goudman is going to pay.

My footsteps are heavy as I make my way back from the tube station to the flat. What is Mum going to say when she discovers I have finally found her nemesis?

I still remember that awful day when I visited her and the guards cut our visit short because another prisoner tried to throw coffee at me. It wasn't even Mum's fault. She was always getting into trouble for everything, she told me, because this prison governor had it in for her. Vicki Goudman. A power-hungry bitch who went after anyone who stood up to her.

Then the accident happened. It was months after her sentence was extended before they let me see my mother again. Until then, I had no idea what had happened, or why I couldn't see her. I hardly recognized her. Her hair was matted, her eyes were glazed, and she struggled to get her words out. But when she did, the only thing she wanted to talk about was Vicki.

"I didn't bloody hit that bitch. It isn't fair. Someone planted that snooker ball and sock in my cell to get me. I had a lot of enemies in that place. Or maybe the guv set the whole thing up, hoping it would get me moved on to another prison. She always had it in for me."

"Why would she try to get herself hurt?"

Mum had shrugged. "Perhaps it went wrong. I don't know. But if she hadn't accused me, I'd have been freed years ago. She has to pay. And you have to help me."

My mind returns to the day I'd collected Mum from prison, just after Christmas. She'd looked so frail, standing there, clutching the plastic bag of clothes that she'd been wearing at the time of her arrest all those years ago in the park.

"The sun hurts my eyes," she'd complained as I guided her to the bus stop. "I'm not used to it."

With every step, she kept stopping to look around, as if she'd never seen a tree before, or a kid on a mobile phone. "You're so lucky to have had all this freedom."

It didn't seem to concern her that I'd been sent to a young offenders unit for a year after setting fire to Dee and Robert's shed, and then passed from one foster family to another. There was the elderly couple who could hardly walk and expected me to look after them instead of the other way round. Then there was a woman who just left food for me on the table and told me to help myself when I felt like it. Once she went away for a fortnight to Florida. I actually didn't mind that too much because I was left to my own devices. But Social Services found out when they made a spot check, and I was put in a youth hostel where the others used to take the piss out of my name. "Come on, Darling. Give us one, won't you? Isn't that what scarlet women do?"

"I shouldn't have given you that name anyway," said Mum when I told her. "Stands out too much. You ought to change it legally. Otherwise someone might link us and that won't do you any favors—especially if you're going to find the bitch responsible for extending my sentence."

So I chose Helen Evans. It felt like a normal, law-abiding name. And I made up a family: two parents who wanted me to make my way in life, and a brother and a sister.

But Vicki Goudman was nowhere to be found—nothing online apart from an old photograph, nothing in the papers. It was as if she had disappeared entirely.

Then one day I had an idea. I might not be able to find her, but I could find her husband. He might know where she was.

From then on it was simple. I did my research. I discovered that David Goudman and the guv had split up. Even so, as Mum said, he might know where Vicki was, so it was still worth pursuing the lead. He was a self-made man, so I told him a story about my life that I thought would appeal. I got the job and seduced him.

Treat them mean. Keep them keen. My mum's advice was spot-on when I told her that I'd found him. "That's what I should have done with your father." Then she stopped.

I held my breath. Whenever I'd asked Mum about my dad in the past, she'd just said it was a long time ago and that she didn't want to talk about it.

"What happened, Mum?"

She sighed. "It doesn't matter."

"Yes, it does. I'm a grown woman. You owe it to me to say."

Something seemed to give in Mum's face. "I've been thinking that myself for a while. Maybe you're right." She closed her eyes. "I met your father on the beach when I was in Trinidad just before going to uni. Then we bumped into each other in a bar later on. It was as simple as that. We didn't even ask each other's names. It was only a couple of months later, when I'd moved on with my friends to another place, that I realized I was pregnant. How naive of me."

She laughs. "A girl from a small Welsh village who'd never thought about contraception. I considered going back to look for him, but I didn't even know his name. If I'd been in the UK, I'd have probably got an abortion—sorry, love. But it was too late, and I had no money. When I asked my parents for help, they went mad. Called me every name under the sun. 'Whore,' 'slut' . . . It was horrible. They told me I'd made my own bed and had to lie in it.

"By then, I felt you were a part of me. So I got a room at a London hostel, and had you at the local hospital. As soon as I looked into your eyes, I knew I'd made the right decision in keeping you." She wiped her eyes. "I fell in love with you—honestly, Scarlet, you've got to believe me. You were—and are—the most important person in my life. I tried to make it on the benefits I got, but it wasn't enough, so I began dealing. We needed the money, love. Even council flats don't come cheap."

I was reeling. "Were those your parents in the photograph you gave me?"

She nodded. Hurt flickered in her eyes. So she did care.

"Where are they now?"

"No idea. And I'm not bothered. Why should I be? They didn't give me any support. It's been just you and me, babe. Remember what I used to say? We make a great team. Keep on playing the game. OK?"

So I did. At first it felt weird being Helen and making up all that stuff about a big family. But the funny thing is that my new identity grew on me. It was easier to sleep with David if I pretended to be someone else. It also helped to erase the memory of Mr. Walter. This time, I was in charge. And then I made the same mistake as my mother. I got pregnant accidentally. When I'd threatened to ring my "dad" during the ensuing argument with David, I'd almost believed my own fantasies.

"Stupid idiot," Mum shouted when I told her. "You're going to ruin your life, just like I did."

"Don't say that."

"We'll make him pay. And her. Keep on looking. Find out where the bitch lives."

And, not knowing what else to do, I did exactly that.

Now I take in Mum's bedraggled appearance as I let myself into the flat. The smell of whisky on Mum's breath. Her dirty fingernails. "I found her."

Her eyes light up. "Go on, then! What happened?"

"She had a fit."

Mum rolls her eyes. "Great."

"You don't sound surprised."

"I'm not. She started having them after the accident."

What? "Why haven't you told me before?"

She shrugs. "Didn't seem important. The only thing that matters is you and me, babe. I'd kill for you."

Then I have a horrible thought. Mum had been furious when I'd told her about David's reaction to my pregnancy. What if she'd hurt him . . . ?

No. She wouldn't do that. Whatever else Mum is, she's always had my best interests at heart. We're a team.

51.

VICKI

12 July 2018

The day is here. My trial. Twelve strangers and a judge are going to decide my future.

The other women prisoners watch as I am taken from my cell. Their silence is far scarier than their usual shouting and swearing. I don't flatter myself that they feel any empathy. Their subdued behavior arises from the incontrovertible fact that one of them will be next.

I am led, handcuffed, toward the courtyard, where I am put in a prison van. After a short bumpy road followed by a smoother surface, or maybe a motorway, we stop. The door is opened. Sunlight blinds my eyes, and I stagger slightly, staring up at the dirty white high walls around me. I don't think I've seen this court before. At least, not from this angle.

"You all right?" asks the officer. She has probably been briefed on my medical condition.

"Just finding my legs after the drive," I say.

I continue to wobble from nerves as I am led in via a back door, through a maze of corridors. "Do you need the toilet?" someone asks.

I nod. An officer unlocks my handcuffs and waits outside the cubicle. She seems relieved when I emerge. More corridors. Up some stairs, through a door, then into a glass box looking down on the rest of the court.

All eyes are on me. I glance up at the public gallery and see a few faces from my old life. Are they here to support me or merely out of curiosity?

There's Frances and Jackie. It's nice of them to come considering I'd ig-nored their texts and phone calls after leaving the prison—I didn't want to be reminded of my old life. And farther to the right is Nicole. I try not to catch her eye. I wonder if Patrick is here. If so, I'm relieved I can't see him. I don't want him to know all the details that are bound to come out about David and me.

Penny is sitting behind Giles, my barrister. She turns round and gives me a smile that is probably intended to be reassuring. I am not fooled. The evidence is stacked against me.

Years ago, as a prison officer, I would be on duty at trials like this. Sometimes we had bets on who would be let off and who would go down. If I was doing that now, I wouldn't wager any money on me.

"Victoria Goudman," says the court clerk. "You are charged with the murder of Tanya Goudman. Do you plead guilty or not guilty?"

"Not guilty," I whisper.

"Can you speak up, please?"

"Not guilty."

I sit down. The room is looming in and out. But my dizziness is not, as far as I can see, a precursor to a seizure. I am simply terrified. Still, at least they haven't charged me with David's murder. Penny had warned me ear-lier that with the evidence they had against me, this might be possible, even though there isn't a body. But clearly, they've decided against it.

A female barrister is outlining the case against me. In my fear, her words go round and round my head in no particular order.

Certain phrases, however, stand out. "You will shortly be told how the defendant was found to have a diary in her possession, declaring her hatred for her ex-husband, David Goudman, and her desire to kill him so no one else could—I quote here—'have him either.'"

There's a gasp from the gallery.

"The jury will also hear how Tanya Goudman was strangled by a dog-tooth chain—similar to the key chain used in prisons. The defendant was once a prison governor, and a chain of this type was found at her home af-ter the murder."

Another gasp.

One of the jurors shakes his head as if he has already made up his mind.

"In addition, the defendant was photographed speaking to her ex-husband in a public place shortly before he disappeared. Initially, she denied this, but she then admitted to having lied."

Members of the jury now shoot me suspicious looks.

"Ladies and gentlemen, you will hear that Victoria Goudman has freely admitted entering the home of Tanya Goudman through the back door, bold as brass. She also admits to 'tussling' with the deceased in anger. To corroborate this admission, the defendant's DNA was found on the body."

I want to put my hands over my ears.

"You will also be told of her history of violence."

What?

"The defense will argue that their client is in far from robust health, but Vicki Goudman is no wilting violet. We will produce witnesses from her most recent prison appointment who will say she had a reputation for being tough and, at times, even aggressive in her demeanor. Clearly, she has brought this trait into her personal life."

I can see from the jurors' faces that I am already guilty.

52.

HELEN

16 July 2018

I ask Mum to stay at home while I go to court. At first, she agrees. But after the weekend, on the third day of the trial, she kicks up one hell of a fuss. "I want to be there to see the bitch get her dues."

We compromise with a coffee shop round the corner, agreeing that I'll go straight there afterward.

As I ease myself into the front row of the public gallery—at seven months gone, I'm getting big now—part of me wishes I hadn't come back to the court today. This place sends shivers through me. How many daughters have sat here and watched a parent being sent down? Or even their own kids? That could have been *me* in the dock.

I remember when I'd got caught shoplifting with the kids from the Walters' house. Then I have a sudden flash of white hands and heavy footsteps coming into my room. Desperately, I stuff my knuckles into my mouth to stop myself from vomiting.

Then the court begins to murmur. Vicki Goudman was being led in by a burly prison officer. You'd never think from her bowed head and lank hair that this was the bully who had made Mum's life hell. At last, with any luck, she's going to get what she deserves.

———————

The guv has given her evidence and is now being cross-examined by the prosecuting barrister. "Mrs. Goudman," she says. "Could you describe your relationship with Tanya Goudman?"

"She married my ex-husband."

"We are aware of that. Did you like her?"

"Would any woman like someone who broke up her marriage?"

There's a ripple of laughter through the court.

"So you hated her, then?"

"I didn't say that."

"What *would* you like to say about the deceased?"

"She wanted David. I realized that from early on. But I was foolish enough to trust him."

Her barrister doesn't look happy. I wonder if Vicki Goudman is enjoying this. It's her moment for revenge. One woman juror's face indicates she's not the only one who's been cheated on. Still, Vicki deserved it.

"From your statement, you admit to going into the deceased's house on the day she was murdered."

"Yes."

"Louder, please."

"Yes."

"Why?"

"I wanted to see if Tanya knew where David was."

"Did she?"

"She said not."

"Did you attack her then?"

"No! She attacked me."

"Did you defend yourself?"

"Yes. But I didn't kill her."

"How do you know?"

"Because she was alive—and shouting at me—when I left her."

"I see. You've had previous experiences of being attacked, haven't you?"

The barrister makes a play of examining her notes. "I believe you were as-saulted in prison by an inmate when you were a governor."

Why are they bringing that up?

"Yes." Vicki Goudman speaks so quietly that I can barely hear her.

"Would you like to tell us what happened after that?"

"I was pregnant." Her voice is dull, as if she's given up. "The attack caused me to lose my baby."

What? A shock of horror zips down my spine. Mum never told me that.

"Why didn't you mention this when you gave evidence earlier on?"

"Because it was too painful. I'd instructed my own barrister to leave it out."

"How else did the attack affect you?"

"The head injuries led to epilepsy. My husband found this difficult to deal with. He said I'd become a different kind of person and he got embar-rassed when I had a seizure in public."

The prosecution's eyes narrow. "Do you still have these fits?"

"Strictly speaking, they are known as seizures."

"I apologize. Please answer the question."

"Yes. I do still have them. I usually take quite strong medication, which reduces the number of episodes, but it hasn't stopped them."

"*Usually* take?"

There's a nod.

"Please speak, Mrs. Goudman."

"Yes, I usually take my medication."

"Are we to conclude therefore that there are times when you don't?"

"Yes."

"Why not?"

"I might forget or . . ."

"Please continue."

"I don't like the side effects."

"What kind of side effects?"

"It can affect my memory."

"Ah yes." The prosecution says this in such a way that she appears to cast doubt on her statement without actually saying so. "Your medical report refers to this on more than one occasion. Would you care to go into more detail?"

"I might forget I've done something, like turn on the cooker. It's why I have a microwave instead for food."

"Might it also make you forget you had hurt someone?"

"Possibly."

"You originally told the police that you hadn't seen your ex-husband for some years. Yet the court has already seen a photograph showing you arguing with him outside a restaurant on the thirtieth of November last year, just two months before he disappeared. Would you like to explain that?"

I begin to feel nervous. That had been an opportunity that had simply fallen into my hands. There I'd been, having dinner with David, and then suddenly, Vicki appeared outside. I knew what she looked like from her old prison profile online. I'd managed to take a quick picture on my phone. Mum had been beside herself with excitement when I'd told her. "Hang on to it. You never know when it will be useful."

After David's disappearance, I had simply handed it over to the police, explaining I'd taken it during a business dinner as part of my "portfolio." The obviously aggressive body language in the picture was perfect "proof" that the ex-wife still had an ax to grind.

"I followed him sometimes," Vicki is saying. "I couldn't get David out of my head. But I was scared of telling the police that I'd seen him in case they thought I was guilty."

Too late. The jury already look as though they've made up their minds on that one.

But where does it all end? I wonder. Vicki had clearly suffered, too. She'd lost her baby. I place my hand protectively on my own stomach.

Then I push the doubt away. It's Mum's side I'm on. Besides, I know what happened on that day with Tanya. Vicki Goudman deserves to go down.

53·

VICKI

16 July 2018

The prosecution is firing relentless questions at me. I want to curl up in a heap and pretend none of this is happening. It's partly my fault for being so open when I'd talked about Tanya. But something had taken me over during the questioning. I wanted to tell everyone what kind of a woman she was. Now I wish I'd kept quiet and been more careful.

"Would you describe yourself as an aggressive person?"

"No."

"Is it true that you attacked a prisoner in your first week as an officer?"

The man who called me in when his toilet was overflowing? "I was defending myself. He yanked my hair by my roots and tried to put my head into the toilet."

"Anything else you'd like to add?"

"No."

The barrister is waving a piece of paper in the air. "I gather from these medical reports that you broke his collarbone at the same time."

I begin to sweat even more. "Like I said, I was defending myself."

"I see."

Several members of the jury are beginning to look even more doubtfully at me.

"I gather that you had to retire from the prison service because of your medical condition."

"Yes."

"Your marriage then broke down. Was there a final trigger for this?"

My nails are digging into the palms of my hands. "Yes."

"Can you tell us what it was?"

"You mean 'who.'" I raise my face, aware it is hot with anger. "Tanya. I told you before. She stole my husband."

"Would you like to go into more detail?"

Despite my earlier thoughts about being more careful, all the old anger comes rushing out. "I'd always suspected them of being close, but then one night, David came home drunk. I asked him where he'd been, and he came straight out and told me that he was in love with Tanya."

"This is the woman you refer to in your diary, I believe."

I nod.

"The one whom you said you could 'happily kill.'"

My mouth is bone-dry. "Yes, but I didn't mean it."

"Why did you write it, then?"

"Because I was hurt. Angry. Upset."

"Enough to murder her?"

"No! I've already said that I didn't do it." I intend on saying this in a reasonable manner. But the prosecution's needling approach has upset me, and it comes out so loud I see the judge flinch.

"Can you tell us more about how you felt when your ex-husband told you he was in love with Tanya, who was then his PA?"

She sounds almost sympathetic even though the prosecution is not on my side. I find myself telling the court things that I hadn't done when my own defense had asked me to tell my story. "It was when he said he loved her. I could have coped with lust, but this was different. I begged him to stay, but he wouldn't. He packed a bag and left, saying . . . saying he had no use for me now."

The jury is gripped.

"What did he mean by that?"

"I asked him the same question." I take a deep breath, trying to steady myself. "He said that my status as a prison governor had given him standing. Now I was no one. He also said that . . . that a baby would have 'sealed' it. But because I'd lost our child, we were finished, too."

Several members of the jury shake their heads.

"Did you feel betrayed?"

"Yes. But I kept hoping," I add, "that the grief from the loss of our child might have made him act in this way. I still loved him. I couldn't believe he was leaving me. So I left the door open, as it were." Tears are blurring my eyes. "It's why I kept ringing him. Letting him know when I moved each time."

The prosecution's tone now becomes steely. "Did you ever threaten to kill him?"

"No! Of course not."

"We've already heard that during your marriage, your husband asked you to sign a document declaring you were buying a house for $3.4 million in the States. You refused because you 'hadn't seen the house and because he was buying it in cash.'"

I nod.

"You also said that you believed he was 'using my status to hide any wrongdoings' and that you had 'prisoners in my care who were in for money laundering. One way of getting rid of dirty money was to purchase houses with it.'"

"That's right."

"So your husband's behavior could have been professionally damaging to your career. I put it to you that you took out your anger at him on Tanya."

"No. That's not true."

But I can see the seed of doubt has been planted in the jurors' minds.

I take a sip of water. I'm not sure how much more I can take of this. And then I see him.

It can't be. I have to be imagining this, just as I imagined him going up the escalator that time. My mind has to be playing tricks. A man who is the spitting image of David has just come into the court. But it can't be him! It had been months since the police had come knocking on my door on that windy, dark February night. Over the last few weeks, I'd more or less reconciled myself to the fact that he must be dead, or else he would have turned up by now. Common sense tells me that his body had probably been buried in a remote place by some unknown adversary. Or maybe he'd killed himself by throwing himself off a cliff or taking an overdose somewhere.

Yet as he sidles up to the prosecution bench, I can see that distinctive face more clearly, and I realize without a shadow of doubt that this is indeed my ex-husband. *What is going on?* I want to yell. But he is busy whispering to the team of lawyers that's determined to take me down. One of them passes a note to the barrister examining me. Her face tightens.

"Mrs. Goudman, do you recognize this man who has just come in?"

"David," I cry out. "Where have you been?"

"Mrs. Goudman," cuts in the judge. "Please address your comments to the barrister. You have been asked if you recognize this man."

My voice cracks. "He looks like my ex-husband."

"Louder please—with his precise name."

"David Goudman. My ex-husband."

As I speak, he looks directly at me. There is a look of triumph about him. How is it that he's appearing *now*? If he isn't dead—and he clearly isn't—why didn't he turn up earlier when Tanya died?

The jury is electrified.

"You seem shocked, Mrs. Goudman."

Anger and relief burst out of my mouth. "Of course I bloody am. I thought he was dead. I want to know what the fuck he's been playing at."

"I suggest that the real reason is that you are now face-to-face with the man you have been stalking for months."

"That's not true."

"I also suggest that you hoped to get him back. Is that correct?"

I want to retreat into my shell now. "Sometimes," I whisper. "Sometimes not."

"But Tanya Goudman was the one person standing in your way. So you killed her."

"No!" I yell. "I'm not like that." Something makes me glance up at the gallery. So he's here, after all. Patrick. I want to throw myself on the ground in self-loathing.

The court is in an uproar. The judge asks for the jury to be sent out and calls for the prosecution and defense barristers to approach him.

David is observing me with a smug expression. He has finally got me.

54.

HELEN

David is here? I don't know whether to be relieved or angry. For once, I feel sympathy for Vicki. What the fuck *does* he think he's been playing at? Maybe someone kidnapped him. He doesn't look in great shape: older, thinner. I try to compose myself during the break. Someone near me is saying loudly that the lawyers need to discuss something with the judge. Eventually, the jury is called back in. According to my neighbor, the judge must have permitted the prosecution to reopen its case and call David as a witness.

I lean forward in apprehension. Until now, it had all been going to plan. But this is something I hadn't bargained on.

"Would you like to tell the court where you have been since the end of January?" asks the prosecution barrister.

He rubs his chin, the way he did that very first time I saw him. "I needed some space."

Hah! That old line. I don't believe him for one second.

"Were you aware that many people had the impression that you were missing, presumed dead?"

"I'm sorry for that." David speaks entirely to the jury. He has that charming look on: the one that has allowed him to get away with so much. "May I be honest here?"

"I would hope so," interrupted the judge. "You are under oath."

David flashes one of his charming smiles. "Of course. I am well aware of that. I went abroad to get away because I had some problems in my personal life. I went to a retreat. I needed to find myself and get some peace."

That's rich, from a man who failed to give me support when I needed it most.

Then David puts his head down. His voice comes out as a sob. "I never thought that my poor wife would be murdered while I was away. I loved her as much as life itself."

Bastard! I wish I could tell the jury about the last time I saw him—the morning of the day he'd "disappeared"—the day I'd told him I was pregnant. How terrifying he'd looked then. But now it seems as though he has everyone eating out of his hand. At least I know Mum had nothing to do with his disappearance now. I feel bad for even thinking it. But what on earth is going to happen next?

55.

VICKI

David. Alive and well. How can this be possible? My mind is reeling. He's been missing since 31 January. How can he have made us sweat for so long?

I'll never forget that night. I'd been at home, just as I'd told the police. I'd finished treating a client and was curled up on the sofa, listening to a radio play. It had just got to the bit where the heroine finally gets to be with the man she'd always loved, and I was suddenly filled with a terrible, cold emptiness. David had behaved appallingly toward me, but I still, for some inexplicable reason, missed him. I couldn't help imagining a different future where we'd stayed happily married and had children together. And I did it again. I rang his mobile in order to hear his voice on the answerphone. I knew my number would come up on his screen and that he wouldn't pick it up. He didn't the first time. But then I tried again, seconds later, and this time he did.

"Please, Vicki." His voice had sounded weary. There was noise in the background as if he was in a busy place. "Just leave it, will you?"

"I can't," I stutter.

"Well after tonight, you won't get hold of me again. So you might as well stop bothering."

What was he talking about? I'd almost rung the police there and then. It even passed through my mind that I should call Tanya. But David wasn't the kind of person who'd kill himself. He was too ambitious. So full of self-belief. I decided he was being melodramatic, trying to get rid of me.

Then he disappeared. I thought back to that noisy call. Had he been at a station or an airport? From then on I tried to tell myself it must be something to do with his dodgy deals.

Nevertheless, I threw away my phone and bought another. Just in case. Thank God I did that, or the police might have traced my calls. I was too scared to tell them the truth in case they held me responsible for his disappearance. Later, when he'd been gone for months, I began to fear that he really had killed himself.

Now it looks as though my original instinct was correct. He'd simply gone AWOL. I listen to my ex-husband with a mixture of hatred and admiration. He always was so convincing.

Still, at least the police can no longer suspect me of his murder. Then the thought strikes me. What if *David* had something to do with Tanya's death?

The prosecutor is still questioning him. "Why didn't you come back earlier? Weren't you aware that your wife had been murdered?"

He rubs his jaw. His voice is raw. "I only found out recently, after leaving the retreat."

"Did your wife Tanya know where you were?"

"I'm afraid I told no one. Not even my daughter. I'd been going through a lot of stress in my personal life, as I said. When I was well enough to come back to the UK, I saw the headlines about the case in the newspaper at the airport. It's why I'm here." Then my skin chills as he looks straight up at me in the dock.

"I believe that my ex-wife is responsible for Tanya's death."

"That's not true!" I yell.

The defense lawyer leaps up to object to David's comment, and the judge agrees, telling the jury to ignore it. He also orders me to keep quiet.

David seems unrepentant. "My ex-wife was violent."

"I was not!"

"This is your final warning, Mrs. Goudman," says the judge.

The defense again leaps up to object about the violent bit. "No," says the judge. "Let's see where this is going."

David looks pleased. "Vicki used to hit me during arguments. It's one of the reasons our marriage broke up."

He's lying, I want to yell.

"So it wasn't because you were having an affair with Tanya, then your secretary?"

He shrugs. "That only started because my wife was impossible to live with. I'm not proud of being unfaithful, but there you are. Vicki, however, couldn't accept it. She would keep ringing me because she said she missed my voice. She even called me at the airport on the night that I went to the retreat. I can prove it with my phone records."

I put my head in my hands. This bit I can't deny.

"Every time she moved, she sent me her address. I'd keep it just in case I needed to contact the police. It was my insurance policy in case she attacked me. Then someone else would know where she was. She used to follow me all the time." He rubs his eyes. "It really upset my poor Tanya."

There's a hushed silence in the court.

The prosecuting barrister is handing him a photograph. "Do you recognize this?"

"Yes. It was taken by a photographer I was having a business meeting with. A woman called Helen Evans who was a work-experience student at my company."

David looks uneasy. Was he having an affair with her? I knew all too well what his "business meetings" usually meant.

"Can you confirm who this woman in the photo is?"

David frowns. "It's Vicki. Which only goes to prove my point about her stalking me." He faces the jury. "It's why I came rushing here as soon as I saw that headline. My ex-wife murdered Tanya out of jealousy. And she should pay for it . . ."

"We're not here to speculate," cuts in the judge.

But the damage is done.

56.

HELEN

The judge calls a brief adjournment. Everyone seems shell-shocked by David's appearance. And no wonder.

I nip outside for some fresh air, keeping my head down in case anyone from the office is there. I hadn't expected the barrister to mention Helen Evans by name. Luckily there's a hat stall outside. Swiftly buying the cheapest—a dull black that won't stand out—I yank it down over my forehead. Still, it's not like I've done something wrong.

Apart from not saying I was at the scene of the murder.

Of course, I could have told the court myself that Vicki had killed Tanya. But it would have meant admitting that Mum and I were at the Goudmans' house, too.

Not that it should have worked out that way.

It was at the end of March when Mum declared she had a brilliant idea.

"You could ring Vicki Goudman to make an appointment. Tell her you need some aromatherapy for . . . I don't know . . . sleeping better or something like that. I'll come down with you."

"Then what?"

She shrugged. "We'll play it by ear."

Yes, said Vicki Goudman when I rang. She'd be delighted to see me. In fact she had a cancellation at nine a.m. for 1 April.

April Fools' Day.

I had a bad feeling about that. "By the way," I said. "I'm pregnant. Is it still all right to have treatment?"

"We'll need to avoid certain oils, but we can go through all that during the consultation. Now what's your name?"

"Helen Evans."

I was nervous. Mum was so unpredictable. "You're not going to hurt her, are you?" I whispered.

"'Course not." Her eyes opened wide. "What do you think I am? Just want to get a few things off my chest, that's all. Give her a piece of my mind."

Mum had dressed up as though we were going to a fancy party, with a flowery skirt from Sue Ryder and a velvet sequined handbag over her shoulder. I'd bought it for her from the market at a reduced price because it was slightly torn, but she paraded around in it like a child in a birthday outfit. Still, maybe that was understandable after years of having to wear prison clothes. In return, she'd insisted on giving me a pair of pretty yellow clip-on earrings. They still had a security tag on them. "The shop must have forgotten to take it off," Mum said lightly.

We took the *Riviera Express* down to Cornwall on the night before the appointment, dozing on and off in our seats as we couldn't afford a sleeper. Mum had a strange grin on her face when we woke up. "I can't wait for this," she said over and over again, with a grim tone to her voice. The other passengers gave us odd looks. But just as we reached Penzance, I checked my phone. There was a text from Vicki. It had been sent last night.

Sorry but I have to cancel for personal reasons.
I'll be in touch shortly to arrange another appointment.

"Fuck," said Mum loudly when I showed it to her. A woman opposite threw us a disapproving glare. "So we've come all the way down here for nothing."

Yet part of me was relieved. Maybe there was another way we could pay Vicki back without Mum needing to see her. It was too dangerous in Mum's unpredictable state. But as we got off the train at Penzance, Mum nudged me in the ribs. "Look. That's her on the platform over there. It's our lucky day. Quick—we'll follow her."

Shit. Mum was already rushing ahead, leaping on the return train. At every station we watched to see if she was getting off. But she stayed put. All the way back to Paddington again. "Stick with me," Mum instructed. "We can't let her out of our sight."

It was when Vicki Goudman took the Wimbledon-bound tube and then changed that I suspected where she was going. "Kingston," I whispered. "David talked about that. It's where he lived with Tanya when he wasn't in central London."

Mum was good at tailing. We stayed close enough not to lose our quarry but sufficiently far away so as not to be noticed. Eventually, Vicki turned down a pretty tree-lined side road and then headed for a house on the right behind a tall hedge.

"Bloody hell," breathed Mum as we peeped round.

I did a double take, too. David and Tanya lived in the poshest place I'd ever seen, with a sports car parked outside a triple garage. There was an alarm box on the front, large diamond-paned windows. Vicki was just walking through a gate at the side of the house that looked as though it led to a back garden.

"What do you think she's doing here?" I asked.

"We won't know if we just stay here, will we?"

"But they'll see us."

"Don't you get it? This is a heaven-sent opportunity. We can tell this Tanya that her husband's got you up the spout at the same time. Maybe she'll give us some money even if he won't."

"But what about Vicki . . ."

Too late. Mum had gone on ahead.

Round the back, there were big open patio doors leading to a conservatory. I could see Vicki and Tanya inside. Swiftly, we hid behind a bush.

"If we get into trouble, do a runner through there," Mum whispered, indicating a wooden gate at the end of the garden.

"Let's leave now. Please."

But she was peeping round. I did the same.

They were arguing fiercely. I could hear the anger, though not the actual words. Then, suddenly, they flew at each other.

Oh my God. Vicki and Tanya were wrestling. There was a hollow crack as Tanya's head hit a table.

"Go!" Mum gave me a push. "Quick."

Through the gate. Past the phone box. Back to the main road. Heart racing. Round the corner. Hide behind a trash bin.

I finally dared to look back. Where was Mum? For a second I was terrified she'd been caught. Then she finally came into sight, puffing.

"Fuck. I haven't run in years." Mum grinned. "Had to stop a few times to catch my breath. You won't believe what happened. Looks like Governor Goudman isn't so good after all."

57.

VICKI

I'm back on the stand, bracing myself for what is to come. My solicitor has admitted to me that she'd told the prosecution about baby Patrick even though I'd told her not to. "I had to, Vicki. I hoped it would get the jury on your side."

I could make a fuss about this, but maybe it's for the best after all.

I could also have asked for a longer adjournment or even a retrial after David's appearance, but I just wanted to get the whole thing done with.

Instead I was recalled to be examined by the defense and now by the prosecution on "matters arising" out of my ex's evidence. I purposefully avoid looking at the gallery. I don't want Patrick's sympathy. I've brought all this on myself.

"You were seen by a neighbor coming out of Tanya's house on the day that she was murdered," says the prosecution barrister. "In addition, another neighbor who declined to be named made an emergency call from a public phone box. Was this indeed you?"

I am feeling dizzy, and there's a humming in my ears. Please, don't let me have a seizure. I need to get this trial over with. "I wanted to ask if she knew where David was."

"Don't you think she would have said if she *did* know?"

"I thought she was covering up for him. When my husband and I split up and we were sorting out our various possessions, I found some deeds in his study showing that she was a cosignatory to a house that had cost millions—rather like the deed that my husband had tried to make me sign toward the end of our marriage. That made me believe she was part of some kind of money laundering scheme and that she knew he was lying low somewhere. But when I told her that, she flew at me."

"I see. What did you do next?"

"I think I probably went into self-defense mode."

"You think?"

The dizziness is getting worse. "It's hard to recall. Like I said, my medication can affect my memory."

"How very convenient."

"I object to that, my lord."

The judge bends his head as if in agreement. "Please keep sarcasm out of my court."

The barrister apologizes.

"What exactly did you mean when you said you went into self-defense mode?"

I know this isn't going to sound good. But it's the truth. "I learned how to look after myself when I was training to be a prison officer."

"Did you hurt her?"

"Not directly."

"Please be clearer than that."

"She . . . well she hit her head on a table when I pushed her away."

I feel too guilty to look at Penny. I should have told her about this earlier. But I'd hoped to get away without talking about it.

"Rather like when you broke a prisoner's collarbone and caused neck injuries to another?"

"Maybe," I whisper.

"Louder, please."

"Maybe. But I don't think I hurt her. Not badly."

"How do you know?"

"She was still talking afterward. She told me to get out. So I did."

"Do you also recall strangling her with a chain?"

"No."

"But is it possible you might have forgotten, owing to your medication?"

"I don't think so."

"Yet you said just now that you forgot things. So how can you be certain?"

"I'm not a murderer."

"I believe that is for the jury to decide. What did you do with the chain?"

"I didn't have one."

The barrister gives a heavy sigh. "The neighbor reported seeing that you were holding something in your hand, which you then put in your bag as you ran."

"Yes. I was."

It's as though the court is holding its breath. I feel embarrassed now. It seems so trivial, although at the time it seemed the right thing to do.

"When I went into Tanya and David's house, I saw something that used to belong to me. So I took it."

"You *stole* something?"

"No. Like I said, it was mine. It must have got muddled up in David's half when we divided our things after the divorce."

"What was it?"

"A wooden love spoon that had belonged to my mother, who died when I was young. It had deep sentimental value for me. Tanya picked it up, and I thought she was going to hit me with it. Later, after she put it down, I grabbed it. I couldn't bear to think of that woman having it. David should have known better. He ought to have returned it."

One of the jurors is nodding as though she agrees.

"That woman?" repeats the barrister. "Clearly, you did not like her."

"Of course I didn't. She stole my husband."

"And where is this so-called love spoon now?"

"It was taken by the prison when I was arrested. But when I told my solicitor this, they said they couldn't find it."

"Really? I put it to you that you were holding a key chain. One similar to that which was found in a packing box, wrapped up in your old uniform in the cellar, by the police when they searched your apartment soon after Tanya's death. It had been wiped clean."

There's a gasp from the jury.

I try to choose my words carefully. "As I said in my statement, I have no idea how it got there. Besides, the police arrested me at the station, before I went home, so it can't be the same chain."

"Not if you asked someone else to take it back for you. Another of Mr. Goudman's employees, perhaps, with a similar ax to grind."

"But I didn't."

"How can you be certain, Mrs. Goudman? We've already established that your condition and your medication can affect your memory."

I think of the other things I'd forgotten. The client appointments in my diary. The misplacing of my front door keys.

"I'm as certain as I can be," I say lamely. Then I feel a surge of anger. "Anyway, if you're so certain, where's your evidence? And why would a so-called accomplice plant the chain back in my flat instead of just getting rid of it?"

"Please answer the questions, Mrs. Goudman. It is not your job to ask them."

The judge intervenes. "We are going over old ground here. I've been very understanding so far in view of the unusual nature of the situation. Is there anything more arising out of Mr. Goudman's evidence?"

There isn't.

But with any luck, I have given everyone something to think about. Including myself.

The jury doesn't take long. Despite that last outburst of mine, I wouldn't hesitate for long either if I was one of the twelve.

"Do you find the defendant guilty or not guilty?"

"Guilty."

The court explodes with shouts and cheers.

I glance up to the gallery. There's Jackie, looking at me sadly. And next to her is Patrick.

My sentence is Life with a minimum term of twenty years.

But my greatest punishment is the fact that I now have to live with myself. Tanya might have stolen my husband. But she didn't deserve to be murdered.

Least of all by me.

58

HELEN

Twenty years! It's no more than Vicki Goudman deserves, I tell myself, threading my way out through the public gallery and down the court steps, past a crowd of journalists buzzing like bees around the lawyers with their flapping black gowns.

"No comment," I hear one say.

Hah! If I was asked, I'd have plenty to say. No length of sentence is too long for that woman.

Breaking out into a run, I make for the coffee shop where I'd left Mum. But she's not there.

Where is she? I try to put myself in her shoes. Then I get it! Bet she's outside the court, keen to hear the verdict. Running out—almost knocking into a passerby—I head back to the large concrete building with its graceful Grecian columns. There are still loads of people there, including a TV crew. No wonder. A disgraced public name. A missing husband. It all made a good story. And then I hear a familiar voice.

"Vicki Goudman was the bitch who stopped me being with my little girl."

It's Mum, talking to one of the journalists. She sounds drunk. "She was power-hungry, that woman. Never showed an ounce of pity . . ."

"I think that's enough." I take Mum firmly by the arm. "We need to go."

"But I was just telling this nice gentleman here . . ."

What if she lets slip we were at the Goudmans' house?

"I said we have to move it."

"Well, I'm not going back to any bleeding coffee shop. We need a drink to celebrate."

When Mum's in a mood like this, there's no talking her out of it. Besides, I'm worried that if I argue with her, we'll only attract more attention.

"Just one. You know what the probation officer said. If you get drunk and make a scene, you could go back Inside."

Mum's lips tighten. "Don't be so boring. This is a great day! Justice has finally been done." She claps me on my back. "Our lives are just starting, love."

We make our way to the nearest pub. There are lots of booths round the side, and luckily, we find an empty two-seater. I buy us each a small white wine.

"Cheers," I say uncertainly.

She knocks it back in one. Then she makes a face. "Not as good as the last lot."

"What do you mean?"

She grins. "When you were at the bar just now, I helped myself to a couple of drinks that a couple left on that table over there."

In the old days, three glasses wouldn't have been enough for Mum to get smashed. But she doesn't have the tolerance she used to.

"Twenty years!" Mum punches her hands in the air and hollers as if she's just won something on one of the gaming machines behind us. "Isn't it great?"

"Shhh." I glance around nervously in case there are any more journalists nearby. "Come on. Let's go home."

"You can if you want. But I'm not."

I need to distract her. But there's something I must ask before I lose my nerve. "Mum, when we ran out of Tanya's house you took a minute or two to join me. What were you doing?"

Go on, I urge her silently. Tell me what you said before about being puffed and not keeping up.

"It doesn't matter."

"Yes, it does." I lean across the table and hold Mum's cold, thin hand. "We're a team, remember. We trust each other. But we can't do that unless we're honest. So tell me."

Mum grips my hand back. "I can't."

"You can," I say.

"You won't love me anymore."

There's a heavy feeling in my chest. "Of course I will."

"I only did it for you, love. She deserved to get punished."

"Mum. What did you do?"

"I . . . well I had one of those key chains from the prison. I nicked one. Just to defend myself in case one of the other women went for me."

"How did you get it out when you were released?"

"I did one of the prison officers a favor." She winks at me. "Nice bloke he was."

My mouth is dry. "Please tell me you didn't take the chain with you when we followed Vicki."

"Only as protection." Mum isn't looking at me. "I didn't know what the guv might do if she saw us."

"But she didn't see us . . . did she?"

"No." She lifts her face again. Defiant this time. "Vicki ran past me, and I was going to follow her when she stormed off, but then Tanya saw me. By then I'd sneaked in through the open patio doors. I was scared so I . . . well, I got my chain out."

The baby kicks inside me as though it, too, is scared.

"Only to frighten her, mind. But then she began yelling, and I knew I had to shut her up."

"You didn't . . ."

"I just told you, love. I did it for you. I thought, well, if she's dead and David's gone missing—maybe dead, too—you'd get all the money once you'd proved it was his child."

"And you thought all of that on the spur of the moment? You've just helped to send down an innocent woman for a crime she didn't commit."

"What about justice? It's what she did to me." Mum's voice rises like a spoiled child's. "I knew David's wife would have Vicki's DNA on her from the fight they'd just had. You pick up a thing or two in prison. Then I stopped at that phone box to dial 999 and leave an anonymous tip-off in a funny voice claiming to be an old neighbor who heard a commotion and recognized David's first wife running from the house. Told them that I thought she now lived in Penzance. Then I knew the police would watch the station and the bitch would get blamed for his murder."

"You lied to me. I thought you said we were a team. How could you be so stupid?" Tears are running down my face.

"Shut up."

"No, you shut up. All I ever wanted was for you to get out of prison, and now you've done it again . . ."

"Zelda, isn't it? Zelda Darling. Thought I recognized your voice."

I take in the broad-shouldered man in a suit who has stepped round the side of the booth. "Who are you?"

"My name's Patrick Miles. I knew your mother from prison."

Mum's face has gone white.

The man steps closer. "'The bitch would get blamed for his murder,' would she? Would the bitch you're referring to be Vicki Goudman, by any chance?"

Oh my God.

"I think we need to speak to the police, don't you?"

"Fuck off." There's a glint. Mum has snatched a knife from the table. "Don't!"

"Police," the man yells, grabbing her wrist. The knife falls to the ground.

"Scarlet," shouts Mum. "Help me."

But this time, there's nothing I can do.

59.

VICKI

I know exactly what is going to happen now. I'm back in the remand prison where I'd been while waiting for the trial to arrive. In a few days, or maybe weeks, I will be assigned to a prison suitable for lifers.

Life. It can mean so many things. If you've never been in prison, you take it for granted. Breathing in fresh air. Being free to walk down the street. To go into a shop. To have a drink. To read a book in companionable silence. To make love to a man who really cares for you . . .

But my sentence means I will never have any of this again, at least for a very long time. I won't have a chance to find the right man, if such a person is out there. I won't have a normal existence. Mind you, my epilepsy has already taught me about that. And worst of all, I will know I have been responsible for taking another life.

For the more I think about it, the less clear I am regarding the exact events after pushing Tanya to the ground.

"Sign in here, please," says the officer. We're in what's known as Reception, the area where prisoners are booked in and out. I am frisked, then I am led to a cell. "Your pad mate refused to share with a lifer, let alone an ex-governor," said the officer tightly. "We took sympathy on her. You're on your own now."

A single cell was usually a luxury with today's overcrowding. But this feels like more of a punishment. There is barely room for the narrow bed, nor is there much light from the tiny window that looks out onto a concrete wall.

"No loo?" I ask.

"You'll have to press the bell if you want to risk the shared bathroom."

Her meaning was clear. It wasn't unknown for lifers to be assaulted—especially ex–prison staff. The showers were a favorite place for this. You're at your most vulnerable.

"Or there's a pot under the bed."

She slams the door behind her. I am alone with my thoughts. My library book from my old cell isn't here. No one, I realize suddenly, has mentioned my medication, which I need to take soon. I hammer on the door. Silence. I haven't had a seizure for some months now—in fact, not since that day in Penzance. Long lapses can sometimes happen, as I know from the consultant. But what if I have one now and no one comes? I could hit my head on the floor when I fall . . .

Panic wraps itself round my throat like an invisible suffocating blanket. "Help!" I call out. "Help!"

Two hours pass. I have been timing every minute on the clock on the wall. Two hours ten minutes. Two hours twenty minutes. Someone had to come soon, if only to feed me.

Footsteps. At last.

It's a different officer.

"My meds," I babble. "I need to take them."

"What meds?"

"Haven't you read my medical notes? I have epilepsy."

Her expression changes. "Right. We'll get that sorted on our way to the governor's office."

"Governor's office?" I repeat. "Why?"

She gives me a strange look. "Your solicitor has rung. She wants to speak to you. Urgently."

60.

HELEN

4 September 2018

"Zelda Darling. You are accused of the murder of Tanya Goudman, the obstruction of justice and attempted grievous bodily harm toward Patrick Miles. On the first charge, do you plead guilty or not guilty?"

I hold my breath. Ever since Mum had been arrested, she'd kept changing her mind about the murder bit. We don't know exactly what Patrick overheard in the noise around us in the pub. She couldn't very well plead not guilty to the second and third, though. There'd been too many witnesses to her attack on Patrick.

Some discussion had gone on about me being a witness, too, but I'd been having some bleeding, and my GP had written a letter to say that, in his view, the stress of taking the stand could be harmful to my pregnancy. Thank God. I didn't know whether I could lie for Mum again.

I have at least managed to find a solicitor for her who does legal aid, which means we don't have to pay anything. He's an earnest young man who keeps checking and rechecking his notes. "It's essential," he told me before the case, "that your mother is honest about what happened on the day she visited Tanya's house."

He spoke as if I had control over Mum, who had been denied bail.

I doubt my mother even knows what honesty is anymore.

As I sit up in the public gallery once again, with the baby floundering around inside me, there's something else that's scaring me. If Mum killed

Tanya, then maybe she has it in her to have attacked Vicki Goudman on the prison staircase all those years ago.

"Not guilty," rings Mum's voice defiantly through the air.

The trial begins. The accusations and questions come thick and fast. We find out that Patrick had been contacted by Vicki's solicitor. When they had found out about Mum's release, they had traced her. They couldn't prove anything, but once the trial started, he had decided to keep an eye on her. He followed us to the pub.

Mum's barrister argues—convincingly, I think—that Patrick overheard the "confession" when she was drunk, so that piece of evidence could not be relied on.

Mum denies it all. But the police found a prison key chain under her bed in our flat that had on it not only Mum's fingerprints but also traces of Tanya's blood.

"I put it to you that the murder was premeditated," declares the prosecution. "You hid the chain in the ripped lining of your handbag. We found Tanya Goudman's DNA in there, too."

The very handbag that I had bought her—the one that she had been so proud of.

"I carried a chain in case I got attacked," snaps Mum. "Prison makes you like that. You're always on the lookout."

It's the same on the estate, I want to say. Loads of people have illicit weapons as protection in the same way that posh people have rape alarms.

But it's clear from the jury's faces that they don't believe her.

Yet it's the next question that really freaks me out.

"Was anyone with you when you went to Tanya's house?"

My ears begin to sing with the pressure. What if Mum says more than she means to?

"'Course not." There's a toss of the head. "I wasn't exactly going to bring my bleeding probation officer, was I?"

One of the jury members sniggers.

"Murder is no laughing matter," thunders the judge. "Any more and I'll declare you in contempt of court."

But I'm trembling at the lie. "If I tell them the truth, you'll be charged as a conspirator," Mum had argued during one of my visits to prison. "If you're sentenced, your kid will be adopted at eighteen months. Do you really want that?"

So I'd agreed. Now, though, part of me feels I should stand up in court and share the blame, even though it would mean losing my child—that's if I decide to keep it. There are days when I am convinced it would be better off with someone else.

I start to get up. Prepare myself to call out the truth. Then I remember Mr. Walter. The young offenders institution. The many foster parents. I sit down again, my hands clenched by my side.

The jury is out now.

"Do you find the defendant guilty or not guilty of murder?"

Blood pounds in my ears.

"Guilty."

Mum gives a little cry and seems to crumple in on herself.

I yearn to run over and hug her, just as I'd done when I was small and things went wrong.

Yet if she hadn't broken the law years ago with our games, we could have had a normal life together.

And now we are right back to where we were when Mum had first been arrested. With one important difference.

I am no longer a child.

But it won't be long before I am responsible for another.

61.

VICKI

16 September 2018

One minute, a life sentence is stretching out before me. The next: the phone call from my solicitor to say that Zelda has been arrested for the murder of Tanya and for attacking Patrick. Thank God my old friend was all right.

Even when Zelda was found guilty, they couldn't release me immediately. Technically, I was a convicted murderer. These things take time. An application has been made for my conviction to be overturned. Eventually, I might even seek compensation, according to my solicitor. But I'm not going to. It's not always easy to decide who is guilty and who is not. When I was in charge, I always knew there were probably a handful of inmates who were there for crimes they had not committed.

In the meantime, an emergency bail hearing was held in my absence, and four days later I am allowed out. The officer hands me a plastic bag with the possessions I came into prison with. As luck would have it, they had found the Welsh love spoon that my father had given my mother. I take out the spoon now and trace its heart-shaped handle with my finger as my mother might have done herself. It calms me, as does the scan of baby Patrick, which reminds me that, once, he really did exist.

I walk through the prison gate, gulping in the fresh air, and head for the taxi rank. The local drivers know a good market when they see one.

A tall figure walks toward me. It's raining, so it's hard to make out the face. My heart gives a little thud inside, but it's not who I thought. It's my solicitor. I'd thought that maybe Jackie or Frances would be here to meet me, or even Patrick. But the girls are probably working, and Patrick likely doesn't want me to interpret his friendship as something else.

"How kind of you to meet me," I say, trying to hide my disappointment. "I was going to get a cab."

"I brought my car." Penny waves her hand toward a dusty navy blue estate car a few yards away. "I thought we could talk. There's something I need to tell you. It's about your ex."

My mouth goes dry. "Is he all right?"

I hate myself for even asking the question. Surely, I don't care anymore—especially after what he said in court.

Penny's lips tighten. "Men like David will always be all right."

We get into her car. She doesn't start the engine. Instead, she speaks. "I've got a good friend or two in the police force. Every solicitor needs one."

There's a short silence. I want to break it, but something makes me wait.

"I've found out a few things. You were right: David was involved in something illegal. In fact, he was dealing in arms. He got into it when he was in the army, apparently, and got chummy with an American serviceman in Afghanistan. Your ex-husband and his American friend set up together using their contacts. They did very well. I'm not an expert on this, I must confess. But from what I can tell, the property business was the perfect front. These men always hide behind a veneer of respectability."

She paused for a minute to let that sink in. "But they needed to hide their tracks. You were right again when you thought David was laundering money through buying houses. It's one of the most common methods."

A burst of adrenaline hits me, along with anger and sorrow. "And the police knew?"

She shook her head. "Only Interpol. They'd been watching him for months, it seems, but it was hush-hush. When he said on the stand that he'd been in a retreat, that was true. But he was actually there because he'd been threatened by one of his arms-dealing clients. This coincided with Zelda's daughter telling him she was pregnant, which gave him even more reason to get out of the country."

He'd gotten her pregnant? It feels like a punch in the stomach.

"Interpol flushed him out of the retreat and offered him a deal," continued my lawyer. "If he gave them details of his arms dealings, they would grant him a safe passage back and offer protection. He wanted to get home to see his daughter. But the police over here got wind of the fact that Interpol had known where he was all the time and were not happy. They were convinced you were guilty of Tanya's murder and still needed more evidence. So to keep the UK police happy, Interpol told David that he had to give evidence against you."

"And lie about me being violent?"

Penny shrugged. "I don't know exactly how the conversation went. I can't say I approve, but it's the way things happen sometimes."

"And now where is he?"

"Staying with his daughter under police protection."

"So he's free?"

There's a sigh. "I'm sorry. I know it's unfair, given that he lied under oath. I wanted you to know from me. Obviously, you could go to the newspapers, but if you want my advice, I'd let it go. You've been given a clean start."

62.

HELEN

2 October 2018

Here again. This prison is different from the last. It's modern, warmer. I hand over my paperwork and place my right forefinger on the identification pad. An officer then takes me to one side, instructing me to hold out my arms so I can be frisked.

It's all too familiar.

The process makes me feel as if I've done something wrong myself. Perhaps I have. I was there at Tanya's house. If I hadn't worked for David, I wouldn't have got pregnant. That would mean Mum wouldn't have gone to the Goudmans' house, and Tanya would still be alive.

I'm joining a queue to get into the visiting room. The person in front moves up to give me more space. I'm well overdue now. I only hope I'm not going to give birth here.

Mum is already sitting at a plastic table; so are a dozen other prisoners. She looks frail. If physical contact wasn't forbidden, I would put my own arms around her and hug her—just as I had tried to do as a young child when the officers weren't looking. Even though she's killed someone, she's still my mother.

"Thank you for not telling them about me," I whisper, not wanting anyone else to hear.

Mum's eyes become fearful. "I don't know what you're talking about."

Of course she does. Yet her denial sounds so convincing. She is a natural liar.

"You know, Mum," I say slowly, "I love you with all my heart. But there are times when I don't know whether you're telling the truth or not. We're a team, remember? And teams need to work together. We can't do that without total honesty. Is there anything else you'd like to tell me?"

There's a flicker in Mum's eyes—I've struck a nerve.

"No," she says hesitantly.

"You're not saying that as though you mean it."

Mum puts her head in her hands. I get a horrible sense of foreboding.

Then she lifts her head. Her face is raw with grief. "I thought someone might bring it up at Vicki Goudman's trial, but they didn't." She wipes her eyes.

"Just tell me. Please."

"I couldn't say before because you were too young, and after that, there didn't seem a right time."

I'm nervous now.

Mum sighs. "When they took me from you in the park that time, I was pregnant."

What?

"The dad was one of my friends."

I think of the various "uncles" who had flitted in and out of the house, giving me fruit-and-nut chocolate or rides on a motorbike.

"Which one?"

"It doesn't matter. The thing is, he didn't want anything to do with it." She sniffed. "Apart from you, the baby was the only thing that kept me going when I was inside. We lived in the prison mother-and-baby unit, but I was only allowed to keep her until she was eighteen months old."

I hadn't been allowed to visit my mother after her sentence was extended because of her behavior, but I do have a dim recollection of her wearing baggy dresses. At the time I hadn't given that much thought. Now I realize she must have been pregnant.

"Her?" I repeat disbelievingly. "I have a sister?"

Mum's eyes are wet. "The prison authorities made me have her adopted. I begged the panel—including Vicki Goudman—to see if she could be fostered instead. That way, I'd be able to keep in touch with her. But they said that with my record and behavior, adoption was 'in the best interest of the child.'"

She gives a little sob. "They wanted to have you adopted, too, but because you'd been in the fostering system and were getting older, they allowed you to carry on. If you *had* been adopted, you'd have been someone else's child instead of mine."

My mind is whirling. "Where is my sister now?"

"That's the thing, love. I'm not allowed to know. Nor are you. She'll be about ten now. We can only hope that when she's eighteen, she'll try to find us."

"What did you call her?"

"Alice." Tears are streaming down Mum's face. "After *Alice in Wonderland*. Remember how it was one of your favorite stories?"

This is too much to bear. A sister? Is it possible that I've actually passed her on the street? Suppose she doesn't try to trace us when she's older? Suppose she does and Mum is dead by then?

And that's when I make my decision. My initial feeling after David had gone missing was that I couldn't possibly go ahead with a pregnancy that hadn't even been planned. But then my body changed. Food started to taste metallic. My breasts became sore. I was sick every morning. How could a tiny seed do this? The picture of "it" sucking its thumb on the three-month scan made me realize I couldn't have an abortion. Instead, I'd go for adoption and give my child a better life. But to be honest, I began to get doubts from the moment I felt the first kick. Now the discovery that Mum had to give up my sister—and the effect on her—has helped me finally make up my mind.

"I'm going to bring up the baby myself," I blurt out.

Mum's eyes instantly brighten. "I'm so glad! A grandchild will give me something to live for."

I feel both relief and terror. How are we going to cope?

"You'll need a DNA test as soon as it's born so you can get support from this David of yours," adds Mum, her eyes narrowing.

I shake my head firmly. "He's not mine. And that's why I'm not going to bother."

"Why the fuck not?"

"I don't want to be constantly chasing him for payments. And if there is an inheritance at some point, I don't want his dirty money. I'd rather manage on our own."

I almost add the words "like we did," but that wouldn't be truthful. We *hadn't* managed.

Instead, I vow to myself, I will do things differently.

Daily Telegraph, *7 November 2018*

The body found at Deadman's Creek in Cornwall has been identified as 49-year-old Jackie Wood, a former prison officer.

A witness saw the deceased hovering at the top before finally leaping to the rocks below. A suicide note was later found at her home. The police are not looking for anyone else in connection with the death.

63.

VICKI

15 November 2018

I've taken my solicitor's advice and stayed put in Penzance. Despite my fears that I'd be the center of curiosity or pity or ridicule (or all three), the town has become almost protective of me.

"Some journalist was sniffing around here yesterday," one of my neighbors informs me. "Sent him packing. Thanks again for the treatment, by the way. I'm sleeping a lot better now. Funny. I'd never have thought of aromatherapy until you moved in."

I've even joined a yoga class, although I have to quietly tell the teacher that I suffer from epilepsy. "I haven't had a seizure for a while now," I say, with my fingers crossed.

"Don't worry," she reassures me. "My niece has it, too, so I know what to do. It's more common than we realize."

I spend my spare time walking up and down the seafront. The open air gives me an immense wave of freedom. I read, but I always avoid the news.

Yet I still can't get rid of a nagging feeling that something isn't right. It's not just that Patrick has failed to get in touch. I thought that his pursuit of Zelda meant that he still cared for me in some way. But obviously not.

And then comes the brown envelope from my solicitor. I receive it one morning when I am sitting at the bay window overlooking the sea. There's a white sail bobbing on the horizon. I open it, expecting a bill. Then I take in the contents, disbelievingly. After that, I do as instructed and read the accompanying letter inside the envelope. It's a photocopy. The handwriting is precise.

To whoever finds this. Please pass the contents to Vicki Goudman. It is self-explanatory.

Vicki,

You might have seen me at your trial. You probably thought I was there as your best friend, to give you support. I know you are short on family, like me. We used to talk about that, remember, during our girly chats. But you had an advantage. You had this strong personality and a certain look about you that made men turn their heads. You just didn't realize it. I admit I was jealous.

No one realizes what hard work it is in prison, do they? The responsibility. The stress. If something goes wrong, the staff are always the first in the firing line. It's hard to relax, so I started taking drugs to help me. But I ran out of money, and I began selling phones and weed to the prisoners.

Then you fell in love and got promoted to governor—a job I could only dream of. But to top it all, you met David. I was so jealous! Not only was he gorgeous, but he was also clever and interesting. It was agony for me to give you away at the wedding. Why couldn't I have a man like him?

It was the "bad boy" bit underneath the charm that I was really drawn to. The bit you didn't see at first. He didn't fancy you. He told me that, too. He fancied me. I'd known that from the moment he held my hand during the dancing at your wedding reception. The touch of his thumb stroking my skin made me melt. It was soon after your honeymoon that he called me. We started seeing each other on the quiet. Did I feel guilty? I should have done. But I wanted what you had. When you got pregnant, I could barely hide my disappointment.

Then came my break. David was furious because you wouldn't sign those deeds. "What's the point of marrying the prison governor if she can't be useful?" he kept saying. "If she's going to be like this, I've got no use for her."

Then he started talking about leaving you for me. I honestly believed him! "Vicki's really getting on my nerves," he said during one of our stolen nights in a motel halfway between the prison and his London place. "I thought that being pregnant might make her more loyal, but if anything, she's become more of a stickler for the rules than before. I should be with you—not her. Sometimes I just wish she was dead."

Prisons were dangerous places. Supposing I "helped" you to have an accident?

It was wrong. I know that. But jealousy took all reasoning out of my head. When you said you'd do outside exercise duty that day, I seized my chance.

It only took a few tenners to convince a friend to switch off the lights at the crucial point. And it wasn't difficult in the dark to grab a ball, put it in a prison regulation sock and hit you with it. All I had to do was sprint upstairs and plant it in one of the troublemakers' cells. Zelda Darling was the obvious candidate—she was jealous of your baby after her own had been taken away. That big bust-up that the two of you had just before the "power strike" made her look even guiltier. Afterward, I stole a prison key chain from your locker and planted it in your box of possessions when you left, along with a nicked mobile, hoping you might get into trouble. The key chain came in useful when you were accused of Tanya's murder later—something I had nothing to do with, by the way.

But then it all went wrong. I thought David would be pleased when I told him that I was the one who had hit you. Hadn't he said that he'd wished you were dead? But he denied it, saying that I'd killed his baby boy. He insisted we couldn't risk seeing each other for a bit *until it all died down. Then he did what I'd always wanted him to do. He left you. But not for me—for Tanya.*

I couldn't believe it. But David soon realized his mistake. Not long after they got married, he rang to say he missed me. He said the sex was "boring." He wanted his "bad girl Jackie." So we went back to our old routine: meeting up every now and then when we could both get away.

This time, I didn't nag him about commitment. I bided my time. I'd wait for years if necessary.

But then he went missing. I was terrified in case the police linked us and came knocking at my door. And I was scared in case something terrible had happened to him.

When David turned up again at the trial, I couldn't believe it. The man I loved was alive after all! I ran up to him outside the court when it was all over. But he'd told me to "get the hell" out of his life.

I returned to my flat, my heart broken. My fiftieth birthday was approaching, and I still didn't have anyone. Just the prison, which had become my life. And an ex whom I couldn't get out of my head.

I've tried calling David so many times. But he never answers. And now I know. He used me for sex just as he used you for your position.

So this is my final act of revenge. It's not an apology. I want that man behind bars. And I know you can put him there. Good-bye.

I read the letter over again, still in shock. My friend and colleague. David's lover. David's dead ex. My baby's killer.

And then I reread the first letter from my solicitor. The bit where she tells me that David has been arrested.

64

HELEN

2 January 2019

"Do you work here?" asks the scared-looking kid with a torn brown rucksack on her back.

"Yes." That's right, I think. I've got a job in a hostel where I once scrubbed the shit off the walls. It's a bit cleaner now, though. New management. They were looking for staff, and they didn't seem to mind at the interview when I told them I was a single mother. Now I'm in charge of adolescents like this one.

"May I help you?" I continue out loud.

She shifts nervously from foot to foot, eyeing the baby in my arms—I'd just been feeding her. My daughter's appetite is, it seems, insatiable. She's wearing a little white cardigan that Mum had knitted her in craft class. I'd never known my mother to knit anything before. "I'm a granny," she keeps saying with a big grin on her face. "It's given me someone to live for— apart from you of course, love."

"I need somewhere to stay," continues the kid. "Social Services suggested I come here."

"Is this the first time you've been away from home?" I ask gently.

The girl shakes her head. "Been in care all my life. My mum—she's in prison. My last foster family was OK but then they had to move." She takes in the brightly colored walls and the lively noticeboard that I've been rearranging. "There's table tennis?"

"That's right. You'll like it here. Just keep your head down and don't do anything wrong."

"I'm not like that." She looks at the noticeboard again. "Cool pictures."

"I took them myself." I try to sound casual. "In fact, I've won a few competitions."

"Wow! I've always wanted to take photographs."

I get a sudden flashback of Robert, my foster father, donating his old camera and showing me how it worked. Taking pictures had somehow made all my anxieties melt away. I contacted them a few months ago to apologize for everything. Dee wrote back saying all was forgiven, but that Robert had been ill and it might be better if we didn't see each other for a while. Maybe this is my chance to go some way toward making up for my terrible behavior.

"I can teach you, if you like," I tell the girl in front of me.

"Cool! Thanks."

And for the first time in a long while, I begin to feel there might be a decent way forward after all.

Later on, one of the hostel kids knocks on my office door. I'm knee-deep in paperwork. "There's someone to see you."

My heart does a little flip. I've never been able to stop wondering where my grandparents are or even if they are still alive. Soon after getting this job, I'd saved enough money to place some "Looking For" personal ads in the local paper after Mum had finally revealed the name of the small Welsh village where she'd been brought up. But there'd been no response. Even so, I can't help a burst of hope every time someone rings and asks for me.

"Says her name is Vicki Goudman."

Shit. How has she tracked me down?

"Tell her I'm busy," I say sharply, looking down at my paperwork again.

"Please. It won't take a minute."

It's her! Standing at my door. There's no getting out of it.

"It's taken me a long time to find you." She seems to be studying my face. "I thought you seemed familiar that time by the sea in Penzance. I could see your mother in you." She shakes her head, almost as if speaking to herself. "I knew something had upset me. I just couldn't remember what."

My heart sinks. "You'd better come in."

Already, I'm cursing my decision. But part of me can't help being curious. "What do you want? How did you find me?"

She ignores the first question and goes for the second. "Online, actually. Your name came up under the hostel. Deputy warden, I believe."

I can't help the note of pride that creeps into my voice. "I was promoted recently."

As I speak, there is a high-pitched cry. I'd been hoping she wouldn't see. But now her eyes are riveted on the baby carrier on the floor by my desk. I pick up my daughter, holding her against my chest and patting her gently. Mum had been right. Even though I'd been terrified about how we'd manage, and despite the fact that I loathed her father, the loving bit just came naturally.

"What have you called it?" she asks with a note of wonder in her voice.

"It's a she," I correct her. "Her name is Hope." I give a short laugh. "It seemed fitting."

Mum's old enemy has tears in her eyes. "That was one of the names on our list." She appears to struggle for a moment, trying to compose herself. "You bring her with you to work?"

"I want my daughter near me, and anyway, I can't afford childcare."

"Actually, that's why I want to talk to you." Her fingers are twisting themselves together as though she's nervous. "I was convinced your mother had attacked me, not just from the ball in her room, but because of her earlier behavior. That was wrong of me."

I think back to last week's prison visit. Hope and I see Mum every Sunday. I owe that much to her. "You're right, so why the hell are you here?"

"Has David offered to help you out?"

She must have known I was pregnant from the statements that came out at the trial.

"That's none of your business," I snap.

There's a nod. "You're right. The thing is, we've all done things we shouldn't have. And that's why I'd like to offer you a monthly allowance, or an annual one, if you'd prefer that."

What? "You think you can buy me off to ease your own conscience?" I stand up, facing Vicki head-on. "I don't want your money. I'm not going to pursue David for it either, because I don't want him in our lives. I've got a regular job with accommodation. We'll manage, my daughter and I."

For a minute, I think of the photograph again and the ads I've placed. It would have been nice to have found my grandparents. But maybe I have to accept that a resolution like that only happens in fairy tales.

"I see." Vicki Goudman flushes. "Of course. I . . . I just thought I'd ask. I'm sorry if I've offended you."

To my relief, she turns to go. But at the doorway, she stops. "Good luck with your baby. Something tells me you're going to be a great mother."

And then she finally goes, leaving just a faint scent of lavender in the room.

65.

VICKI

24 January 2019

David is in Dartmoor Prison. It's miles from anywhere. You have to go for miles through the moor past wild ponies and stony tors, then suddenly you come to a forbidding stone castle-like building. I follow the officer down the steep steps and feel my blood chill. This place has a bad feeling about it.

And now my ex-husband is here. It didn't take the jury long to convict him of his role in my attempted murder. He might not have instructed Jackie to do it, but he'd finally admitted to telling her that he wished I was dead.

The visitors room is surprisingly pleasant, with modern chairs and tables. To be honest, I was amazed that my ex agreed to see me. But now here he is, being brought in by an officer. He looks like his old charming self. Somehow, he actually manages to suit the serge prison uniform.

"Vicki," he says, stretching out a hand as if we are old friends. I am taken aback. There's no sign of remorse. No guilt. We could almost be friends, meeting up at a cocktail party.

"No touching," snaps a prison officer. Too late. The feel of my ex's flesh makes my stomach contents curdle. Quickly, I step away.

"Only trying to be civilized," says David. He looks around at the other men, and for a minute I see the fear in his eyes. "I like to keep up my standards in a place like this."

If he's expecting polite conversation, he can forget it.

"Do you know why I'm here?"

His voice is smooth. "Why don't you tell me?"

Tears fill my eyes. "I need to know how you could have encouraged Jackie to hurt me—a crime that caused the death of our child. I thought you wanted to be a father."

I need to face him, to see the man who was indirectly responsible for murdering my son. *Our* son.

He leans toward me over the table. His face is deadly serious. "I *did* want to be a father, believe it or not."

"Because you thought it would add to your credibility?"

"No. Not just that." A haunted expression comes into his eyes. "I thought it would be a chance to start again. To get it right this time. I didn't tell Jackie to attack you."

"Don't." I feel my voice rising and have to fight to keep it down. "Jackie was wrong, but you said you wished I was dead."

"Look, Vicki." That charm has gone now. His eyes are hard. "It's your fault for not being a loyal wife. If you'd helped me out of that sticky financial patch I was going through, none of this would have happened."

"You really mean that, don't you?" Tears are running down my face. "You're a bastard, David. You're not just evil. You're selfish. Look what you've done to me."

"And look what *you* did to Zelda Darling! You were so convinced it was her who attacked you that you didn't consider the possibility of it being anyone else."

He was right. Innocent until proven guilty—isn't that what our justice system is all about? Yet I had based my own suspicions on circumstantial evidence.

There is no excuse.

Little Patrick will always stay alive in my heart, I tell myself as I sign out. But at least I am over David. I am finally free.

66.

VICKI

Three years later

"They're here," says Patrick, putting his arm around me as we go out to greet them.

I can hardly believe it. We've been waiting so long for this day.

Everything is ready. The bedroom upstairs that I've decorated with such care. The desk so she can do her homework. The school uniform, which I hope will fit.

When Patrick had first suggested long-term fostering, I'd assumed I wouldn't be suitable because of my epilepsy. But the new drug has worked better than anything else I've tried.

Patrick found me soon after that last time I saw David. Just when I'd persuaded myself that I really did have to put him out of my head, he rang out of the blue and suggested dinner up in London.

It felt so natural to be together that it was as if we'd never been parted. "I can't tell you how many times I almost rang before," he said as he took me back to my hotel. "But I felt you needed some time and space."

"I could have done with some friendship," I blurted out.

"I'm not talking about that," he said quietly. Then he kissed me. It felt as though I had finally come home.

"You know," he said afterward, "there's nothing I'd like more than to ask if I can stay over with you, but some things are too important to rush."

After that, we saw each other as often as his work would allow. But we both agreed to take it slowly. Once bitten, twice shy. When we finally had sex after four months, it was totally different from my experience with David. There was real love there instead of raw animal passion. "I think," he said, looking down on me in bed, "that it's the right time to get married now. Don't you?"

I didn't want to leave Penzance, and luckily he had fallen for its charms as well. So we bought a cottage on the outskirts in order for me to continue as an aromatherapist. Luckily, he found a post as a psychologist at a hospital not far from here. But now we are about to change our lives all over again.

"It will be all right," says Patrick, sensing my nervousness.

I lean into his shoulder and breathe him in. "What if I'm not good at this?"

"You will be. All she needs is a loving home and some structure. We can do that."

Together we walk toward the car. The social worker gets out of the driver's seat. It looks as though the little girl with dark plaits wants to stay put. Poor kid. She must be terrified, after everything she's been through.

"Hello," I say, crouching down by her open window. "My name's Vicki. You're Rhiannon, aren't you?"

She nods, her large brown eyes a pool of fear.

"We've got chickens in the back," I say. "Would you like to help me feed them? We could collect some eggs for tea."

And slowly, very slowly, she opens the door, gets out and places her small, warm hand in mine.

EPILOGUE

*T*here's just one more thing. I need to let it out or I will burst. So I'm going to write it down instead. My very last diary entry. Then I'm going to burn it before anyone can read it. I've learned my lesson about putting pen to paper.

Lavender is absorbed through the skin and into the bloodstream. This is true for other essential oils. Once inside the body, they can't be removed. My tutor told us this on more than one occasion.

I love aromatherapy. Its magic is both stimulating and calming. Yet if used in the wrong way, the effects can be catastrophic. My tutor was very clear about the safety aspects and contraindications. She taught us which oils can aggravate certain health conditions—and not just epilepsy.

Before I went to visit Tanya on the day she died, I had massaged my hands well with oil. Always good for the nails and your skin. But that isn't why I did it. David's wife had a permanent tan, courtesy of the sunbed she'd installed in my old house. I knew that because she boasted about it on Facebook. But the special citrus oil that I'd blended myself and rubbed into my hands just before seeing Tanya can cause allergic reactions to UV light. It can make skin blister and cause discoloration. It can also make you burn more easily, especially if it's undiluted. Luckily, it doesn't affect me.

I didn't mean any harm. Well, not long-lasting. I just wanted to do something that might make Tanya feel uncomfortable and less attractive. I wasn't even sure it would work, because it normally only reacts in the sunlight or when you are actually on a sunbed. How lucky for me that this is exactly what she was doing when I visited! Even better, it was a warm, sunny day—unseasonably so for that time of year. That's why I'd grabbed both her arms when I arrived. It worked faster than I thought. Within minutes, her skin had turned blotchy and perhaps painful. Did it affect her so much that she couldn't defend herself when Zelda attacked her?

The autopsy didn't mention it. I suppose an allergic reaction doesn't matter much when someone's been strangled. But what if one day it somehow comes to light? I've tried to tell myself that this is just my guilty conscience talking. But the truth is that I just don't know.

Meanwhile, I've kept quiet, convinced that the police will come knocking on my door, just as they had done before, when David had gone missing. But this time it would be to charge me with complicity in Tanya's murder.

But they haven't.

At least, not yet.

**Read on for a
selection from Jane Corry's
debut novel** ...

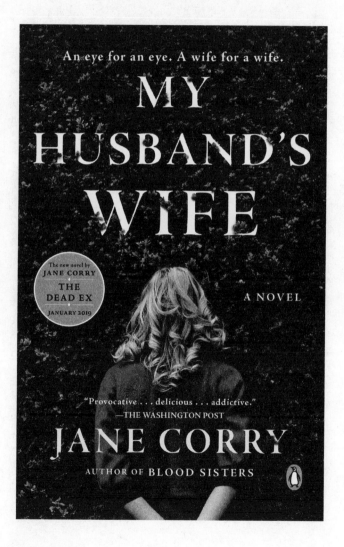

Prologue

*F*lash of metal.
      Thunder in my ears.
"This is the five o'clock news."

The radio, chirping merrily from the pine dresser, laden with photographs (holidays, graduation, wedding); a pretty blue and pink plate; a quarter bottle of Jack Daniel's, partially hidden by a birthday card.

My head is killing me. My right wrist as well. The pain in my chest is scary. So, too, is the blood.

I slump to the floor, soothed by the cold of the black slate. And I shake.

Above me, on the wall, is a white house in Italy, studded with purple bougainvillea. A honeymoon memento.

Can a marriage end in murder? Even if it's already dead?

That painting will be the last thing I see. But in my mind, I am reliving my life.

So it's true what they say about dying. The past comes back to go with you.

THE DAILY TELEGRAPH

Tuesday 20 October 2015
The artist Ed Macdonald has been found stabbed to death in
his home. It is thought that . . .

PART ONE

❦

Fifteen Years Earlier

1

Lily

Late September 2000

❧

"**N**ervous?" Ed asks with a note of sympathy in his voice.

He's pouring out his favorite breakfast cereal. Rice Krispies. Usually I like them, too. As a child, I was obsessed by the elfin-faced figures on the packet, and the magic hasn't quite left.

But today I don't have the stomach to eat anything.

"Nervous?" I repeat, fastening my pearl earrings in the little mirror next to the sink. Our flat is small. Compromises were made.

About what? I almost add. Nervous about the first day of married life, perhaps. Nervous because we should have taken more time to find a better flat instead of one in the wrong part of Clapham, where both bedroom and bathroom are so small that my one tube of Rimmel foundation and my two lipsticks (rose pink and ruby red) snuggle up next to the teaspoons in the cutlery drawer.

Or nervous about going back to work after our honeymoon in Italy? A week in Sicily, knocking back bottles of Marsala, grilled sardines and slabs of pecorino cheese in a hotel paid for by Ed's grandmother.

Maybe I'm nervous about all these things.

Normally, I love my work. Until now, I've been in employment law, helping people—especially women—who've been unfairly sacked. Looking after the underdog, that's me. I nearly became a social worker like Dad, but, thanks to a determined careers teacher at school, here I am. A twenty-five-year-old newly qualified solicitor on minimum wage. Struggling to do up the button at the back of my navy-blue skirt. No one wears bright colors in a law office, apart from the secretaries. Or so I was told when I started. And the fact that I was advised to wear a *skirt* suit, not trousers—don't even get me started.

"We're moving you to criminal," my boss announced by way of a wedding gift. "We think you'll be good at it."

So now, on my first day back, I'm preparing to go to prison. To see a man who's been accused of murder. I've never been inside a prison before. Never wanted to. It's an unknown world. One reserved for people who have done wrong. I'm the kind of person who goes straight back if someone has given me too much change in the newsstand when I buy my monthly copy of *Cosmo*.

Ed is doodling now. His head is bent slightly to the left as he sketches on a notepad next to his cereal. My husband is always drawing. It was one of the first things that attracted me to him. "Advertising," he said with a rueful shrug when I asked what he did. "On the creative side. But I'm going to be a full-time artist one day. This is just temporary—to pay the bills."

I liked that. A man who knew where he was going. But when he's drawing or painting, Ed doesn't even know which planet he's on. Right now, he's forgotten he even asked me a question. But suddenly it's important for me to answer it.

"Nervous? No, I'm not nervous."

There's a nod, but despite that earlier kind tone, I'm not sure he's really heard me. When Ed's in the zone, the rest of the world doesn't matter. Not even my fib.

Why, I ask myself, as I take his left hand—the one with the shiny gold wedding ring—don't I tell him how I really feel? Why not confess that I feel sick and that I need to go to the loo even though I've only just been? A shiver passes down my spine as I spray duty-free Chanel No. 5 (a present from Ed, using another wedding gift check) on the inside of both wrists. Last month, a solicitor from a rival firm was stabbed in both lungs when he went to see a client in Wandsworth.

"Come on," I say, anxiety sharpening my usually light voice. "We're both going to be late."

Reluctantly, he rises from the rickety chair that the former owner of our flat had left behind. He's a tall man, my new husband. Lanky, with an almost apologetic way of walking, as if he would really rather be somewhere else. As a child, apparently, his hair was as golden as mine is today ("We knew you were a 'Lily' the first time we saw you," my mother has always said), but now it's a sandy brown. And he has thick fingers that betray no hint of the artist he yearns to be.

We all need our dreams. Lilies are meant to be beautiful. I look all right from the top bit up, thanks to my naturally blond hair and what my now-deceased grandmother used to kindly call "elegant swan neck." But look below, and you'll find leftover puppy fat instead of a slender stem. No matter what I do, I'm stuck on the size fourteen rail—and that's if I'm lucky. I know I shouldn't care, and Ed always says he doesn't, but I just do.

On the way out, my eye falls on the stack of wedding cards propped up against Ed's records. Mr. and Mrs. E. Macdonald. The name seems so unfamiliar.

Mrs. Ed Macdonald.

Lily Macdonald.

I've spent ages trying to perfect my signature, looping the *y* through the *M*, but somehow it still doesn't seem quite right. The names don't go together that well. I hope it's not a bad sign.

Meanwhile, each card requires a thank-you letter to be sent by the end of the week. If my mother has taught me anything, it is to be polite.

One of the cards has a particularly flamboyant *look at me!* scrawl, in turquoise ink. "Davina was a girlfriend once," Ed explained before she turned up at our engagement party. "But now we're just friends."

I think of Davina with her horsey laugh and artfully styled auburn hair that makes her look like a pre-Raphaelite model. Davina who works in events, organizing parties to which all the "nice girls" go. Davina who narrowed her violet eyes when we were introduced, as if wondering why Ed would bother with a too-tall, too-plump woman like me.

Can a man ever be just friends with a woman when the relationship is over?

I decide to leave my predecessor's letter until last. Ed married *me*, not her, I remind myself.

My new husband's warm hand now squeezes mine. "It will be all right, you know."

For a minute, I wonder if he is referring to our marriage. Then I remember. My first criminal client. Joe Thomas.

"Thanks." It's comforting that Ed wasn't taken in by my earlier bravado. And worrying, too.

Together, we shut the front door, checking it twice because it's all so new to us, and walk briskly down the ground-floor corridor leading out of our block of flats. As we do so, another door opens and a little girl with long, dark, glossy, curly hair—looking as though it's trying to escape from that ponytail—comes out with her mother. I've seen them before, but when I said "hello," they didn't reply. Both have beautiful olive skin and walk with a grace that makes them appear to be floating.

We hit the sharp autumn air together. The four of us are heading in the same direction, but mother and daughter are now slightly ahead because Ed is scribbling something in his sketchbook as we walk. The pair, I notice, seem like carbon copies of each other, except that the woman is wearing a too-short black skirt (while carrying what looks like a uniform) and the little girl—who's whining for something—is dressed in a navy-blue school blazer. When we have children, I tell myself, we'll teach them not to whine.

I shiver as we approach the bus stop; the pale autumn sun is so different from the honeymoon heat. But it's the prospect of our separation that tightens my chest. After one week of togetherness, the thought of managing for eight hours without Ed is almost scary.

Not so long ago, I was independent. Content with my own company. But from the minute that Ed and I first spoke at that party six months ago (just six months!), I've felt both strengthened and weakened at the same time.

We pause and I steel myself for the inevitable. My bus goes one way. His, the other. Ed is off to the advertising company where he spends his days illustrating slogans to make the public buy something it never intended to. Just before our wedding, he'd presented me with a beautifully designed box of expensive hand cream. I'd thought it was a gift he had picked out for me, but it had turned out to be a "freebie." Now he is tearing a page out of his notebook and handing it to me. It's a sketch of a four-leaf clover inside a heart with the words *Good luck* below. "Thank you," I say, with a catch in my throat. He makes an *it's nothing* gesture.

"You know, it won't be so bad when you're there," adds my new husband before kissing me on the mouth. He tastes of Rice Krispies and that strong toothpaste of his that I still haven't gotten used to.

"I know," I say before he peels off to the bus stop on the other side of the road.

Two lies. Small white ones. Designed to make the other feel better.

But that's how some lies start. Small. Well meaning. Until they get too big to handle.

2

Carla

"Why?" Carla whined as she dragged behind, pulling her mother's hand to stop this steady, determined pace toward school. "Why do I have to go?"

If she went on making a fuss, her mother might give in out of exhaustion. It worked last week, although that had been a saint's day. Mamma had been more tearful than usual. Birthdays and saints' days and Christmas and Easter always did that to her.

"Where has the time gone?" Mamma would groan in that heavy, rich accent that was so different from all the other children's mothers' at school. "Nine and a half years without your father."

For as far back as she could remember, Carla had known that her father was in heaven with the angels. It was because he had broken a promise back when she was born.

Once, she had asked what kind of promise he had broken.

"It was the sort that cannot be mended," Mamma had sniffed.

Like the beautiful blue teacup with the golden handle, Carla thought. It had slipped out of her hand the other week when she had offered to do the drying. Mamma had cried because the cup came from Italy.

It was sad that Papa was with the angels. But she still had Mamma! Once, a man on the bus had mistaken them for sisters. That had made Mamma laugh. "He was just flattering me," she'd said, her cheeks red. But then she had let Carla stay up late as a special treat. It taught Carla that when Mamma was very happy, it was a good time to ask for something.

It also worked when she was sad.

Like now. The start of a new century. They'd learned all about it in school.

Ever since the new term had started, Carla's heart had ached for a caterpillar pencil case, made of soft green furry stuff, like everyone else had at school. Then the others might stop teasing her. Different was bad. Different was being smaller than any of the others in class. *Titch!* (A strange word which wasn't in the *Children's Dictionary* she'd persuaded Mamma to buy from the secondhand shop on the corner.) Different was having thick black eyebrows. *Hairy Mary!* Different was having a name that wasn't like anyone else's.

Carla Cavoletti.

Or "Spagoletti," as the other kids called it.

Hairy Carla Spagoletti!

"Why can't we stay at home today?" she continued. *Our real home,* she almost added. Not like the one in Italy that Mamma kept talking about and that she, Carla, had never even seen.

She stopped briefly as their neighbor with the golden hair walked past, shooting her a disapproving glance.

Carla knew that look. It was the same one that the teachers gave her at school when she didn't know her nine times table. "I'm not good with numbers either," Mamma would say dismissively when Carla asked for some help with her homework. "But it does not matter as long as you do not eat cakes and get fat. Women like us, all we need is to be beautiful."

The man with the shiny car and the big brown hat was *always* telling Mamma she was beautiful.

When he came to visit, Mamma would never cry. She'd loosen her long dark curls, spray herself with her favorite Apple Blossom perfume and make her eyes dance. The record player would be turned on so that their feet tapped, although Carla's weren't allowed to tap for long.

"Bed, cara mia," Mamma would sing. And then Carla would have to leave her mother and guest to tap their feet around the little sitting room all on their own, while pictures of her mother's family glared down disapprovingly from the cracked walls. Often their cold faces visited her in the nightmares that interrupted the dancing and made Mamma cross. "You are too old for such dreams. You must not bother Larry and me."

A little while ago, Carla had been given a school project called "My Mummy and Daddy." When she'd come home, fired with excitement, Mamma had done a lot of tongue-clicking followed by a burst of crying. "I *have* to bring in an object for the class table," Carla had persisted. "I can't be the only one who doesn't."

Eventually, Mamma had taken down the photograph of the stiff-backed man with a white collar and strict eyes. "We will send Papa," she announced in a voice that sounded as though she'd gotten a hard candy stuck in her throat. Carla liked hard candy. Sometimes the man with the shiny car brought her some in a white paper bag. But they stuck to her hand and then she had to spend ages washing off the stain.

Carla had held the photograph reverently in her hand. "He is my grandfather?"

Even as she spoke, she knew the answer. Mamma had told her enough times. But it was good to know. Nice to be assured that she had a grandfather like her classmates, even though hers lived many miles away in the hills above Florence and never wrote back.

Carla's mother had wrapped the photograph in an orange and red silk scarf that smelled of mothballs. She couldn't wait to take it into class.

"This is my nonno," she'd announced proudly.

But everyone had laughed. "Nonno, nonno," one boy had chanted. "Why don't you have a granddad like us?"

That had been just before the saint's day when she'd persuaded her mother to phone in sick to work. One of the best days of her life! Together they had taken a picnic to a place called Hyde Park where Mamma had sung songs and told her what it was like when she was a child in Italy.

"My brothers would take me swimming," she had said in a dreamy voice. "Sometimes we would catch fish for supper and then we would sing and dance and drink wine."

Carla, drunk with happiness at having escaped school, wove a strand of her mother's dark hair around her little finger. "Was Papa there then, too?"

Suddenly her mother's dancing black eyes stopped dancing. "No, my little one. He was not." Then she started to gather the Thermos and the cheese from the red tartan rug on the ground. "Come. We must go home."

And suddenly it wasn't the best day of her life anymore. Today didn't look too good either. There was to be a test first thing, the teacher had warned. Maths and spelling. Two of her worst subjects. Carla's grip on her mother's hand grew stronger.

"You might be small for your age," the man with the shiny car had said the other evening when she'd objected to going to bed early, "but you're very determined, aren't you?"

And why not? she nearly replied.

"You must be nice to Larry," Mamma was always saying. "Without him, we could not live here."

"Please can we stay at home together? Please?" she now begged.

But Mamma was having none of it. "I have to work."

"But why? Larry will understand if you can't meet him for lunch."

Usually she didn't give him his name. It felt better to call him the man with the shiny car. It meant he wasn't part of them.

Mamma turned around in the street, almost colliding with a lamp-post. For a moment she looked almost angry. "Because, my little one, I still have some pride."

Mamma's work was very important. She had to make plain women look pretty! She worked in a big shop that sold lipsticks and mascaras and special lotions that made your skin look "beautiful beige" or "wistful white" or something in between, depending on your coloring. Sometimes Mamma would bring samples home and make up Carla's face so that she looked much older than she was.

That's how Mamma had found Larry. She'd been on the perfume counter that day because someone had been sick. Sick was good, Mamma had said, if it meant you could step in instead. Larry had come to the shop to buy perfume for his wife. She "wasn't feeling very well, which made Larry sad." And now Mamma was doing the wife a favor because she was making Larry happy again. He was good to Carla, wasn't he? Didn't he bring her candy?

But right now, as they walked toward the bus stop where the woman with golden hair was waiting (the neighbor who, according to Mamma, must eat too many cakes), Carla wanted something else.

"Can I ask Larry for a caterpillar pencil case?"

"No." Mamma made a sweeping gesture with her long arms and red fingernails. "You cannot."

It wasn't fair. Carla could almost feel its soft fur as she stroked the caterpillar in her mind. She could almost hear it, too: *I should belong to you. Then everyone will like us. Come on, Carla. You can find a way.*

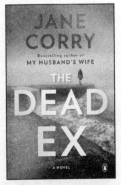

THE DEAD EX

Vicki works as an aromatherapist, healing her clients out of her home studio with her special blends of essential oils. She's just finishing a session when the police arrive on her doorstep—her ex-husband David has gone missing. Vicki insists she last saw him years ago when they divorced, but the police don't believe her. And her memory's hardly reliable—what if she *did* have something to do with it?

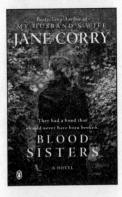

BLOOD SISTERS

Three little girls set off to school one sunny morning. Within an hour, one of them is dead. Fifteen years later, Kitty can't speak and has no memory of the accident. She lives in an institution, unlikely ever to leave. Art teacher Alison looks fine on the surface, but she's struggling to make ends meet—and to forget the past. Meanwhile, someone is watching both Kitty and Alison. Someone who never forgot what happened that day. Someone who wants revenge. And only another life will do . . .

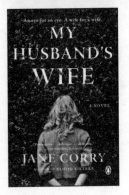

MY HUSBAND'S WIFE

When young lawyer Lily marries Ed, she's determined to make a fresh start. To leave the secrets of the past behind. But then she takes on her first murder case and meets Joe, a convicted murderer for whom Lily soon will be willing to risk almost anything. But Lily is not the only one with secrets. Her next-door neighbor Carla may be only nine, but she has already learned that secrets are powerful things. That they can get her whatever she wants.

🐧 PENGUIN BOOKS

Ready to find your next great read? Let us help. Visit prh.com/nextread